WILD SAVAGE STARS

KRISTINA PÉREZ

[Imprint]
MAKE YOUR MARK

NEW YORK

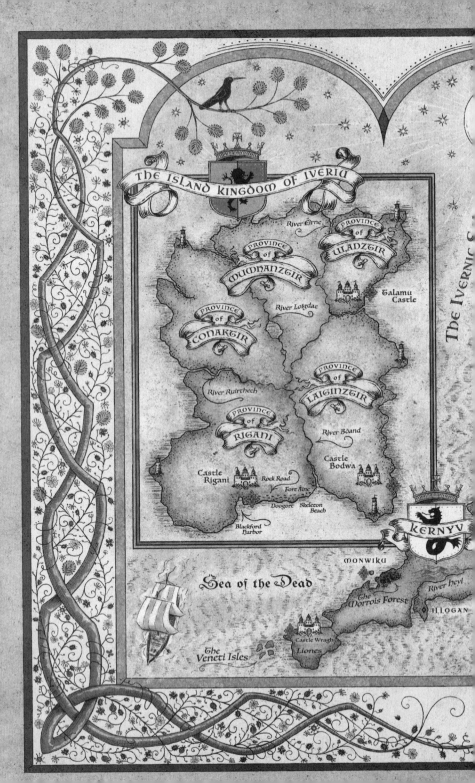

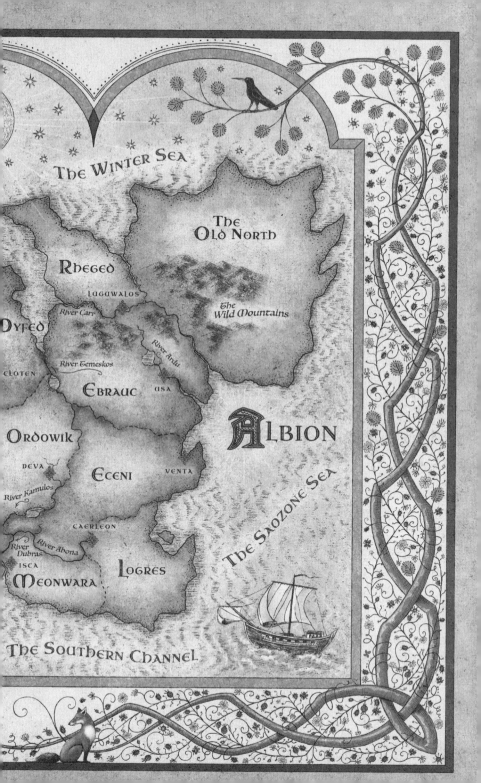

[Imprint]
MAKE YOUR MARK

A part of Macmillan Publishing Group, LLC
120 Broadway, New York, NY 10271

Library of Congress Cataloging-in-Publication Data is available.

ISBN 978-1-250-13283-3 (hardcover) / ISBN 978-1-250-13284-0 (ebook)
ISBN 978-1-250-25284-5 (international edition)

Our books may be purchased in bulk for promotional, educational, or business use. Please
contact your local bookseller or the Macmillan Corporate and Premium Sales Department at
(800) 221-7945 ext. 5442 or by email at MacmillanSpecialMarkets@macmillan.com.

Book design by Ellen Duda

Map by Virginia Allen

Imprint logo designed by Amanda Spielman

First edition, 2019

1 3 5 7 9 10 8 6 4 2

fiercereads.com

An té a dhéanfadh cóip den leabhar seo, gan chead, gan chomhairle,
dhíbreodh é go Teach Dhuinn.

For Bernice Dubois,

a true Wise Damsel, mentor, and friend

DRAMATIS PERSONÆ

IVERNIC ROYAL FAMILY

KING ÓENGUS, HIGH KING OF IVERIU—father of Princess Eseult, uncle to Lady Branwen, holds his court at Castle Rigani in the province of Rigani

QUEEN ESEULT OF IVERIU—mother of Princess Eseult, aunt to Lady Branwen, sister to Lady Alana and Lord Morholt, originally from the province of Laiginztir

PRINCESS ESEULT OF IVERIU—fiancé of King Marc of Kernyv, daughter to King Óengus and Queen Eseult, cousin of Lady Branwen, niece to Lord Morholt

IVERNIC NOBILITY

LADY BRANWEN CUALAND OF LAIGINZTIR—heir to Castle Bodwa, cousin to Princess Eseult, niece of Queen Eseult and King Óengus, daughter of Lady Alana and Lord Caedmon

LORD DIARMUID PARTHALÁN OF ULADZTIR—heir to Talamu Castle, descendant of High King Eógan Mugmedón, son of Lord Rónán and Lady Fionnula, former love interest of Princess Eseult

LORD CONLA OF MUMHANZTIR—nobleman from the province of Mumhanztir, former love interest of Princess Eseult

LADY ALANA CUALAND OF LAIGINZTIR (*deceased*)—mother of Branwen, Lady of Castle Bodwa, sister to Queen Eseult and Lord Morholt

LORD CAEDMON CUALAND OF LAIGINZTIR (*deceased*)—father of Branwen, Lord of Castle Bodwa

LORD MORHOLT LABRADA OF LAIGINZTIR (*deceased*)—uncle to Branwen, former King's Champion, brother to Queen Eseult and Lady Alana

MEMBERS OF THE ROYAL IVERNIC HOUSEHOLD

SIR KEANE OF CASTLE RIGANI (*deceased*)—member of the Royal Ivernic Guard and bodyguard to Princess Eseult, from a coastal village along the Rock Road

SIR FINTAN OF CASTLE RIGANI—member of the Royal Ivernic Guard and bodyguard to Queen Eseult

TREVA OF CASTLE RIGANI—head royal cook

DUBTHACH OF CASTLE RIGANI—servant at the castle, son of Noirín

NOIRÍN OF CASTLE RIGANI—castle seamstress, mother of Dubthach

MASTER BÉCC OF CASTLE RIGANI—the royal tutor to Princess Eseult and Lady Branwen

SAOIRSE—from the coastal village of Doogort, becomes an assistant to Queen Eseult in the infirmary at Castle Rigani

GRÁINNE—an orphan girl from the Rock Road befriended by Princess Eseult

KERNYVAK ROYAL FAMILY

KING MARC OF KERNYV—fiancé of Princess Eseult of Iveriu, uncle to Prince Tristan of Kernyv, brother to Princess Gwynedd, son of King Merchion and Queen Verica of Kernyv

PRINCE TRISTAN OF KERNYV—heir to Castle Wragh and the protectorate of Liones, nephew of King Marc of Kernyv, Queen's Champion to Princess Eseult of Iveriu, son of Princess Gwynedd and Prince Hanno, grandson of King Merchion and Queen Verica of Kernyv, cousin to Ruan, Endelyn, and Andred

PRINCE RUAN OF KERNYV—son of Prince Edern and Countess Kensa, King's Champion and cousin to King Marc, heir to House Whel, older brother to Princess Endelyn and Prince Andred, cousin to Tristan

PRINCESS ENDELYN OF KERNYV—daughter of Prince Edern and Countess Kensa, lady-in-waiting to Princess Eseult of Iveriu, sister to Prince Ruan and Prince Andred, cousin to King Marc and Prince Tristan

PRINCE ANDRED OF KERNYV—son of Prince Edern and Countess Kensa, king's cupbearer and cousin to King Marc, younger brother of Prince Ruan and Princess Endelyn, cousin to Tristan

COUNTESS KENSA WHEL OF ILLOGAN—head of House Whel, widow of Prince Edern, mother of Prince Ruan, Princess Endelyn, and Prince Andred, aunt to King Marc and Prince Tristan, sister-in-law of Queen Verica; Villa Illogan and the other lands belonging to House Whel are located on the south coast

DOWAGER QUEEN VERICA OF KERNYV—mother of King Marc and Princess Gwynedd, grandmother of Prince Tristan, widow of King Merchion, originally from the kingdom of Meonwara, currently resides at Castle Wragh in Liones

KING MERCHION OF KERNYV (*deceased*)—father of King Marc and Princess Gwynedd, husband to Queen Verica, older brother to Prince Edern

PRINCE EDERN OF KERNYV (*deceased*)—younger brother of King Merchion, husband of Countess Kensa, father of Prince Ruan, Princess Endelyn, and Prince Andred

PRINCE HANNO OF LIONES (*deceased*)—father of Tristan, navigator with the Royal Kernyvak Fleet who became a prince through marriage to Princess Gwynedd of Kernyv; his ancestors came to Kernyv with the Aquilan legions from Kartago

PRINCESS GWYNEDD OF KERNYV (*deceased*)—mother of Tristan, older sister to King Marc, daughter of King Merchion and Queen Verica

GREAT KING KATWALADRUS (*deceased*)—king at the time the Aquilan Empire withdrew from the Island of Albion to the southern continent; decreed that southerners could remain in Kernyv; started the raids on Iveriu that have persisted for a century

KERNYVAK NOBILITY

BARON ANIUD CHYANHAL—head of House Chyanhal, one of the five largest baronies in Kernyv granted by Great King Katwaladrus; House Chyanhal's lands lie in the north, bordering on the kingdom of Ordowik

BARON BRYTAEL DYNYON—head of House Dynyon, one of the five largest baronies in Kernyv granted by Great King Katwaladrus; House Dynyon's lands are adjacent to Liones and used to comprise some of Prince Tristan's territories

BARON CINGUR GWYK—head of House Gwyk, one of the five largest baronies in Kernyv granted by Great King Katwaladrus; House Gwyk's lands lie to the east, bordering the kingdom of Meonwara

BARON MAELOC JULYAN—head of House Julyan, one of the five largest baronies in Kernyv granted by Great King Katwaladrus; House Julyan's lands are located close to Monwiku and the Port of Marghas

BARON RYD KERDU—head of House Kerdu, one of the five largest baronies in Kernyv granted by Great King Katwaladrus; House Kerdu's lands are located on the north coast

MEMBERS OF THE ROYAL KERNYVAK HOUSEHOLD

SEER CASEK—chief *kordweyd* of the temple in Marghas

SEER OGRIN—*kordweyd* who runs a rural temple on the moors

MORGAWR—Captain of the *Dragon Rising*, member of the Royal Kernyvak Fleet

LOWENEK—an orphan girl rescued by Branwen from the mining disaster

TALORC—an Iverman who resides at Seer Ogrin's temple

TUTIR OF MONWIKU CASTLE—member of the Royal Kernyvak Guard

BLEDROS OF MONWIKU CASTLE—member of the Royal Kernyvak Guard

XANDRU MANDUCA—friend to King Marc, Captain of the *Mawort*, and a member of the powerful Manduca family, a mercantile dynasty from the Melita Isles; distant cousin to Queen Yedra of Armorica

ARMORICAN ROYAL FAMILY

KING FARAMON OF ARMORICA—father to Crown Prince Havelin, Prince Kahedrin, and Princess Eseult Alba

QUEEN YEDRA OF ARMORICA—mother of Princess Eseult Alba, stepmother of Crown Prince Havelin and Prince Kahedrin, originally from the Melita Isles and a distant cousin to Xandru Manduca

CROWN PRINCE HAVELIN OF ARMORICA—son of King Faramon, older brother to Prince Kahedrin and half-brother to Princess Eseult Alba

PRINCE KAHEDRIN OF ARMORICA—son of King Faramon, younger brother to Crown Prince Havelin, older half-brother to Princess Eseult Alba

PRINCESS ESEULT ALBA OF ARMORICA—daughter of King Faramon, younger half-sister to Crown Prince Havelin and Prince Kahedrin

QUEEN RIMOETE OF ARMORICA (*deceased*)—mother of Crown Prince Havelin and Prince Kahedrin

PART I

UNTO THE BREACH

THE QUEEN'S CHAMPION

THE WAVES MOCKED HER.

Discordant laughter swelled in Branwen's mind and twisted her heart. She couldn't remain on the ship one moment longer. Her skin itched.

Branwen rubbed her thumb along the raised flesh of her right palm, trying to quell her anger. She couldn't. The gangway creaked beneath her feet as she disembarked the *Dragon Rising* at a brisk pace. She needed to get away from everyone on board.

With a shallow breath, Branwen took her first step onto dry land—the land of her enemies.

The kingdom of Kernyv had terrorized her beloved island of Iveriu for generations. Kernyvak raiders were responsible for the deaths of Branwen's parents, and countless other Ivermen. But she wasn't here for revenge.

She was here to make peace.

And she had already killed for it.

Her eyes skittered over the cliffs that towered above the Port of Marghas; their lurid green had faded to a melancholy hue in the hour it had taken to make landfall. The rocky vista reminded Branwen deceptively of home, of the view from the beach below Castle Rigani.

She quashed a pang of longing. She couldn't afford to look backward; Branwen had been sent across the sea to ensure that the future would be brighter than the past.

The late-autumn breeze coming off the waves was warmer than it would have been in Iveriu. The Kernyveu called the body of water that separated their two kingdoms the Dreaming Sea. Branwen scoffed. Her voyage had been filled with nothing but nightmares.

Loosening her fur-lined shawl, she panned her gaze across the fishing boats and other merchant vessels moored in the sheltered harbor. Kernyv occupied the southwestern peninsula of the island of Albion and, being so close to the southern continent, it owed much of its wealth to trade. Both legal and illegal. Kernyvak pirates were feared throughout its neighboring seas.

The din of bartering and gossiping lured Branwen toward the jetties, which were littered with stacks of crates, wicker baskets, and ceramic pots. Albion had been ruled by the Aquilan Empire until a century ago. At the empire's peak, it had dominated half the known world, and Kernyv maintained strong trading ties with its distant corners.

Farther inland, near the end of the pier, Branwen spied a market where fishermen were selling their fresh catch. Also, she reckoned, where foreign merchants were trying to tempt the locals into purchasing jugs of sweet Mílesian liqueur or weapons forged from the toughest Kartagon steel.

Her throat tightened. Those weapons would never be used against the Iverni again. Branwen would die before she let that happen.

She glanced back at the sail of the *Dragon Rising*. A swath of red cloth was stitched between the white. Branwen had risked everything for the deepest magic known to her people because she'd rashly believed she could mend the rift between Kernyv and Iveriu in the same way.

Blood and bone, forged by fire, we beseech you for the truest of desires.

To bind the peace with love, she had conjured the Loving Cup. This morning, the streak of red looked like blood on the moon.

The Land, Goddess Ériu herself, had chosen Kernyv as her Champion in a sacred ritual, but Branwen had wanted more for the Princess of Iveriu—for the sister of her heart—than a political alliance. She had wanted her cousin to know love.

Her aunt, Queen Eseult of Iveriu, had cautioned Branwen that forced fruit is nearly always bitter.

She hadn't listened.

The Old Ones, the Otherworld-dwellers who guarded her homeland, had sent her warnings.

She'd ignored them.

And now . . . no one could ever know the Loving Cup had existed. No one could know the potion intended for the Princess of Iveriu and the King of Kernyv had been imbibed by the wrong couple. Not even the new lovers themselves.

The knowledge could only bring ruin—to Iveriu, to Kernyv, to everyone Branwen cherished. When she'd discovered the golden vial empty, she hurled it to the bottom of the sea, disposed of the evidence. In trying to break the cycle of war, Branwen had led others into treason: both her cousin and the only man she had ever loved.

The truth threatened to strangle her from within, but, if that was the price of her transgression, she accepted. The burden of this secret was hers alone.

Lost in her thoughts, Branwen continued walking toward the market. *Thud.* She smacked straight into a solidly built chest.

The man she'd stumbled into regarded her shrewdly, silver eyes gleaming, and Branwen studied him right back. Light brown hair and a precisely trimmed beard framed his pale, slightly sunworn face. The angles of his cheekbones were too severe to be handsome, but not unappealing. He was at least a head taller than Branwen, and she ventured a guess he was also about ten years her senior.

"*M-Mormerkti,*" she stuttered.

"*Mormerkti?*" the stranger repeated.

Branwen flushed. *Mormerkti* was the Kernyvak word for "thank you." His eyes remained steady on hers, not unkind, no doubt puzzling at why she would offer thanks for barging into him. Scrambling to recall the few other words of Kernyvak she knew, Branwen tried again.

"*Dymatis,*" she said, tentative, her pronunciation halting. It was a greeting that translated as "good day." The stranger must have realized Branwen was a foreigner from her accent, but could he tell she was an Iverwoman?

The Iverni had also spilled much Kernyvak blood. Branwen had come to the land of her enemies, but she was their enemy, too. She braced herself to be rebuffed. Unconsciously, she touched the brooch pinned to her shawl. It had belonged to her mother and bore her family motto: *The right fight.*

Slowly, the corner of the stranger's mouth lifted in a guarded quarter smile.

"*Dymatis,*" he said in return, and Branwen released a small sigh of relief. Pointing toward the other end of the dock, in the direction of the ships, the man launched into a torrent of Kernyvak words.

Branwen couldn't keep up. His tone was friendly and, from his cadence, she thought he was asking a question—although she had no notion as to what that question might be. The heat on her cheeks intensified. Biting her lips together, she dropped her gaze, landing on the sash that the man sported across his tunic.

In the center of smooth white silk, a sea-wolf had been embroidered in shiny black thread. The hybrid beast was the royal emblem of Kernyv. Morgawr, the captain of the *Dragon Rising*, had informed Branwen that King Marc would send an envoy to meet them at the port. This man must be in the king's service. His leather trousers and sumptuous linen tunic indicated affluence, perhaps even nobility.

An idea sparked in Branwen. The language of the Aquilan Empire was still spoken at most royal courts across their former territories. Ivernic nobles also learned the language so as not to be at a disadvantage in diplomatic negotiations.

Steeling herself with a deep breath, Branwen said to the man in Aquilan, "I beg your pardon, but I'm not fluent enough in Kernyvak to be able to understand your question."

His eyebrows shot up in surprise, followed by a tensing of his features. He stroked his beard.

Tamping down on her nerves, Branwen summoned a smile of encouragement. She hadn't been graced with the same natural charm as some other members of her family. She was less interested in public life than her patients in the castle infirmary.

But that had been in Iveriu. Branwen was in a new land, and she needed to become someone new. She needed to make allies for her people—to do everything in her power to secure the peace and prevent the chaos of her magic from being unleashed.

"Forgive me," the envoy replied in Aquilan after a moment. His voice held something close to trepidation. "You've arrived on the ship that just landed?"

"Yes." She nodded.

"From Iveriu?"

Another nod.

His agitation mounted. "Forgive me," he said again. "I'd planned to meet you on deck. A pressing matter . . . delayed me."

"You were sent by the king?" Branwen inferred.

The envoy didn't answer, just worked his jaw. He began to bow from the waist. "I—" Branwen stopped him, touching a hand to his shoulder.

"There's no need to bow before me," she said.

He looked like he was about to protest when he was distracted by something over Branwen's shoulder.

"Brother!" he exclaimed. His face relaxed into a brilliant smile, and she suspected that this was a man who smiled less often than he wanted. He looked younger when he smiled. Affinity, instant and unexpected, rippled through Branwen.

Intrigued, she turned, following the envoy's eye line, to see who had inspired his sudden joy.

Her heart liquefied.

Tristan.

The man with whom she'd shared her first kiss—with whom she'd wanted to share her life until a few hours ago—raced toward them.

And behind him, still on deck, was the woman whose happiness Branwen had prized above an entire kingdom.

"Marc!" Tristan called out as his feet pounded the dock, and Branwen failed to suppress a gasp. She swung her gaze back toward the other Kernyvman.

Marc. *King* Marc. The man destined to wed her cousin. The man for whom the Loving Cup had been devised.

She staggered back a pace and raked her eyes over him with fresh scrutiny, guilt and fear roiling inside her. And hate.

During the voyage, Branwen had been tormented by images of horror sent to her by Dhusnos: The Dark One who ruled the Sea of the Dead. He'd used a *kretarv*—a carnivorous bird—to send her a vision of her parents' deaths.

A young Kernyvak raider had watched Branwen's mother die. He'd seen the blood spurting from her chest and run away. A raider named Marc.

Was it truly the king? Had it been recognition rather than affinity she'd felt a moment ago?

Dull sunlight shimmered on Tristan's warm brown skin as he halted before them, and Branwen couldn't stop her eyes from seeking out the small scar above his right eyebrow, concealed by dark, messy curls. When she'd first rescued him, half-drowned from the waves, that tiny imperfection had endeared him to her.

For a moment, Branwen was back on that beach.

For a moment, he was all she could see.

The moment passed.

King Marc wrapped an arm around Tristan, clapping him on the back, pulling him into a hearty embrace. Although he'd called Tristan brother, the Prince of Kernyv was actually his nephew. He was the son of Marc's older sister who had died in childbirth. With only seven years between them, the pair had grown up together, raised by Tristan's grandparents. Tristan had always spoken fondly of Marc to Branwen— when she was still interested in hearing anything he had to say.

Wind whipped her long black tresses across her face, the air instantly colder than the song of a Death-Teller, the Otherworld women whose laments foretold your end.

Hugging his nephew, the raw affection on King Marc's face didn't tally in Branwen's mind with the ruler who had sent raiders to decimate Ivernic villages; nor with the gangly pirate she'd seen ambush her parents.

Tristan's expression was uneasy as he broke his uncle's embrace, the edges of his smile brittle. Marc didn't appear to notice. Branwen could read Tristan only too well. She'd spent too long mastering the meaning of each different smile, dreaming of him, begging the Old Ones to keep him safe—learning to love her enemy.

But that was done. He was a Kernyvak prince and she would accord him the respect that his status required. Nothing further.

Glancing between Branwen and the king, Tristan wet his lips. "You've met Marc?" he asked her in Ivernic. There was a quaver in his voice.

"I was just making his acquaintance." Branwen's answer came in Aquilan, and she struggled to keep her words from stinging like nettles.

She no longer wanted to share her native tongue with Tristan. Angling her shoulders toward Marc, she commanded her lips to part in another polite smile. She pictured a wooden shield between them, protecting her from the past.

Lowering her eyes deferentially, Branwen added, "Although I hadn't realized he was the king," and sank into a curtsy. She needed to ingratiate herself with the monarch for Iveriu's sake, and yet, as her gaze flitted over her right palm, over the purple welt that ran the length of her heart line, rebellion stirred.

To protect the Land, the Old Ones had imbued Branwen with

terrifying power: the Hand of Bríga. Ancient magic. She could set Tristan alight with her fire where he stood. She could kill the king. It wouldn't be the first time she had burned a man alive.

Marc reached forward, resting a hand lightly on Branwen's elbow. "There's no need to bow before me, either," he said. He sounded sincere. Drawing back, she tugged on the sleeve of her dress, covering her palm.

"I'm not as fluent in Ivernic as I'd like to be," Marc went on, apologetic. "Perhaps we can teach each other, Princess—"

"Branwen," she interrupted. "I am Branwen."

Confusion puckered his brow. "I—I thought you were named Eseult? Like your mother?" The king shot Tristan a quizzical look.

"The princess *is* called Eseult." Branwen was the one to reply. "But that's not me."

Despite the bustling of the port, a strange silence descended on the three of them. Branwen wondered if Tristan's mind had also darted back to the night when he returned to Iveriu for the Champions Tournament. He'd thought she was the princess at first, too.

Memory was more dangerous than any quicksand.

"There she is," Tristan told the king, directing a glance toward the *Dragon Rising.*

Eseult loitered at the end of the gangway, hesitant to leave the relative safety of the ship. Having felt Tristan's gaze settle upon her, she canted her head. Her golden hair was gathered hastily into a braid tossed over one shoulder. Without Branwen's expert fingers to tame her locks, they ran wild. And yet, it suited her.

Branwen looked at Eseult and saw her own broken heart.

Tristan raised his hand, beckoning.

The princess began processing down the dock as if she were walking toward her own execution. Indeed, if anyone learned what had passed between Tristan and Eseult on the ship, it *would* mean death for them both. As well as untold numbers of Iverni and Kernyveu.

When Branwen discovered Eseult in his bed, Tristan had offered to confess his crime, to die for the peace. Branwen had forbidden it. She wouldn't allow anything to throw the alliance into question. Tristan would have to learn to endure his own disgrace. A clean conscience wasn't worth a war.

The awkward silence that cloaked Branwen, Marc, and Tristan as they watched Eseult approach was sheared by a booming voice.

Ríx was the only word Branwen could pick out. *King.* She wheeled around to face the speaker. The two men did likewise. A few of the hawkers and their customers shot curious looks in the king's direction.

"*Ríx!*" called the newcomer again as he strutted from the market to meet them. He seemed closer to Branwen's age than Marc, and he carried himself with confidence, shoulders back. He had donned a tunic and sash that matched the king's, but his face was clean-shaven and his dirty-blond hair reached his shoulders. A guard, perhaps.

He flashed Branwen a ready smile.

The guard was undeniably attractive, but, unlike Marc, she surmised this man smiled too much. When he addressed Branwen, he took her aback by immediately speaking Aquilan.

"You must be the reason why my king left me in the dust," the guard said with a laugh. There was something haughty about the sound. Cutting Marc a look, he said, "He bolted from the stables like a colt as soon as the ship was sighted by the spyglass." Another laugh. "It's hard to protect the king when he's nowhere to be found."

Marc shrugged at the mild chastisement, unbothered. Branwen bristled. None of the Royal Guard at Castle Rigani would take such a liberty, even in jest, with her uncle, King Óengus. Marc's court at Monwiku must operate very differently.

"Not that I blame him." Sliding his gaze from the king to Tristan, the guard said, "I'm glad you're back, cousin." He squeezed Tristan's shoulder. *Cousin?* Tristan had never mentioned this man to Branwen. "Otherwise," he continued, "the ladies might start complaining that taking your place as King's Champion is aging me prematurely."

Branwen restrained a snort. Pompous noblemen had never been to her liking, and this one had let his strong jaw, dazzling topaz eyes, and prominent dimple make him vain.

"*Bran*—Lady Branwen," Tristan said. "May I introduce my cousin, Ruan?"

"*Prince* Ruan," he corrected him, and his eyes danced as he met Branwen's. "Delighted to meet you, Lady Branwen."

"And you," she lied. Men impressed with their own titles didn't impress her at all.

Ruan's smile twisted in question. "But, where is Princess Eseult?" he said, running his thumb along his lower lip.

A small cough. Eseult had sidled next to them quietly, positioning herself halfway behind Tristan. Her creamy cheeks were splotchy, and she shifted her weight anxiously from one foot to another, skittish as a doe. She looked wretched.

Up close, Branwen could see her cousin's eyes were puffy from crying—those emerald eyes that glittered like Rigani stones; they always made Branwen think of her mother, Lady Alana. *Essy*. Her first impulse was still to kiss away her baby cousin's tears. She had always felt the princess's sadness as her own.

Branwen clenched the hem of her shawl. She could no longer concern herself with her cousin's wants or needs.

The princess remained silent, worrying her hands together.

Branwen forced herself to speak instead. "Princess Eseult is still recovering from the attack last night, my Lord King," she said directly to Marc.

She shuddered, and it wasn't feigned. The *Dragon Rising* had been attacked by Shades: unclaimed souls of the dead transformed by Dhusnos into half-*kretarv*, half-human creatures. The ship was nearly lost.

"It . . . it was horrible," Eseult rasped.

Alarm streaked King Marc's face. "*Attack?*" He pivoted toward Tristan. "What happened?" he pressed his nephew.

Branwen saw Ruan's hand drop to the sword at his waist, posture becoming rigid as he leaned toward his king. Marc was unarmed. The King of Iveriu never bore arms, either, because his retainers were supposed to protect him. Carrying a weapon would indicate that he didn't trust them. It would make him appear vulnerable, as if he had something to fear. They likely had a similar custom in Kernyv.

"Pirates," Tristan lied through gritted teeth.

"Ours?" Fury underscored Marc's question but not surprise.

Had Kernyvak pirates grown so bold that they dared attack royal vessels?

Tristan dashed a glance at Branwen. He had promised to keep knowledge of her magic to himself—of the fire that had sent the Shades fleeing back to the merciless depths. She had saved the ship, but something inside her had been unleashed that scared Branwen even more than the Shades.

"Not ours," Tristan said to Marc, holding Branwen's gaze.

The king nodded, jaw relaxing a fraction. Under his breath, he muttered a Kernyvak phrase often shouted by the crew of the *Dragon Rising*. A curse, to be sure.

"When Captain Morgawr has finished unloading the ship," Marc instructed Tristan, "tell him I expect a full report."

"Of course."

Would Marc even believe that they'd been lost in the Otherworld, that they'd crossed the Sea of the Dead and been set upon by its inhabitants?

The king clasped Tristan's shoulder. "I'm glad you're home, brother." Tristan only ducked his head in response.

Marc took a step toward Eseult, and the princess sucked in a breath.

Branwen should have gone to her cousin on the ship, coaxed and cajoled her to play her part, to do her duty to Iveriu despite her indiscretion. But she hadn't. She couldn't push the image of Eseult's legs wrapped around Tristan from her mind.

Had either of them had a moment's hesitation before they betrayed her?

"It grieves me that your journey was so menaced," Marc told the princess, searching for the words. "But you're safe now in Kernyv. I swear it."

Eseult's lips trembled. Gesturing at Ruan, Marc explained, "Prince Ruan is to be your Queen's Champion. He won't let any harm befall you."

"It will be my greatest honor to serve you, *Rixani*." Then, "My queen," Ruan translated, bowing before Eseult with a flourish of the hand.

The princess swept her gaze from Ruan to Marc to Tristan.

"I want . . . Tristan—*Prince* Tristan—to be my Champion."

The words punched Branwen in the gut. She pressed her mouth into a line as bile rushed up her throat. Rage obliterated any guilt or pity she had for her role in Eseult and Tristan's treason.

Consternation creased Tristan's forehead, and Branwen prayed that nobody else could read the conflict in each line.

Eyes widening, Ruan straightened to standing. He looked to the king.

Marc rubbed his beard, glancing between his nephew and his future wife.

"If Tristan is agreeable," he said, a trace of reluctance in his voice. "I, of course, want you to feel welcome in your new homeland, Princess Eseult. You *are* very welcome here. You will be safe and . . ." He faltered. "Happy. I hope."

Tristan sought Branwen out once more with his gaze. She held her breath as she waited for him to give his answer.

"Thank you," Eseult said softly. She fidgeted with her braid, scratching at the base of her skull. "The prince saved me last night. He is my only friend in Kernyv—except for Branny."

When the princess had been thrown overboard wrestling with a Shade, as she vanished beneath the inky blackness, Branwen had thought her world would evanesce.

Now the shadow-stung part of Branwen's heart whispered that it might have been better for Iveriu if the Dark One had swallowed her cousin whole.

"I understand," Marc told his bride-to-be. "I trust Tristan with my life, too."

The edges of Tristan's mouth went taut. Branwen willed him to decline the request. He simply stared at his boots.

From the corner of her eye, Branwen saw Ruan grimace for less than the space of a breath. Laughing, he said, "Well, I'm happy to accept the permanent promotion to King's Champion," and slapped Tristan on the back, dispelling the renewed tension. "Thank you, cousin!"

"What about the ladies at court?" Branwen said, playful and acerbic at once. "I thought you were afraid to disappoint them." She knew she shouldn't antagonize a member of the royal family, especially within her first hour in Kernyv. But it felt good.

Ruan barked another laugh at her barb. It was fuller than the last, more open. "I think you'll find I'm never a disappointment, Lady Branwen."

"That remains to be seen, Prince Ruan." Branwen felt Tristan's eyes on her, but she ignored him.

"It's decided, then," Marc declared. "Tristan will be the Queen's Champion and poor Ruan will go gray looking after me." He peered at the nobleman sidelong, and his lips quirked. Ruan chuckled, then gave a swift nod of acquiescence.

"Always, *Rix*." The levity faded from his voice. "Kernyv forever."

After a stunned moment, Tristan bowed formally to Eseult.

"I am your servant," he said, and she blushed.

"My Champion," the princess said, a longing note to the title.

As Branwen watched Ruan watching the future Queen of Kernyv and her Champion, narrowing his gaze, the tide surged against the dock, splashing Branwen's feet.

She had been naive to hope her nightmares might end with the voyage.

They were just beginning.

LAND OF GIANTS

BRANWEN FOLLOWED THE OTHERS FROM the dock through the noisy marketplace. She heard a flute battle against the haggling vendors, its cheery tune utterly at odds with her mood. Passing by a baker's stall, she caught a whiff of an unknown spice. It tickled Branwen's nose, and she sneezed.

The baker, a woman who had seen at least forty summers, laughed, smiling broadly. Her skin was a rich shade of brown. The Iverni were all pale like Branwen, but many different peoples had settled on the island of Albion during the Aquilan occupation. Tristan's own father had descended from the legendary warriors of Kartago. She inhaled shortly and sneezed again.

Branwen wouldn't think of him; he was nothing to her. She mustered a lukewarm smile for the baker and continued wending her way through the stalls.

Four horses waited at the edge of the market square. Their leather saddles had been finely crafted, the seats dyed white and the skirts black. Royal Kernyvak colors.

Marc presented a gorgeous mare with a coat like starlight to the princess.

"A first wedding gift," he said.

"What's her name?" Eseult asked, voice shy.

"I thought I'd let you choose."

"It's nice to be able to choose," she replied, looking forlornly at Branwen, but she would get no sympathy. Ice flowed in Branwen's veins.

"It is," Marc agreed. He also shifted his gaze to Branwen. "I'm afraid I didn't bring enough horses. I didn't realize I would be welcoming two Ivernic ladies at my court."

"Branny is my only cousin and my most loyal companion," Eseult informed him. "We've never been parted. I'd—I'd be lost without her."

Branwen could barely stand to look at the princess. She'd only just set foot in Kernyv and already she'd risked the peace by making Tristan her Champion.

"I am indebted to you, Lady Branwen, for leaving your homeland to accompany my bride," King Marc said. He dipped his head.

"I always do my duty," Branwen replied. The king met her gaze and Branwen felt an understanding pass between them.

"When we reach the castle, please take your pick of my horses from the stables. As a small token of my gratitude."

"You're too generous." Branwen broke eye contact. She didn't want gifts from the man who had destroyed her family—if it really was him.

"Well, I for one am beginning to regret not entering the Champions Tournament myself," Ruan said, tone light. "Tristan, what's your secret?"

He startled. "Secret?"

"To setting off for Iveriu to win one bride, and coming home with two!" Ruan exclaimed, arching a brow. Tristan merely shook his head at his cousin.

"I am nobody's bride, Prince Ruan."

Ruan winced at the ferocity of Branwen's words, before releasing yet another laugh. This Kernyvak prince found life altogether too entertaining for Branwen's liking.

"Perhaps not, my lady," he said. "But may I offer you a ride? Since we seem to be short a horse?"

Tristan stepped between them. "Branwen will ride with me." It was practically a growl. Eseult's face pinched, and Marc pursed his lips, surveying the exchange.

Tristan's hands were curled in loose fists. Odd that a man who had remained unflappable while surrounded by enemy warriors should be rattled by his own cousin with such a little effort.

"As you prefer," Ruan relented with what Branwen assumed was characteristic nonchalance. He mounted his steed. "Make haste, cousin," he told Tristan, "while the horses can cross the causeway."

If she and Tristan were still friends, Branwen would ask him the source of his rivalry with Ruan. As adversaries, she should also want to know it.

She would not ask. She needed to become less than a stranger to him.

Marc helped his future queen onto the nameless mare before swinging a leg over his own stallion. Ruan urged his horse forward, riding out first. He waved at the villagers entering the market—the young women, in particular. Otherworld protect them from his wiles, thought Branwen.

The king and Eseult followed closely behind on their mounts, inciting many stares and bows.

Tristan dawdled, untying his steed slowly from a timber post.

Branwen knew he wanted a moment alone with her, and that was precisely what she was afraid of. "Branwen—" he started.

"We should go," she said. "We'll lose sight of the others."

"I know how to find my way home."

"The tide is coming in," she insisted.

"Fine." With a sigh, he hoisted himself astride a dappled gray stallion and extended his hand toward her. She hesitated before reluctantly accepting.

His callused palm sent tingles through her—her body didn't yet understand that this was the touch of a man who was no longer hers.

The lacerations on her stomach from the beak of a one-eyed Shade smarted as Branwen lifted herself onto the saddle, and she flinched.

"Did I hurt you?" Tristan said, panicked.

In so many ways. Shaking her head, Branwen touched the nape of her neck. "It's from the Shades." She would carry the scars from their monstrous beaks on her flesh for the rest of her life. "I'll heal." She positioned herself sidesaddle in front of him, her mouth growing parched at the contact. Their faces were too close.

"You were a warrior last night," Tristan said. He reached a hand to her cheek out of habit, then stopped himself. Instead, he took the Hand of Bríga in his own.

Tristan had witnessed Branwen destroying the Shades with abandon, reveling in it. She hadn't known the extent of her power until she was confronted with the Dark One's creatures. A power she had never asked for. Still, she couldn't deny its exhilaration.

"Thank you for not telling the king," she said, even though it cost her to thank him. Many of the Kernyveu adhered to the Cult of the Horned One, which barred women from its Mysteries. Her aunt had implored Branwen to be discreet with her magic.

"I would never betray you," Tristan replied. Branwen could only release one brutal laugh. "I deserve your wrath, I know I do." The hazel flecks in his dark eyes sparked to life. "I still don't know *what*—how . . ." He trailed off, his voice rife with disgust and disbelief, and Branwen yearned for nothingness. To go numb.

"But I also deserve the chance to make things right," Tristan said with a hint of the stubbornness she'd once admired. "To regain my honor."

"By being the Queen's Champion?"

"I didn't have a choice," he pleaded. Tristan didn't know how right he was, and Branwen hated him for it.

She hated herself.

He leaned toward her until their lips were almost touching.

"*Odai eti ama*," he breathed. *I hate and I love.*

"I have no love for you, Prince Tristan." Branwen would lie and lie and lie until it became the truth.

"Don't call me that," Tristan told her, switching into Ivernic.

"Oh? Would you prefer *king*?" she said in Aquilan. "*Ríx*?" Branwen goaded him in Kernyvak.

He recoiled, offended, and she took more than a little satisfaction from it. Tristan had inherited the territory of Liones—the southernmost tip of Kernyv—from his mother, Princess Gwynedd. Technically, he could be its king. He had confided in Branwen that there were those at the court of Monwiku who disapproved of Tristan's mother marrying a commoner, especially one of Kartagon ancestry, and feared that he would challenge Marc for the throne.

"Bedding the king's bride is an excellent way to start a civil war," Branwen said, and swung her head forward.

She heard a sharp intake of breath. Then Tristan lifted the reins, warm shoulders brushing hers, and nudged the stallion into a trot. Branwen had made it to Kernyv, Tristan's arms were around her, and yet she had never felt so far away from him—or herself.

Flames flickered in her hand, just beneath the surface of her skin. Fire that demanded release.

✠ ✠ ✠

The coastal path reminded Branwen of the Rock Road in Iveriu that she had traveled so many times. Tristan's breath teased the back of her neck as they shared a mount in simmering silence; hoofbeats mimicked the surf buffeting craggy rocks.

She scanned the lush cliffs, hoping against hope to spot a familiar, unnaturally red coat and white-tipped ears. Queen Eseult had promised that the Old Ones would send Branwen a teacher when one was needed. But that was before she had failed them. In her bones, she knew the fox wasn't coming back.

She was on her own in a strange land.

Up ahead, King Marc rode beside the princess, stance guarded. Branwen traced the grooves on the underside of her brooch, almost like a meditation. For all the years after her parents died, faceless raiders had stalked Branwen's dreams, but the Dark One had given those nightmares a face. She rubbed the scabbing claw marks on her forearms.

Branwen had never divulged to either Tristan or Eseult what had been revealed to her in the vile *kretarv*'s eyes. She hadn't wanted to upset her cousin with what she'd seen, and—if Branwen was being truly honest with herself—she'd also been afraid Tristan might not believe her, or make excuses for the man he considered his brother. Now she was glad she'd kept her own counsel.

"Look, Branwen," Tristan said. "Monwiku." The breath caught in Branwen's throat as the road curved.

Captain Morgawr had pointed out the castle from the ship, but then it had only been an indistinct silhouette. From this distance, the structure was awe-inspiring. Not only had Monwiku been set upon an island, it had been carved into what appeared to be a small mountain. Turrets and towers grasped at the sky, impossibly high.

Trees and shrubbery enveloped the base of the castle, growing from the bedrock, leading down the slope toward the water. Although it was nearly winter, the branches had not yet shed all of their leaves. Blossoms like gemstones flecked the green expanse.

A series of round stone dwellings with thatched roofs dotted the circumference of the island. Smoke swirled from the hearths contained within. Rowboats and square-sailed dinghies suitable for shallow water were moored around the shoreline, bobbing as the tide began to rise.

The scale of Monwiku completely dwarfed Castle Rigani, and Branwen found herself humbled by the seat of Kernyvak power. It would also be a fool's errand to besiege it. Branwen thanked the Old Ones that her late uncle Morholt and the other Ivernic nobles who had agitated for an invasion had failed to sway King Óengus to their cause.

"It's an entire city on an island," she said, unable to keep the amazement from her voice. There was nothing in Iveriu that qualified it as a city, but she'd been taught by the royal tutor about the maze-like streets, densely packed dwellings, and throngs of people thrown together throughout the Aquilan Empire. Master Bécc would sorely regret missing this sight.

Tristan shifted in the saddle behind her, releasing a laugh. "The island was created by giants," he said.

Branwen turned her head to show him her skepticism. "*Giants?* You believe in giants?"

"Why not?" He shrugged and there was defiance in the set of his shoulders. "With all that we've seen?"

Her attempt at indifference was marred by a scowl. There had been a time, not so long ago, when Branwen didn't believe in magic or the Otherworld. Or love. A time when she had known her place in *this* world and been content with it.

"We call them the Koranied—the giants," Tristan said in a rush to fill the fraught quiet. "The island of Albion is named after the warrior-giantess Alba who led their conquest."

"I see. Should I fear becoming a treat for a hungry giantess, then?" Branwen used to adore Tristan's regaling her with tales of his people, starting when she had believed him to be a shipwrecked bard named Tantris.

Maybe they had never known how to do anything but lie to each other.

"The Koranied were driven from our shores," Tristan assured her. "They made their last stand here, at Monwiku. As they made their retreat, Alba, their leader, demolished the land between Kernyv and Monwiku with her bare hands." Despite his restless manner, Tristan always enjoyed telling stories. Branwen could see it in the way his eyes shone.

It would be too easy to be lulled into familiar patterns, to picture herself sitting by the fireside, listening to him sing ballads of epic battles.

"For several decades," he told Branwen, "the Koranied continued to terrorize the coastline until one day a Kernyvman named Lugmarch saw a giant stung by a wasp drop down dead."

She leaned closer. A traitorous part of Branwen's heart wanted to hear how this Lugmarch had outwitted the giants.

"Lugmarch gathered all of the wasp nests in Kernyv and ground them into dust. Then he laced vats of honeyed mead with the fine powder."

Tristan paused for dramatic effect. "The greedy Koranied accepted the offering as their due. One by one, the poisoned giants fell into the sea. Dead. For his ingenuity, Lugmarch was made the first king of the Kernyveu, and he built his castle upon the rock of Monwiku."

Tristan risked a smile, and Branwen felt the air leave her chest. The smile was too much—it made her want to turn back the wheel of time. It made her want impossible things. Flattening her lips, Branwen dug her heel into their mount's side.

The stallion broke into a gallop, and she gripped the front of the saddle to avoid being thrown off.

Her shawl billowed as they rushed toward the beach where Ruan, King Marc, and Eseult waited. Their horses were halted at one end of a cobblestoned path that traversed the causeway. Ruan and the king were speaking with a young man who wore a black tunic embroidered with a crest in red thread that Branwen didn't recognize.

Ruan jerked on his reins, and his steed's front legs lifted from the ground and crashed back down in two plumes of sand.

Tristan slowed their mount to a trot. As they drew nearer, Branwen saw the muscles of Ruan's neck stiffening as the man in the black tunic relayed his message. She couldn't understand more than a few words, but, from Ruan's reaction, it was troubling news.

Begrudgingly, Branwen whispered to Tristan, "What is it?"

"There's been an accident," he answered. "Ruan's family owns many mines." She tucked that information away as their stallion walked toward the others.

Ruan ran a hand along his sash several times, stress rolling off him. Pronounced ridges had also formed on Marc's forehead as he questioned the messenger. Eseult's lips were drawn, her hand wrapped tightly around her braid, flicking its tail against her shoulder.

The princess coughed, and Marc returned his attention from the messenger.

"Forgive me, Lady Princess," he told her in Aquilan. "We've just received word of a mining accident. Prince Ruan must leave us to inspect the damage."

"*Sire—*" the newly appointed King's Champion began to protest.

"I'm within view of the castle, Ruan. And I'm quite confident Tristan can keep me safe while you're gone."

The muscles in Ruan's jaw tightened before he vaunted a smile at his cousin.

"I would be so very grateful," he said to Tristan.

"I'll go with you." The words flew from Branwen's mouth before she knew what she was saying.

Ruan raised both eyebrows, equally shocked. "Where I'm going is no place for a lady."

"I'm not a lady, Prince Ruan. I'm a healer." She twisted her torso to face Tristan. "Tell him," she said, throwing out a hand in frustration.

Tristan swallowed. "Lady Branwen has saved me many times over."

"And me," Eseult said, voice filled more with apprehension than appreciation.

Ruan looked to his king for permission, and Branwen followed his gaze to make her appeal. "King Marc," she said. "I was trained by Queen Eseult herself—the most renowned healer in Iveriu. Let me help your people." His silver eyes deepened to pewter as he considered her request.

It galled Branwen to ask anything of the king—of the boy from her vision—but a more profound need compelled her.

"Let me show the Kernyveu that we have come here to heal the wounds of the past," she persisted.

A long moment passed. Branwen felt Eseult's gaze upon her cheek as surely as if it were a touch, but she refused to look her way.

"With my heartfelt gratitude, Lady Branwen," Marc said at last.

"Thank you, my Lord King."

"Branny, if it's dangerous, perhaps you shouldn't—"

Branwen directed a hard stare at the princess, and she went quiet.

"I need to ride fast," Ruan told Branwen. "And you have no horse."

Branwen looked back at Tristan. "You don't mind walking from here, do you? After such cramped quarters on the ship, I'd think you'd be happy to stretch your legs."

His nostrils flared. Ruan laughed. "You're astride a stallion, my lady. Are you sure you can handle him?"

"You have no idea what I can handle, Prince Ruan."

"I'll remember that." Shifting his gaze to his cousin, he lifted his chin. "We must away."

Tristan huffed as he dismounted and landed in the sand. Branwen grabbed the reins, triumph teasing her lips. She'd never liked being a passenger.

"I won't stop, so don't lose me," Ruan warned her. He bolted inland, toward a forest.

Branwen cast a parting glance at Marc, Tristan, and Eseult. She was only too happy to turn her back on all three of them.

She spurred her stallion forward and tasted a heady moment of freedom as she left them behind.

DOORS TO NOWHERE

TRUE TO HIS WORD, PRINCE Ruan didn't slow his steed for a moment. Branwen galloped after him into a densely thicketed wood. Like the greenery that surrounded Monwiku Castle, the odd flower still clung to the branches overhead. She lowered herself closer to the stallion's neck as the forest floor sloped upward and her mount began to climb.

Hooves thundering against the moss and dirt, the steed exhaled steam through his nostrils. Branwen had almost caught up to Ruan when the path narrowed into a tunnel of hazel trees. All at once, the branches pressed in on her. As children, she and Essy had declared themselves to be like the honeysuckle vine that wraps around the hazel tree, ever entwined. One could not survive without the other.

An almost uncontrollable urge possessed Branwen—to summon her fire and set the hazel trees alight. To burn the entire forest down.

She heard Dhusnos's laughter.

With a shiver, she clutched a thatch of the horse's mane to steady herself. Her cousin's passionate nature had always balanced Branwen's contemplative one; her brightness had assuaged the pain of Branwen's other losses, opened her heart. That was in the past. She would learn to live without her best friend. She would seal off her heart and hurl it to the bottom of the sea like she had the Loving Cup.

Pearly sunlight blinded Branwen as she emerged from the forest. Lifting her hand as a shield, she saw Prince Ruan a few horse lengths ahead, his blond hair flying in the wind.

He didn't look back to see if she followed.

Branwen's muscles were weakened from a month without exercise during the sea journey, her energy sapped from last night's attack. Nevertheless, she wouldn't give the conceited nobleman the satisfaction of losing her.

Vast moorland expanded in front of her. Even as heat from the sun warmed Branwen's face, she spied fog rolling in from the south. Chasing after Prince Ruan, she realized that the moor, in fact, lay on one side of a valley. On the opposite hill sat a lake surrounded by stones of burgundy. It didn't look natural.

And, what was more, in the distance, she glimpsed a similar, smaller lake on her side of the valley. A bridge spanned the distance between the two lakes. *Bridge* seemed like too lowly a term for the structure. Branwen had never seen anything like it.

Dominating the landscape, rose seven enormous, rounded arches. Each was at least a tower tall, fashioned from the same rubicund rock as the walls surrounding the lakes. There didn't appear to be any roads leading either to or away from the massive bridge. Branwen struggled to think of its purpose. She could well believe this monument had been constructed by the Koranied of which Tristan spoke.

Captivated, Branwen made a clicking noise from the side of her mouth, prodding her steed to quicken its pace. When she was less than half a horse length behind Ruan, she called out, "What is it?"

"Aquilan technology," Ruan replied, staccato, voice still raised as they rode into the wind. His mount eased beside hers. Pointing at the impressive arches, the prince said, "The bridge channels the water from one dammed lake to the other. Then we release the water into the valley. It washes away the rock to reveal the minerals."

Branwen marveled at the archways stamped against the sky like doors to nowhere.

"Ingenious but dangerous," Ruan remarked, pulling her gaze away from the imposing edifice.

"Dangerous?"

"You'll soon see for yourself." The reply was gruff. He made a clicking sound at his horse and sped away again. Inwardly, Branwen sighed. Although she preferred impatience to false flattery. She touched her middle—her cuts were weeping fresh blood.

Another quarter hour of hard riding later, Branwen spotted a black chasm against the green of the valley. A wound in the earth. The force of the water released from the smaller lake had split the land, exposing its veins like secrets. Did the Kernyveu not fear disturbing the Old Ones who dwelled in the Otherworld beneath *ráithana*—hills and mounds—such as these?

Branwen knew that Kernyv exported minerals, especially white lead, to the southern continent, yet this bordered on plundering. Robbery. She quivered at the sheer violence of it. If the Aquilan Empire had set its sights on Iveriu, her small island would have been child's play to conquer. Master Bécc had taught Branwen that the greatest empire the world had ever known disintegrated through the folly and tyranny of its own leaders.

She was glad of it.

Ruan halted his steed at the edge of the moorland. When Branwen reached him, the breath buckled against her rib cage.

Down below was carnage. Shouts and screams pierced the air.

The prince looked ashen. "The gate must have broken," he said, mostly to himself.

Branwen saw people—bodies—strewn on either side of the man-made gorge. Mud had swept away everything in its path. The water from the small lake had caused a landslide. If miners had been working in the crevasse when the dam burst . . . Branwen swallowed. The poor men would have drowned where they stood.

King Marc had said there had been an accident. This was a disaster.

Water continued to stream into the valley.

Branwen probed Ruan with a glance. He scrubbed a hand over his face, anguish tightening his lips. "Stay here," he barked as he met her gaze.

"I came to *help*."

"I won't be responsible for injuring the queen's lady's maid," he said and, without waiting for her response, raced his mount down the hillside. Dirt spewed into the air from its hooves.

Branwen's temper spiked. Lady's maid she might be, but she was *not* Ruan's to command. She gave her mount a swift kick and descended into the shadow of the great arches, the howls of the wounded erasing any fear she might have for herself.

Before Branwen discovered her magic, she had medicine. The healing arts she had painstakingly studied for years were skills she could trust. Helping these people was something she knew how to do— something to balance the scales of her grievous mistake.

As Branwen advanced toward the chasm, the screams and groans multiplied. Some muffled. Her ears struggled to hear them. *Buried.* Men were trapped beneath the wreckage—alive. Others were digging through the piles of rubble to free them with their bare hands. Many would hear a Death-Teller's shriek before they were unearthed.

Branwen's mount began to stumble in the thick, uneven ground. She pulled up on the reins. The stallion nickered in something like complaint. Patting his shoulder, "*Mormerkti,*" Branwen said and jumped down to the soggy ground.

Debris was flung in all directions: broken tent poles, chairs, tools, ceramic jugs. There must have been makeshift resting places for the miners here before the flood. She spotted a banner floating in a dirty puddle: the same red hand on black as worn by the messenger at Monwiku.

A higher-pitched, female scream broke through Branwen's thoughts. She spun toward the sound and launched into a sprint. She picked her way through the ruins, tripping several times.

Her gaze caught hold of the mud-spattered skirt first. It wasn't a woman. It was a girl. Twelve years old at most. What was she doing here?

The girl writhed on the ground, skirt twisting around her. Her ankle was pinned between two large stones.

Branwen froze, just for a moment, as if she were back on the deck of the *Dragon Rising*. Cadan's corpse haunted her. The cabin boy had been her friend, and Branwen hadn't been able to save him last night.

She shook her head. Despair was futile. Branwen heard her aunt's calm voice telling her to find those she could help, to focus on what she *could* do.

She dropped to her knees beside the girl. Thrashing her limb would surely be making her injury worse. Placing a firm hand on the girl's shoulder, "*Stop,*" Branwen said in Aquilan. The girl stopped to stare—but not in comprehension. Of course a peasant wouldn't speak the language of the court.

Did she also fear Branwen's Ivernic accent the way little Gráinne in Iveriu had once feared Tristan's?

Holding the girl's gaze, Branwen willed her to understand that she wanted to help, that she meant her no harm. The Kernyvak girl released a shaky breath and nodded. Branwen brushed a reddish-brown lock from her face, then turned her attention to the girl's trapped ankle.

The weight of the stone would doubtless have broken it. If the girl was fortunate, the bone would only be fractured, not fragmented. But it was impossible to assess the damage while her leg was still pinned under the rock.

Branwen gave the stone a firm shove. Her shoulders ached, and the wounds on her neck and stomach chafed. The rock didn't budge. She swore.

Tears streamed from the girl's dark blue eyes. Her freckled cheeks were white with pain.

Branwen pushed again with all her might. Still the stone resisted her. She beseeched the Old Ones to help this Kernyvak girl.

"I thought I'd told you to stay put," Ruan said, squatting beside her. Branwen glanced up, leery. She'd lost sight of him in the chaos.

"As you said, I'm the *queen's* lady's maid. I don't take orders from you."

"Clearly."

The self-satisfied prince wasn't the aid she'd hoped the Old Ones would send, but she'd take it. "Help me get this rock off the girl," Branwen said.

He cocked his head. "I think you like orders just fine when you're the one giving them." She snorted at that. "Together," he said.

Ruan and Branwen shoved the stone, and their combined strength was enough to topple it into the mud. Branwen leaned back on her heels, panting. The girl's yellow skirt was soaked with blood around her right calf.

The girl cried out at the sight and immediately tried to get up. "Tell her to lie still," Branwen barked at Ruan. Without the pressure from the stone, the blood flowed freely.

"And ask the girl her name." Branwen cursed her inability to communicate. Just speaking in Aquilan was taxing enough while a thousand other thoughts swirled in her mind.

Ruan seemed dubious, but he did as she asked. "Lowenek," the prince told her a moment later. "It means 'joy,'" he added. *Joy*. Branwen's chest pinched.

"Lowenek," she repeated, pressing a hand to the girl's wet cheek, shushing her. Then, to Ruan, Branwen said, "Give me your sash." He puzzled at her. "I need to stop the bleeding." Why hadn't she thought to bring any of her herbs or bandages with her?

As Ruan whipped the sash over his head, Branwen told him, "Find me a stick. Or something firm. I need to splint it." He arched a brow at her curt tone, glanced around them, then dashed away.

Branwen worked quickly, tying the sash tightly around Lowenek's calf. The girl mewled. The swelling around her ankle was the size of Branwen's fist. Branwen detected the bone just below the surface of the skin, almost pushing through.

When Ruan returned brandishing a broken piece of tent pole, Branwen snatched the wood from his grasp. A few splinters bit her skin.

"Hold her shoulders and keep her still," Branwen said. Ruan nodded. "I'm going to set the bone." Setting it would be agonizing for Lowenek, and she dearly wished she had some Clíodhna's dust to put the girl to sleep. Clíodhna was an Otherworld queen whose song was believed to heal the sick.

Instead, Branwen began humming an Ivernic lullaby as she placed the shaft of wood beside Lowenek's calf. *The wild moon is high, my love, come away with me.* In a distant recess of her mind, Branwen could hear Lady Alana's dulcet contralto singing the melody to her, night after night. *The wild moon is high, my love, follow me into the Otherworld of sleep.*

Aiming her gaze at the spot where the bone pressed against the skin, Branwen positioned one hand above it and one below.

She flicked her eyes at Ruan. "One . . . two . . . *three*."

The snap ripped through Branwen, reverberating in her skull. Lowenek cried out—a bloodcurdling scream—before she slumped into unconsciousness. Branwen tied the tent pole to the girl's leg, her breathing labored.

Feeling Ruan's eyes on her, Branwen tilted her head in his direction. He wore a mystified expression.

"What?" she demanded.

Before Ruan could answer, there was a commotion from farther into the center of the gorge. The valley quaked as if a thunderclap had come from the earth itself. Ruan sprinted toward the fracas.

Branwen gave Lowenek a rapid assessment. The girl was safe enough for now. There was nothing further that Branwen could do for her, and there were others who needed her help. Following Ruan's lean form with her eyes, she leapt to her feet.

She wiped the girl's blood on her dress as she ran.

The rumbling had been a fresh landslide. Rescuers had become victims. The flood must have destabilized the exposed soil.

Branwen rushed toward the edge of the chasm and saw a man

trapped in mud up to his chest. He flailed his arms as if he were drowning.

"Help!" he bellowed. "Help!"

It took Branwen a moment to realize she'd understood him. The man was calling out in Ivernic. This was one of her countrymen.

Ruan ran headlong toward the man, putting himself in the path of the burst dam. Several other miners rushed alongside him. The prince's feet disappeared into the mud, then his knees. He waded toward the Iverman, fighting against the sludge.

Another tremor passed through the valley.

Branwen watched in suspense as Ruan reached the Iverman first, looped his arms through the miner's, and yanked. The trapped man hollered.

He was calling on the Old Ones.

A cascade of falling rock showered Ruan and the Iverman from above.

One of the other miners, also shouting in Ivernic, secured his arms around Ruan's waist. Five other men joined them, forming a chain of bodies, and, several great heaves later, the submerged Iverman was free.

Once Branwen saw that Ruan and her countryman appeared unscathed, she scouted for other patients.

Walking among the injured, Branwen heard groans and prayers in both Kernyvak and Ivernic. She stopped beside a white-haired man. A thin tree branch protruded from his belly. It was a mortal wound.

His eyes opened and latched onto Branwen's. Smiling, he reached for her hand.

"Goddess Ériu," said the man in her native tongue. "Have you come to take me home?"

Branwen felt a jolt in her chest. Another Iverman. He was delirious, close to death. The numbing kindness had already relieved him of his pain. She folded her hand around his weathered, age-spotted one.

"How long is it since you've seen Ivernic shores?" she asked, voice placid.

"Twenty-five winters. I was taken by raiders near Bodwa." He coughed, blood leaking from the corner of his mouth.

Anger roiled in her heart. Branwen fell to her knees beside him. Castle Bodwa was her family stronghold. This man had been under her family's protection.

"Did you know Lord Caedmon?" she said.

"I pray to the Old Ones daily for his safekeeping."

Branwen touched the brooch on her muddied cloak. "I'm his daughter," she said. This man had been captured before Branwen had been born, before her parents were even wed. "I am Lady Branwen of Castle Bodwa." She decided not to tell him of her father's death. Squeezing the old Iverman's hand, Branwen said, "I offer you my protection."

"Thank you, Lady Branwen." He coughed again. His eyes were glazed as he looked at her, as if he were already peering through the Veil to the Otherworld. "I am Talorc. My son is Ném. If he survives, ask him to drink my Final Toast."

"I will."

Branwen stared down at her scarred palm. Only magic could save Talorc now. Her fire began to stir. Magic was his only hope, and yet Branwen didn't want to use it. She was afraid to loose that part of herself—afraid of the elation she'd felt fighting the Shades.

If she did nothing, Talorc would soon be in the Land of Youth.

Coming across a man who had served Branwen's father on her first day in Kernyv was more than a strange coincidence, and she knew what her father would want her to do. "Forgive me, Talorc," she said.

Branwen's heart made the decision before her mind knew what her hands were doing. She ripped the branch from the old man's abdomen, and his blood spurted across her chest and face. Branwen's skin heated as she felt her magic rise. A flame appeared in the center of her right palm. It wavered, danced, growing higher.

The Hand of Bríga could heal as well as destroy, but Branwen didn't know which aspect she was summoning. When she'd saved her cousin's life on the *Dragon Rising*, it had been more luck than skill.

Goddess Bríga, I implore you, guide my power.

Breathing hard, Branwen pressed her palm to Talorc's wound. Astonishment filled her as she watched the flesh begin to close. Sweat dripped from her temples. She still couldn't quite believe what she was capable of.

Light-headedness deluged Branwen and she swayed on her knees. Talorc convulsed, the Iverman's eyes rolling into the back of his head. Branwen prayed he wouldn't remember what she'd done for him.

"You are Otherworld-touched, daughter."

Branwen cringed. Fear shot through her as she lifted her gaze, glancing over her shoulder.

The resonant voice belonged to a woman whose red hair was flecked with silver strands. She too had spoken in Ivernic. Branwen gaped as she approached her from behind. The woman's skin glimmered like moonlight. A few crow's feet surrounded her eyes, which were so brown they appeared black.

"I haven't been anyone's daughter in a very long time," Branwen replied, tiny hairs prickling all over her body. The woman halted beside her.

Squinting down at Branwen, the stranger lifted one corner of her mouth. "Healers are daughter, mother, sister to each other in turn—as the need arises."

"I am not in need of a mother."

The woman grabbed Branwen's right hand, exposing the newly inflamed scar.

"If you wield your power bluntly, like a weapon, it will begin to wield you. You will become a weapon, daughter."

Branwen tried to pull her hand back, but the woman held firm.

"I am a healer. Nothing more." Looking the woman in the eye, Branwen told her, "I have no power."

Covering Branwen's palm with her own, the woman closed her eyes. Elation rushed through Branwen and she gasped in fright. When the woman removed her hand again, the scar on Branwen's palm was nothing but a threadlike line, smooth and white. It looked like a childhood injury.

The healer woman croak-laughed at Branwen's wonderment.

"My name is Ailleann. Some call me the Wise Damsel. Those in need are always welcome in my home."

"You're an Iverwoman?"

Not answering, Ailleann looked at Talorc, whose eyes were closed, his chest rising and falling in slumber. "He'll live."

Branwen rubbed the white line again, licking her chapped lips.

"I can help you tame your power," the Wise Damsel said.

"I don't want to tame it—I don't want it at all." The Old Ones had made a mistake. Her power was a curse.

The other woman furrowed her brow. "We don't always want

what we need." Another shout for help rose above the din. "When you're ready to accept your gift," she said, "you'll find me at the White Moor."

The Wise Damsel held Branwen's gaze for a long moment before turning on her heel and striding away.

THE WILD MOON

THE SUN HUNG LOW IN the sky, traveling westward toward
Iveriu as Branwen moved between the survivors, helping those
she was able. The last of the daylight on the great Aquilan water bridge
made the stone shine like rubies. Branwen felt woozy on her feet, and
she welcomed the sensation. If the Old Ones were merciful, they would
let her remain in this hazy, dreamlike state forever.

She stumbled on a loose rock and slipped backward.

She never hit the ground.

"It's time to go, Lady Branwen," Ruan said, his strong arms supporting her. She relaxed into him before realizing her mistake.

Immediately, she pulled out of his embrace. Branwen regarded
the Kernyvak prince. His tunic was crusted with mud and blood, his
hair matted with sweat and dirt. He didn't resemble the smug nobleman who had met Branwen at the Port of Marghas in the least. The
warm light highlighted his cheeks invitingly. She tossed the thought
aside.

"There are still wounded that need tending," Branwen protested.

"Night is falling."

"I'm not afraid of the dark."

Ruan laughed. "I don't think you're afraid of anything," he said, and Branwen scoffed at how wrong he was. Her fears were too numerous to count. He extended a waterskin in her direction. "Here. You must be parched."

Accepting the waterskin, she murmured, "*Mormerkti*," as she put it to her lips.

His amber-brown eyes glinted. "With Lugmarch's blessing."

"The king who killed the giants?"

A nod accompanied a sly smile. "Since Lugmarch defeated the giants with tainted mead, it's customary in Kernyv to offer a drink with his blessing," Ruan explained as Branwen took another gulp. "When you're a guest in someone's home, the host will take a sip first to prove it isn't poisoned."

She lowered the waterskin from her mouth. "I didn't see you take a sip," she challenged, but it was halfhearted.

Ruan whisked the waterskin from Branwen's grip and guzzled the remainder. "Satisfied?" he asked as he wiped his mouth, a single drop clinging to his lower lip.

"I suppose, my prince."

Catching her eye, he said, "Would you do me the favor of calling me Ruan? We've already been through mud together." He motioned with the waterskin at Branwen's ruined dress and shawl.

"So we have," she agreed; his intense gaze provoked a flush. "But I thought you were fond of being called *Prince*?"

"Sometimes." Ruan took a step toward her, closing the space between them. "Sometimes I like to be just Ruan."

He licked his thumb and raised it to Branwen's cheek.

"What are you doing?" she said.

"You have blood on your cheek, Branwen." She schooled her features, compressing her lips, and nodded. She hadn't given Ruan permission to call her by her name, and she shouldn't be allowing him the liberty of touching her, either. But, just for an instant, she craved physical contact. "I like your freckles," he told her. Branwen said nothing as he dabbed away another splotch of blood with a tender gesture.

"*Mormerktí*," she breathed.

"*Sekrev.*" Ruan kept his thumb on her cheek. "That means you're welcome," he added in Aquilan.

"I know." Tristan had taught Branwen its meaning the day after the only night she'd ever spent in his bed. If she had given all of herself to him that night, would he have been able to resist the power of the Loving Cup? Could love ever be stronger than magic?

Branwen winced at the memory, and Ruan dropped his hand. He stepped back, misinterpreting Branwen's reaction.

Clearing his throat, the prince cast his gaze to where the sun had just dipped below the horizon. "I must insist that we return to Monwiku," he said. "I have duties there to attend to—and so do you."

Branwen didn't need the reminder, and she didn't want to go back. Nothing filled her with more dread. Not the Shades. Not even the Dark One.

For the first time, she understood how the princess had felt on the night of the Farewell Feast. Her cousin had called Kernyv a prison. Perhaps it was. But she and Branwen were imprisoned here together.

Branwen had vowed to the Queen of Iveriu that she would place the interests of her kingdom above all else. She would redeem herself to the Land. Her mission was all she had left.

"Very well," she told Ruan. He offered her an arm, and, although Branwen was mistrustful, exhaustion obliged her to take it. "Who will tend the wounded?" she asked as they began to retreat from the center of the gorge.

"You mean you aren't going to do it single-handedly?" Branwen tensed, then released a laugh-sigh. "Fear not," Ruan said. "A messenger has been sent to the nearest temple of the Horned One."

"There are healers at the temple?"

Now it was Ruan's turn to look at her askance. "There are no temples in Iveriu?"

"The New Religion has not yet come to our land. We are devoted to the Old Ones."

Ruan tapped his thumb against his thigh, considering. "I wouldn't call it *new*. The Cult of the Horned One came to Albion in the era of the Aquilan Empire."

"You're a believer?"

"As much as I believe in anything," he said, almost under his breath. "But to answer your first question, the *kordweyd*—seers of the Horned One—are all skilled healers. The temples have cared for the sick since the time of the plague."

Questions buzzed in Branwen's mind. She knew that forty or so years ago the island of Albion and the southern continent had been ravaged by disease. The Iverni believed that the Old Ones had protected them from the plague because it never came to their island. The raids on Iveriu were fewer and farther between during that period.

"Only the *kordweyd* dared to enter the plague-ridden villages," Ruan expounded. "If the seers died in service of the afflicted, the Horned One would resurrect them for their sacrifice."

Branwen kept quiet. She could understand why the New Religion was adopted so eagerly in the wake of such devastation.

"I met a woman the miners call the Wise Damsel," she said. "Is she also a *kordweyd*?"

Ruan gave a small snort. "Wise Damsels, gifted women—the peasants go to them for herbs and charms. Fool's hope."

"And you scorn these women?" Branwen's tone grew caustic.

"I meant no offense." Ruan met her gaze. "The *kordweyd* at the temples have studied the medicine of the Aquilan Empire and beyond. They deal in facts, not superstitions."

She herself had once spoken with condescension of things she couldn't explain. Using the Hand of Bríga to save Talorc had been a risky, impetuous thing to do. Branwen understood better why Queen Eseult wanted her to keep her magic hidden.

"You hold the conquerors of your island in very high esteem," Branwen pointed out.

Ruan lifted a shoulder. "They never conquered Kernyv—and we learned much from them."

She made a noncommittal noise, wondering if everyone in Kernyv shared the prince's views. Ruan came to a stop in front of the horses. He must have collected them during the afternoon and tied them to a lone tent pole sticking up in the mud. In the coming evening, the coat of Branwen's dappled gray stallion glowed like a storm cloud.

"Allow me to help you up?" Ruan said.

"Thank you." Branwen grabbed ahold of the mane. The prince gave her a boost into the saddle before launching himself onto his own mount.

Branwen surveyed the field of broken bodies and debris. She prayed to the Old Ones that Lowenek and the others would not be taken by infection during the night.

Ruan made a clicking noise and both steeds began to ascend the slope onto the moor. Branwen was grateful their pace was barely above a walk. She pressed a hand to her middle. She would need to clean her own wounds when they reached the castle.

They rode across the moor for a few minutes before Branwen restarted the conversation. "There were Iverni among the miners," she said. "Men captured in raids."

Ruan glanced at her sidelong. "Yes. And there are Kernyvak prisoners in Iveriu, are there not?"

"Yes." Branwen swallowed. Prisoners of war were enemies of Iveriu and they were put to work, usually hard labor. There were fewer Kernyvak prisoners in Iveriu solely because Ivernic raids on Kernyv had been less successful.

"The man you saved from the landslide," she said to Ruan. "He was Ivernic. A prisoner, I dare say. Why did you risk your life for him?"

The moon began to rise over the moor as Ruan answered.

"He may be a prisoner, but he's still a man." The prince's inflection was heated.

Branwen blinked twice, taken aback, and recalled the day her father had saved a drowned fisherman with the kiss of life. "We Iverni believe that if you save someone's life, your honor becomes tied to theirs until they return the favor," she said.

"In that case, Lady Branwen, your honor must be pulled in very many directions."

Branwen went quiet. Her honor was tied to both Tristan and Eseult in more ways than Ruan could ever discover. Cheeks warming, she raised her eyes toward the moon. "I would like to check on my patients tomorrow," she told him.

"I'll see what I can arrange."

He kicked his stallion into a trot, and Branwen's mount followed suit. Her joints ached as they rode a while longer in a mostly companionable silence.

"This is called the Morrois Forest," Ruan remarked as they reentered the wood. Thin light through the arches of bowed branches made the contours of his face appear jagged. "When we were younger, Tristan used to follow me and Marc when we came here to hunt, challenging us to duels with scraggly sticks."

Essy, too, had shadowed Branwen until she had become as essential as a limb.

"You're older than Tristan, I gather?" Branwen said.

"By four summers." Which made Branwen wonder why Ruan hadn't been selected as King's Champion from the start. Surely being older made him the natural choice?

"My father, Prince Edern, was the younger brother of King Merchion—Marc's father," Ruan added, supplying a partial answer to her unvoiced question. "He passed away a year after his brother."

"I'm sorry for your loss."

He nodded in acknowledgment before a false smile crossed his face. "And what of you, my lady?" He tapped his lower lip. "Your family in Iveriu must be missing you already."

For all his rakish charms, Branwen could almost believe Ruan's interest was genuine.

"I'm an only child," she began. "My mother was Queen Eseult's younger sister. My parents . . . died when I was a girl." Branwen choked on the sanitized words, but she decided it was better if the courtiers at Monwiku didn't know all the reasons she had to hate them. "I was raised by Queen Eseult and King Óengus at Castle Rigani."

"Princess Eseult is like a sister to you," Ruan said.

"Yes." Barely a whisper.

At that moment, they emerged from the forest onto the beach. The horses skirted shallow tide pools where serpent-stars crawled on the bottoms. Dark waves lapped against the glowing sand. Branwen would never be able to look at the sea in the same way. Now she knew what lay beneath.

Dhusnos had told Branwen she was made of destruction. She didn't want to believe it—and yet the waves tugged at her.

Goddess Ériu had banished Dhusnos from Ivernic shores long before Branwen's ancestors were born. The Dark One thrived on Iveriu's grief, on strife. Had he only let Tristan and Eseult survive the night because he wanted to watch the Land's carefully laid plans fall apart? War for Iveriu meant more unclaimed souls, more darkness on which Dhusnos could feed.

"We'll leave the horses here," Ruan said, jarring Branwen from her thoughts. "The tide is still too high—" He showed her a wicked grin. "Unless you fancy a swim?"

She gave a tired laugh. "Not tonight."

"Lucky for you, I have a boat."

The journey across the causeway took less than a quarter hour and suddenly Monwiku Castle loomed above Branwen. Ruan threaded a rope through a small mooring ring. Securing the knot, he jumped onto the dock.

"Welcome to your new home, Branwen."

He pressed a hand briefly to the small of her back as he helped her onto the dock. "It's been a long day. Can you manage the hike up the hill, or should I carry you?"

Regaining her balance, Branwen pulled away. "I can stand quite well on my own two feet."

"In that case I'll live in the hope that one day I can sweep you off them," Ruan said with a wink. Branwen's lips formed a smile without her permission.

Pointing at the stone huts along the shoreline, she asked, "Who lives there?"

Ruan led them along the slipway. "The castle servants," he replied. "The island has everything the king could need. Livestock, gardens, a granary, a brewery, barracks, stables . . . Everything."

Branwen had to admit it was remarkable. Her eyes strained to make out all the details in the faint light. The dock led to a cobblestoned path that passed through an imposing granite archway. Two stone sea-wolves guarded either side of the entrance.

"Why isn't the island fortified?" she said.

"The castle is, my lady. But there's no need to worry. Monwiku has never been attacked."

"That must be a nice feeling. Security has been hard to come by in Iveriu."

At her side, Ruan strummed his fingers against his thigh but made no reply. Branwen's legs ached as they followed the path, climbing as it twisted and turned through a canopy of trees. Lanterns were hung at regular intervals to light the way. Her nerves tightened with each step she took closer to the castle, closer to Tristan and Eseult.

They reached the gate of the first perimeter wall and Branwen drew down a long breath. "The king lives at the top," Ruan said. "As will the queen. Only a little farther."

Two guards saluted the prince as they opened the gate. He greeted them in Kernyvak. Continuing up the hill, they soon arrived at the last of the terraced levels. The design of the castle was circular. Five rounded towers protruded from the sides, almost like petals on a flower, surrounding the inner bailey.

"The north-facing tower belongs to the queen," Ruan informed Branwen, following her gaze. "I'll escort you there before I find my king. I'm sure you're eager for a hot bath."

"Are you implying that I smell?" she said.

He sniffed at Branwen's hair. "You do, my lady. But so do I."

She couldn't help but laugh. Today had been full of horrors, yet Ruan still managed to make her laugh.

"Branwen!"

A rough voice carried her name across the courtyard that lay beneath the Queen's Tower.

Speaking so only Branwen could hear, Ruan muttered, "I think you're in trouble."

Tristan rushed toward them. He had changed into a black velvet tunic and leather trousers. The white sash that cut his chest at a diagonal was almost too bright. He'd trimmed the curls that had grown long during the voyage.

He looked magnificent. She took a step backward.

"Branwen, are you all right?" Tristan said, stopping only when their toes were almost touching. Then he turned a glower on Ruan.

"I'm perfectly fine, Prince Tristan." She kept her reply cold and curt, again refusing to use her mother tongue.

He skimmed her profile with worried eyes. "Is that blood?"

"It's not mine."

Tristan speared Ruan with another glare. "How is it that you let Lady Branwen come to be spattered with other people's blood?"

Branwen spied something shutter behind Ruan's eyes.

"Lady Branwen is rather better at giving orders than taking them," he told Tristan. "I'd like to see you prevent the lady from doing something on which she's set her mind."

His smile was hard. This was the Prince Ruan who had greeted Branwen at the port, not the Ruan of the moors.

Tristan's shoulders slouched forward. "I've never had much success at that, either," he admitted to his cousin, capturing Branwen's gaze.

"Nor is it your responsibility to try," she told him. "You're the Queen's Champion. Not mine."

Tristan flinched, and Branwen scolded herself for caring. "Be that as it may," he said. "I'll escort you to Princess Eseult's apartment." He stared down Ruan until he relinquished Branwen's arm.

Taking her hand instead, Ruan raised it to his lips. "Come find me if you'd like a private tour of the castle." His mouth lingered on her skin. "I'll make sure it's extensive."

Branwen retracted her hand as if she'd been bitten, refusing to be used like a pawn in whatever battle was taking place between the royal cousins.

"I can find my own way around the castle, thank you, Prince Ruan." There was the tiniest flicker of the muscle in Ruan's jaw as she emphasized his title.

"Good night, my lady." He bowed in a supercilious fashion and exited the courtyard.

Branwen started toward the entrance of the Queen's Tower. Tristan barred her path. "Did you use your magic?" he asked in a whisper. He fingered a strand of her hair: white.

"I'm exhausted, Tristan. Please, leave me be."

"I'm only concerned for you. Let me help."

She leaned into him. "You've done enough."

"*Branwen.*"

"I was wrong in Iveriu when I said you could never fail me. You failed us both." *And so did I.* Choking down a sob, Branwen shoved Tristan's chest, hard, and barged past him toward a spiral staircase.

"It's the third *land*—" he called after her. Branwen blocked him out. Her tears sluiced through the dirt on her cheeks as she broke into a sprint. Racing up the tight, candlelit stairwell, face hot, she only stopped to catch her breath at the top.

Branwen leaned her forehead against the cool stone wall until her breathing had returned to normal.

Blotting her cheeks, she walked toward the susurration of voices and, unwillingly, knocked on the door at the end of the corridor. The murmuring ceased abruptly.

A finely attired woman opened the door. She appeared to be the same age as Branwen, her light brown hair arranged in stylish plaits. A bejeweled golden torque adorned her milky neck. Sapphires studded her ears.

"*Dymatis,*" said Branwen.

The woman took one look at her and wrinkled her nose. Disdain dripped from the reply in Kernyvak, which Branwen didn't need to understand.

"I am Lady Branwen of Iveriu," Branwen told her in Aquilan. The woman's expression changed to incredulous.

"Branny!" exclaimed a familiar voice from inside. Eseult raced to the door, pushing the Kernyvak woman aside.

Taking in Branwen's disheveled appearance, the princess's face fell. "What happened?" she said, anxious, in Ivernic. "Are you hurt?" She grabbed Branwen's hand and pulled her across the threshold as if the other woman didn't exist.

Branwen wanted to resist her cousin's touch, but she had nowhere else to go.

"I'm unharmed, Your Highness," Branwen said. "Thank you for asking. There were many wounded at the mine."

The princess squeezed her hand so hard it hurt, eyes doleful.

"Who is this?" Branwen tore her gaze away from her cousin, still speaking in Ivernic. She put on a smile for the other woman's benefit. Her eyebrow was arched. Branwen determined that the Kernyvak woman didn't speak her language, either.

"That's Endelyn. She's been assigned as my lady-in-waiting," the princess said. "She won't stop hovering."

Branwen turned toward the woman. "A pleasure to meet you," she said to Endelyn.

"And you. I am Princess Endelyn." She smiled, and her blue eyes were as cold as the sapphires in her ears. "It seems like you've been on quite the adventure with my brother. Ruan never misses the opportunity to welcome the newest lady to court." Endelyn looked Branwen up and down. "I hope you didn't fall from your horse? Or were you rolling around in the mud for fun?"

The words were a slap, but Branwen had endured too much to be affected by the spite of some spoiled Kernyvak princess.

"Not at all," Branwen said to Endelyn in a cloying voice. "It's hard to tend wounded men and women without getting your hands dirty." She peered down the length of her body. "Or your clothes."

Eseult brushed her hand against Branwen's tangled, knotty curls. "I've been so worried, cousin." She spoke urgently in Ivernic.

"I was in no danger," Branwen lied.

"Maybe not, but I'm glad you're back," Eseult said, lashes fluttering. "Endelyn has just poured me a bath. You go first." Before Branwen could protest, her cousin whirled toward her new lady-in-waiting. "Branwen is here now," she said in Aquilan. "You may retire."

Shock smoothed Endelyn's brow. She opened and closed her mouth. The Kernyvak princess was obviously unaccustomed to being dismissed.

"Of course, Lady Princess." Endelyn curtsied. "My chamber is on the floor below if you require anything in the night."

"*Mormerkti*, Princess Endelyn," Branwen said. Eseult barely acknowledged the other woman's departure. As she retreated toward the doorway, Endelyn threw Branwen a smile over her shoulder that was as deadly as any blade.

A bathing tub cast from copper was positioned in front of a large window with a view of the sea. Eseult led Branwen by the hand and began helping her undress. Branwen didn't want her cousin's help. She wanted even less to speak with the princess, however, so she didn't stop Eseult from loosening the laces of her dress. Branwen's tunic and under sheath slipped to the floor, pooling around her ankles.

"Branny!" The princess gasped when she saw Branwen's assorted injuries. "You said you were unhurt."

Branwen's hand drifted across her naked torso, examining the marks left by the Shade's cruel beak.

"They're from last night."

Eseult's fair complexion had gone green. "All day I've been trying to convince myself that they were just men. Just pirates. But I thought I saw Keane—as one of those . . . those *things*. I don't know how that could be."

Branwen shuddered thinking about the night she fed Keane to the waves. To protect her cousin's honor, she had killed the former bodyguard, condemned him to an eternity as a Shade. But Branwen hadn't burdened her cousin with the knowledge. And during the attack on the *Dragon Rising*, the Hand of Bríga had ended his afterlife.

Eseult pinched the bridge of her nose. "My memory from last night is so patchy." Branwen skewered her with a glance. "I—I mean, I remember . . . *that*," the princess said. "Branny, what happened with Tristan, I—"

"*Don't.*"

"But we need to talk about—"

"*No.* We don't. There's nothing to discuss. You will become Queen of Kernyv as the Old Ones have ordained. If you don't remember all of the horrors that took place, consider it a blessing." Branwen herself considered it a blessing that the princess hadn't witnessed her using her magic against the Shades.

Tears welled in Eseult's eyes. Without another word, Branwen stepped into the tub. The bathwater was pleasantly warm. She hissed as it splashed her wounds. Sinking into the tub, Branwen felt older than Kerwindos, the Mother of Creation, herself.

She dunked her head beneath the surface of the water.

The princess washed Branwen's hair and dabbed a soapy cloth around her injured flesh. Eseult's touch was loving, gentle, and the familiarity made Branwen sigh despite herself.

Her heart had been rent into a thousand shards.

She soaked until the water turned brown with grime.

Eseult wrapped Branwen in a linen blanket, drying her limbs as if she were a babe. Branwen tore the blanket from her cousin's grasp and tucked it securely beneath her arms. "Has my trunk been delivered?" she asked. "I need my salves."

The princess drummed her fingers on her chin. "I'll check." She scurried through a side door and into an adjoining room. Branwen clutched the covering, gaze wandering toward the waves breaking against the rocks below.

"Here. *Here*—" Eseult rushed back. Her voice warbled.

Branwen took a small, intricately carved wooden box from her cousin's hands. She had filled it with remedies from Queen Eseult's infirmary at Castle Rigani. The supplies were running low after treating the princess's injury during the sea voyage.

Branwen selected a paste made of ground birch bark to prevent infection. It burned as she applied it to her open wounds. She clenched her jaw, eyes stinging as well. She struggled to reach one in the center of her back.

"Let me—" Eseult started, extending a hand. Sullenly, Branwen passed her the small ceramic jar. "A little goes a long way," she admonished.

"I remember Mother's advice."

"Do you?" Branwen said. Her cousin had abandoned the healing arts years ago. She hissed as the princess applied the salve.

"I'm sorry, Branny. I didn't mean to hurt you." Eseult spoke to her back. "I'm *so* sorry." Branwen refused to turn around and let her cousin see the tears beading her own lashes.

When Eseult was finished, she handed Branwen a nightgown. "There's only one bed," she said, indicating the tastefully appointed canopy bed. Curtains could be drawn on all sides for privacy. "I told the king we're used to sharing."

"I think you've had your bed warmed quite enough," Branwen said. "You don't need me."

Eseult pulled a strand of hair taut around her forefinger. "But I *do*, Branny. I need you more than ever." Her voice began to rise, eyes shining. "You ran away from me the minute we were off the ship—I was afraid you wouldn't come back." A few blond hairs wafted to the floor.

"Believe me, I thought about it!" Branwen roared, losing her patience. She flattened her right hand against her thigh. It itched. Her power simmered.

"Please, Branny. Don't abandon me."

"*You* abandoned *me*. You abandoned peace. Duty. Honor."

Eseult buried her face in her hands and began to weep.

Branwen walked over to the bed and plucked a plump pillow from atop the quilt, which was lavishly embroidered with golden thread. A skilled weaver had decorated the thick silk with an intertwined sea-wolf and lion: the royal standard of Iveriu. This was a bed fit for a queen. Hugging the pillow to her chest, Branwen walked methodically around the apartment and blew out each candle. The princess continued to cry.

"You are to be my queen," Branwen told Eseult before she extinguished the last candle. "And I will serve you as such." The flame fizzled on the wick. "But that is all you are to me." Smoke rose upward in the darkened room.

Eseult stood in place, bewildered.

Branwen placed the pillow on the floor beside the bed and lay down on the stone. The floor was nippy, yet she felt feverish. A sliver of moonlight tickled her nose.

When she closed her eyes, she sensed the Dark One more keenly.

A few moments later, she heard feet padding toward her. The princess lay down beside Branwen, resting her head on her pillow, and took Branwen's hand.

"Not you without me," Eseult said stubbornly. "Not me without you."

The princess traced the symbol for hazel on the back of Branwen's hand as she had done since they were children. "I love you, Branny." And yet her cousin's love hadn't been stronger than her desire. Branwen shook her off with a grunt.

The princess's body trembled beside her as she wept; Branwen kept her back turned. Eventually, the princess cried herself to sleep.

Branwen stared out the window as the hours passed. *The wild moon is high, my love, come away with me.* Her mother sang to her in the back of her mind. Could her parents still watch over her from the Otherworld now that she was in Kernyv?

Branwen fought the spell of night as long as she could. The last time she'd allowed herself to rest, she had woken to find her world on fire.

Finally, Branwen's body once more betrayed her, and she plunged into a void filled with wild, savage stars.

RED-HOT ASHES

THE PRINCESS WAS SNORING LIGHTLY when the first rays of dawn disturbed Branwen from her dreamscape. She tried and failed to cling to the balmy strands of sleep as disquiet pricked each of her nerves awake.

Drawing in a shallow breath, Branwen raised herself into a sitting position. The stone floor had not been kind to her sore muscles. She stretched her arms above her head and stifled a groan. She didn't want to wake her cousin.

A few wisps of blond hair rose and fell as the princess continued to snore.

The princess hadn't changed from her traveling dress or detangled her plaits before crawling next to Branwen. As lady's maid, Branwen should have done that for her.

Watching her cousin sleep, dawn touching her brow, she could almost make herself believe that this was any other morning. That Eseult had stolen into Branwen's bed at Castle Rigani like she'd done so many times when she was lonesome or had a nightmare. That nothing could ever come between them.

Longing sliced her deep. Longing for a closeness she had never experienced with anyone else, not even Tristan. Without her cousin to chase away her dark moods, Branwen didn't know who she would become.

She pushed silently to her feet. Plucking a knitted blanket trimmed with lace from the end of the bed, she laid it atop the princess, who didn't stir.

Dressing herself promptly, Branwen braided her hair and rushed down the stairs of the Queen's Tower. Her shawl was filthy, so she'd selected a cerulean cloak, pinning it closed with her mother's brooch. The inner bailey was deserted.

She turned in a circle, admiring the five towers and the sculpted wolf heads that decorated the crenellations.

She glimpsed an alleyway on the other side of the courtyard and decided to explore. The passage opened up into several levels of manicured gardens. Yesterday, when Branwen had spotted the island of Monwiku from the coast, the greenery sprawling up from the bedrock had seemed chaotic, unruly.

On this side of the castle, looking out toward the Dreaming Sea, someone had imposed order. A steep set of granite steps took Branwen to the first of the terraced gardens. Trees with long, slender trunks and leaves like spikes lined either side of the staircase. She didn't know what they were called.

Her eyes roved across the neatly arranged rows of blooms of bright pink amaranthine, opalescent teals, and rain-flecked sage, as well as shrubs bursting with every other color Branwen could imagine. Tristan had told her that Kernyv possessed flowers that she'd never seen, nurtured by a southerly wind from the Mílesian Peninsula. He was right. And like so much else here, they were a mystery.

Wind chimes dangled from many of the spear-leafed trees, their silence unsettling.

Branwen crouched down to press her nose into an enormous dark purple blossom. The scent was almost smoky. It made Branwen think of mornings sitting beside the hearth in the kitchens at Castle Rigani, drinking tea with Treva and Dubthach, waiting to rouse the princess for the day.

"Childhood's end."

Branwen jumped up, bashing her head against someone's chin.

"Forgive me—" King Marc rubbed his jaw, grimacing ever so slightly. "For startling you, Lady Branwen." His eyes were as serious as they had been the day before.

"My Lord King." Branwen curtsied. "I'm so sorry." Without stopping to consider what she was doing, she placed two fingers beneath the king's chin to inspect the damage. The bristles of his beard were softer than they looked, the brown interspersed with sorrel. Branwen exhaled, assuring herself that she hadn't broken the skin.

"I'll live?" King Marc said, and for the first time Branwen spied mischief in his countenance.

"You'll live." She dropped her hand as mortification began to set in.

"And your head?" the king asked.

"I've been told it's hard."

Marc laughed heartily, and it resounded through the garden. "Mine, too." He stroked his beard again. Pointing at the purple blossom, he said, "It's called childhood's end."

The petals were layered like a crown. "It's beautiful," Branwen said. "Is it common in Kernyv?"

The king shook his head. "I know a merchant—he's a friend . . ." His face smoothed in a faraway look. "He travels throughout the southern continent, across all of the known seas. He sends me the seeds." A small smile. "He says the garden is my only indulgence."

Branwen let her gaze skip down the cascading levels of bright plants and trees toward the sea. This was not the indulgence she would have envisaged from the king of a land of pirates. She fingered her mother's brooch. Lowering her nose to the bloom once more, Branwen struggled at how to describe it.

"The scent, it's . . ."

"It makes me think of campfires," said King Marc. "When my father would take me hunting in the Morrois Forest."

A vise twisted Branwen's stomach. King Merchion had only died four years ago—he'd been responsible for sending Kernyvak raiders to Iveriu for most of Branwen's life.

"Red-hot ashes are easily rekindled," she muttered.

"What's that?"

She straightened up. "Oh, nothing. Just an Ivernic saying."

"I fear you're right, Lady Branwen." Marc's expression darkened as he pinched one of the petals between his fingers. "Tristan's mother and I used to play in these gardens," he said. "He has her smile. I wish he'd known her."

Quiet stretched between them. Branwen's uncle had also slain Tristan's father on the night of his birth. Their families had taken much from each other, left so many embers, so many potential sparks of hatred.

"At the mine yesterday," King Marc began again. "Ruan says you helped many of the wounded."

She shifted her gaze from the sea to the king. "I've never seen such a disaster," Branwen blurted. "And I've treated many of the war victims." She paused. "I helped those I could."

Marc's eyes dimmed. "I am grateful to you, my lady, for using your skill to help my people," he said.

"And *my* people," she said, with unthinking boldness. "The Iverni captured in raids."

"The Kernyveu and Iverni are to become one people. There will be no more raids."

Branwen nodded, bunching her skirts between her fingers. "No, no more raids," she said in a muted tone. That had been the entire purpose of the Loving Cup—to unite the kingdoms, forge an unbreakable bond. "I would like to check on my patients as soon as possible," Branwen told the king. Then she added, "With your permission, of course."

"Granted, with thanks."

"*Mormerkti.*"

Marc observed Branwen in the same canny way he had at the port.

"Tristan told me how your parents died."

She held his gaze, blood pounding. Did King Marc know he'd watched them die? Or had he killed so many since then that their faces had faded from his mind?

"I want you to know, Lady Branwen," he said, "that I am not my father. I loved him, but I don't want to be the same kind of ruler as he was."

Branwen bit her bottom lip to stop it from trembling. Marc plucked the purple flower and presented it to her.

"There has been too much bloodshed," he said. "I don't want my legacy to be one of violence. When Tristan proposed entering the Champions Tournament, he had my full support."

The Iverni believed that the man chosen by the Land as king must possess the Truth of the Ruler. He must be selfless and honorable. Would the Old Ones have selected a murderer to protect Iveriu?

"I want to make something grow," King Marc told Branwen. "Like this garden."

She showed the king an open palm and he placed the flower atop her scar. The petals were both soothing and ticklish on her skin.

"You come here when you can't sleep," she said.

He glanced at the sun still perched on the horizon. "Is it that obvious?"

"I couldn't sleep, either."

"I have many regrets, my lady." The king ran his hand along the inside of his forearm, which was covered by a dark green tunic.

"We all do."

A breeze came off the sea, almost a moan, and the wind chimes tinkled all around them. The sound was haunting. Branwen shivered, and Marc noticed.

"In Kernyv, we believe the laments of the sea must be answered," the king told her. "Otherwise the water will get lonely and overwhelm the land."

She let out a short laugh. The Dark One was hungry for souls to join the Sea of the Dead, but Branwen didn't think he was lonely.

"It's true," Marc said. "Well, perhaps not. But it's said that the Veneti Isles were once connected to Liones until the land in between was claimed by a lonely sea." The king shrugged. "Why take the chance?"

"Why indeed," she agreed.

"I would beg a favor," King Marc said, after a moment.

"Of course. You're my king now." The blossom in her palm felt instantly heavy.

"Not as your king. As a new friend—if you'd have me?"

Branwen hesitated. Part of her wanted to accept his friendship. A part that made her feel like a traitor to her parents, despite her mission of peace.

"What's the favor?" she asked.

"I hear that you're a master of Little Soldiers," said Marc, showing her a rare grin. "And my regular partner has recently left court. Since we're both restless sleepers, perhaps you might play with me?"

Her eyebrows lifted. "We call the game *fidkwelsa* in Iveriu," Branwen told him.

"*Fidkwelsa*," he repeated. The grin spread across his face. "Do we have a deal?"

Strangely, she found herself returning his smile. "We do."

"Excellent." The chimes jangled again. "Oh, there will be a feast next week to celebrate the Seal of Alliance," King Marc said. "I wanted to ask, does Princess Eseult have a favorite flower? I would like her to feel welcome in her new home."

Branwen raised the childhood's end to her nose and inhaled. It was as melancholy as the laments of the sea. Whenever she smelled it, she would think of this morning.

"Honeysuckle," she told the king. "My cousin loves honeysuckle."

"*Mormerkti*, Lady Branwen. I will do my best to make her happy."

"I'd better go see if the princess needs me," Branwen said, fleeing back up the stairs toward the Queen's Tower without begging her leave.

If King Marc ever found out what she had done for her cousin's happiness, he would never have cause to thank Branwen again.

A TRUE QUEEN

BRANWEN HELD HER BREATH AS she entered the Great Hall of Monwiku Castle for the first time. Tonight was the official introduction of the Princess of Iveriu to King Marc's court. Endelyn had informed Branwen and Eseult that all of the prominent Kernyvak noble families would be in attendance. She had spoken of little else all week.

The Kernyvak princess had also insisted on dressing her future queen for the feast. Her cousin's mournful looks notwithstanding, Branwen had been happy to be relieved of her duties as lady's maid. She did grant Eseult's request that she be the one to treat the new scabs on her cousin's scalp with juniper ointment, however. The princess didn't want Endelyn to see the marks left from the hair pulling that quelled her nerves. Branwen had applied the ointment in silence; she grimaced when her cousin hissed at the sting, pained by her distress, but she didn't have the will to console her.

When Endelyn escorted Eseult to the Great Hall half an hour ago, Branwen was grateful for a few moments alone in the Queen's Tower.

A cot had been hastily installed in the cupboard of a room that adjoined Eseult's bedchamber which, Branwen had to admit, was better than the alternative of sharing quarters with Endelyn. Her most precious possessions were laid out on a small table: the miniature *fid-kwelsa* set that had belonged to her father, the moon-catcher gifted to her by Queen Eseult, and the wooden practice sword that Uncle Morholt had fashioned for her when she was girl. Reminders of home that reminded Branwen how very far she had come.

Tiptoeing along one side of the Great Hall, Branwen surveyed the throng of courtiers. At the back of the hall, she glimpsed a long table on a raised dais. The king's table. Honeysuckles were out of season, but the table had been draped in yellow silk of a similar shade. King Marc's attention to detail was impressive.

Would he ever be able to win the princess over? Or had the Loving Cup destroyed any chance of that?

Branwen's gaze continued traveling over the tapestries that decorated the walls; it wended up the ornate capitals of the pillars and climbed toward the vaulted ceiling. The interior stonework was carved from the same material as the Aquilan water bridge. Florid stone shimmered in the light of the oil lamps that dotted the chandeliers and sconces.

Ruan had explained to Branwen that lamps fueled by oil were another Aquilan invention. The Kernyvak prince enjoyed explaining things to Branwen—and she didn't mind nearly as much as her frequent scoffs implied. The oil for the lamps in the castle was pressed from nuts foraged from the Morrois Forest, he'd told her. The scent filling the Great Hall was toasted, inviting.

Branwen raised her guard.

Growing up as the niece of the King and Queen of Iveriu, she'd attended many formal banquets, of course, and was well versed in the habits and customs of a royal court. Branwen had always understood what was expected of her. And yet, everyone at Castle Rigani had also known Branwen her entire life. It was easy to float in the background.

Here, there was no place to hide.

Branwen's heart hiccupped as her eyes landed on Tristan. He stood near the king's table, in between Marc and Eseult, together with a cluster of other guests. He was dressed in a turquoise tunic and black leather trousers, the white sash that indicated his status in the king's service proudly displayed across his chest. He must have felt Branwen's gaze on him, because Tristan lifted his eyes to hers.

He had moved into the apartment at the bottom of the Queen's Tower, his duties requiring him to be near Eseult at all times. Still, Branwen had managed to exchange as few words with him as possible. She'd also absented herself from the pair's presence whenever she could. The fact that Endelyn was permanently welded to the princess's side allayed Branwen's fears that the couple might succumb to the power of the Loving Cup again.

She had no idea how long the effects might last. *A night? A year? A lifetime?*

"Might I offer you a drink, Lady Branwen?" a flirtatious voice whispered into her ear.

Even if she hadn't recognized it, the scowl that immediately creased Tristan's features would have revealed the voice's owner.

"Thank you, Prince Ruan." Branwen pivoted toward him, showing Tristan her back.

Ruan took a sip, smiling, and handed her a silver goblet. "With

Lugmarch's blessing," he said, holding Branwen's gaze, then took a drink from his own.

The saffron-dyed piping of his black tunic complemented his dirty-blond hair. Branwen tasted the mead prudently. There were no vats of red ale, the Ivernic drink of kingship, being offered by King Marc to his guests. This mead was sweeter than what was served at Castle Rigani—and spicier. She coughed.

"I recommend that you develop a tolerance, my lady," Ruan told her. "I find that mead makes these gatherings . . ." He circled his gaze around the hall. "Well, more tolerable."

"I prefer to keep my wits about me. Besides, I thought you enjoyed life at court. Especially the ladies, from what your sister tells me."

"Ah, Endelyn is a tad possessive."

"I can't fathom why."

"That's a shame."

"What's a shame?" asked an elegant woman as she joined them. She was dressed in a gown of cherry velvet, and she wore her caramel-hued locks long. Heavily jeweled combs held it back from her face. Branwen recognized the pattern: a red hand made of precious stones. The same sigil she'd seen as on the discarded banner at the mining site.

"Lady Branwen," said Ruan, "it's my singular pleasure to introduce you to my mother, Countess Kensa Whel of Illogan." Something in the enunciation of his consonants conveyed the opposite sentiment.

Looking from Ruan to his mother, Branwen could see the resemblance not only in the matching dark blond hair, but also the set of their eyes and the slope of his mouth. Branwen forced her eyes not to fixate on his mouth.

"Pleased to meet you, Countess Kensa." Branwen curtsied.

"So *you* are the famous Lady Branwen." The countess observed

Branwen like a hawk does its prey. She had the same cold blue eyes as her daughter. "Your reputation precedes you."

Branwen's hand tightened on the stem of her goblet. "It does?"

"Rumors have reached me across the peninsula that an Ivernic lady has been visiting the miners—*my* miners. Is such a thing common in Iveriu? Do noblewomen do the work of peasants?" The countess's smile was harder than the granite upon which the castle had been built. Ruan cut his mother a cautioning glance.

Temper flaring, Branwen pressed her right palm against her skirt and prayed she wouldn't set herself on fire in the middle of the feasting hall.

"Healing work is done by whoever has the skill," she informed Countess Kensa as civilly as she could. "Queen Eseult is renowned throughout our island for her healing abilities. My aunt cares for her subjects as the Goddess Ériu protects the Land."

"How peculiar." The countess cast a look toward King Marc and Eseult. "My nephew will learn many new traditions from his bride, I suppose."

She pinched the end of Branwen's shawl between her fingers. "Ivernic lace? So quaint, just charming." She let the fabric fall. "Just think what your weavers could produce with modern, Aquilan technology."

Branwen counted to ten before speaking. She had anticipated that not all the Kernyveu would welcome the Iverwomen with open arms.

After a moment, Branwen told the countess, "With peace between our kingdoms, there will be many opportunities for Iveriu and Kernyv to improve each other." Her cheeks hurt from smiling.

Countess Kensa laughed. "Ruan, I can see why you find Lady Branwen so . . . diverting. Oh look, there's Baron Dynyon." She glanced diagonally at a mustached man. "Excuse me, I must greet him." Cupping

Ruan's cheek, Kensa told her son, "We'll speak later," and sauntered away.

Branwen blinked several times. Humiliation scalded her. Ruan touched her elbow, speaking low. "Don't mind Mother. Now that we have Ivernic noblewomen at court, she's hoping the great Kernyvak Houses will forget that she comes from a family of wreckers."

"Wreckers?"

"The Whels got their start by luring ships onto the rocks near Illogan. My forebearers used their ill-gotten gains to purchase land that turned out to be mineral rich. We were the first to trade with the Aquilan legions." Ruan grinned. "Pragmatic, my ancestors. The red hand on my family crest is even said to represent the hand that the first Whel cut off and threw onto the site of Villa Illogan—in order to keep it from being claimed by a rival."

Branwen wrinkled her nose. The Kernyveu were overly fond of fanciful stories.

"Mother was also hoping to make Endelyn queen," the prince said, an afterthought, and sipped his mead. "Don't look so shocked," he said, reading Branwen's face. "Cousins marry all the time."

At least now she understood Endelyn's animosity. Being lady-in-waiting to a queen was a far cry from being queen herself. Did Endelyn harbor feelings for Marc? Or merely covet the title?

"Why are you spilling all of your family secrets to me, Prince Ruan?" Branwen asked.

"There are very few secrets at court." He clinked his goblet against hers and leaned forward. "How about a dance?" Ruan smiled broadly, and Branwen could see how many women might be enticed by that smile like flies to honey. A reckless part of her, a caged part, wanted to dance like it was Belotnia, the Festival of Lovers; whirl her body around bonfires, laugh long into the night.

"I'm afraid I'm a quaint, backward Iverwoman, Prince Ruan," Branwen replied instead. "I don't know how to dance." She foisted her goblet into the prince's free hand. "But I suspect you excel at dancing with yourself."

Ruan let out an enormous sigh as Branwen strode in the direction of the king's table. Much as she might want to, she couldn't avoid Tristan or Eseult forever, and there no longer seemed to be nearly enough room between her and Ruan, either.

The Princess of Iveriu was swathed in an emerald-green gown. Its trim had been embroidered with freshwater pearls by a seamstress at Castle Rigani who was also the mother of their childhood playmate, Dubthach. As a girl, Eseult had adored playing practical jokes on poor Dubthach. She'd been quite the terror.

Tonight, standing beside King Marc, her cousin didn't look like she knew how to smile, much less pull pranks. She was pallid; demeanor careworn.

Branwen resented the ache that it caused in her chest.

"*Dymatis*, my king," she said, sinking into a curtsy. Endelyn glared at Branwen from the corner of her eye. Like her mother, she too wore red.

Beside the king stood another man whom Branwen hadn't yet met. He had a shaven head, and he was cloaked in dark brown robes. She judged that the man had seen fifty summers.

King Marc inclined his head at her. "*Dymatis*, Lady Branwen."

Neither Branwen nor Eseult had seen much of Marc this week. He was constantly cloistered in the King's Tower, meeting with his advisers.

"Lady Branwen," Tristan greeted her.

"Prince Tristan." She didn't meet his eyes as she nodded her response. Endelyn watched them with more than idle interest. Perhaps she was a tad possessive of Tristan, too.

"Oh, Branny," Eseult said breathily, in Ivernic. "Thank goodness you're here. Everyone's speaking Aquilan and it's making my head hurt." Her cousin never had been Master Bécc's most diligent student. She'd preferred vexing Dubthach to conjugating Aquilan verbs. Taking Branwen's hand, she murmured, "You look lovely."

"Thank you, Lady Princess."

"Lady Branwen, this is Seer Casek." King Marc motioned toward the man with the shaven head. "He is the chief *kordweyd* at the temple in Marghas."

The man fiddled with an antler shard that hung around his neck. Branwen knew that followers of the Horned One used it to invoke his protection, that it represented his sacrifice: leaping in front of an enraged stag to save his father's life. Captain Morgawr wore such an amulet and had called upon the Horned One when the Shades attacked.

The fragment that rested against Casek's robe, however, was ornamented with diamonds and dangled from a golden chain.

"*Dymatis*, Seer Casek," Branwen said.

"It is evening, Lady Branwen," Casek replied in Aquilan. "Therefore I should bid you *Nosmatis*." He smiled pleasantly, light from oil lamps reflecting off his bald head.

His greeting set her teeth on edge. The king didn't see fit to correct her but apparently this man did.

"*Nosmatis*, Seer Casek," she told him.

"*Nos-ma-tís*," he repeated, emphasizing the second syllable. "The pronunciation of Kernyvak can be tricky." Casek smiled another terribly pleasant smile. "When I first arrived from the southern continent, it took me several years to master it."

"*Mormerktí*, Seer Casek. I'm a quick study."

Marc interrupted smoothly. "How do your patients fare, Lady Branwen? Do you have all the supplies you need?"

"Yes. Thank you," Branwen replied. "My patients are mostly improving. Some will require a few more weeks to fully heal."

Lowenek and Talorc, thankfully, had survived their injuries. Others—including Talorc's son, Ném—were not so fortunate. Branwen had watched the old man cry as he drank his son's Final Toast.

King Marc angled his body toward Casek, saying, "I didn't realize so many were injured so grievously," in a leading way.

"The *kordweyd* have the situation well in hand," he assured the king, slanting a less than friendly glance at Branwen.

"I was curious," Branwen said to Marc. "Are there no royal infirmaries in Kernyv?"

Casek was the one to reply. "The temples care for the sick in Kernyv, my lady." His tone was intended to silence. "We are men of learning."

"In Iveriu, healers are men—and women—of learning," Branwen countered, trying to imagine what Queen Eseult would say to this man. "But our king and queen are also responsible for providing aid to those in need."

"Lady Branwen," Casek charged, "you insult the king."

The wind rushed from her lungs. Had she gone too far? Marc's expression was inscrutable.

After what felt like an eon, during which Branwen counted each heartbeat, King Marc announced, "The lady has caused no offense. I am grateful for her help and her counsel. Perhaps, Lady Branwen, you can share your Ivernic learning with Casek and the other *kordweyd*?"

"Of course."

"A wonderful suggestion, sire," Casek agreed through a thin-lipped smile. Branwen clutched the sleeve of her dress. She would need to be careful around this man.

A boy of perhaps thirteen or fourteen approached the king from behind. He was clothed in royal colors, and he hobbled slightly, favoring his left leg. The foot was curved partially inward.

"The boar is ready to be served," said the boy.

Marc's face brightened. "Thank you, Andred." He mussed the boy's hair. "Princess Eseult, Lady Branwen. This is my cousin, Prince Andred. Ruan and Endelyn's brother." Andred shared the same nose as his brother, but, unlike his mother or siblings, he had thick, curly dark hair.

"Also the king's cupbearer," the young prince piped up, pride in his voice. He smiled shyly at the Ivernic ladies, reminding Branwen of Cadan.

"Also my cupbearer," Marc corrected himself with a laugh. "Fill it high tonight, Andred. We have much to celebrate. Now, let's eat!"

As they took their seats for the meal, Branwen was shown to a chair between Tristan and Ruan. Immediately, she lost her appetite.

Eseult, as Marc's future queen, was seated on his right, and next to her sat the Queen's Champion. Branwen would have expected the King's Champion to sit on Marc's left, as her uncle Morholt had always done for King Óengus. Instead that honor went to Countess Kensa. She was the king's aunt and the oldest member of the royal family present, Branwen supposed. The countess smiled like a snake as she assumed her seat next to the king. Casek and Endelyn took their places beside her.

"Miss me?" Ruan asked, coming up behind Branwen, then pulled out her chair.

"Hardly."

He laughed, taking his own seat. "Hello, scamp," he said to Andred, and his brother blushed. Andred gripped the table and swung his lower body into the chair beside Ruan. Ruan's face was full of warmth as he looked at his brother, and it was the first genuine emotion Branwen had seen from the prince all night.

There was much fanfare as the boar was presented and Branwen spent the rest of the meal concentrating on cutting her meat into bite-size pieces and not on the proximity of the men on either side of her.

Most definitely not on how much Tristan's vivid tunic reminded her of the iridescent seaweed known as mermaid's hair, which she'd been collecting on the day they met. She had saved a single, dried strand. It was in her room even now. She hadn't yet been able to discard it.

Branwen did not recall the feel of the finely packed muscles she knew lay beneath his tunic, how they were at once hard and soft.

Nor did she remember how she had once looked into Tristan's eyes and seen her best self reflected.

✣ ✣ ✣

When the platters of honeyed fruits and dates were passed throughout the Great Hall, King Marc stood and commanded the attention of all those present.

A respectful quiet slowly descended over the assembled guests.

Branwen was seated close enough to see a muscle flicker in his neck. At twenty-seven, Marc was a young king. He didn't yet wear his mantle of power with the same ease as King Óengus did. "Friends," Marc began, speech stilted. "Tonight, I have invited you here to celebrate the beginning of a new era for Kernyv."

He waved a hand at Andred. The boy collected something from a sideboard behind the king's table and limped toward him. In her peripheral vision, Branwen saw Countess Kensa's face pinch.

King Marc lifted a scroll from Andred's hand into the air. He held it high so that all could see. "With this Seal of Alliance, hostilities between Kernyv and Iveriu are at end." He took a breath. "All prisoners of war in both kingdoms are to be freed."

Silence.

Tristan was the first to clap.

He grabbed Branwen's gaze as she put her hands together. Was this his doing?

From what she had seen at the mine, Ruan's family—and undoubtedly many others—depended on the prisoners' labor. Only polite applause followed from around the hall, and a chill skittered down Branwen's spine. The king had said the Iverni and Kernyveu were to become one people, but not everyone would benefit from the peace.

King Marc directed his attention at Tristan, his affection unguarded.

"I owe a debt I can never repay to my nephew, Prince Tristan of Kernyv and Liones, for bringing us this Seal of Alliance. He has served me and Kernyv with loyalty and honor." Marc rested a hand on Tristan's shoulder. Branwen saw color rise in his cheeks at the compliment. Not in a thousand lifetimes would Tristan have willingly dishonored his king.

"He is the truest brother any man could want," Marc declared.

Acid churned in Branwen's gut. She had always known that using magic on a foreign king was an act of war. She hadn't wanted to make Tristan complicit in her treason, even though she had fully believed her treason would bring peace. She had believed all would be right in the end. She had *believed* . . .

The chair beside hers creaked as Ruan refilled his goblet to the brim.

"Because of Tristan's bravery," the king continued, "it gladdens me to introduce you, my friends and countrymen, to the Princess Eseult of Iveriu—your future queen!"

Eseult sat statue-still through another round of tepid clapping.

"The wedding and coronation will take place at Long Night. We will start the darkest part of the year with the brightest joy."

Marc cleared his throat. His fingers tensed minutely on the scroll. "In accordance with the treaty I have made with the High King of Iveriu," he went on, "Princess Eseult will not be solely my Queen Consort. Instead, she will be a True Queen in her own right."

Countess Kensa was only partially successful in concealing a gasp. Others less so. Casek coughed as if he were choking.

Branwen glanced at Tristan with trepidation. The corners of his mouth tightened.

This was even more explosive news than the freeing of the prisoners.

A True Queen held the same status as a king. She was a full sovereign and retained the throne if her king died.

King Marc's older sister, Tristan's mother, had been unable to inherit the throne of Kernyv because she was a woman. Even in Iveriu, a woman couldn't rule in her own right. Only a True Queen could. Queen Eseult embodied the Land, but the Land was the Consort of the High King.

Branwen unfurled her right hand beneath the table. There had been no True Queen of Iveriu since the legendary Queen Medhua. Branwen's eyes traced the snow-white scar that bisected her heart line. According to her aunt, Queen Medhua had also been the last woman known to possess the Hand of Bríga.

Why hadn't Tristan warned her?

Throughout the voyage, Branwen had felt her secrets wind around her like a noose. Yet Tristan had still been keeping his own.

King Marc set down the scroll and extended a hand to Eseult.

"Kernyv and Iveriu are equals from this moment forward," he said. "Likewise, my future queen and I will be partners."

Eseult accepted Marc's hand, but Branwen saw the fear in her eyes. Branwen shared that fear. The implications were momentous. Dangerous. Why had King Marc agreed to this? Did he really regret the past so much?

Marc showed Eseult a tentative smile. "Let us raise a glass to the future True Queen of Kernyv, and to peace!"

Andred had refilled the king's solid gold drinking cup without being asked.

"With Lugmarch's blessing!" Marc declared. "*Kernyv bosta vyken!* Kernyv forever!"

To sons! To peace! To the queen! Kernyv forever!

The shouts reverberated in Branwen's ears as dread coiled around her heart. The Kernyvak nobility toasting to the union had nothing to gain by Eseult's elevation to a True Queen. They only had personal power to lose.

King Marc lowered himself back into his chair, pressing a chaste kiss to Eseult's cheek. She stared blankly at the myriad guests. Her future subjects. Conversation swiftly resumed and much mead was poured.

Ruan rested his head against Branwen's. "The Ivernic king must be incredibly persuasive," he muttered. "Peace has only just been agreed to and already you're rewriting all our laws." The prince smiled as he drank from his goblet.

Not the Ivernic king, thought Branwen. The Ivernic *queen*.

Only Queen Eseult would be bold enough to suggest such a risky gambit.

Her aunt had seen the opportunity to endow her daughter with more power than she would ever possess—and she had seized it. The treaty may have been signed by two kings, but its terms had been orchestrated by a queen. Noblewomen rarely got the chance to control their own destinies. Queen Eseult had moved the men—Tristan, Marc, her own husband—around the board as if she were playing *fidkwelsa*.

With a True Queen, an Ivernic queen, upon the throne of Kernyv, the power and influence of Iveriu would become manifold.

But in augmenting Iveriu's might, Queen Eseult had also painted a target on her daughter's back. Enemies would crawl out of the woodwork. Branwen had always hoped her cousin would grow into being a leader, but the weight of being a True Queen might break her. Branwen peered down the table at her cousin, who had gone whiter than a Death-Teller.

This was why her aunt had at last agreed to conjure the Loving Cup, she realized. It wasn't so that Eseult would know love or happiness. It was insurance against King Marc changing his mind.

Branwen recalled how, on the day of their departure, Queen Eseult had said that the Land must think of all her children. Her aunt was the Queen of Iveriu first, a mother and aunt second. She couldn't afford to rule with her heart.

Still, why hadn't her aunt trusted Branwen with her plans? Why, when she knew everything Branwen was willing to risk for the Loving Cup?

A second realization punched her, swift and painful.

Queen Eseult must have feared that, deep down, Branwen loved her cousin more than her kingdom. And Branwen had proved the queen's fears justified. She'd jeopardized peace by loving her cousin too much. She took an imprudent gulp of mead.

"So much for your wits," Ruan remarked.

"To the Otherworld with my wits."

He lowered an eyebrow and laughed.

Branwen drained the goblet dry.

KERNYV FOREVER

EACH OF THE NOBLE KERNYVAK Houses approached the king's table in turn and offered their congratulations to the future True Queen of Kernyv.

Branwen observed them carefully as they introduced themselves, keeping in mind the details that Endelyn had provided to the princess before the feast. The five oldest and largest baronies had been created by King Katwaladrus who ruled Kernyv at the time of the Aquilan withdrawal from Albion. Emboldened by the departure of the Aquilan legions, Kernyv's neighboring kingdom to the east, Meonwara, had staged an invasion.

Katwaladrus and his allies beat them back across the River Dubras and burned half of the Meonwaran capital of Isca to the ground. The Kernyveu called him Great King Katwaladrus, but he was also the king who began the raids on Iveriu. The Iverni didn't call him Great, and Branwen couldn't bring herself to, either.

The descendants of Katwaladrus's victorious allies now bowed their heads before King Marc and Princess Eseult.

Baron Gwyk and Baron Dynyon offered perfunctory salutations to the king and his bride-to-be. The head of House Gwyk was an exceptionally tall man with one piercingly yellow-brown eye, like a cat's; the other was made of cloudy glass from the Serene Republic, Ruan whispered in Branwen's ear. He had lost it fighting the Iverni.

Branwen wanted to say he'd lost it raiding her homeland, but she smiled at him instead. Baron Dynyon made a habit of touching his carmine mustache as he talked and, if he was a friend of Countess Kensa, Branwen was predisposed to dislike him.

Baron Kerdu offered his congratulations to Eseult in Ivernic, eliciting a small smile from the princess. They sounded sincere. He lingered a few moments to ask Tristan about his journey from Iveriu.

"You're a true Kartagon warrior," the baron said with approval, wrinkles creasing his dark skin as he smiled, and shook Tristan's hand. "You've made us proud."

Tristan thanked him, seeming touched, and Branwen tried not to be touched as well. His happiness was no longer her affair.

Baron Chyanhal also appeared to be of Kartagon descent. When the Aquilan military left Albion, Tristan had explained to Branwen during the sea voyage, King Katwaladrus allowed the legionaries to stay if they wished. Which struck her as a strange decision. Why allow trained, foreign fighters to remain in his kingdom?

Branwen wondered if, perhaps, the price of remaining was to join his campaign against Meonwara.

The head of House Chyanhal was younger than the other barons, tall and slim, amicable but self-contained. Branwen couldn't ascertain his allegiances.

The last baron to come forward had a long, white beard. His waxen skin was flecked with liver spots. He walked with some difficulty and seemed to resent the finely whittled cane on which he leaned.

"House Julyan offers our very best wishes on your engagement." The baron smiled at King Marc in a grandfatherly way. Indeed, he was more than old enough.

"I never thought I'd live to see peace with Iveriu," he said. "Perhaps that is why the Horned One has yet to call me for judgment." He rattled a warm laugh and shifted his smile to Eseult. "Long may you reign, Lady Princess."

Pressing his cane toward his heart, the elderly baron declared, "*Kernyv bosta vyken!*"

"Kernyv forever," King Marc repeated, and Branwen detected a hint of relief in his tone. Tristan's shoulders also noticeably slackened. Baron Julyan's support must carry great weight at court.

Tristan and Marc were attempting to change Kernyv's future with this marriage—and it was evident they hadn't consulted the barons beforehand. King Marc wanted to make peace grow like his garden but, glancing around the Great Hall, Branwen wondered how many weeds would first need to be pulled up by the root.

The king stood. Gazing down at Eseult, he held out a tentative hand.

"Would you do me the honor of a dance?"

Eseult nodded, eyes downcast. She took his hand, and Baron Julyan released another chesty laugh. Dutifully, Branwen and the others followed them down from the dais to the space that had been cleared for dancing.

King Marc gestured at the musicians and they broke into a

boisterous tune. The instruments looked almost identical to those used by the *kelyos* bands in Iveriu. Before she'd met Tristan, Branwen had never considered that the music of her enemies could be so like her own. She swayed to the beat.

The nobles formed a ring around the king as he began guiding the princess through the steps of a Kernyvak dance. Marc held Eseult as if she were a bird who might fly away. Eseult stared at her feet. The awkwardness between them was palpable, painful to watch.

"Join us!" King Marc invited the crowd. "Join us!"

Several of the courtiers answered his call. Eseult's eyes sought out Tristan, but he didn't notice because Baron Dynyon had him engaged in what appeared to be an animated conversation. Branwen spied Endelyn trying to capture Tristan's attention as well. While Endelyn's mother might have wanted to see her married to Marc, the Kernyvak princess had evidently set her sights on his nephew. She settled for an invitation to dance from Baron Chyanhal whose features were angular, yet pleasing.

Ruan cocked an eyebrow at Branwen, and she edged backward through the crowd as more couples joined the king and future queen on the dance floor.

"Lady Branwen?"

Andred appeared at her side. "*Nosmatis*, Andred," she said.

His jaw tightened as he shifted his weight onto his right leg. "*Nosmatis*," the young prince echoed. "I've heard you're a healer."

"I am." Discreetly, Branwen marked his profile. She had assisted her aunt in treating a girl with a similarly twisted foot. "But I don't know of any cures—"

"No," Andred interrupted. "Not for me. I—I've been studying—

reading..." He ran a hand over his dark curls. "I grow herbs in Marc's—the king's garden. I was wondering if you would teach me?"

"Teach you?"

"Healing. Medicine. I'd like to go with you when you visit your patients." He scrunched his lips together. "I know all of the herbs in Kernyv, and I can suture wounds. I can help." Determination in his eye, Andred told her, "I'd make a good apprentice."

Branwen was taken aback. She still considered herself to be Queen Eseult's apprentice. "You don't want to learn from the *kordweyd*?"

Andred frowned. "The *kordweyd* don't share their knowledge outside the temple. They also don't marry or have families. Once a *kordweyd* is Consecrated, he has no family apart from the Horned One." The boy rubbed his left hip, which appeared stiff. "I'm not ready to be Consecrated. Give me a chance, Lady Branwen," he said.

Branwen didn't know if she was in a position to teach anyone anything, but she said, "I would be very happy for your help, Andred."

He showed her a heartrending grin. "Thank you, my lady." The grin grew cheeky, making him look even more like Ruan. "Maybe I can teach you something, too?"

"Oh?"

"Kernyvak. You're living here now. You need to speak our language."

"Yes, I do," Branwen agreed. "I think Prince Ruan is tired of playing translator."

"I think he likes the excuse to speak with you."

"*Mmm*. Your brother likes hearing himself talk."

"You're not wrong." They shared a laugh.

The courtiers clapped as the dance came to an end and King Marc bowed to Eseult. He led the princess toward where Countess Kensa, Ruan, and Seer Casek were standing. The musicians struck up another song, and the dancing continued, accompanied by cheers and laughter.

The princess's cheeks glowed from twirling. She looked almost like the cousin Branwen remembered. Catching Branwen's eye, Eseult beckoned her to join them, and she was in no position to refuse.

Resigned, she excused herself from Andred's side. Ruan smiled, running a thumb over his mouth, as Branwen joined their group.

"Lady Branwen," King Marc said. "There is another matter to do with the treaty that concerns you."

"There is?" She clutched the sleeve of her dress, sneaking a glance at her cousin. Eseult looked as mystified as Branwen felt.

Countess Kensa and Seer Casek leaned forward as the king spoke.

"You are the heir to Castle Bodwa and lands in the Laiginztir province of Iveriu, are you not?" Branwen nodded. "Your uncle, King Óengus, requested that you also be provided with territory in Kernyv for a dowry that befits your status as cousin to my queen."

"I . . ." Branwen took a deep breath. "I have no interest in marriage."

Ruan laughed. "I've never heard of a woman with no interest in marriage."

"Perhaps you don't know what women truly want," she said, and the words came out more snappish than she'd intended. Ruan's smile faltered.

"Which lands are to be gifted to Lady Branwen?" Countess Kensa prompted the king. Her voice was breezy and false.

King Marc's gaze traveled across the room to Tristan. "My nephew has bequeathed Lady Branwen estates in Liones, near his own Castle Wragh."

"He did?" Branwen whispered.

"I hope these are welcome tidings," King Marc said. She swallowed. If not for the Loving Cup, it would have been. Just then, Tristan walked toward them, Baron Dynyon at his heels.

Countess Kensa looked over Tristan's shoulder, meeting the baron's eye. "You've missed the happy news," she told him. "Prince Tristan has gifted some of the estates near Castle Wragh to Lady Branwen."

Baron Dynyon's face turned as red as his mustache. Tristan froze.

To Branwen, the countess said, "House Dynyon originally controlled much of Liones—a reward from Great King Katwaladrus."

"In the time before House Whel existed," Ruan remarked, and his mother glared at him.

"I suppose Liones is Prince Tristan's *sovereign* territory," Kensa continued, ignoring her eldest son. "He may do with it as he pleases."

Tristan's jaw tightened. Only a monarch had the power to redistribute lands. King Marc spoke before his nephew could take the countess's bait. "Liones has been under the protection of Kernyv since Tristan pledged his fealty to me—as you well know, Countess. I authorized all of the terms of the treaty with Iveriu, including the land bequest to Lady Branwen."

There was a hard edge to his words. "Furthermore, we are looking to the future," King Marc said, shifting his gaze between Countess Kensa and Baron Dynyon. "Not the past."

"And as we look to the future," said the baron, "will the Houses be compensated for the loss of labor from the freed prisoners—whom we have clothed and sheltered? Or will our taxes to the crown be reduced?"

Branwen marveled that the nobleman would make such a thinly veiled threat.

Tristan stepped closer to his king, taking umbrage on his behalf.

"My esteemed baron," said King Marc. "I am building a new future for Kernyv. The Iverni are free to remain in Kernyv or return to Iveriu. If they choose to stay, I expect them to be compensated for their labor."

"And you expect the Iverni to treat the Kernyveu in Iveriu so fairly?" he spluttered. "Didn't the King's Champion cheat in the Final Combat? I heard he coated his spear with poison."

Outrage shone on Eseult's face as she drew in a breath. Branwen felt a spark in her right palm. The marriage ceremony hadn't yet been performed and there were already so many ways this alliance could unravel.

"My uncle Morholt acted with dishonor, Baron Dynyon," said Branwen, trying to restrain her own ire. "The Queen of Iveriu denounced him and denied him entrance to the Land of Youth."

"Yes," Eseult said. "We're all grateful Prince Tristan survived. Do not suppose you know the heart of the Ivernic people." Branwen barely masked her surprise at the princess's words. Before she'd drunk from the Loving Cup, her cousin had sworn she would never forgive Tristan for slaying their uncle.

Tristan turned on Baron Dynyon. "King Óengus is a man of honor," he said roughly. Gesturing at Eseult and Branwen, he continued, "As is his daughter and his niece. Lady Branwen purged the poison from me herself."

"Indeed," said King Marc. "I am beholden to the Iverwomen for bringing Tristan back to me. He's as dear to me as my own life."

The baron's flush deepened to purple.

"I see why Princess Eseult chose you as her Champion, Prince Tristan," he said. Looking at the king's crossed arms, Baron Dynyon bowed his head. "Forgive my impertinence, my Lord King."

"It isn't my forgiveness you need," King Marc told him.

The baron angled his shoulders toward the princess and bowed from the waist. "I apologize for my rash words, Princess Eseult," he said, although a vein thrummed near his temple.

"I accept your apology, Baron Dynyon," Eseult said. Her voice was chilly. "Prince Tristan has saved me from pirates and will always defend my interests. That is why I have chosen him as my Champion."

For the first time since their arrival in Kernyv, the princess resembled Queen Eseult. She sounded like a True Queen. Branwen looked between her cousin and Tristan. If Eseult's interests ran counter to those of Kernyv, of peace—which would Tristan defend?

"And now, I would ask my Champion to perform another service," said Eseult.

"Of course, Lady Princess." Tristan ducked his head.

"A dance?"

He glanced at Marc. "With my blessing," said the king.

Fire flickered beneath Branwen's flesh as Tristan escorted Eseult onto the dance floor. How could her cousin be so foolish?

The princess wrapped her hand around Tristan's shoulders with none of the hesitation with which she'd allowed herself to be held by her future husband. She showed Tristan the delighted, tempestuous smile that mesmerized so many. He maintained an appropriate distance between them, but there was an ease between the pair that all could see. The same ease Branwen had once felt in Tristan's arms, by Eseult's side.

"Prince Tristan seems to be much beloved of the Iverni," remarked Countess Kensa, creeping closer to Branwen. "He and the princess look well together."

The warmth between the couple as they danced wasn't real, but the lovers believed it was. Did the truth make any difference?

"As a queen and her Champion should look," Branwen told the countess.

"The Iverni must be equally beloved by the prince. The entire court was astounded to learn Tristan had relinquished his position as King's Champion. He and the king have been inseparable since they were boys," Countess Kensa said, flicking a glance at Marc, before returning her gaze to Branwen.

Branwen took a breath. "Prince Tristan does his queen—and all of Iveriu—a great honor."

"Of course. He also parted with profitable lands for you, Lady Branwen. Lands teeming with white lead." The countess pricked her with a glance. "Tristan must have been made to feel extremely welcome in Iveriu."

"I hope so. The prince is very generous."

"Very."

"In fact, I should go thank him," Branwen said, deciding to put an end to Eseult's folly, and strode toward the couple.

"Mind if I cut in?"

"Branny, we're just dancing—"

"Dance with your betrothed," she said in a warning tone.

The cousins stared at each other; Branwen recalled a thousand childhood struggles between them, but there had never been this—this friction, like whetting a blade against a stone, until the day Tristan had washed up on the Ivernic coast.

"Or would you like the entire Kernyvak fleet to assault our homeland after they learn the truth?"

"I—I'm sorry," Eseult whispered. "I needed a moment away from the others." Branwen didn't—*couldn't*—respond. Hanging her head, the princess told Tristan, "*Mormerkti,*" and retreated toward the king's side.

The music transitioned into a song with a strong, insistent tempo. Tristan proffered a hand. "I thought you were cutting in," he said. Circling his gaze around the Great Hall, he added, "The nobles are watching." Not just the noblemen and noblewomen, but also Seer Casek.

Branwen painted on a smile and seized Tristan's hand. He slid his arm around her waist, and she tried to ignore the feelings his touch fomented. This man who had once been her refuge.

They began to dance. "Have you lost all sense?" she scolded under her breath.

"I couldn't refuse my queen's request."

"You're never to blame, are you, Tristan?" *You know who's to blame,* snarled a voice in Branwen's mind.

Tristan twirled Branwen farther into the dance floor. "I *do* blame myself. I blame myself for everything." His voice was mixed with sand. "I was supposed to protect the princess and I disgraced myself. *I'm* responsible for what happened. But I will protect Eseult now. However unworthy I am. I owe her that, and so much more."

Branwen's hands trembled in his. His self-loathing made her sick. *Hate me,* she nearly said. *Hate me instead.*

But she only demanded, "Why didn't you tell me Eseult would be a True Queen?"

"Your aunt and uncle insisted I tell no one before Marc. I gave them my word." Tristan's palm was warm on her back.

"You're very good at keeping secrets."

"I think we both are."

Branwen felt the beat of the drum in her bones. Her body followed

Tristan's lead. She didn't know the steps, but it was as if she had been performing this dance her entire life, as if there were no beginning and no end, as if it were a dance that would be performed again and again. Sweat trickled from Tristan's temple; it glistened in the mellow light of the oil lamps.

The compulsion to wipe it away, to stroke his face nearly shattered her.

"What about the lands?" she said. "You couldn't have told me about that?"

Tristan dipped Branwen low, his chest pressing against hers. "I wanted them to be a wedding present. I thought we would share them."

Tears stung her eyes.

"Take the lands back. Take them back, Tristan. I don't want—I don't want to share anything with you."

He raised her up from the dip, their chests still pressed together. "I can't. I've signed the deeds. They're yours. And I don't want to." He dragged down a breath and Branwen could feel it on her lips. "The lands are yours—and so am I."

She wanted to feel more than his breath.

No. Branwen broke his embrace and rushed for the exit. The heady, nutty smell of the oil was nauseating.

She was almost out the door when Ruan stepped in her way.

"I thought you didn't know how to dance?" he said. Branwen was too overwrought to come up with a witty retort. Her face fractured from the effort of holding back her tears.

For a moment, Ruan's façade crumbled. "What's wrong?" he asked, and he actually sounded like he wanted to know.

"Nothing." *Everything.*

Branwen raced through the courtyard and down the passageway

toward the gardens. Tristan might want to belong to Branwen, but he was fighting the urge, the pull he felt toward Eseult. She could see it. Countess Kensa could see it.

How could she protect Iveriu, protect the princess, when Eseult flaunted her affection for Tristan before King Marc's entire court?

Branwen could only hope Marc loved Tristan too much to sense the betrayal.

Her feet skidded over the stone steps, descending along the tree-lined path. She wanted to run far, far away from this island.

Reaching the second terraced garden, Branwen let her tears flow. She had loved her cousin before she had loved herself; now she felt enmity like venom eating it away. She had put a naive, childlike faith in the Loving Cup—and in the Queen of Iveriu. She had trusted too much. She had loved too hard. She'd delayed her own happiness until it turned to ash.

Branwen lifted the Hand of Bríga, allowing the spark she'd suppressed all evening to surface. Her fire warmed her. Her sigh became a strangled laugh.

The flame continued to grow, climbing like a vine against the sky until it competed with the brightest star.

Odai eti ama. Branwen was starting to hate more than she loved.

She wanted to jump from her skin, throw herself into the sea, become the flame.

Ecstasy streamed through her. She could feel this way all the time—if only she let herself. This power was hers.

Gazing out onto the moon-glazed waters that surrounded Monwiku, Branwen saw flames erupt and dance upon the waves. In the distance, sails winked as the wind chimes moaned. The sails were there, then gone: a whisper of silver against an ebony sky.

Branwen only knew of one kind of ship with tattered sails like broken promises. Ships that didn't exist wholly in this world.

They were coming. The Shades were coming for *her*. She had to warn the princess, Tristan, the king . . . everyone.

She looked back at the castle, and it was already on fire. *Let them burn.*

Branwen let out a hoarse scream. She squeezed her eyes tight as the Dark One's laughter filled the cavern of her mind.

When she opened them again, the Shades were gone. The sea was calm.

There was no fire save the flame in Branwen's hand.

A WAR IN THE OTHERWORLD

BRANWEN ANSWERED THE KNOCK AT the door with impatience.

"*Dymat*—"

Tristan stood in the doorway, morning light slicing the corridor behind him in two. Branwen had managed to avoid him for three days since the feast.

"It doesn't seem right for me to keep it," he said, and her gaze dropped from Tristan's face, sleepless circles beneath his eyes, to the *krotto* in his arms: the harp that had once belonged to her mother.

Branwen could almost see Lady Alana's fingers plucking its silver strings.

"Queen Eseult gave it to you," she said tonelessly.

Her aunt had known how Branwen and Tristan felt about each other. When she presented the harp to him at Castle Rigani, the queen had been giving them her blessing.

"Your aunt wanted it to stay in the family," Tristan said as he extended the *krotto* across the threshold. "If—if that's no longer possible, then the harp should be yours." Their eyes met; his gleamed with sadness, dark wells into which Branwen could let herself fall.

"You know I don't play well," she said.

He stepped into the chamber. "Does that mean there's a chance Emer will let Tantris sing for her again?"

The weakness in Branwen wanted to let him more than she wanted her next breath.

"Emer never existed."

"She did." Tristan drew closer until only the harp lay between them. "She *does*. And the Hound is still devoted." His hand grazed her cheek, and something in her core quivered.

"Share a song with me, Branwen." It was a plea.

His lips brushed hers, and Branwen drove her fingers through Tristan's curls as if clinging to a precipice. He kissed her more ardently. A moan escaped her lips.

But when Tristan closed his eyes, Branwen couldn't help but wonder if it was Eseult he pictured. She broke the embrace, pushing on the *krotto*, sending him staggering backward.

"You can't share a song with me *and* with my cousin, Tristan!"

"I don't want to share a song with anyone else, Branwen. What can I do to make you believe me?"

"You can't."

"Then *take* it." He offered her the harp with more vehemence, his voice thin, near breaking.

"No. Unlike you, I don't disobey my sovereign's wishes."

"*Branwen*." Tristan's fingers flexed on the bend of the harp. "Your heart has never been cruel." He brimmed with the sadness of the seas.

"You don't know my heart." The thrill of the flame, vibrant and delicious, wavered in her breast even now. It frightened her. Excited her.

Branwen sidestepped Tristan and shimmied past him through the opened door.

"My patients are waiting."

"You have time to heal everything except *us*." He spoke to her back.

"I can't raise the dead," she said, and walked away.

✠ ✠ ✠

Branwen made haste for the royal stables, which were located near the base of Monwiku island, close to the granary and some of the servants' dwellings. She clutched her cloak against the gusts of wind that came off the water, fighting the memory of the kiss. *Foolish. Impulsive.*

She picked up her pace. The causeway would be closing soon. Andred and Ruan were waiting at the stables to accompany Branwen to the temple where the injured miners had been taken.

The younger prince from House Whel knew the name of each of the groomsmen and appeared to be well liked by all of the castle inhabitants. Andred possessed the same charm as his older brother but it was tempered with a dose of humility and kindness. Somehow his company always cheered Branwen.

She heard footsteps from behind as she followed the path that wound beneath the covering of trees.

"Branny! Branny, wait!"

The princess's voice carried over the rustling leaves. The lanterns squeaked as they swayed on the branches. A hand grabbed Branwen's elbow from behind, jolting her to a stop.

"Branny, would you please wait!" Incensed, Branwen turned toward her cousin. The princess's shoulders heaved from her sprint, blond hairs escaping the plaits that Endelyn had arranged atop her head.

"I'm in a hurry, Lady Princess. I'm sure Endelyn can provide you with whatever you require."

"No, she can't." Eseult threw her hands to her sides. "Please, Branny. I know you're furious with me. But on the ship, you made me promise that I would tell you—that if I was feeling . . . *desperate*, I would tell you." Her voice was strangled. "This is me telling you."

The image of her cousin bleeding in her cabin aboard the *Dragon Rising* immediately surfaced in her mind. When the princess had stabbed herself, Branwen had felt the blade pierce her own heart. The Hand of Bríga had saved the princess—but it could only heal her physical wounds.

"What are you saying?" she asked.

"I'm scared, Branny. I'm so scared." Eseult tugged at a loose strand of hair. "I didn't want any of this—and now I'm supposed to be a True Queen? I *can't*."

Branwen opened and closed her mouth, frustration and fear stealing her words. Wasn't that why she had created the Loving Cup in the first place?

At last she said, "This isn't about what you want, Essy. It's about what Iveriu needs." The Wise Damsel had told Branwen the same thing about her magic, and yet it was Branwen's magic that had ruined everything.

"But I'm *not* what Iveriu needs," Eseult countered. "I never have been. I'm not talented. Or especially clever. I wasn't born to rule. My mother has overplayed her hand." The princess gave Branwen a plaintive stare. "We both know it was her."

"The Old Ones chose you," she said, softening her tone somewhat. "They believe in you."

"How can they? I don't believe in myself." Eseult clutched at her chest. Her breaths grew shallower, tiny wheezes. "I can't do this without you."

Instinct, or habit, propelled Branwen to gently drop a hand on her cousin's back. She drew soothing circles between Eseult's shoulder blades. After a minute or two, the princess's posture relaxed, and she blew out a deep breath.

Swiping at her tears, Eseult said, "Not you without me. Forgive me, Branny. I'm so alone."

So am I. "All I ever wanted was for someone to love me for me," her cousin went on. "Not for my titles. But not like this, not by hurting the only sister I've ever known. Tristan won't even look at me, either."

"That's not how it seemed when you asked him to dance."

"It was the only way I could get him to say more than two words to me. I'm sorry—I didn't think." Eseult's face crumpled. "He told me to forget what happened between us. But I can't."

"Neither can I."

The princess dropped her gaze to the cobblestones. If Branwen told Eseult that Tristan didn't really love her for her, she would devastate her cousin. She would start a war. And it wouldn't change anything. Countless people would perish for nothing.

The lanterns overhead squeaked, reminding Branwen of the *kretarvs'* caw.

"When I was recuperating after my . . . accident," Eseult said in a hush, "Tristan told me I was brave. That marrying for peace required a hero's sacrifice."

Branwen dug her fingernails into the pads of her palms as if they were talons. She remembered the morning when she'd encouraged Tristan to play the harp for her cousin.

"No one had ever called me brave before. A hero. More like you, Branny."

I'm not a hero. Each word was a sword running her through.

"The only thing special about me is my royal blood, I've always known that." The princess raked a hand through her plaits. "But Tristan saw the best in me. Someone worth admiring—loving, even. I think that's when my feelings began to change. I didn't mean for it to happen, I swear I didn't."

A breath shuddered through Branwen, magic stirring. The night the Shades attacked, Eseult stole the golden vial from Branwen, unaware it was anything more than a special liqueur prepared by the head royal cook. Yet she had still brought it to Tristan's cabin. She had still sought solace from him.

What if the Loving Cup had merely incited them to act on impulses they'd already harbored? Tristan asked Branwen to be handfasted aboard the *Dragon Rising* because he felt the distance growing between them. She had thought it was her secrets driving them apart.

Had Tristan only kissed Branwen this morning to make himself forget the princess?

Her pity for her cousin turned to smoke.

Searching the trees, making sure they weren't being overheard, Branwen stepped in close to Eseult. "Then *be* the hero Tristan sees in you. Be brave." Her voice was somewhere between a growl and a rasp. "Make the sacrifice and *be* the hero Iveriu needs. As a True Queen, you have the power to ensure a better life for the Iverni—and the Kernyveu. A peaceful life."

"Don't you ever get tired of duty, Branny? Don't you want anything for yourself?" Eseult said. Her words were whispered, ragged around the edges.

"Tristan was the one thing I ever wanted for myself," Branwen said.

The truth stretched between the cousins, a fraying rope about to snap.

Branwen turned to leave.

"Where are you going?" Eseult asked.

"To visit my patients."

"I'll go with you."

That was the last thing Branwen wanted. She squeezed the Hand of Bríga into a fist. "You can't stand the sight of blood." Ever since they were little girls, the princess had had no stomach for treating the war-wounded. She'd always avoided the infirmary at all costs.

"I'll be brave," said the princess. Defiance rang from her words. Branwen no longer had the energy to fight her.

"Fine. But hurry. The tide is coming in."

A few minutes later, the warm smell of hay wafted over Branwen.

"You're late," Ruan admonished as she entered the stables. She raised her brows at the prince. "I have company," she said.

Ruan straightened. "Lady Princess." He performed a swift bow. Andred, who was feeding an apple to his mount, did the same.

"Good morning," Eseult said. "I'm visiting the injured with Branwen today." She looked around the stable, which had stalls for the horses on either side of the entrance. "Do you know where the mare is that the king gifted me?"

Andred beamed a smile. "I do, Lady Princess. This way." He pointed toward the end of the left-hand row of stalls.

"Does the king know you're leaving the castle?" Ruan asked the princess.

"The king is in one of his many meetings. I don't think he'll even notice."

Ruan frowned as Eseult turned on her heel, following Andred. Although it was true that Marc had made himself scarce outside of official functions.

Branwen and Ruan trailed a few paces behind. "If I told you that the blue of your cloak brings out the coppery tint of your eyes," Ruan said, "would that make you less likely to wear it?"

"No." Branwen met his gaze. "Because I only brought one cloak with me from Iveriu, and I don't fancy freezing to death on the moors."

Ruan hadn't mentioned seeing her on the verge of tears the night of the feast, but it unnerved Branwen that he knew she'd been so upset.

"It does seem like this winter will be colder than usual," he noted.

"Perhaps there's a war in the Otherworld."

"What's that?"

"Oh, nothing but a backward Ivernic superstition." Branwen tilted one corner of her mouth upward.

"You know, it's funny, I'm finding myself quite enamored of all things backward and Ivernic these days."

Branwen could only laugh. "I see. Well, when there's a particularly cold winter or a meager harvest, we Iverni say it must be due to a war in the Otherworld." As she spoke, the tiny hairs on her forearms tingled. She wished she hadn't mentioned it.

The click of boots on stone resounded off the roof. Branwen turned to see Tristan rushing toward them. "There you are, Lady Princess," he said, relief washing over him.

The stable was suddenly much too crowded.

Ruan barked a laugh. "Already lost our future queen, have you, cousin?" A line formed on the bridge of Tristan's nose. "Fear not, I can provide a sufficient escort to the temple," Ruan taunted. "Go back to whatever it was you were doing—"

Endelyn entered the stables just behind Tristan and, looking between them, Ruan added, "With my sister."

Much, *much* too crowded.

Endelyn's cheeks erupted like wildfire. "*Ruan*," Tristan said, a coarseness to the name. "Endelyn is practically my little sister as well." At the proclamation, Endelyn's face flamed brighter, and Branwen almost felt sorry for the snobbish Kernyvak princess. Apparently Tristan was the only one oblivious to Endelyn's infatuation.

"I'm going with Branwen to visit her patients," Eseult said to Tristan, ignoring the others. Tristan looked toward Branwen, but she refused to meet his gaze.

"As you wish, Lady Princess," he said stiffly. "I'll accompany you."

"Me too," Endelyn said.

"Endelyn tending the wounded? This I have to see," Ruan said, earning himself a thorny look from his sister. To Tristan and Andred, he said, "Let's saddle the horses before we need a boat."

Eseult stroked the muzzle of the stark white mare, which had popped her head out of the stall. "Lí Ban doesn't need a boat. She can transform into a fish."

"Lí Ban?" said Tristan.

"Yes, I decided on a name for my palfrey," she replied. The princess gazed at her Champion a long moment.

Branwen's next breath cut her from the inside like broken glass.

She had listened to Tristan sing the ballad of Lí Ban to her cousin on the day he'd called her a hero. Had Branwen always been a fool?

"And how exactly will the mare transform into a fish?" Ruan asked, a roguish quality to his voice, breaking the tension.

Eseult tousled the palfrey's forelock. "Lí Ban is an Otherworld goddess of the sea—and a mermaid."

The prince laughed. "The Iverni believe in mermaids, too?" He directed the question at Branwen.

"The Kernyveu believe in giants," she replied.

Ruan let out a whistle at the fierceness in her tone. "Fair enough." Glancing at Tristan, he said, "Lady Branwen has been riding your stallion. But I'm happy to have her astride mine."

"Branny can ride with me," Eseult said.

Branwen darted her gaze from her cousin to Ruan and, fleetingly, at Tristan. Turning to Andred, she said, "King Marc offered me a horse of my own. Help me find a suitable mount?"

"I know just the one."

"*Mormerkti*, Andred." Speaking to everyone and no one, Branwen said, "I prefer to ride alone."

THE ONLY HOSTAGE

ANDRED SELECTED A MARE WITH a lustrous, umber coat
and a headstrong disposition for Branwen. The palfrey bolted
out in front of the other horses as they crossed the causeway, which
suited Branwen just fine.

Her mount was named Senara, after a princess from the southern
continent who had apparently been thrust into a barrel and cast onto
the sea by an evil husband. She washed up on the coast of Kernyv, pregnant, and gave birth to none other than Lugmarch, who eventually
defeated the giants. Branwen had smiled as Andred told her the tale,
and she'd forced herself not to wonder how Tristan might recount it.

A guard dog barked as soon as Branwen entered the village. The
stone dwellings were arranged in a defensive ring. The settlement had
been built on a hill somewhat elevated from the surrounding moors,
and Branwen spied the rest of her traveling party below.

The temple of the Horned One was positioned in the center of the
village—a humble, horseshoe-shaped structure. Its walls were made

from slabs of granite interspersed with the oxblood stone that supported the Great Hall, which, on closer inspection, was flecked with black. The Kernyveu called it snakestone because it resembled a serpent's skin.

The roof was thatched like the others in the village, and, from the outside, the only attribute that distinguished the temple was a finely carved statue of a man with horns above the entrance.

Talorc spotted Branwen first and called out a greeting. Thanks to the Hand of Bríga, the elderly Iverman had sufficiently recovered to help with chores around the temple. As he raised himself from a stool, the ache in his joints was plain. Even without his newer injuries, his days as a miner should have been long since past.

Branwen dismounted from Senara and tied the mare to the post of a wooden fence, which enclosed the temple's pigs.

"Good morning, Talorc," said Branwen. She withdrew a satchel filled with salves and bandages from the saddlebags. Talorc released a phlegmy cough, and Branwen's ears pricked at the sound. "There's a chill in the air," she chided him. "Be sure to keep warm."

"I will, Lady Branwen." His smile was indulgent. "The Old Ones haven't let me pass through the Veil to the Land of Youth yet but, when they do, I'll see Ném there."

Branwen nodded, slinging her satchel over her shoulder. The loss of his son anchored Talorc's words. A parent shouldn't have to drink the Final Toast for his child, but Branwen had seen many young men felled by raiders. She glanced back toward Eseult as the princess brought her mount to a stop, Tristan at her side. Her marriage to King Marc would save many fathers from Talorc's grief.

The Iverman bowed as Ruan walked over to them. "*Penaxta*," Talorc said, which Branwen had learned meant "prince" in Kernyvak.

Ruan launched himself from his stallion and bade Talorc good morning in Ivernic, provoking a skeptical look from Branwen. "There have always been Iverni on my family estates," Ruan said to her in Aquilan. "I've picked up a bit of your language."

The guard dog barked again, racing toward Branwen and nipping at her ankles. She looked down, shooing it away, and saw that it was only a puppy. Its hair was a mottled white and brown, its ears floppy, and the skin crinkled around its flat nose. "Off, off," she said.

The puppy snorted and scampered behind Branwen. A moment later she heard a familiar, delighted squeal. Eseult leaned down to pet the puppy, stroking its saggy jowls, not minding the muddy paw prints it left on her finely embroidered gown.

Endelyn observed the dog with considerably more displeasure.

Tristan stood behind the princesses as he tied up the horses, posture wary. He glanced around the village for any threats to his future queen.

"Andred!" Branwen called to the boy who was also admiring the puppy. "Let's see to our patients." She'd had enough delays for one morning.

Andred straightened at her surly tone. He grabbed his own bag of herbs from his mount and moved toward her. The boy's left leg lagged half a breath behind his right with each step, and Branwen could see the discomfort etched into his stride, but she'd noticed that Andred disliked when others offered sympathy. He never appreciated being treated as any less capable than he was. True to his word, his knowledge of the medicinal properties of the local plants and wildflowers was exhaustive.

Eseult sprang up and rushed toward Branwen, too. "Wait for me."

Branwen exhaled a frustrated breath. "Another Iverwoman?" said Talorc.

The princess dashed a glance at Branwen when she heard the man speaking Ivernic.

"Talorc," Branwen began, "may I introduce you to Princess Eseult of Iveriu. Lady Princess, this is Talorc. He comes from Laiginztir, near Castle Bodwa."

The elderly Iverman ran a hand over his white hair and sank into a bow.

"May the Old Ones favor you, Lady Princess. It's a great honor to meet you." Raising himself upright, Talorc added, "You have brought us peace. One Iveriu." He pressed a fist to his heart.

Branwen heard her cousin inhale a startled breath. "One Iveriu," Eseult said. Competing emotions crossed her features. "How did you come to be here?" she asked.

From the corner of his eye, Talorc looked hurriedly at Ruan before answering. "I was captured by raiders when I was a much younger man, Lady Princess."

Branwen wondered how much Ivernic Ruan understood as the Iverman spoke.

"I've been working the prince's mines ever since," Talorc explained. "But now the war between Kernyv and Iveriu is over. Thanks to you, Lady Princess, I will die a free man."

Talorc took Eseult's hand and kissed it.

"May the Old Ones protect you always," he said.

The princess turned her head toward Branwen, and she saw fury, sympathy, and helplessness in her cousin's eyes.

Eseult clasped her hands together. "I am glad you can go home now, Talorc."

"My son is in the Land of Youth, Lady Princess. As is my wife. I am too old for anyone in Iveriu to remember me," Talorc replied. "I will stay in Kernyv."

The princess cut a glance at Ruan. "This man is too weak to work in your mines," she told him in Aquilan, raising her voice.

"That is entirely the man's choice, Lady Princess. House Whel will abide by the king's decree to pay the Iverni who remain for their labor. They may even remain dwelling on our lands in exchange for a small rent."

Eseult rested her hands on her hips, and Branwen tapped her mother's brooch. If the Iverni paid rents to the noble Houses as well as working their mines and fields, she couldn't help but wonder whether their lives would change at all?

"I am the King's Champion," Ruan said, looking from Branwen to his future queen. "And I will enforce his laws without question." Tristan walked to Eseult's side, listening intently, but said nothing.

"Talorc," Eseult said to the Iverman. "Are there other injured Iverni here?"

"There are, Lady Princess."

She threw her shoulders back. "I would very much like to meet them."

"They will hardly believe their eyes." Talorc smiled. "Follow me."

The puppy chased after Eseult as Talorc led her through the temple courtyard and inside the low doorway. The Horned One was also known as the Lord of Wild Things, and animals were always welcome within the temple walls. Branwen had been alarmed the first time she noticed a hare caper in and out, but she'd grown used to it over the past few weeks.

The entrance to the temple was situated at the midpoint of the horseshoe design, Aquilan oil lamps casting a warm light on an altar where offerings were left for the Horned One. Behind the altar, the wall had been plastered and decorated with ceramic tiles depicting scenes from the god's life. Branwen averted her eyes from the fox in the corner of the mosaic—it made her stomach cramp. She no longer deserved any Otherworld messengers. The Wise Damsel had said she could help Branwen with her power, but Branwen just wanted it to disappear. She had seen what her magic could do.

The infirmary lay on the left side of the temple, although patients had also been accommodated in the living quarters of the seer who resided here. Being a small, rural temple, there was normally only one who maintained it. Branwen let Talorc introduce Eseult to the Iverni housed in the infirmary while she and Andred began their rounds on the opposite side. Tristan and Ruan followed the princess, with Endelyn trailing behind, closest to the Queen's Champion.

"My brother is as good as his word, Lady Branwen," Andred said to her. "You should know that. The Iverni who stay on our family lands will be well treated."

"We're not here to talk about your brother." Branwen gestured toward a middle-aged man with a poultice on his arm. "Check for infection and clean his wound. Use the lichen salve." She began to root around her satchel.

"I—I ground a new paste of lichen and garlic—the Aquilan treatises say it wards off fever." Andred's cheeks blazed.

Nodding, she said, "Well done. Go on, then," and returned to her own patient. Branwen changed bandages and inspected the stitches she'd made on several Ivernic and Kernyvak miners before she came to Lowenek.

"*Dymatis*," Branwen said to the girl.

"*Dymatis*, Branwen."

The first time she'd visited Lowenek after the accident, the girl hadn't remembered it was Branwen who had helped her at the mine, which was just as well. She was glad to see Lowenek's pallor steadily growing rosier. Unfortunately, it would be at least another moon before the girl would be able to put her full weight on the ankle that had been trapped beneath the rock. Branwen pushed the end of Lowenek's skirt up around her knees so she could inspect the flesh around the fracture.

The tent pole splint had been replaced with a smoother piece of wood. With any luck, the bone would heal straight.

Branwen pressed her fingers to different places on Lowenek's calf to check for infection—the flesh was inflamed, but it wasn't hot, which was a positive sign. Branwen spied Andred blush when Lowenek caught him staring. Andred turned his back, and Lowenek snuck a quick peek herself.

"Healer Branwen, good afternoon."

Branwen glanced up from Lowenek as a jolly-faced man entered the room.

"Good afternoon, Seer Ogrin," she replied in Aquilan.

His hair was shorn like Seer Casek's but already gray and sparse, and his dark brown robes rustled as he walked toward Lowenek's cot. A belt of wooden beads was secured around his waist, and he worried the antler shard that dangled from it.

"*Dymatis*, Lowenek," Ogrin said, placing a hand on the girl's forehead, and a smile shone on her freckled face. "She's been looking forward to your visits," he said to Branwen. "Prince Ruan told me that Lowenek owes you her life."

Branwen shrugged as she massaged a pain-relieving ointment into the girl's ankle. "Her parents were both lost in the disaster," Ogrin continued. "I wondered if, perhaps, you could find an occupation for her at Monwiku?"

"She can't even stand."

"Once she's recovered, Healer Branwen." He possessed a childlike laugh.

"Why do you insist on calling me Healer Branwen?"

Ogrin simply smiled. "You are a healer, are you not?"

The seer had been extremely friendly to Branwen and yet, knowing that women were not permitted to join the ranks of the *kordweyd*, made it difficult for her to drop her guard around him.

"I'm sure we can find a place for her," Andred interjected from across the room. "She could help me prepare remedies—for you, Lady Branwen." Branwen lowered an eyebrow at the young prince. "I'll ask King Marc," he said to Ogrin.

"Wonderful, wonderful," said the seer.

Branwen sighed. "Go see to the patients in the infirmary," she told the boy. Andred gave her an obedient nod and saw himself out.

Lowenek was a watchful girl, Branwen had observed, and she was not unaware that she was being discussed—even if she didn't understand Aquilan.

Branwen finished massaging in the ointment. "Better? *Dagos?*" she asked.

"*Dagos,*" Lowenek assured her. She took Branwen's hand and squeezed. "*Mormerkti.*"

"You're very welcome. *Sekrev.*"

Ogrin smiled and followed Branwen toward the infirmary. Tension crackled in the air as they entered.

Eseult was perched on the edge of a cot where an Ivernic boy about the same age as Andred lay. He'd lost his right forearm in the avalanche.

The princess stared daggers at Ruan. "It was an *accident*, Lady Princess," he protested, and clearly not for the first time.

"What's going on?" Branwen asked.

Ruan showed her a pleading look. "I was explaining that the gate on the dam broke, flooding the gorge. It was a horrible, tragic *accident*."

Eseult gestured at the boy and then at Talorc, who leaned against the wall beside the cot. "The miners say the accident happened because they were being pushed to go too fast—that white lead is becoming harder to find."

"Is this true?" Branwen glanced crossly at Ruan, then Tristan.

"It's true that we're having to dig deeper to find white lead," Ruan replied. "But we're looking into the causes of the accident. I swear to you, Lady Princess, Lady Branwen, I will find out what happened."

"I would hope so," said the future True Queen of Kernyv. "It's only a shame you didn't care for these people sooner. I'm going to speak to the king about the working conditions of the miners."

"House Whel has always managed its own affairs," Ruan told her, chest expanding. "I am responsible for these people and I take that responsibility seriously."

"The wounded in this room would indicate otherwise."

Ruan recoiled as if Eseult had slapped him. To her own surprise, Branwen found herself coming to his defense. "Prince Ruan put himself in harm's way to save an Iverman from drowning. He does care."

"Not enough, Branny." Her cousin began to lose her composure, speaking rapidly in her native language. "No one cares enough. I'm supposed to be the only Ivernic hostage in Kernyv!"

Earsplitting silence rent the room. Ruan's eyes bulged, speechless, and Branwen realized that he'd understood Eseult's outburst.

Then, from the far end of the infirmary, a woman moaned.

"Everyone needs to leave," Branwen declared. "I need to see to my patients, and they don't need an audience while I tend to them. Everyone except for Andred, please leave."

Shock splayed on Endelyn's face. Eseult sulked while Ruan looked disconcerted, and Tristan—Tristan didn't look at Branwen at all.

The puppy scuttled into the room, its nails clacking on the stone floor. Ogrin rumbled with laughter. "The Lord of Wild Things has given this creature an extra dose of wildness." The puppy barked, pawing at Eseult's skirts. She scratched it behind its floppy ears as the others exited.

The princess waited a beat before she left. "I'm sorry, Branny. I didn't mean to lose my temper. Seeing our people wounded, imprisoned—how can I be queen of the kingdom that did this to them?" Her chin wobbled. "I don't know how to do this."

Neither do I.

Branwen blinked back a tear and turned to her next patient with a smile.

STONE OF WAITING

RUAN'S STALLION CANTERED TO BRANWEN'S side as they began to traverse the moor in the direction of Monwiku, leaving her apprentice in the rear. Tristan had escorted Eseult and Endelyn back to the castle earlier while Branwen remained at the temple with Andred. Ruan had insisted on staying behind as well, but he'd kept out of Branwen's way, uncharacteristically taciturn.

"Your cousin isn't happy about being in Kernyv," he said.

Every muscle in Branwen's body tensed, and she took a moment, composing her thoughts.

"She's . . . overwhelmed."

Ruan leaned closer. "She thinks she's a hostage."

"Your Ivernic is better than you let on."

"I told you the day we met that I'm never a disappointment." He grinned. "But," he said, turning serious. "There are many at court who wouldn't take kindly to their True Queen thinking herself a hostage."

"The princess is only seventeen and she's been sent to marry a man she's never met in a kingdom that has been at war with ours since before we were born. Eseult will do her duty." Branwen looked Ruan in the eye. "I would simply ask you to make some allowances for her . . . misgivings."

Defending her cousin, Branwen felt a pang. She had always known the sacrifice being asked of the princess—and her magic had only made it worse. Yet she still couldn't find the strength to forgive Eseult.

"Spoken like a true politician, Lady Branwen." Ruan gave a small laugh. "But you make a valid point. Consider her words forgotten."

"*Mormerkti*," said Branwen, although she doubted she had truly persuaded him so easily.

"And what about you?" he asked. "Did you have qualms about coming to the land of your enemies?"

"Of course."

"And now? Do you think you could be happy here?" Ruan looked at her, the wind wreaking havoc with his burnished hair.

Branwen touched her mother's brooch. "I take satisfaction in helping my patients," she said. "But I didn't come to Kernyv seeking happiness."

Liar, whispered a voice in her head.

"See there." Ruan pointed to a tall, dark green standing stone. It was tilted at an angle, like a crooked forefinger. "That's the tallest long-stone in Kernyv."

"What's its purpose?" Branwen said. The stone stood alone on the moor with nothing else around it. "Who carved it?"

Ruan shrugged. "Giants, perhaps. We call it the Stone of Waiting."

"Waiting for what?"

"Nobody knows who erected the stone or why," he admitted. "But some people believe if you wait there long enough under a full moon, you'll see the face of your true love."

Could it be a place of in-between? Neither this world nor the Otherworld, like Kerwindos's Cauldron.

"I don't believe it," she told him.

"It's just a story."

"No. I don't believe true love is something you find by waiting." Branwen's whole life had been waiting: waiting for her parents to return when she knew they never would, waiting on the princess's every whim and mood, waiting to share herself with the man she loved—waiting too long, waiting until it was too late, waiting for *nothing*.

"Oh no? How do you propose to find it, Lady Branwen?" Ruan asked.

"I don't plan to find it at all." She kicked Senara into a gallop, letting dirt and heather spew toward the prince.

When Branwen, Ruan, and Andred returned to the stables some time later, the grooms informed them that the Queen Mother had arrived at the castle that afternoon. They were all expected immediately in the King's Tower.

Branwen's heart beat rapidly as she ascended the hill—and not solely from following the steep path. The Queen Mother was Marc's mother and Tristan's grandmother, the woman who had raised him. He had described her as formidable. Branwen tucked the flyaway strands into her plaits as she walked and smoothed her skirts.

Noticing her fidgeting hands, Ruan commented, "Don't worry, my lady. You look more than presentable."

Branwen didn't respond. Andred, who was keeping pace beside her, said, "Queen Verica lives at Castle Wragh now, in Liones. She hasn't traveled much since King Merchion died. But of course she would come for the wedding."

Long Night was still several weeks away, and Branwen wondered if there was some other purpose to her trip. Or perhaps the Queen Mother simply wanted to get a closer look at the Ivernic princess before she wed her son? The Seal of Alliance had already been signed, but the approval of the king's mother could only help Eseult's standing at court.

This was Branwen's first invitation to the king's quarters since she'd come to live at the castle, and she was glad to have Andred by her side.

She and the princes entered a large reception room. Branwen noticed a desk and a few bookcases at the far end, as well as an oblong table for council meetings. In one corner, she spied a finely carved *fidkwelsa* set on its own table. The king must use this room as his study.

"Forgive our lateness!" Ruan boomed in a jovial voice as he strode across the room. His self-confidence seemed an inexhaustible font. Several people standing with their backs toward the door turned to greet him.

"Ah, my Champion returns at last!" said King Marc, one of his rare smiles on his face.

Tristan stood beside his uncle, his bearing far more pensive, while Seer Casek regarded the newcomers with scant interest, not sparing a glance for Branwen. Light glittered off the precious stones that encased the antler shard around his neck. While his robes were the same brown as Seer Ogrin's, Casek's were cut from brocade silk. Endelyn had positioned herself beside Tristan, but she had a pout on her face, and paw prints covering the front of her gown.

Eseult immediately hooked Branwen with her gaze, her shoulders rigid, as if she'd stepped into a hunter's trap. She was standing as far away from the king as she could manage, and she made a discreet beckoning motion at Branwen with her hand.

"Let me see my nephews," said an older, female voice.

Marc stepped to the left, revealing a stately woman seated in a velvet armchair. Her once dark hair was now mostly silver, and age had softened the line of her jaw, but the resemblance to the king was immediately apparent. She surveyed the room with the same inscrutable, gray eyes.

"*Dymatís!*" Andred exclaimed, and rushed to embrace the Queen Mother. She kissed the boy fondly on the cheek. Branwen presumed that she saw him as another grandson, even though he was truly her nephew. Countess Kensa must have been considerably younger than her deceased husband.

Ruan bowed dramatically before the Queen Mother, taking her hand and kissing it.

"You're looking lovelier than ever, Queen Verica," he said, beaming her a smile. The old woman laughed, bemused.

"You certainly didn't inherit your charm from Edern." Ruan's smile froze for a fraction of a moment at the mention of his father. "It must be from the Whel side of the family," she said.

"It must be."

Queen Verica turned her attention to Branwen. "And who is your companion?"

"I am Lady Branwen of Iveriu, Queen Mother." Her eyes flicked to Tristan as she sank into a curtsy.

"Ah, the healer."

She nodded. "Yes, Queen Mother." From the corner of her eye, Branwen saw Seer Casek sneer. Ogrin appreciated her help at the temple, but the chief *kordweyd* showed Branwen nothing but contempt.

"Welcome to Kernyv." The Queen Mother shifted her gaze between Branwen and Eseult. "I was a foreigner, too, when I first arrived from Meonwara to wed Merchion, but now I see myself as a Kernyvwoman."

Tristan hadn't mentioned that his grandmother had also been a foreign queen, sent to forge an alliance with Kernyv. She must be at least sixty summers old. When the Queen Mother was a girl, the older Meonwarans would have remembered King Katwaladrus setting their capital city alight.

"In time," the Queen Mother said to Eseult, "I hope you will, too." Then to Branwen: "And you."

Marc had told Branwen that he wanted to build a different legacy from his father. What did his mother think of the raids King Merchion had sanctioned against Iveriu? She didn't comport herself like a woman used to holding her tongue.

Tristan took a step toward his grandmother, dropping an affectionate hand on her shoulder. "Lady Branwen and Princess Eseult are proud Iverwomen, Grandmother." He held Branwen's gaze, his expression pained. "But their hearts are big enough to bear Kernyvak colors as well."

He touched a hand to his own heart, to the spot where Branwen had sewn it back together. She looked away.

"My favorite grandson is quite the poet," Queen Verica said.

"I'm also your *only* grandson."

Wrinkles formed around the Queen Mother's lips as she smiled. "A mere technicality," she said. The closeness between them was tangible, and Branwen dropped her gaze. If not for her magic, this introduction could have been to her grandmother-in-law. She'd never known any of her own grandparents.

"King Marc," Eseult said, her consonants crisp. He instantly gave her his full attention, as did everyone else. "My Lord King," she started again. "I would like to ensure that the Iverni in Kernyv are able to celebrate our marriage."

"Of course." He took a hesitant step toward her. "What would you suggest, Lady Princess?" The king smiled at Eseult, but it was the kind of smile given to a passing stranger in the marketplace.

"After visiting the injured miners today," she said, "I am concerned for their welfare. They are no longer prisoners—they shouldn't be forced to work in dangerous conditions."

Marc slanted a gaze at Ruan. "As I told the princess," the King's Champion began, "we're investigating the cause of the accident and how to prevent it in the future." He skated a knuckle over his lips.

"Good. I'll go with you to inspect the mines in the coming weeks." Ruan nodded, touching his Champion's sash, and the king glanced back at Eseult. "Your people are my people now," Marc told her. "I will protect them as my own."

Branwen heard conviction in the king's voice. Yet she wondered how difficult the other Kernyvak nobles would make it for him to keep his promise.

"I would also like to offer hazelnut bread to the Iverni across the land," Eseult said, which Branwen hadn't expected. "And the Kernyveu," she added, after a moment. A genuine smile parted Branwen's lips. It was the kind of gesture that her aunt would make. What a True Queen would do.

"It's customary to serve hazelnut bread at royal weddings in Iveriu," the princess explained to Marc. "I would like to carry on the tradition."

Branwen felt Tristan's gaze on her, but she kept her eyes averted.

When he was close to death in her cave, she had brought him hazelnuts to eat. He had told her it was the food of poets in Kernyv. It was also how he'd gleaned that she was a noblewoman, since hazel trees were sacred to the king.

"An excellent idea, Princess Eseult," Marc said. "I'd be happy to share in your customs."

"Thank you, my Lord King." Her shoulders deflated, and she smiled weakly. Branwen recognized when her cousin was braced for a fight, but no fight came.

Seer Casek coughed in a deliberate manner. "This returns us to our earlier discussion of the marriage ceremony. As chief *kordweyd* of the largest temple in Kernyv, I will perform it."

Branwen swiveled her gaze toward the seer. She hadn't given any thought to the wedding itself. She had assumed it would be in keeping with Ivernic tradition.

"What does a Kernyvak wedding ceremony entail?" she asked Casek.

"It will be performed according to the rites of the Horned One."

Eseult flashed Branwen a worried look. "But the Iverni do not follow the Horned One," Branwen said to Seer Casek. "We believe in the Old Ways."

"We're living in a new era, Lady Branwen," the seer replied. "And surely the queen will take up her husband's beliefs?"

"I was under the impression that there were Kernyveu who still worshipped the Old Ones," Branwen said, shifting her gaze to Tristan.

"There are," he agreed, voice strained.

"But the king follows the Horned One," Casek told her.

He did? The question must have been written on Branwen's face, because Marc said, "I do, but my people may worship whom they choose."

Casek angled his body toward the king, blocking Branwen from his line of sight.

"My Lord King," he said. "This is a momentous occasion. You must show Kernyv that its king adheres to the teachings of the Horned One. You are their shining example. You will lead them to his truth."

Marc visibly swallowed. He was someone who hid his emotions well—a useful quality in a leader—and the shadow passed over his face in an instant. Branwen thought the *kordweyd* perilously close to giving the king an order.

"I am to be a True Queen, Seer Casek," Eseult said. Her voice grew in strength as she spoke. "I would have my own beliefs honored. Bríga is the goddess of the hearth and marriage. I wish her favor on my wedding day."

Eseult appealed to her future husband. "If my people are your people, King Marc," she told him, eyes gleaming, "then my people's beliefs are also yours."

Seer Casek's eyes rounded, and he opened his mouth to object, when Queen Verica silenced him by pushing to her feet.

"I agree with the future True Queen," she said, leaning on the back of the chair for support. "I see no reason why we can't honor all of the gods at the wedding."

Casek pivoted toward Queen Verica. "You follow the Horned One, Queen Mother."

"Indeed, Seer Casek. And I do not find my beliefs shaken by allowing another to follow hers." The Queen Mother's voice rang with authority. "When I was anointed, I accepted the Horned One's mercy.

Nothing changes that." She paused, then intoned: "*From his blood, I know mercy; in my blood, I am worthy.*"

The Queen Mother cut the air twice with her right forefingers, in two diagonal lines that intersected. Captain Morgawr had often done the same aboard the *Dragon Rising*. He'd explained to Branwen that it represented the stag's antlers upon which the Horned One had been impaled.

"Of course, Queen Mother," said Seer Casek hurriedly. "His mercy is eternal."

With a bracing breath, King Marc declared, "Then it's agreed. My wife—" He captured Eseult's gaze. "My wife and I will honor our gods together on our wedding day."

The Queen Mother raised her chin, satisfied. "Andred, my dear boy. Let us toast," she said. Andred moved toward the court cupboard and returned with a silver tray of exquisitely crafted goblets and Mílesian spirits.

"Yes, with Lugmarch's blessing, let's drink," said Ruan with an exuberant laugh. Marc looked at him appreciatively. As Andred passed out the glasses, Ruan wandered to Branwen's side. Taking a sip, he whispered in her ear, "*Overwhelmed* isn't the word I would use to describe the princess."

Branwen's throat burned as the strong desert spirit slid down it. A True Queen would have many enemies—starting with several people in this room.

When the glasses had been distributed, King Marc raised his and said, "To all the gods."

"To all the gods," murmured everyone in response.

Seer Casek took a sip and lowered his goblet. "Of course, we must ensure that the Mantle of Maidenhood is observed." He spoke directly to Marc, and it seemed far too close to a threat for Branwen's liking. "The temple must be satisfied that the maiden's sacrifice has taken place."

The king's eyes took on a pewter cast, the skin of his neck reddening. He stared into the bottom of his glass. Queen Verica pursed her lips.

"What is the Mantle of Maidenhood?" Eseult asked.

"Lady Princess, the Cult of the Horned One is built on a foundation of sacrifice and self-denial. The most glorious service is to die protecting another," Seer Casek said. "Because women were not created for battle, they cannot perform this service, and therefore do not take part in our Mysteries."

The princess bristled. "There are many Ivernic queens who led their warriors into battle, Seer Casek."

Proceeding as if she hadn't spoken, Casek said, "Women are meant to refrain from knowing the touch of a man so that they may present their maidenhood as a sacrifice to their husband on their wedding night. The morning after the consummation of the marriage, the *kordweyd* will inspect the bedclothes to determine whether the bride's sacrifice was pure."

An acrid taste filled Branwen's mouth together with the too sweet Mílesian spirits. In Iveriu, they believed that the joining of the Land and her chosen Consort was a sacred marriage. A union. The Goddess Ériu bestowed kingship on her Champion—and she could take it away if he was deemed an unfit ruler. *She* was the kingmaker.

What Seer Casek described was akin to submission. Violation. Forcing a goddess to her knees.

Branwen wouldn't stand for it. "You would abuse the True Queen's privacy?" she said, outraged. She aimed a terrified look at Tristan. His face drained of all emotion.

The love-tossed sheets in Tristan's cabin on the *Dragon Rising* tormented Branwen's mind. The sheets stained crimson like a vengeful dawn.

"It is no abuse, Lady Branwen," retorted Seer Casek. "The blood symbolizes the blood that the Horned One shed for his father. It is sacred. It is the only Mystery women can know."

Branwen's own blood boiled and went cold. Her right palm tingled.

She glanced at King Marc, who raised no objection, and the desire to tear up all of his precious flower beds rushed through her.

The arrival of a True Queen—an Ivernic queen—threatened not only the Kernyvak nobility, but the *kordweyd* as well, and Seer Casek in particular. He could see his own influence on the king fading, and Branwen had no doubt he would undermine Eseult at every turn. The power inside her began to hum, seductive—demanding.

"After the Mantle of Maidenhood has been presented to the *kordweyd*, the union will be sanctified, and you will be a True Queen, Lady Princess," Casek told Eseult. He turned to Queen Verica, and then Marc. "Not before."

THE INTOXICATING ONE

After dinner, which Branwen could barely keep down, she hurried back to the Queen's Tower, her skin itching, fire swirling in her veins. She'd had no idea when she left Iveriu just how entrenched the Cult of the Horned One already was in Kernyv, or how powerful. The future of her kingdom lay in the hands of a man she trusted less than a destiny snake.

Nearing the door to Eseult's apartment, Branwen heard barking and the sound of nails against wood. She frowned. Why was there barking? She opened the door without knocking, and the ugly puppy jumped up to Branwen's knees. She hardly noticed.

Her eyes were fixed on the princess—who was embracing Tristan, sobbing into his shoulder. He soothed her, stroking her flaxen hair.

"By the Old Ones, what do you think you're doing?" Branwen roared. Tristan's head snapped up, and his arms fell from around the princess. Branwen flung the door closed behind her with a bang. Barking, the puppy scurried toward Eseult.

She stalked toward the couple, her heart an open flame. "Are you so eager to betray your treason?" Branwen reproached them.

Tristan's jaw dropped. "*Branwen.*" He spoke her name sternly. "I'm comforting your cousin. Nothing more."

Eseult peered up at Branwen, eyes red, cheeks splotchy. She looked desolate—and in that moment Branwen hated her for it. She hated the magic she saw between the princess and her Champion—*Branwen's* magic.

"It's your *comforting* of my cousin that's brought us to the brink of war," she hissed, and shoved Tristan backward, away from the princess, with her full force.

"Why didn't you tell us?" Branwen thrust her right hand in the air, accusing. "The princess left her Mantle of Maidenhood in your bed, Tristan!"

Queen Eseult had told Branwen she'd been gifted the Hand of Bríga to guide mortal affairs, but she could burn down Monwiku Castle with her magic. With her rage. Part of her yearned, *begged* her to do it.

"I didn't know!" Tristan shouted back. "Branwen, I didn't know!"

"How could you not know?" She matched his volume.

He exhaled, raking a hand through his curls. "Only followers of the Horned One normally adhere to that ritual. I had no idea the *kordweyd* would ask it of a non-believer—an Ivernic princess, no less!" Tristan cursed in his native tongue. Eseult moaned, burying her face in her hands. The puppy pawed at the princess's hem as she wept.

"Seer Casek scorns our gods. He'll take any excuse to prevent Eseult from becoming the True Queen of Kernyv. Can't you see that?" Branwen exclaimed.

Tristan's shoulders heaved. "I'll go to the king," he said. "I'll explain it's my . . . fault. I dishonored him. I'll accept any punishment."

"*No*," Branwen and Eseult said at the same time. Their eyes met in surprise.

"Tristan, no," said the princess. "He'll execute you. And I don't . . . I *won't* let you say you did something heinous, turn what happened . . . between us . . . into horror."

Branwen glanced from her cousin to Tristan, ice in her eyes.

"There's more than your honor at stake, Prince Tristan," Branwen cut in. "Would you condemn both of our peoples to endless war?"

King Marc could have overruled Seer Casek—he was the king, after all—but he hadn't. He must believe the Mantle of Maidenhood to be necessary. Under no circumstances could he learn the truth. Especially not when the *kordweyd* believed he was already making too many concessions to the Iverni.

Tristan retreated a pace from Branwen's glare. "Then what would you have me do?" he asked her.

"Nothing." The princess—the peace—was caught like a fly in the laws of men. "*I* will be my cousin's Champion in this." If the noblemen and seers discovered Eseult was no longer a virgin, it would annul the Seal of Alliance and result in more bloodshed.

"Please leave us, Prince Tristan," said Branwen. "I need to speak with my cousin alone."

Confusion crinkled his brow. He looked to Eseult for permission, and Branwen's heart kicked. True, he was her Champion. She needed to dismiss him. But Branwen saw the emotion in his eyes.

"My life is yours," Tristan whispered to Branwen, leaning in close as he walked toward the door. "Do with it what you will."

Tristan would gladly die for the peace, Branwen knew. It was harder to live with his own dishonor. Uncle Morholt had made the same choice during the Final Combat.

The dog barked as the door closed behind Tristan. Yaps filled the bedchamber as the cousins stared at each other. "Hush, Arthek," Eseult chided the creature, sniffling.

Some of the rage bled from Branwen. She saw her cousin as a girl again, stealing milk from the kitchens at Castle Rigani to nurse an orphaned kitten that she'd hidden under her bed.

Pointing at the puppy's rumpled face, Branwen said, "How did this happen?"

The princess sighed. "Seer Ogrin gave him to me. He said the Lord of Wild Things wanted me to have a companion." She crouched down, and the dog ran into her arms, licking her wet cheeks. She scratched him between the ears. "Arthek means 'bear' in Kernyvak. The seer said he got his name because he barks so loudly he must think that's what he is."

Eseult gave a small laugh that dissolved into a whimper. The wind rattled the windows in sympathy.

Branwen peered down at her cousin as sobs racked her body.

"It's ruined ... it's ..." The princess's teeth started to chatter. "*I'm ruined ...*"

Branwen crossed toward Eseult and sank onto the floor in front of her. "*Shh,*" she said, pushing the hair from her cousin's eyes.

"You should go, Branny. Escape back to Iveriu before the wedding, while there's still time." Eseult's eyes shone. She clutched Branwen's hand tightly in hers. "You've always been my other half. Let me die knowing you're safe."

"Oh, Essy." Her anger broke like a storm at sea. Branwen gathered the princess onto her lap. In her heartache, Branwen had forgotten how deep Eseult's love ran.

"Today, at the temple," her cousin said, "our people looked at me like a hero. They're free because of the alliance." She leaned back on her heels. "I'd decided to be brave." Looking Branwen in the eye, she said, "But now I can't even do that."

"You can." She stroked her cousin's forehead, the skin almost feverishly hot.

Eseult shook her head, tearing out a strand of hair. "I can't. It's over." She clutched at another strand.

"Stop. Essy, *stop*," Branwen said, wrapping her hands around her cousin's wrists and pulling them down to her sides.

After a moment, Eseult's rib cage hitched in a ragged breath. "What will King Marc do to our people when he finds out?" Terror frayed her whisper.

Branwen shut her eyes and saw the faces of her parents. She felt the brutality the Land had shown her bubbling beneath the sea: the starless tide threatening to drown her beautiful island once more. The same poison she had drained from Tristan.

Her aunt had once told Branwen that natural healers could heal kingdoms. That the magic of the Land flowed through her. But she had set this chain of events in motion. *She* had ruined the peace.

A numbing resolve began to spread through Branwen's veins as a plan took form. A terrible plan.

"He won't find out," she told her cousin, opening her eyes again. "King Marc will know a maiden on your First Night, Essy."

"How?"

Branwen's gaze dropped to the scar on her palm. Aboard the *Dragon Rising*, she would have sacrificed her life to save the princess. To save the peace. She wouldn't let any other children's parents be taken from them. There was still one way to stop the violence.

Branwen locked eyes with her cousin: the same green as her own mother's, as the hills of Iveriu. "The *kordweyd* want a sacrifice. Blood. I will give them mine."

Wonder turned to disbelief as realization dawned on the princess's face.

"No," said Eseult.

"I have never known a man."

"No. I won't let you do this for me."

"It's not just for you. Our people need this peace. Our people need you to become the True Queen." She grabbed the princess's hand. "Not just the Iverni here. Saoirse and Dubthach at home deserve to start a family without risk of capture." Branwen's words grew more urgent. "Graínne should grow up without fear of being murdered by the same raiders who murdered her parents."

"Of course she should." Eseult's lower lip trembled. "But not this way."

"There is no other way," Branwen said, voice rising, convincing herself. Arthek barked. If the Old Ones saw another way to save Iveriu, they weren't sharing it.

"I don't want this for you, Branny."

"I don't want this, either." The words turned to dust in her mouth as the reality of what she was proposing deluged her. Her chest hitched.

Branwen would lay her naked body down before a man she barely knew. A man who might have ambushed her parents. She would open herself to him as she never had to the man she had loved.

Goose bumps broke out across her flesh; sourness coated her tongue. This was the reality the princess had always faced. Branwen had conjured the Loving Cup because she had thought she understood the depth of the sacrifice. She had thought she could make it easier.

Now she felt Eseult's plight in her bones. Visceral. Her cousin pressed a hand to Branwen's cheek. The tenderness made her shiver.

The peace would be made with her flesh and blood.

When the Goddess Ériu took her chosen king to her bed, she renewed the Land, made it lush and fertile. Those were the Old Ways.

Tristan was able to drink from the Chalice of Sovereignty at the Champions Tournament on King Marc's behalf because they shared the same blood. Branwen and Eseult, too, were of the same line. When Branwen consummated the marriage with King Marc, she had to pray the Old Ones would be satisfied. That she would be enough.

"What I shared with Tristan—"

"Don't you dare talk to me about that," Branwen warned.

"It was beautiful because it was a choice."

Branwen gritted her teeth against a wail. *A lie. It was a lie.*

"I won't take that choice away from you, Branny." Her cousin's voice was raw. "I love you, and I won't let you do this."

Eseult was as stubborn as ever. She meant what she said. She would let the peace collapse rather than ask Branwen to take her place in Marc's bed.

"*One* person—*one* choice isn't worth the lives of so many innocents."

And Branwen was far from innocent. She would make the sacrifice asked of her cousin because her magic had already taken away Eseult's choice. She would redeem herself to the Old Ones. To the Land.

It was all she had left.

Eseult wiped a tear from Branwen's cheek. She hadn't noticed she was crying.

"Branny," she said, tone pacifying, as if trying to reason with a child. "We don't look anything alike. I think King Marc would notice it's not me in his First Night bed."

"Medhua's tears," she murmured.

A small breath escaped Eseult. "I didn't think it was real."

Queen Medhua had been the last woman to possess the Hand of Bríga. She was also known as the Intoxicating One. On the night that Branwen and Queen Eseult cast the Loving Cup, her aunt had doctored a draught known as Queen Medhua's tears to disguise their absence. It made whoever drank it highly suggestible—enough that King Marc might not know which woman came to his bed.

"It's real." Sir Fintan, the queen's bodyguard, had no recollection of helping to dispose of Keane's body or of drinking his Final Toast. It wasn't foolproof, but it was the only chance they had.

Branwen rubbed her scar. Deceiving King Marc in this way would be a far graver betrayal than what Queen Eseult had done to Fintan. Could she do something so completely dishonorable to save her cousin's life—to save her kingdom?

Eseult brushed away another of Branwen's tears. Marc knew the princess no better than he knew Branwen. He was marrying her for peace, but he was also allowing his seers to demand her blood.

"It's too dangerous, Branny," cautioned her cousin. "If you're found out, you'll be charged with treason."

"If I do nothing, it will be you, Essy," Branwen said. "Not you without me." King Marc had made his choice tonight. He was the king. He held his future wife's life in his hands, and he had chosen to give the *kordweyd* what they wanted.

Death was easier than peace, but peace was what her people needed.

Branwen gripped Essy's shoulders. "If my plan succeeds, you must promise me something in return." The princess inclined her head. "You must never again look at Tristan as anything but your husband's nephew."

"I don't know how to stop what I feel." Misery weighted her words. "I wish I did."

"It doesn't matter how you feel, Essy. It only matters what you *do*."

Eseult took Branwen's hand in hers. She sketched the symbol for hazel.

"I loved you first, Branny. Not me without you."

"Peace above all." Branwen added the honeysuckle.

Tears watered the vine.

THE WHITE MOOR

THREE WEEKS HAD PASSED AND the mornings remained dark as Long Night approached. Branwen started up the stairwell toward Andred's room, which was located in the King's Tower on the same level as the king's study.

Branwen had nearly everything she needed to concoct Queen Medhua's tears. Nearly. She couldn't allow herself to think ahead to the wedding night itself. Whenever she did, she became a ship lost at sea, its mast snapped, waves rocking her to and fro.

Branwen focused on the ingredients. The measurements. The things she could control. She regretted turning her apprentice into her accomplice, but there was little choice.

Sucking down the wintry air, Branwen knocked on Andred's door. She tapped her mother's brooch as she waited for him to answer. The silver was cold to the touch.

"Lady Branwen?" The door squeaked open on its hinges. "Were we supposed to meet?" Andred asked, tugging at one of his curls.

"No, no. Don't worry. You're not remiss in your apprentice duties." She showed him a playful smile. "I wanted—" Branwen broke off her words as her eyes caught on something glittering behind him. "What's that?"

The boy turned to follow her gaze. Set atop a table by the window was a rectangular box made from translucent stone. The stone twinkled in the brightening day. It was as if a thousand tiny stars had been caught and trapped within it.

Andred's eyes sparked to a similar brightness. "It's my flowering box," he said. "Come see." Branwen followed him toward the window. She ran a finger along the luminous stone: strangely hot.

"Careful," Andred said, grinning. He leaned his hip against the table, letting it take some of his weight. "The plant needs a very warm climate to thrive. It's Aquilan technology. Xandru brought me the box from the southern continent on his last visit. And the seeds."

At the look of confusion on Branwen's face, the boy explained, "Xandru is a merchant, a good friend of King Marc's."

"Xandru sends the seeds for the castle gardens," Branwen said, thinking back to her discussion with the king on the morning after her arrival.

Another excited head bob. "From all over. Xandru has his own ship. He stayed at Monwiku last winter and hopefully he'll return soon—he promised me another box." Nervously, almost apologetically, Andred added, "I like to experiment with growing plants. This one"— he pointed through the stone to a small green stalk sprouting from a bed of dirt—"is called gods' blood. I read in an Aquilan treatise that its oil can cure a blood infection."

"That's very industrious of you, Andred." Branwen smiled.

"Sometimes Marc helps," the boy told her. "When he's not too busy."

To be chosen as the king's cupbearer, Andred must have Marc's absolute trust. The bond between the two seemed very strong. Branwen pictured Marc working with the boy to make a flower grow. She pushed the image from her mind. She couldn't think of King Marc that way. Until Eseult had been recognized as a True Queen, Branwen must continue to think of him as her enemy. He had taken the side of the *kordweyd* over the princess.

"Is there something I can help you with, Lady Branwen?" Andred asked, distracting Branwen from her thoughts.

"Yes. I need to find a place called the White Moor. Do you know it?"

"Why would you want to go there?"

Branwen curled her hands around the edge of her cloak and delivered the lie that she had prepared.

"The princess has problems sleeping," she began. "Back in Iveriu, I would blend a special tea for her. I'm missing a key ingredient, and I believe the Wise Damsel may know where to find it. She told me I could find her at the White Moor." Branwen turned a serious look on Andred. "I'm only telling you because you're my apprentice. As healers, we must respect our patients' privacy."

"Of course, my lady. Only . . . perhaps I can find you a substitute for what you're missing? You shouldn't go to the White Moor. It's not safe. It belongs to the Old Ones."

"We have such places in Iveriu, Andred. The Old Ones must be respected, but they don't scare me." The Iverni were leery of Death-Tellers, but the Old Ones were neither wholly good nor bad—like humans. "I honor them," Branwen told the boy.

"I didn't mean to offend you, I—"

"I know you didn't," she interrupted him. "Now where can I find the White Moor?"

The boy coughed. "When you head in the direction of Seer Ogrin's village and you see the Stone of Waiting, follow the tip of the stone northwest. About a league. It's nearly always shrouded by fog. I'll go with you."

"I need to go quick—" Branwen stopped herself the moment Andred cringed, but it was too late. Guilt sliced her as his face fell. "I know you can ride fast, Andred." She touched a hand to his shoulder. "But I need to keep this errand discreet. I don't want to embarrass the princess. You understand?" He nodded, but his shoulders slumped forward.

"*Mormerkti*, Andred."

She pecked the boy on the top of his head and exited the King's Tower.

✚ ✚ ✚

Following Andred's directions, Branwen clung to her palfrey's mane as the forest whizzed by her.

After she'd proceeded northward from the Stone of Waiting, an icy fog stole over the moor from the sea to the west. The sun had reached its highest point for the day, but it merely caused the mist to shimmer. The White Moor deserved its name.

Between the sea and the moor lay another thicket of trees. Branwen steered her mount toward the wood. Senara threw her head back, stomped her front hoof in protest. Animals were often more attuned to the presence of the Old Ones than people.

Branwen kept her eyes peeled for smoke swirling from a hearth or any other sign that the wood was inhabited. A few minutes later, she heard chimes tinkling. Dangling beside them in the branches were strips of fabric and ribbons strung with tiny bells. Hundreds of them. The cloth was dark blue like ripe elderberries, pink as a baby's cheeks, bleached as sorrow. As Branwen's gaze wove from strand to strand, Senara came to a halt.

Branwen dug in her heels. The palfrey nickered. She would go no farther.

A gust of wind blew Branwen's cloak up over her face, ringing all the bells. She struggled with the fabric, yanking it back down, and found that she was no longer alone.

"I expected you sooner."

Branwen released a small gasp. Recovering, she said, "Greetings, Wise Damsel."

The older woman wore her hair long, the dark garnet and silver strands whorling around her. Her tunic and cape were sewn from a thick wool, dyed a similar shade of green to Rigani stone. She was taller than Branwen remembered and she radiated supreme self-possession. Branwen speculated the Wise Damsel to have seen at least fifty summers.

"Call me Ailleann." Wrinkles formed around her eyes as she narrowed them. "You're a Wise Damsel, too," she said, and Branwen felt a frisson of foreboding. The woman stepped closer. "Are you going to dismount?"

Branwen slung her leg over Senara and dropped to the ground. She patted the mare's shoulder and tied the reins to a low branch. "I won't be long," she murmured, and the horse neighed. Pivoting to face Ailleann, she said, "I came to ask for help."

"Yes," the Wise Damsel said. "Come, daughter."

Enigena. Hearing the Ivernic word for daughter gave Branwen pause. Would her mother approve of the woman Branwen was becoming? Of the deceit and subterfuge? The extremes that peace required of her?

The Wise Damsel retreated farther into the thicket of trees and Branwen followed.

Beneath her feet, the soft dirt became a path of slick, moss-covered stones. The path crossed a small stream, and water seeped into Branwen's boots.

Shrouded in the mist, appearing as if from nowhere, emerged a circular hut made from snakestone. Before the hut, stood a well, red stones gleaming dully.

The tiny hairs lifted on Branwen's arms. "Where are we?" she called to Ailleann.

Her aunt had once described the Otherworld as love. She couldn't see it, yet it always surrounded her. In some places, however, the Veil between the worlds grew thinner, and Branwen had the creeping sensation this was just such a place.

Pausing beside the well, the Wise Damsel shrugged. "People have come here for healing since before the Aquilans came to Albion. Since before the longstones were carved. They hang offerings in the trees to the spirits of the waters."

Branwen approached the well and noticed that there were beeswax candles in various stages of melting around its base. "Whom do you worship?" she asked.

"I think, gods or Old Ones, they care little for the names mortals give them," Ailleann said, her tone brisk. "I tend the well now, and I heal those I can."

She scanned her with her eyes, and Branwen would have sworn the other woman could see right down to the bone.

"Including you, Branwen of Iveriu."

Alarm streaked through her.

"I never told you my name."

The Wise Damsel croaked a laugh. "Seer Ogrin is a friend of mine. He told me you've been helping at the temple."

Oh. "I didn't come here to be healed," Branwen said, irritation and relief eddying inside her. "I need *derew* root."

"There are plenty of pain-relieving herbs in the Morrois Forest."

"It has to be *derew* root."

"I see." She crossed her arms. "I have what you seek. I'll give it to you if you agree to train with me."

"I told you I don't *want* my power." On Whitethorn Mound, Branwen thought she'd been wrong to reject the Old Ways, the healing magic she shared with the other women in her family. But Branwen's magic had wronged both Tristan and Eseult, wronged her kingdom.

"Stop lying, daughter. You feel the power humming inside you— the thirst to unleash it. Your instincts are at war."

"I don't have time to barter," Branwen spat. "And I'm not your daughter!"

The moor grew very still.

The Wise Damsel moved so fast Branwen didn't have time to breathe before the older woman grabbed her hand and pain shot straight to her heart. Chest spasming, she fell to her knees. She screamed as she stared down at the Hand of Bríga.

The scar on her hand had been transformed into a bilious black. Beneath the surface, it appeared to writhe like the Sea of the Dead.

"What did you *do*?" Branwen shouted.

Steam rose from the center of her scorching palm.

"I did nothing but reveal the truth you feel." The Wise Damsel pointed at the midnight line. "From the same source comes creation and destruction—from the in-between. Primordial magic won't be ignored."

Tears of agony ran down Branwen's cheeks.

"Rejecting your gifts won't make them go away," the Wise Damsel said.

They're not gifts, thought Branwen. *I'm cursed, and I curse those who love me.*

"Magic like yours attracts dangerous forces, *enigena*. Either you control your power, or it controls you."

Branwen tried to breathe through clenched teeth, her chest heaving. She couldn't deny the constant pressure of magic under her skin, the desire to break free, to run away and char the ground beneath her. When she'd fought the Shades, she'd been terrified, but she had also felt alive. Exquisitely alive.

She could reduce the Dreaming Sea to salt with her fire. Her wrath.

"Make it stop!" Branwen pleaded. She hated herself for whimpering. "I accept your terms!"

Once again, Branwen didn't see the Wise Damsel move, and then the pain was gone. The other woman kneeled before her, pressing her palm to Branwen's. When she removed it, the scar had returned to its threadlike appearance. Pale as the echo of nightmare.

Fresh tears leaked from Branwen's eyes at the absence of pain.

"Come inside," Ailleann said. "The wind's growing bitter."

Branwen remained on her knees, steadying her harsh breaths, as the other woman rose and walked toward the hut.

It was too late to back down now. Branwen pushed to her feet. She needed the *derew* root.

When she entered the cottage, Ailleann was pouring boiling water from a kettle into two ceramic mugs. She motioned for her guest to be seated.

The interior of the stone hut was more sumptuously appointed than Branwen would have expected for a dwelling in the middle of a wood. But, then, she was not altogether certain that she hadn't passed into the Otherworld.

Branwen sat opposite the Wise Damsel at a table carved from oak.

Her host took a sip of her tea. Branwen watched the crushed, dried petals floating on the surface of the water.

"Primordial magic is not given lightly," Ailleann began. "To obtain this kind of power, you must have killed and saved."

Branwen swallowed. The tea burned her throat. Queen Eseult had warned Branwen that the Loving Cup was primordial magic and its cost would be unpredictable. She had been naive to think the Hand of Bríga stemmed from a less potent source.

"Tell me your story, Branwen," said the Wise Damsel. "Tell me your heart."

A broken laugh escaped her. Branwen had accused Tristan of not knowing her heart, but she didn't know it, either.

Ailleann waited for Branwen to speak.

"My aunt always said I was a natural healer, like my mother," she started, tentative. "My mother died when I was young. I never believed in the Old Ones until—"

"Until?"

"There was a man. He was poisoned." Branwen flinched at the memory of Tristan's motionless form on the tournament pitch. "He would have died without Otherworld magic. I offered the Old Ones my blood in exchange for their help."

The Wise Damsel listened impassively. After a moment, she said, "So, that is the life you saved. Which is the life you took?"

Branwen turned the red-glazed mug in a circle against the grain of the wood. Revulsion washed over her as she remembered the stink of spirits on Keane's breath, the dampness of the stones on her back as he cornered her in the stairwell.

"I was defending myself," she said, her tongue sluggish, tasting the chalky memory of her fear. "I begged the Old Ones for help." She held up her palm. "The flames erupted before I realized what I was doing."

"It wasn't only yourself you were defending, was it? It was someone you loved."

Panic gripped her. No one knew that Branwen had killed Keane because he discovered Eseult's affair with Diarmuid. Not even Queen Eseult. Tristan knew Branwen had condemned Keane to be a Shade, but he didn't know why.

"The—Land," she stammered. "My aunt said the Hand of Bríga was awakened when I felt the Land under threat."

The Wise Damsel stared at her a long moment. "Your love is as deep as the well outside."

Branwen's eyes dropped back to her palm. She could almost feel Eseult's finger drawing their secret symbol. Before Branwen understood duty to her kingdom, she felt devotion to her younger cousin.

Had Queen Eseult suspected all along it was Branwen's love for the princess, not the Land, that had truly brought forth the darker side of her power? That it was the air that fueled her fire?

"And the man?" asked the Wise Damsel. "Why did you offer your blood for him?"

Tristan's death on Ivernic soil would have spelled disaster, but it wasn't the only reason. And, despite everything, she could never regret saving him.

"For the Land," Branwen repeated, as obstinate as the princess.

The Wise Damsel inhaled. "You've killed for love, and you were willing to die for love. The power you've been granted, daughter, comes from the time before magic was bound by rules. Before this world and the Otherworld were split. It can create or destroy—just like you."

Branwen rested her hand on the table, palm up. "My aunt is the most renowned healer in Iveriu, but she couldn't teach me how to wield it. She only knew legends about the Hand of Bríga. No one has carried it since ancient times." She curled her fingers toward the scar. "How did you learn?"

"There is always a guardian at the well." Branwen heard a door close in the Wise Damsel's voice. She stroked Branwen's scar.

"Your heart is divided," Ailleann said. "As long as you remain at war with yourself, you will not wield the magic. The magic will wield you."

The Wise Damsel pushed to her feet and retrieved an Aquilan oil lamp from above the hearth. Its wick was unlit. She placed it before Branwen on the table.

"Like this lamp, you only have so much magic, so much fuel. Your fire burns bright, Branwen, but there are forces that would use you like fuel until your fire burns out."

She plucked one of Branwen's white hairs between her fingers, held it up to the light.

"The miner you healed with your power. Why did you save him?"

"Because I could." Ailleann snorted. "Because he came from my family's lands in Iveriu," Branwen admitted. "We should have protected him."

"So you are responsible for all of the Iverni captured in raids? You have magic, but you're not a god. Branwen, your power and your life are joined now. Once it's gone, it's gone—and so are you."

She ran a tongue over her lips. "My aunt told me there would be a cost to using the Hand of Bríga . . ." Branwen hadn't realized exactly what that meant, but she had asked much of the Old Ones. No power was infinite.

"The Aquilans have a goddess named Menrva. Like Bríga, she is the goddess of fire. But she is also the goddess of wisdom. You must use your fire wisely."

"If I use it in the service of Iveriu, then I've spent it wisely."

The Wise Damsel exhaled through her nose.

"There is room in your heart for an entire kingdom, Branwen—but not for yourself." She returned to her seat and put her mug to her lips. "I want you to light the wick of the lamp," said Ailleann.

Branwen stared down at her hand. The only times she'd summoned her magic, she'd been angry or afraid. The Wise Damsel sipped her tea. Waiting. Branwen chewed her lip.

Ailleann began to drum her fingers on the table, impatient, and Branwen's heart beat faster and faster. Finally, "I don't know how," she said, frustration chiseling at her words. "I'm afraid I'll make it explode."

With a grunt, the Wise Damsel set down her tea and extended her own right hand. "Your magic was born from love. Love that is boundless, but wild. You only know how to find your power in a place of frenzy." She held Branwen's gaze, and fear quickened Branwen's pulse that the Wise Damsel could pluck the very thoughts from her head.

A tiny blue flame appeared in the palm of the other woman's hand. She touched it gently to the wick. As she transferred the fire, a warm glow was cast on the terracotta lamp. "When I summon my magic, I think of the heat on my face from a bonfire. You only need the impression of the fire, not the fire itself. You must learn to find strength—and magic—in stillness."

The Wise Damsel closed her hand, and the flame vanished. "I'll get you the *derew* root."

"But I couldn't do what you asked."

"Nothing is mastered in a day."

GAMES OF CHANCE

BRANWEN FILLED THE BOWL OF oats in Senara's stall high as she whispered words of thanks in her ears. Her palfrey had remained on edge until they'd put the White Moor behind them, and she couldn't help but share the horse's relief.

"I've been looking for you," said a worried voice.

Branwen glanced over her shoulder at Tristan. For a half a breath, she glimpsed the old warrior she'd seen in the in-between. The life they might have shared.

"Is the princess well?" she asked and surprise registered on Tristan's face. Branwen was so drained from her meeting with the Wise Damsel that she'd slipped into Ivernic. *Dymatis, nosmatis* had been the extent of the conversation between them since the Mantle of Maidenhood had been decreed.

"Yes. The princess is fine." Tristan scratched the scar above his eyebrow. "I've been looking for you. No one knew where you were."

He entered the stall and tousled Senara's forelock. "You shouldn't be outside the castle alone after dark, *Bra*—my lady."

"I can take care of myself." Branwen raised her right palm. Tristan stepped in closer. The mare neighed.

"You always have," he said, taking her hand lightly. Branwen's body tensed; then she sighed.

"What did you want, Tristan? Why were you looking for me?"

He released her hand. "It's my grandmother. She fainted at lunch with Marc. She says it's nothing, doesn't want us to send for the *kordweyd*, but—" Tristan swallowed. "Would you check on her for me?"

"I'll come now."

"Thank you," he said.

The words rang with more than gratitude. Branwen ignored the quiver in her chest as she followed him from the stables.

Tristan went first up the twisty stairwell of the West Tower. Branwen's eyes strayed to the waning moon through the small slits in the stone. Long Night would also be a new moon this year.

A moonless sky on the shortest day of the year was a rare occurrence. Children born in Iveriu on that day were said to be more easily stolen into the Otherworld because their souls had never entirely left it.

Branwen herself felt torn between this world and the Otherworld. Much as the White Moor had put each of her nerves on alert, she'd also felt a sense of recognition there. Welcome. As if it wasn't solely the Wise Damsel who'd been expecting her.

"*Damawinn?*" Tristan called, opening the door to the apartment where Queen Verica had been installed. Only Tristan was so familiar with the queen as to call her *damawinn*—grandmother. Even King Marc, Branwen had noticed, addressed his mother using her title.

Branwen heard an odd *plink-plink* noise coming from inside. Almost like rain, yet more solid. *Plink-plink.*

Finally, a female voice answered, followed by a prolonged cough. Tristan frowned, but he motioned at Branwen to enter.

Queen Verica was seated beside the hearth at the opposite end of the drawing room. Buttercup-yellow draperies framed the windows, giving the room a cheerful appearance.

Plink-plink.

Squinting, Branwen detected the source of the sound: dice. The Queen Mother was throwing dice cut from alabaster onto the small table in front of her. Despite the light of the glowing embers, Tristan's grandmother looked sallow, more haggard than when she'd first arrived at Monwiku. The dice landed beside a glass of Mílesian spirits.

"*Damawinn.*" The distress in his voice affected Branwen more than she wanted it to. "I thought you were going to rest." Tristan looked back at Branwen, speaking in Aquilan for her benefit. "I've found Lady Branwen. She's kindly agreed to see if she can help."

"My grandson fusses too much," the Queen Mother said to Branwen. She took a harried breath. "My body is resting. I said nothing about my mind." Then, patting Tristan's arm affectionately, she told him, "I'm the old woman, not you, *karid.*"

"*Nosmatis*, Queen Verica," said Branwen with a curtsy. "I would be happy to assist you in any way I can."

The Queen Mother smiled, looking between her and Tristan. Then another cough racked her frame. It sounded watery. She covered her mouth with a lace-trimmed handkerchief. As the queen withdrew it again, Branwen noticed it was smeared with black spittle. Their eyes met briefly before the queen hid it in her lap, beneath the table.

"Prince Tristan," Branwen said. "Would you mind retrieving my healing satchel from the Queen's Tower? There's an herbal tea I believe will help with your cough, Queen Mother."

"I prefer Mílesian spirits but I'll drink your tea if you insist," replied Queen Verica.

"I insist, *damawinn*," Tristan told her. He kissed his grandmother's cheek. "Thank you, Br—Lady Branwen. I'll return directly."

She nodded, top teeth digging into her lower lip. She sensed the Queen Mother watching their interactions closely. Unlike with Countess Kensa, Branwen didn't detect hostility. It was more of a fierce protectiveness.

Plink-plink. Queen Verica threw another round of dice as Tristan left.

"Do you play?" she asked Branwen.

"No, Queen Mother."

"Please, Lady Branwen, take off your cloak. Sit with me."

Unfastening her mother's brooch, Branwen draped her cloak on the back of the chair opposite the queen's and did as she was told. Queen Verica collected the dice. The alabaster reminded Branwen of sea foam.

The old queen held up one of the dice, admiring it, worrying it between her fingers.

"These dice have six sides," she said. "They're etched with the Aquilan numerals for one through six. When I throw one, I have a one in six chance of landing on the six. Throw two and the odds become much more complicated. How much would you wager that they'll sum to six?"

"I don't know, Queen Mother."

"Being queen is like gambling. You have to play and you can't control the outcome."

Branwen thought of her aunt. "I've always thought ruling was more like a game of strategy."

"Ruling is only a game of strategy if you're extremely lucky." Queen Verica's gray eyes sparkled. "The same goes for life. It's a game of chance."

She raised her blackened handkerchief from beneath the table.

"We both know I've lost, Lady Branwen."

"Prince Tristan doesn't know," she inferred. Branwen adopted the carefully neutral demeanor her aunt always used when discussing a dire prognosis with patients.

"Neither does my son," Queen Verica confided. "I don't want to distract from the wedding. Kernyv must appear strong to the guests who come from abroad to celebrate this union with us." The queen leaned forward in her seat. "Can I trust you with my secret?"

The weight Branwen had felt on her chest since her visit to the White Moor grew heavier. She should be used to keeping secrets from Tristan by now.

"Yes, Queen Mother," she said with a nod. "I will keep your secret. I am a healer first, and your condition is not mine to share."

"Thank you, Lady Branwen. My grandson thinks very highly of you."

Branwen pulled the handkerchief gently from the queen's grasp, examining it. "When did the wasting sickness begin?" she asked.

"In the summer." Queen Verica tossed one of the dice. "The kord-weyd in Liones removed a tumor from my abdomen. I seemed to be doing better—then the black cough began. I'd hoped to be here to celebrate the Seal of Alliance, but the weather turned, and I grew too weak to travel."

She coughed. "I told the Horned One he couldn't call me for judgment until after the wedding."

"I can help ease your suffering, Queen Mother. If you'll let me."

Once a wasting sickness had spread, there was little to do besides make a patient comfortable. This wasn't an injury like Talorc had sustained at the mine or a poisoned spear; this was an illness that came from within the body. Magic couldn't mend everything. And after her conversation with the Wise Damsel today, Branwen was afraid of how the magic might try to wield her if she tried.

Queen Verica tilted her head. "I would be grateful for your help, Lady Branwen." The embers crackled in the hearth as a log shifted and fell. "When Tristan was lost off the coast of Iveriu," she began, "everyone told me he was dead. But I knew better. He is my *karid*—my beloved." The queen gave Branwen a look that made her hold her breath.

"I love my son, but I knew I had to raise a king. With Tristan, it's different." The queen's expression turned wistful. "When Tristan did not return to our shores, I implored Marc to send the ships to Iveriu looking for him. I knew in my heart that he was alive."

A knot formed in Branwen's stomach. She was sitting opposite the woman responsible for sending the raiders who killed Graínne's parents, for the villages that were massacred along the Rock Road. But the Queen Mother had done it for someone she loved.

Branwen could no longer pretend that she wouldn't do the same. Or worse.

"The Horned One answered my prayers," Queen Verica continued. "And when, at last, Tristan came home, he told me that I had a young Ivernic healer to thank for his safe return. A fair maiden, like something out of legend. And that he'd promised her he'd bring peace between our peoples."

Branwen squirmed beneath her gaze. The queen pinched one of the dice between her fingers.

"Tristan, like me, is a gambler. The chance for peace was a risk worth taking, he said." The other woman sipped her spirits.

"No one else knows you helped Tristan before he entered the Champions Tournament, do they?"

Branwen met her eye. "Do you think me a traitor?"

"I think you helped a man in need, regardless of the fact that he was your enemy. If that makes you a traitor, then let us all be traitors." The Queen Mother cough-laughed.

She raised her glass to Branwen. "To traitors!"

Branwen pinched her thigh to stop from crying. She was a traitor many, many times over.

"We will keep each other's secrets, won't we?" said the Queen Mother as footsteps echoed from down the corridor. "For that is what we women do."

A YEAR WITHOUT DEATH

THE FOREST THRUMMED WITH ANTICIPATION. Branwen was on foot, as were the other wedding guests. Fanned out through the trees, courtiers from all over Albion walked softly in search of a small, russet-colored bird.

Over the past five days, foreign dignitaries and Kernyvak nobles had been arriving at Monwiku Castle. The island was filled to bursting, and the dread coiled inside Branwen threatened to rip from her skin.

It was a Kernyvak custom, she'd been told, to hunt the *rixula*—the little queen—on the day before Long Night. The Kernyveu believed whoever was first to kill the bird would have protection against death for the coming year.

Tomorrow, the Princess of Iveriu would marry the King of Kernyv, joining their kingdoms forever and warding the Iverni from death for many years to come.

Branwen froze as her foot snapped a twig. A pair of wings flapped rapidly overhead, and a speck of reddish-brown darted skyward.

"Bad luck," said Ruan, sidling up next to her. "The *ríxula* are cunning. They know how not to be caught."

Branwen spread her hands. "I have no bow or arrow."

He flicked his bowstring. "It'll be hard to shoot without those." Grinning, Ruan leaned closer, and Branwen could feel his body heat. She resisted the urge to lean into him.

"I've scarcely seen you these past weeks. How do you fare?" Ruan asked, concern in his gaze. "Branwen." He truly wanted to know.

And she could never tell him. She had started to like the arrogant prince, and she wouldn't blame him for despising her if her treason were uncovered.

"Once the wedding is over, I think I'll sleep for a month." Branwen laughed uneasily.

Ruan waited a beat before accepting her deflection. "I've never seen Endelyn work so hard," he agreed. Glancing around them, he said, "Princess Eseult didn't fancy joining the hunt?" A slight edge had crept into his voice.

"My cousin hates to see an animal in pain," Branwen replied. "When we were girls, she freed a rabbit from a trap. It bled out in her arms. Ever since then, she's hated blood—and hunting. She's with Queen Verica, playing dice."

Ruan snorted. "Then she'll lose. The Queen Mother cheats."

"It's a game of chance."

"Not if the dice are weighted," he said, and Branwen gave a laugh.

A rustling of wings caught Ruan's attention. He targeted his bow, which was made of heartwood, to the north. New footsteps joined them, and the *ríxula* flew off.

He cursed under his breath.

"Hail, Prince Ruan," said a man, about Branwen's age, whom she hadn't met yet. He spoke in Aquilan, as all the wedding guests would.

A look of chagrin passed over Ruan. "Hail, Prince Kahedrin." Lifting his bow, he said, "Be careful that no one mistakes you for our prey," and leveled the arrow at the other man's vibrant red hair.

"I think there's little danger of that." He slung his own bow over his shoulder. To Branwen, the redhead said, "I am Prince Kahedrin of Armorica." He was only just taller than her, with a stocky build.

He bowed his head at Branwen with respect. "Lady Branwen," she said in response. "From Iveriu." She curtsied.

The Armorican prince had a strong jaw, yet his smile was warm. "Delighted to meet you, my lady." His eyes were steady on hers—a hazy blue like a late summer's evening.

Ruan glanced between them, the corner of his mouth betraying the slightest frown.

"Ruan!" called King Marc from farther back in the wood.

He clinched the curve of his bow with his fingers. "I'll win the *ríxula* for you, Lady Branwen," Ruan said. Arching a brow, he added, "Maybe then you'll save me a dance tomorrow night? I'm keen to learn your unenlightened, Ivernic ways." He winked and dashed off.

Prince Kahedrin stared after him. "Ruan has always been charming," he said.

"You know him well?" Branwen prompted.

"I don't know if anyone knows him well, my lady." Kahedrin turned a serious look on her. "But I've known him since we were boys. The Whel family stronghold at Illogan is only a few days' sail across the southern channel from Armorica. We used to trade with them for white lead."

"No longer?"

Kahedrin began to walk, and Branwen fell into step beside him. "White lead has been found in the kingdom of Míl. The supply is plentiful and the price is cheaper."

Branwen absorbed the information. This new competition would explain the pressure on the miners to work faster. Without minerals to export, Branwen didn't know how Kernyv would sustain itself.

Could Marc have needed Eseult's dowry in addition to wanting peace? She had always assumed the kingdom was far wealthier than Iveriu.

"You look troubled, Lady Branwen," Kahedrin remarked.

"No, that's just how I look when I'm thinking." She laughed. "When did you arrive at Monwiku?"

"The day before yesterday. My father sent me as emissary. The pirate raids usually become less frequent in the winter. Not so this year." He blew out a breath. "We're refortifying all of the old Aquilan city walls."

"I'm sorry to hear that," she said.

"If my older brother had won the Champions Tournament last summer, we might be celebrating a union between Armorica and Iveriu tomorrow."

Branwen folded her hands together. "Crown Prince Havelin fought bravely." She maintained a neutral tone, remembering how Eseult had complained about Havelin's crooked nose.

Kahedrin grunted. "Havelin didn't even advance to the single combat. I would have done better," he boasted, catching Branwen's eye.

"Spoken like a younger brother."

The prince laughed. "I suppose."

"And you have a younger sister? Also called Eseult, I believe."

He nodded. "But don't call her that. She prefers her middle name—Alba."

"Like the giantess?"

"She has the attitude of one." Kahedrin laughed more broadly. "You'll know what I mean, if you ever meet her."

"She didn't want to come to the wedding?"

His face clouded. "She prefers sailing to entertaining, and we could only risk one member of the royal family setting foot in Kernyv with things . . . the way they are. Sending Havelin was out of the question— so here I am." The words speared Branwen with panic. She dug her fingernails into her palm. "It's a shame Iveriu and Armorica couldn't unite to fight the Kernyvak pirates together."

A frightened birdcall pealed from the trees.

"The Land chose her Champion," Branwen told Kahedrin. "My father taught me to turn enemies into friends, and a new era of peace for Iveriu is about to dawn."

"For Iveriu, maybe. Not Armorica."

"It's not for us to question the Old Ones."

Liar. Branwen heard that acid-washed voice in her head again. It was her questioning of the Old Ones that had left the peace balanced on a knife's edge.

Kahedrin stopped mid-stride and angled his body toward her. "Kernyv's enemies become Iveriu's tomorrow. I very much hope they won't number more than their friends," he said.

An arrow whizzed overhead and lodged in the tree trunk a few hands' widths away.

"Beg your pardon!" Ruan called out. "I thought I saw a *ríxula.*"

Kahedrin grimaced. Branwen pivoted toward Ruan and saw King Marc a pace behind.

Dead leaves crunched beneath the king's boots as he came to a halt.

Branwen glanced at him sideways, her gaze drifting to his hands. There was dirt from the forest beneath his fingernails, but they were precisely filed. Almost too short, as if they'd first been bitten.

"Your Majesty," said Kahedrin. "Congratulations on your upcoming nuptials." He bowed from the waist.

"Thank you, Prince Kahedrin."

Stealing another look at King Marc's nails, Branwen wondered if he was at all apprehensive about the wedding night? She dug her own into the flesh of her palms and dropped her gaze.

Marc adjusted the bow slung over his shoulder. "I trust King Faramon is in good health," he said to the Armorican prince.

"My father's health is as good as can be expected." Kahedrin widened his stance, as if preparing for a fight. "Given the relentless assaults on our northern coast."

Ruan moved closer to Kahedrin and Marc pulled him back.

"I have no quarrel with Armorica," said the king.

Kahedrin's nostrils flared. "And yet you allow pirates to plague our shores."

"You forget yourself," Ruan barked, grazing the hilt of his sword with his bow hand. "You're speaking to my king."

"I know exactly to whom I'm speaking, Prince Ruan."

"Prince Kahedrin," said Marc, deepening his voice. "The pirates do not sail under my banner. I don't condone their actions." The Armorican prince only sneered.

Branwen tapped her mother's brooch, pulse accelerating. "Prince

Kahedrin," she interjected. His eyes caught on hers as if he'd forgotten Branwen was there.

Holding her nerve, she said, "My prince, the king's own nephew, Prince Tristan, was on a vessel attacked by pirates and thrown overboard. Surely you don't believe that King Marc would authorize such an action?"

The king's gaze shifted to Branwen, and the corner of his mouth ticked upward. She didn't want his gratitude. The king had taken part in raids; he was no more innocent than she. Branwen only defended him to defend Iveriu.

The damp air grew heavy.

Prince Kahedrin puffed out his chest. "My people are slaughtered by pirates who reside in your kingdom, King Marc, and my father's patience is at its limit. The raids have only grown worse since you succeeded King Merchion." He looked between the king and his Champion. "Either you are not willing—or not able—to curb the pirates' attacks."

Ruan hissed a breath. He couldn't assault an invited wedding guest without breaching all rules of hospitality and risking a war, but Branwen saw how much he wanted to do just that.

"If you refuse to leash your pirates, King Marc, Armorica will have to take matters into its own hands."

"And if you sail the Armorican fleet into Kernyvak waters, Prince Kahedrin, I will view it as a declaration of war."

Branwen heard the cold steel in the king's voice.

"Don't force my father's hand," Kahedrin shot back.

A high-pitched trill rang out from above. In the blink of an eye, it had stopped. Ruan had nocked his arrow against the bowstring and let it soar.

The *ríxula* fell from its branch and landed at Branwen's feet.

"I always catch my quarry," Ruan said to the Armorican prince, stone-faced. He crouched down and collected the little creature, pulling the arrow from its breast. "Striking first is far more effective than making threats."

"I'll remember that," said Kahedrin.

Ruan held out the bird to Branwen. "I offer you a year without death, my lady," he said. Blood from the *ríxula*'s wound trickled between his fingers.

Branwen looked from Marc to Kahedrin, and she knew it was a lie.

✛ ✛ ✛

King Marc dined in his study that evening with only Tristan and the Queen Mother for company. Branwen could guess at their topic of conversation.

The mood in the Great Hall was generally subdued, the wedding guests tired from the day's hunt. Prince Kahedrin seated himself beside the King of Ordowik, who was also no great friend of Kernyv. Branwen recalled how fearsomely he had clashed with Tristan at the Champions Tournament, with true rancor.

Kahedrin was unmistakably sending a message in his choice of feasting companion. He and Ruan watched each other with razor-sharp glances. If Armorica and Ordowik allied against Kernyv, they could squeeze the kingdom from both above and below.

When Eseult feigned a headache to leave the feasting hall, Branwen was only too happy to accompany her. Her own temples throbbed.

The princess's marriage would end one war for Iveriu; but what if it was the beginning of a new one? Branwen hadn't considered the possibility of an alliance between Kernyv's other enemies before.

Arthek jumped into Eseult's arms the moment she pushed the door to the suite ajar. The lifeless *ríxula* was laid on the vanity where Branwen had left it, out of the puppy's reach. Her cousin screwed up her nose at the sight of the bird.

"What in the Otherworld is that?" she said.

"It's the bird we were hunting. The Kernyveu call it *ríxula*. A little queen."

The princess shivered, and Arthek licked her cheek. "It's horrid. Why do you have it?"

"Ruan caught the *ríxula*. He offered it to me—it's meant to ward against death."

"Oh." Eseult's face softened. "He . . . He seems eager for your company." She set the puppy down on the bed. "Are you eager for his?" Her cousin's question was a mixture of doubt and hope.

"No," Branwen said dismissively, although that wasn't entirely true. At least Ruan could make her laugh. But she couldn't think about the company of other men while the wedding night loomed before her.

Branwen shuddered. Better to divorce her mind from her body.

"No," she repeated.

The princess was quiet, chewing her lips, and then she nodded. "I understand."

She crossed toward Branwen, and Branwen saw her cousin reflected in the looking glass on the vanity. For a moment, she glimpsed two Eseults, one on either side of her.

She shook her head, trying to clear the double vision. It was the same as the premonition she'd been given on the night she stole the traitor's finger for the Loving Cup. The portent she had failed to recognize.

"Branny," said Eseult, barely above a whisper. "Branny, tonight's my last night as an unmarried woman. And tomorrow night, you'll—" She choked on her breath. "Let me take care of you tonight. Can we just forget—pretend that what's happened hasn't happened? Just for tonight?"

The princess ran a hand over Branwen's knotty, windblown curls. "Let me brush your hair," she offered.

"You never brush my hair, Essy."

"Let me start now."

Her cousin plucked the brush from the vanity and began to detangle Branwen's dark locks. She didn't resist.

"I hated Tristan for making you so ill after the tournament," Eseult said quietly. "I hated that you suffered—but I liked taking care of you. I liked you needing me."

Eseult still believed the lie that her mother had told her. The Queen of Iveriu had spread the tale that it was an accident Branwen had been poisoned while she was treating Tristan's wounds; not that her niece had summoned Otherworld magic to leech it from his veins. Her aunt had wanted to protect Branwen, and Branwen hadn't wanted to burden her cousin with her newfound powers. Now it seemed too late to tell her.

The princess sighed, stroking the brush through Branwen's curls. "I wish you'd—I want to take care of you more, Branny. If you'll let me."

Branwen didn't know if they'd ever find their old ease together. But tonight she needed comfort.

"I'll try," she said. Tonight, Branwen would let herself be loved.

Once her hair was as smooth as it ever was, Branwen and Eseult dressed for bed. Branwen crawled into the grand canopy bed without being asked.

So many nights of their childhood, the cousins had held hands as they fell asleep. Branwen intertwined their fingers one last time. She felt her baby cousin's breath on her face as she began to snore.

She kissed the princess on the forehead and closed her eyes. This was childhood's end.

DRESSED IN FIRE

TRISTAN'S RICH BARITONE ECHOED OFF the fire-washed walls of the Great Hall.

Goddess Bríga was the patroness of poetry as well as marriage, and a bard always performed a ballad at Ivernic weddings.

Princess Eseult processed slowly, with grace, toward her waiting husband as Tristan's fingers teased the strings of the *krotto*. The cousins had embraced for a long, silent moment before the doors to the hall were flung open. They were both afraid, but they weren't alone in their fear.

Branwen walked behind the princess, carrying the train of her gown. She willed her hands to remain still. She forbid her thoughts from racing ahead to what came after the ceremony.

Seer Casek stood in the center of the dais where the king's table usually lay, King Marc to his left and Tristan to his right. His expression was solemn yet victorious.

The guests watched in silence, lining either side of the hall. Their faces were earnest as they listened to the music.

Odai eti ama

Tristan had selected a song in the Aquilan language so that all those assembled would understand. But Branwen knew he was singing for her—for Emer.

I hate and I love

In another life, he might have serenaded her at their own wedding. Each of Branwen's choices had led them to this moment.

Dark as dawn, light as midnight

Because she loved too wildly.

Fire that numbs, rain that burns

Brides in Iveriu dressed themselves in the color of fire, seeking Bríga's favor for a long and happy marriage. They hoped their love would be as eternal as a flame, as warm as winter evenings by the hearth. Fidelity in its purest form.

This love that I hate

Eseult reached the end of the hall. Torchlight flickered on King Marc's face as he flashed his wife-to-be a nervous smile.

And hate that I love

Tristan captured Branwen's gaze as he held the last note of the song. It reverberated in her very core. Taking her place beside him, she pivoted to face the audience. She and Tristan would bear witness to the marriage. Every detail of the ceremony had been painstakingly negotiated with Seer Casek.

Branwen would represent the Iverni, and Tristan would represent the Kernyveu. With a full and open heart, their peoples would give their consent to the union of Princess Eseult and King Marc.

With no knowledge of why the marriage should not take place.

The song ended, Tristan passed the *krotto* to Andred for safekeeping. The feasting hall had been cleared of tables for the ceremony, standing room only.

King Marc stepped forward and joined Princess Eseult, turning his back toward the wedding guests. He was dressed in a tunic and breeches of thick, white velvet. Marc's crown was simple, made from solid gold. It was the first time Branwen had seen him wear it.

Seer Casek raised his hands toward the ceiling. He wore opulent robes. Staring out at the wedding guests, he began, "We give praise to the Horned One for bringing us together this Long Night." He made a small noise in his throat. "And to the Old Ones revered by the Iverni." The *kordweyd* couldn't entirely mask his distaste at mentioning the Old Ones. At least, not to Branwen's ears.

"Under the eyes of all the gods," he continued, "we are assembled to join together King Marc of Kernyv and Princess Eseult of Iveriu as husband and wife until the end of their days. As well as to crown a new True Queen of Kernyv."

Eseult glanced at Branwen sideways, seeking reassurance. *Not you without me*, Branwen mouthed. It was the first, the oldest—the deepest vow Branwen had ever made.

The princess nodded, and a diadem of Rigani stones winked atop her blond plaits.

"Princess Eseult," said Seer Casek, focusing his gaze on her. "Do you consent to love and honor King Marc without impediment or guile, and to bleed for him if the Horned One wills it?"

Tristan shifted his weight, his elbow grazing Branwen's for the briefest moment. She couldn't look at him.

"I do," answered the princess. Branwen felt a tremor of relief even as she saw a tear glide down her cousin's cheek.

"King Marc," intoned Seer Casek. "Do you consent to love and honor Princess Eseult without impediment or guile, and to bleed for her if the Horned One wills it?"

For a moment, Marc's eyes grew unfocused. Then, "I do," he said with conviction.

The *kordweyd* reached behind him to where a small altar had been positioned on the dais. He selected a silver knife with a jeweled hilt, and a matching goblet.

"The marriage will be sanctified with blood, because blood flows from the heart," Seer Casek pronounced. He handed the blade to Tristan. "First, the blood of the witnesses," he said. As Tristan accepted the knife, a ribbon of light cut his face.

"Prince Tristan of Kernyv, on behalf of the people of Kernyv, do you give your blood willingly in support of this union?" asked Casek.

Tristan lifted the blade and traced its point across his left palm. "I do," he said.

He squeezed a trickle of blood into the chalice. Branwen saw Eseult begin to pale.

"Lady Branwen of Iveriu," Casek said. "On behalf of the people of Iveriu, do you give your blood willingly in support of this union?"

"I do," Branwen declared. She held out her right palm. Tristan looked between Eseult and Branwen before his dark eyes locked with hers. She could no longer stop her hands from trembling.

Quick and gentle, Tristan reopened her scar. The blade was so sharp it didn't hurt.

Her blood mixed with his in the chalice, and Branwen was transported back to Kerwindos's Cauldron. She would give anything to return to that moment—to never have conjured the Loving Cup. But no one had that power. Not even the Old Ones.

Marc took the knife from Tristan. "I offer you my blood and my life," he said to Eseult as he cut himself. His blood swirled into the cup.

The princess chewed her lip. Branwen was afraid her cousin might be sick.

"I—I offer you my blood and my life," Eseult stuttered. She looked away as the king pricked her skin. Then he handed the knife back to Tristan.

King Marc pressed his bleeding palm to his bride's, and Seer Casek wrapped them together in a length of white satin that he'd taken from the altar.

"With your shared blood, you begin your life together as husband and wife." He dipped his forefinger into the chalice.

"With the blood of the witnesses, you are anointed in love and made anew." The *kordweyd* drew the mark of the Horned One on each of their foreheads in blood. The princess paled further.

Branwen took two more lengths of silk from the altar. She tied one around Tristan's hand before tying the other around her own.

"Princess Eseult," said Casek. "You are now the true wife of our king. He will make you a True Queen."

Following the instructions that the *kordweyd* had previously given her, Branwen approached the couple. She carried a fourth length of silk in her hands. Carefully, she untied the knot that bound Marc's and Eseult's hands together, then retied it tightly around just Eseult's. Her cousin flinched. "Sorry," Branwen whispered.

Next, Branwen turned to Marc and secured the last bandage around his palm. His hand was clammy, as was hers. From the altar, he picked up an elegant golden crown studded with onyx and diamonds.

"Princess Eseult of Iveriu," said the king. "Please kneel."

Eseult's eyes flitted once more to Branwen. She sank to her knees.

"You arrived in this land as the Princess of Iveriu. From this day forward you will be the True Queen of Kernyv."

Branwen plucked the diadem of Rigani stones deftly from her cousin's head. She saw her chin tremble. Branwen stepped backward and replaced the tiara on the altar.

"My wife," said Marc. "I offer you my blood, my life, and my crown." His hands shook once as he laid the crown upon Eseult's head.

"Arise, Queen Eseult of Kernyv."

Seer Casek peered at Branwen sidelong. His smile was ruthless.

She's not a True Queen yet, it said.

Peace was made with women's bodies. Branwen had spoken the words as she offered her magic for the Loving Cup.

She hadn't asked herself why. Who made the rules? Was it the gods, or was it merely men?

Her cousin had been crowned, and yet she still needed to bleed to become a True Queen. She still needed the seer's permission.

Branwen smiled back at Casek, imagining it to be a razor that could slice him from ear to ear.

Tonight would be the last time that either of the women bled for him.

✢ ✢ ✢

Queen Verica insisted that Branwen be seated next to her at the wedding feast, much to the annoyance of Countess Kensa. The wedding guests were treated to mead, ale, and Mílesian spirits as the servants rearranged the tables in the Great Hall for the meal. Platters of hazelnut bread in the shape of lions were also passed throughout the hall.

Branwen's breaths grew more and more shallow as the evening

deepened into night and dancing replaced eating. She reached for the stillness of which the Wise Damsel had spoken—she only found anger, and she clung to it tightly.

The Queen Mother showed Branwen a watchful smile. "You're young, Lady Branwen," she said, nodding toward the laughing guests. "You should be out there dancing, not sitting here with an old woman."

"I'm happy where I am," Branwen replied.

"Are you?"

Branwen took another sip of mead. Her eyes roamed involuntarily toward King Marc, who was standing at the edge of the dance floor with his wife by his side, together with Ruan and the King of Ordowik.

"My son's not much of a dancer. Too like his father in that respect." Queen Verica rattled a cough. "Perhaps your cousin can change that?"

"Perhaps."

The Queen Mother's gaze landed once more on Branwen. "The beginning of a marriage between rulers is always a delicate dance in and of itself," she said, and Branwen met her stare. "You needn't worry for your cousin. She and Marc may disagree, but I have raised a kind son."

"He has been very generous since we arrived in Kernyv," Branwen told the queen, the words sticky against the roof of her mouth.

The Queen Mother leaned into Branwen. "I wanted to thank you for keeping my secret this past week." The stomping feet and rowdy laughs from the revelers made it hardly necessary to lower her voice.

"And I've been impressed at how you've handled Seer Casek. The True Queen will need a trusted friend by her side," she said. "Your cousin is blessed to have you."

Guilt stabbed Branwen. This woman had been nothing but welcoming, and Branwen was about to betray her son.

"Thank you, Queen Mother," she said in a small voice. "I will do my best."

"You objected to the Mantle of Maidenhood—"

"I—" Branwen interrupted, fear cooling her anger.

Queen Verica lifted a hand. "I don't rebuke you, Lady Branwen. These are not your ways," she said. "For true followers of the Horned One, the ritual is a joyous occasion—a bond between husband and wife. It ought not to be otherwise."

The Mantle of Maidenhood, if offered willingly, could perhaps be something joyful, as the Queen Mother believed. But this . . . this was fetid, rotten. Branwen's courage faltered. She beseeched the Old Ones to show her a way out of this evening that didn't compel her to choose between compromising her honor—her very self—and starting a war.

The Queen Mother touched Branwen's shoulder. "Seer Casek loves his own power more than he loves the Horned One, I think. My son did not consult the *kordweyd* before agreeing to make your cousin a True Queen, and he had to make this concession. A ruler's life is full of compromises."

"Of course," she replied tightly.

Yet men had made these compromises, bartered with the bodies of women without consulting them. Branwen herself had conjured the Loving Cup in an attempt to make her cousin's heart better suited to the world in which they lived.

Until now, she hadn't considered changing the world to better suit her cousin's heart instead.

"Not all the seers are like Casek," said the Queen Mother, her scrutiny overt. "And the seers were not always men."

Branwen's eyebrows lifted. "They weren't? But I thought women couldn't take part in the Mysteries?"

"When I was a girl, we could. Some places in Albion, we still can. In the center of Isca, the city where I was raised, there is a shrine to Matrona—the Mother of the Horned One," the Queen Mother said. "Women pray to her in their hours of need. In childbirth, in grief."

"I haven't heard of her," said Branwen.

Queen Verica sniffed. "Matrona gave birth to Carnonos when she thought she was past her childbearing years. He was a miracle. A bit like me with Marc." Affection threaded through the old queen's words. "When Carnonos was first resurrected as the Horned One, he went to visit his mother. He revealed himself to her as a god in order to comfort her. Women were the first to spread the Cult of the Horned One throughout the Aquilan Empire," she went on. "But men like power. Now that the Cult is powerful, they want it for themselves."

Branwen touched a hand to her throat. "I am too old not to speak frankly, Lady Branwen," said the Queen Mother. "And when the Horned One calls me for judgment, I won't be afraid to tell him my thoughts on the matter."

Branwen laughed. She didn't doubt that the Queen Mother would do precisely that. Thinking of her aunt, of everything that she had done to put her daughter on the throne of Kernyv, Branwen said, "I don't think it's only men who like power."

"No, indeed." Queen Verica gave her an astute look. Branwen shifted in place. "Be careful of Seer Casek once I'm gone, Lady Branwen. And those close to him. He has fought for every shred of his power— and he won't be easily pushed aside."

Branwen placed her uninjured hand atop the queen's. The old woman's skin was thin, her veins protruding. "I will take your warning to heart," she said, although she was all too aware of the danger he posed.

"*Nosmatis*, Queen Verica. Lady Branwen."

Branwen was greeted by a familiar face. "*Nosmatis*, Captain Morgawr. It's good to see you again."

His charcoal whiskers were more neatly trimmed than Branwen had ever seen them on the ship, and he had donned a black tunic and leather breeches, the standard of the Royal Fleet embroidered over his heart.

"And you." To Queen Verica, Morgawr said, "You look radiant, Queen Mother."

"I'll take the compliment, Morgawr," said Queen Verica. "Although calling me Queen Mother makes me feel even older than I look. It seems like just the other day that you and Hanno were joining the fleet."

She and the captain exchanged a smile, lamplight warming his dark brown skin, their rapport easy. Of course, Branwen had forgotten that Morgawr had sailed with Tristan's father as young men. He would have known Tristan's mother as well.

"We are older than we were," Morgawr said. "Seeing Princess Eseult become the True Queen tonight makes all of our losses easier to bear. We have peace at last."

"Indeed, Captain," said the queen. "Thank you for bringing Tristan safely home."

"Lady Branwen deserves some of the thanks." Fear rippled down Branwen's spine. Morgawr had seen her use the Hand of Bríga against the Shades, but he'd said he wouldn't speak of it.

"We have much to thank her for." Queen Verica patted Branwen's hand. "Now, I think it's time for me to rest my weary bones. Captain Morgawr, could I impose upon you to help me to my rooms? Lady Branwen is young and should be dancing."

"It would be my honor." He performed a small bow. "Take care of yourself, Lady Branwen. Cadan would be proud to see you tonight. This is what we were fighting for."

Branwen remained rooted to the chair as the captain escorted the Queen Mother from the hall. She cradled her bandaged hand.

Dhusnos had chased them across the Dreaming Sea because of Branwen, because of her power and her mistakes. Seeing Eseult safely in Kernyv, married to King Marc, provided Captain Morgawr with the comfort that his men's lives were lost for a greater good.

If Branwen didn't betray his king tonight, she would take that comfort away. How could she do that to him? To Cadan's memory? Too many sacrifices had already been made to unite Iveriu and Kernyv.

For peace, for her people, Branwen would sacrifice whatever of her innocence remained.

BEFORE THE BEGINNING

THERE WAS NO MOON AS Branwen crossed the courtyard to the Queen's Tower.

Eseult had left the feast to ready herself for the First Night a quarter of an hour ago, but Branwen had been delayed by a request to dance from Ruan. She denied him, but there was a part of her, a large part, that didn't want to.

When she reached the entrance to the tower, a figure stepped out into the torchlight.

"Branwen," said Tristan.

"*Nosmatis*," she replied, barely audible.

Glancing up at the invisible moon, he said, "We're in the shadow of the short days now."

"The queen is upstairs?"

"She is." Tristan stepped closer. "Branwen," he repeated. The breath from her name grazed her face. "I sang for you tonight."

She clenched her fists and fresh blood leaked from her injured hand.

"I must attend to the queen, Tristan. I'm late."

Branwen couldn't let him delay her, not when she wanted so much to be delayed, for time to stop, to be given any excuse to shirk her duty to the Land.

Tristan took her bandaged hand with his own. He pressed their palms together, and Branwen's entire body tingled.

"I still love you," he said. She cast her eyes to their bloodied hands. "I will carry the shame of what I did with me for the rest of my days."

Tristan pulled her closer. The desire to devour him and to destroy him weren't nearly so different as Branwen might want.

"Eseult—*Queen* Eseult told me what you're planning." He fingered one of her errant curls. "Please don't do this. Don't make my shame yours."

Branwen stilled. This secret was only meant to be carried by Branwen and Eseult. A secret between only them, like so many others in their childhood.

Tristan didn't need to know. Nothing good could come of Tristan knowing this truth. But Eseult had *told* him.

Branwen broke free of his embrace. "I have no choice but to give King Marc what you took," she said in a quiet roar. "He wants blood."

She raised her right hand as a drop fell to the cobblestones. "Seer Casek wants blood."

"Then let him have mine."

"It is not the blood of men that the *kordweyd* want. I told you I was my cousin's Champion. I will save her life, and yours. *And* the peace."

Even if her cousin had betrayed Branwen yet again, this was what Iveriu needed.

"You're a healer, Branwen. If you do this, it will change you—there will be no going back. No undoing this. Not for you, not for Marc— Marc, he . . . he doesn't deserve this."

"Marc is the king. He makes the rules. He could have chosen differently."

"Seer Casek—"

"Enough excuses have been made for the king!" she spluttered. "The men wouldn't accept any excuses for their queen not being a maiden! I'd bet my life Marc has known a woman before, and the seers don't care about the purity of *his* sacrifice!"

Tristan didn't contradict her. A tiny blue flame began to eat its way through the bandage on Branwen's hand as her rage mounted.

"You can either denounce us all as traitors, Tristan," she said as the Hand of Bríga smoldered, "or you can let our kingdoms have peace."

"You know I would never do anything to hurt you."

Branwen pushed past him. "If you want to help, Tristan, go back to the feast and keep Endelyn distracted," she said, over one shoulder, tone colder than a frozen spring. "Consider it an order from the queen, if you like."

"This isn't a game of *fidkwelsa*, Branwen."

She turned her face so Tristan couldn't see the sweat pebbling her forehead or the tears in her eyes. "No, it's a game of chance."

Branwen walked toward the stairs and a very uncertain fate.

✠ ✠ ✠

Branwen was waiting in Eseult's—Queen Eseult's—apartment when King Marc arrived. She had rebandaged her hand, and everything was in order.

"*Nosmatis*," she greeted him.

"*Nosmatis*, Lady Branwen," he said. The king's pallor was closer to the white of his tunic, the creases around his eyes deeper as he attempted a smile. Anxiety radiated from him. It tugged at her own.

At the Champions Tournament, surveying the competitors who had come to Iveriu for glory, Branwen had realized that no amount of gold or jewels could ever tempt her into trading places with the princess.

Sheer desperation had driven her to change her mind.

"Thank you for adhering to the traditions of the Iverni tonight, my king," Branwen said, not quite meeting his gaze. Apart from the Mantle of Maidenhood, King Marc had deferred to Branwen regarding all other matters.

She motioned for him to be seated in an armchair by the window. The room was illuminated by the glow of Aquilan oil lamps and beeswax candles. He toyed with the bandage around his hand as he walked toward the chair.

Branwen retrieved a crystal decanter and a single silver goblet from atop a chest of drawers in the corner of the room. There was a small water bowl on the floor beside it. Arthek had been exiled to Tristan's quarters for the night.

"For we Iverni," Branwen began, "our Goddess Ériu is not only the goddess of the Land, she is the Land itself. Her body is our island. As Princess of Iveriu, my cousin also embodies the Land."

"Yes," Marc said.

"Ériu has a sister named Bóand, the goddess of rivers." Branwen poured mead from the decanter into the goblet as she spoke. The tart and sweet spice with which the Kernyveu flavored their wine would mask the taste of Medhua's tears.

"To celebrate the love between the goddesses," Branwen continued, her voice growing thick with emotion, "on a woman's wedding night, her sister or other close female relative offers the new husband a drink before they share the marriage bed."

Whomever Eseult had wed, Branwen had always known she would perform this ritual for her younger cousin. When she left Iveriu, she'd believed it would be an uncomplicated matter to serve King Marc the Loving Cup. Branwen's own arrogance knocked the wind from her.

But was there truly a difference between the love potion and Medhua's tears?

Both were conceived in despair, an attempt to reclaim power where it had been stripped away. The herbs required for Medhua's tears were not commonly held knowledge, but Branwen's grandmother must have taught her daughters. In a world ruled by men, women shared knowledge like warriors donned armor.

Would women always need magic or potions to take back a shred of control?

Girding herself, Branwen went on, "The drink is both a blessing and a request that her sister's husband supports his wife the way the rivers nourish the land." The king looked from the goblet to her. "Eseult has been my sister since the day she was born," Branwen told him. "King Marc, I offer you this drink with my blessing. I trust you to take care of her as I have."

The king stood. "*Mormerkti*. On my blood, I will hold your cousin as dear as my own heart," he said, pressing his hand across it.

As she leaned forward to offer him the goblet, Branwen noticed a tiny cut right where his beard met his earlobe. King Marc must have nicked himself shaving. Was it from nerves?

Branwen smothered her empathy. If she wavered, many more deaths would be on her head. "*Sekrev*," she told King Marc. "Please, sit."

She didn't know how quickly the Medhua's tears would take effect. She could only hope she'd mixed the proportions correctly. Her grip tightened on the neck of the decanter. "With Lugmarch's blessing," Branwen added, and the king's lips twitched in a partial grin as he noted, "You're learning our customs, too."

She answered with a modest smile. Her knuckles began to ache from clutching the tainted drink.

Lowering himself back onto the chair cushion, Marc said, "You look like you want to ask me something, Lady Branwen." He took a long sip of the mead.

Her pulse pounded in her ears. Branwen pressed her tongue against the back of her teeth and held her breath as she watched him swallow his drink. After a moment, the question that had been troubling her for weeks spilled from her lips.

"Why did you agree to make my cousin a True Queen?"

Marc's shoulders grew even more taut as he drained the rest of the mead in one gulp, and Branwen feared she'd been too bold. He set the empty goblet on the window ledge.

Then the king surprised her. "From the time I could speak, I knew what was expected of me." Marc lifted the crown from his head. "That I was born to rule." He turned the golden circle in his hands. "And, I imagine, it was the same for my new wife."

The word *wife* was formed uncertainly on his tongue.

Branwen could only nod. She would never reveal how hard Eseult had fought her fate. How she fought it still. And Branwen could no longer blame her cousin for that as much as she once had.

"We . . . ," the king started. "We've both been raised to put our peoples first, as it should be." He coughed. "I believe that my wife and I carry equal burdens. Therefore we should have equal power."

Something wrenched violently inside Branwen at his words. That was not an answer she'd anticipated. King Marc was completely sincere. She heard it in his voice. She saw it on his face. And yet she mistrusted her own senses.

"But why?" she challenged him. "Why give up your power when Kernyv was in a position of strength? You have superior ships, superior numbers. If you'd sailed the Royal Kernyvak Fleet into Blackford Harbor, I don't know what King Óengus would have done."

"You sound like my barons." Marc gave one bleak laugh. "I've heard the rumors that Tristan negotiated the treaty without my consent. Unhappy nobles who want to blame him. But it's not true."

The king's eyes were beginning to dilate—the silver replaced by hungry black, becoming two new moons.

"I didn't give up my power, Lady Branwen. I'm *sharing* it," he said. "I know that I will rule better with . . . a partner. It's what I wanted."

Blinking back tears, she turned to the window and picked up the goblet. Branwen had never heard of a king *wanting* to share power in this way.

Could she have been so very wrong about Marc's character? Had the Dark One sent her the vision of her parents' deaths merely to torment her?

She blew out the candle on the windowsill.

"I didn't mean to upset you, my lady. Forgive me if I spoke harshly."

"You didn't. You haven't," she assured him, throat raw. Branwen carried the goblet and decanter back to the chest of drawers, then snuffed out the oil lamps in that section of the room as well.

She hated that King Marc hadn't overruled Seer Casek, yet she could see that he had changed the rules as much as he dared. If given the chance, he and Eseult might bring about a lasting peace for both their peoples.

But only deception would give them that chance.

"Lady Branwen?" said the king. Fighting for her composure, she pivoted to face him. Marc was on his feet. He took a step toward her, and he wasn't unsteady, but—in the same way that Sir Fintan had walked and talked without issue on the night of the Farewell Feast—King Marc didn't seem to wholly inhabit his body, either.

"Lady Branwen, I know that you and my wife are the closest of sisters," King Marc said. "Now that we are wed, I consider you my sister, too. I hope you might come to see me as a brother."

Branwen bit the inside of her cheek, pinched the flesh tightly between her teeth. She blew out the rest of the candles until only a solitary flame remained.

Light glowed on the intertwined sea-wolves and lions that decorated the bedspread.

"After tonight, you will be my brother," she said.

He nodded. As if only just occurring to him, he said, "Why have you blown out all the candles, Lady Branwen?"

Offering a drink to a sister's new husband was a true Ivernic tradition. What Branwen told King Marc next was a lie.

"In Iveriu, the groom awaits his bride in total darkness. The darkness represents the time just before the beginning of the world, before Kerwindos created us all in her cauldron. Before the land. Before the sea. Before the stars. The queen will come to you soon."

Branwen extinguished the final flame, leaving only smoke behind.

✦ ✦ ✦

The True Queen of Kernyv admired her First Night gown as she slipped it over Branwen's head. Branwen quivered, the silk soft and cold, barely able to speak.

The cousins were concealed within a secret room between the castle walls. Few people knew of its existence. The hollow was designed to protect the queen in the event of an attack. Capture was often worse than death for a royal hostage.

Branwen wished she could hide here forever.

She ran her forefinger along the scalloped neckline of the gown she'd meticulously embroidered for her cousin. She remembered how she'd pricked a finger as she'd been sewing. How she'd worried her blood would mar the white silk.

"*Shh,*" Eseult soothed. She stroked Branwen's shaking shoulders. "*Shh.*"

"I'm not scared!" Branwen's whisper was barbed—and it was a bigger lie than the one she'd fed the king. "I'm furious."

"But, I—last night . . . I thought you'd forgiven me?"

"And today you betrayed me again."

"What? How?"

"You told Tristan." The reply was frost-covered.

"He—he was worried for me. For *us.*" Eseult touched Branwen's elbow, and Branwen jerked away. She cursed as the bone hit the wall. "I didn't think it'd matter," her cousin insisted. "We're all in this together."

"And whose fault is that?" Branwen retorted. *Mine. All mine.* She pulled loose the first of her plaits.

"I only wanted to reassure him," Eseult said weakly.

"You wanted to reassure him that I would fix your mess? Or did you want to make sure he knew I planned to lie with his uncle? That

I would deceive his king and dishonor myself?" Branwen jabbed a finger at her cousin. "Were you *jealous*?"

Eseult's mouth fell open. "*No*, Branny. Please, don't say such a thing. How could you even think it? If you don't want to do this, I'll go to Marc right now and throw myself on his mercy."

"You've done enough, Queen Eseult. Your husband is waiting for me. Stay here until I return. By the Old Ones, don't let yourself be seen."

Eseult threw her arms around Branwen, crushing her in an embrace.

"I love you, Branny. I love you." She squeezed Branwen harder. "It's natural to be frightened."

"I'm not." *I'm terrified.* Branwen suppressed a wail, but it still racked her body.

"From Kerwindos's Cauldron was I born." Branwen met Eseult's eyes as she began to recite the Royal Ivernic Guardsmen's oath. "I serve the Land against all those who seek to harm her. Until I return from whence I came."

FIRST NIGHT

SHE CLICKED OPEN THE LATCH. The bedchamber was dark as pitch. Branwen's heart thudded in her throat.

"M-Marc?" she called out, teeth chattering. No answer. "M-my king?"

Wood creaked. "Eseult," he answered in a hush. Branwen heard a rustle of fabric as he stood and walked toward her. He stopped short of trampling her toes. He must be a very capable warrior; his instincts were well honed in the dark.

"I am not your king tonight," Marc said. "I come to you just as a man." She heard him gulp. "And a timid one at that."

"I-I—" Dread made Branwen's tongue useless. Her cousin often described the moments when her anxiety overpowered her as a frantic drunkenness. Branwen hadn't fully comprehended what that might feel like until now.

"I'm grateful for the Ivernic tradition of darkness, Eseult—not that you're not beautiful." The king paused. "That's not what I meant."

Marc released a sigh. "I wish I could speak to you in your language.

Or in mine. My thoughts don't come as readily in Aquilan. What I meant is . . . sometimes it's easier to be honest in the dark."

"Yes," Branwen forced out. "It is."

He pressed something into her hand. It was winter-bitten. "Careful. It's the blade of our binding. In Kernyvak tradition, the groom gives it to his bride. It's a symbol of his honor. You're now the keeper of my honor now, Eseult."

Branwen was glad for the dark, so that he could not see her face. She had already jeopardized the honor of those she held most dear. She couldn't be trusted with anybody else's.

"*Mormerkti.*" She laid it on the table beside the bed.

"*Sekrev.*" Marc touched his bandaged hand to her shoulder. "Eseult, I know we've barely had a moment alone. Barely spoken since you arrived in Kernyv. That's my fault," he said. "I tend to avoid things when I don't know how to handle them."

Branwen couldn't help a laugh. "And you don't know how to handle me?"

"Not at all."

"I—I don't know what to make of you, either," she admitted, and Branwen was speaking for herself.

Who was King Marc really?

"Eseult," Marc said, his voice serious. "You've become my wife without first becoming my friend. I regret that. I know you know that's how it is for rulers—but I wish it were otherwise."

He reached a tentative hand to Branwen's brow. Gently, he brushed at the wisps that lined her face. Her knees quaked together, and King Marc felt it.

"We—we don't have to . . . *be* together tonight. I won't compel you. I don't want to hurt you. We can wait."

Truth echoed from his words. Fear and relief twined around Branwen's heart.

"We c-can't," Branwen protested, bitterness filling her mouth. "The *kordweyd* won't declare me a True Queen until they've examined the Mantle of Maidenhood."

She didn't want to do this—not now, not ever—but she could only chance giving the king Medhua's tears once. Branwen couldn't forsake her people, no matter how terrified she was.

"Forgive me, Eseult. I didn't want to impose our customs on you— or to embarrass you." Marc cursed softly in Kernyvak. "We've not yet been married a day and already I've failed you." His frustration was palpable, and a thousand pins pricked Branwen from the inside.

"You're not powerful enough to rule without the support of the seers," she said, and it wasn't a question.

King Marc inhaled deeply. "I won't lie to you. My rule is precarious. Many factions formed among the nobles when my father died. Yes, I need the *kordweyd*'s support to rule."

"My father always said that a king's subjects keep him in power."

"King Óengus is wise."

Branwen swallowed, grateful Marc hadn't recognized her mistake— that she'd spoken in the past tense. Her father would have liked this man, she thought, and the realization cut her to the quick.

Branwen took Marc's injured hand with hers. "Iveriu needs me declared a True Queen in the morning."

"Tristan told me that you had a will of steel beneath your slight frame."

Branwen flinched. "He knows me well," she said. What else had Tristan told the king?

They both remained standing. "You're strong," Marc said. "But you're young yet."

"Not too young to be queen."

Hands shaking, Branwen pulled Marc's tunic over his head and made herself walk toward the bed. Aside from her patients, Tristan was the only man Branwen had ever seen half-dressed. The king came to sit beside her atop the quilt.

"Eseult," Marc said, and the sadness in the way he said the name made Branwen's heart cramp. "Eseult, I've never been married before, but it seems to me that secrets don't make for a solid foundation."

Her throat constricted. "I have no secrets."

"No, but *I* do."

Branwen clasped her hands together in her lap. She rubbed her thumb against the bandage. The chafing anchored her.

"Before our marriage was agreed, I was in love with another."

"Oh," she said. "I understand."

"I've sent him away," Marc assured her. "I swear that I will put all that I am into making our marriage a success. For our kingdoms, and for ourselves."

Branwen took a quick breath. "Him?"

"Yes. Eseult, I have lain with both men and women. But I have only ever fallen in love once. I've only had one *karid*. I don't regret anything that passed between him and me. But, before we share our bodies, Eseult, I thought it only fair that you know the truth of my heart."

Tristan was right that Marc would be a good husband to her cousin because he was a kind man—far kinder than Branwen. She hid her face in her hands. The Loving Cup had been doomed from the start, for more reasons than she could have ever foreseen.

Branwen had been selfish. Prideful. She had tried to tame hearts that did not belong to her, and she had lost her own. The king stroked Branwen's back as she wept.

"I'm sorry," she said.

"What do you have to be sorry for, my wife?"

That I'm not your wife. More than she could ever say. Branwen scrubbed her eyes, letting shame wash over her.

"I am sorry, Marc, because I had never truly considered that the king of my enemies could love. Or that I would be the reason he would lose that love."

Even as they crossed the sea, Branwen had only ever seen the King of Kernyv as an obstacle to her cousin's happiness. She hadn't seen him as a man. She'd hated the faceless ruler who'd sent raiders to her island.

Branwen had never considered that Marc might also have a *karid*, a beloved of his own, or that *his* happiness might lie in someone else's arms. Someone he couldn't make a life with because Kernyv needed an heir. It hadn't occurred to her that a man—a king—could be equally caught by the demands of peace.

Marc kissed Branwen's wet cheek. "*Mormerkti.* Thank you for understanding, for accepting who I am. Tell me your secrets, Eseult, and I promise to accept who you are." He pulled Branwen against his chest and they lay back on the bed together.

Branwen couldn't tell him her secrets, even though an unexpected part of her longed to do just that.

Instead, she asked for more of his. "No one knows about the man you love?"

"Only Tristan," Marc replied, and Branwen held her tongue as new tears leaked from her eyes. One more secret. One more reason she and

Tristan had never been free to love each other first. "Others may suspect—including Seer Casek," he said, exhaling. "Tristan is my brother. He would never betray me."

"Others would use it against you?"

"In the days of the Aquilan Empire, love between men was common. Accepted. The seers don't approve, and some of the Kernyvak nobles agree. The *kordweyd* value self-denial above all and foreswear romantic love." Marc swallowed. "The seers only condone physical love for procreation. They see physical love for . . . its own sake as beneath them. As weakness."

Marc dragged in another heavy breath. "If they knew, my opponents would use my love as a weapon against me." Pain stretched his voice thin as his arms grew rigid around Branwen. "I'm sorry about the Mantle of Maidenhood, Eseult. Truly. I couldn't let the *kordweyd* have a reason to think our marriage wasn't genuine. The seers and the Horned One aren't the same, but I do need them to rule."

Branwen felt for her mother's brooch as his words sank in. Missing its presence, she fidgeted with a pearl stitched into the silk.

"I believe in the mercy of the Horned One," Marc continued. "And I have many things for which I need to make amends." He went quiet, and the *kretarv*'s vision filled Branwen's mind. Surely it was false. It must be. Dhusnos wanted her to question the peace, that was all.

"I would never judge you, Marc," Branwen told him, iron in her voice. When she fell in love with Tristan, she'd feared her family's scorn, her people's wrath. "We love who we love."

"Do all the Iverni feel this way?" he said.

"The Old Ones are immortal," she began. "In our legends, they find love in all forms. The Hound of Uladztir, one of our greatest heroes, had a *kridyom*—a heart-companion—who was a man before he married Emer." Branwen found it hard to speak the name by which Tristan had first known her. "I think a heart-companion is the same as your word, *karid*."

"Yes," Marc said quietly. "Perhaps our languages are not so different."

Fiddling with the pearl on the collar of her gown, Branwen said, "You've made a great sacrifice to give up your *karid*. That makes you strong. Not weak. Your people have a good king—a king who puts their needs above his own heart."

"Our people," he said.

"Our people." Branwen dared to cover Marc's hand with hers.

He shifted onto his side, facing Branwen in the dark. "The gods, both yours and mine, have favored me by making you my queen. I will endeavor to be worthy of you."

"And I of you," she whispered. Her lashes grew heavy with tears. Marc brushed his thumb across her cheek.

Branwen loved Iveriu more than she loved herself, but this . . . Branwen couldn't betray this man more than she already had. If she did, she would be no better than the Dark One who enslaved unclaimed souls.

Seer Casek had dictated the terms of Eseult's First Night. He had also dictated to the king. Branwen had been so trapped by fear, by tradition, that she'd allowed the *kordweyd* to corner her in her own mind. She'd lost herself in the fog.

And she had failed to see the power in her own hand. She saw clearly now. Revelation blazed behind her eyes. Incandescent. It made her almost giddy.

Branwen lifted herself up, pushing at Marc's shoulder. She rolled her body on top of his so that she was straddling him.

"Eseult—"

"I need you to do something for me," she said.

All Branwen needed to keep the peace was an illusion.

"Anything," Marc said into the stillness. "Tell me what you need."

The illusion was still a risk, but it was a risk worth taking. The seers could have her blood. They couldn't have her soul.

"I need you to look into my eyes," Branwen said to the king, remembering how her aunt had influenced Sir Fintan. "Only my eyes. Can you do that?"

"Yes," Marc told her, and Branwen lowered her face to his until their noses were touching. Determination coursed through her.

Why had she let Seer Casek make the rules? She had magic running through her veins like the rivers that nourished the Land. She had looked to the Old Ones for answers, but the answers had been inside her all along.

Holding her right hand aloft, Branwen pictured herself as the echo of fire, just as the Wise Damsel had instructed. For the first time, she didn't feel frenzied as she summoned her power.

A blue flame created a halo above them.

Marc's eyes were round and dark, and fixed to hers. Silently, she begged his forgiveness.

"Tonight you lay with your wife, Eseult," Branwen told him. "You decided to wait to tell her the full truth of your heart until you know each other better. In the morning, you will only remember that as you consummated the marriage, you promised to become friends."

Branwen cupped his cheek. "You will remember tonight as a sweet, dark dream. Do you understand?"

"I do."

She pressed her lips to his forehead. "Go to sleep now, my king."

"Good night," Marc said as he closed his eyes.

Branwen would reopen the wound on her hand. Let Seer Casek have his blood. She lifted herself from Marc's chest, gently easing from the bed to the floor. His form was prone, trusting, like Tristan on the raft.

She gasped as if she'd been struck in her chest.

By the light of the Hand of Bríga, Branwen's eyes made out a howling sea-wolf inked on Marc's forearm.

The flame rising from her palm began to grow.

It was true.

It was all true.

King Marc *was* the young boy who had attacked her parents, who had watched her mother plunge a *kladiwos* blade into her own breast.

The tattoo was proof. Branwen didn't want it to be true—especially not after tonight, but she couldn't pretend otherwise. She had known it since the *Dragon Rising*. She had made excuses. Told herself lies. Because the truth could be far more cruel.

She couldn't think. She heard only the Dark One's laughter in her mind.

Her flamed danced higher as she grabbed the blade of binding from the bedside table. She rushed toward the king.

Branwen stood over Marc, her blade pressed to his throat. His breathing took on the rhythm of sleep, and her fire slithered toward the ceiling.

Lady Alana and Lord Caedmon never came home to six-year-old Branwen because of this man—because of this man for whom she had just cried, from whom she'd sought absolution.

Branwen forced back a scream and tilted the tip of the blade against the king's fragile, exposed flesh. A scream would send guards running through the door.

One liquid-quick movement and she could avenge her family.

Do it, urged the darkest part of her heart. *Do it now.* The part that was shadow-stung, like Keane had been.

Her flames licked at her curls—she could free herself, lose herself in dark fire.

Branwen's hand warmed the jewels on the hilt of the knife. It trembled.

Take your revenge. She could burn the kingdom, starting at its heart—with its king. Turn Monwiku to cinders and ash.

Destruction was power. *Her* power. She could show the seers, show the Kernyveu what one Iverwoman could do.

Lady Alana had killed herself rather than be taken by this man. The chance to kill the king was unlikely to present itself twice. *Now, you only have now.* The voice was lyrical, lulling, like a lethal undertow.

No. Her father's voice resounded through the darkness, staying her hand. If Branwen killed her enemy, she could never turn him into her friend. She would destroy everything so many had given their lives for.

As Branwen struggled to control the flame, sweat collected on her brow. She gripped the knife tighter.

The moment had come for Branwen to decide: take Marc's life now, or defend it as her king until her own dying breath.

Branwen's years of fury fueled the flame, even as she hesitated. The scar on her right hand glistened like the dead of night.

"Stop," she whispered aloud. Vengeance wasn't justice.

Marc stirred, but he didn't open his eyes.

The Land had chosen her Champion, and Branwen understood why. This was a man with regrets. A man who wanted to leave a different legacy than his father.

Whoever Marc had been as a boy, he was now a king who wanted peace with her homeland.

She didn't forgive him, not yet, but she believed he would fight for peace. She believed he wanted to be a just king, a good king. For now, that was enough.

Enough.

The fire at last sputtered, flickered to nothing as Branwen closed the Hand of Bríga into a fist and tore off what remained of the singed bandage.

Her shoulders heaved with exhaustion. Nerves flayed, Branwen used the blade to reopen the wound that Tristan had made. She trickled her blood over the sheets.

Branwen bled for Iveriu, for the Old Ones, offering her magic to heal the rupture between kingdoms. *Bind it with my blood.* She felt the Otherworld pressing in on her; the hairs on her arm lifted.

The marriage between Goddess Ériu and her Consort had not been consummated according to the Old Ways. *Please, accept my offering. Take what you must. Let it be enough to renew the Land.*

Branwen did not bleed for the *kordweyd*, but they had their sacrifice nonetheless.

Marc would believe it. Eseult would believe it. Tristan would believe it.

Branwen would *make* them believe.

The reign of King Marc and Queen Eseult depended on it. She

would defend them against Prince Kahedrin of Armorica and all other comers.

She would help Marc become a better king for her people—for their people.

No one would ever know that the peace had been won with Branwen's blood and lies.

LIGHT ME FROM THE INSIDE

BRANWEN WAS STILL SHAKING AS she slinked back into the Great Hall unnoticed by the remaining wedding guests. Some continued to dance, their movements sloppy; others were slumped at the banquet tables, hands curled around half-drunk cups of ale.

A ferocious energy coursed through her. Not a darkness, but something heady. She scoured the many ruddy faces in the feasting hall. She pushed thoughts of the queen—of her apologies as she left to take her place beside King Marc—from her mind. Branwen had given all she could tonight. Before the night was done, she wanted something for herself.

She'd changed back into the dress she'd worn for the ceremony, ultramarine with red lace trim, but she had left her black curls loose, untamed. They fell halfway down her back.

Moving closer to the dance floor, Branwen spied the dark blond head she was after.

Ruan was dressed in royal Kernyvak colors: a suit of black velvet and the white sash of the king's service. He filled out the velvet rather splendidly.

Desire welled inside her. A desire she'd been fighting since she'd first spotted him at the port. She was done fighting it.

She tapped him on the shoulder. Ruan spun around, his face bright with amusement. When his eyes landed on Branwen, however, his expression grew dubious. "Lady Branwen?"

"I thought you wanted to dance," she told him.

"And you've made it abundantly clear that you don't."

"Am I not allowed to change my mind?"

Branwen had tried to ignore the prickle of excitement she always felt in Ruan's presence. It didn't make sense. Their allegiances would always be at odds. Tonight, Branwen didn't care about sense or reason.

Ruan leaned closer. "Are you drunk?"

"Does a lady need to be drunk to want you as a partner, my prince?"

He sniffed her breath. Branwen laughed and put her hands on her hips. "Oh." Ruan's jaw relaxed. "You're not drunk."

"No. I'm not." Branwen had taken only the smallest sips of mead during the toasts earlier in the evening, needing to keep all her senses sharp. What she felt now was free—like a prisoner who had slipped the noose.

"I'm not drunk, but I *do* want to dance," she told the prince.

Ruan gave her a look that was equal parts lust and confusion. He held out a hand. "Then it would be my honor, Lady Branwen."

She closed her right hand around his. The new bandage was red. She had torn a strip of fabric from the train of Eseult's wedding gown.

Ruan kissed her knuckles and led Branwen into the center of the dance floor, pulling her tight against his body. She pressed her hand against his back, feeling the muscles, and imagined the smoothness of his skin. Branwen's hair swung free, a few strands draping themselves across Ruan's chest.

He pinched a lock between his fingers. "It's beautiful," he said. His other hand cinched Branwen's waist. "Like waves at night." A trill of pleasure traveled from the warmth of Ruan's hand to something low in her body.

She released a small gasp and twisted her finger around one of Ruan's dirty-blond strands. "So is yours," she said. "Gold like the sun. Or, perhaps, like a chicken?"

The prince threw his head back with laughter.

"You're in fine form this evening."

"I don't know what you mean. You promised me a private tour of the castle—an *extensive* tour. Or was your offer not sincere?"

"No, it was very sincere," Ruan replied. His eyes roved over her. Branwen smiled. She liked being pursued, but she liked doing the pursuing even better.

"I'm glad to see you've finally realized I'm the more charming of the royal cousins," he added.

Branwen stopped dancing. "I won't be batted between you and Tristan like kittens with a ball of string. I'm not here to settle some childhood grudge."

"I bear Tristan no grudge. He has me to blame for the scar on that pretty face of his, though, so he may feel differently."

"I don't want to talk about Tristan." She struggled to keep her voice light. The last thing Branwen wanted was to think about Tristan.

"What *do* you want, Lady Branwen?" Ruan's gaze captured hers. "Really?"

It might be only for a night, the happiness might be fleeting, but

Branwen had earned herself a sliver, like a waning moon. Happiness that had nothing to do with her queen or her first love.

The music died away and a few other revelers groaned in complaint. The prince didn't move a muscle. He waited for Branwen to reply.

She wanted to forget herself. To know what it was that lovers shared. To know the feel of someone else beneath her skin.

To break the rules. To make the rules. To *choose*.

Branwen pressed her lips to the shell of Ruan's ear.

"I want you to light me from the inside."

✝ ✝ ✝

Ruan intertwined his fingers with hers as Branwen followed him to his apartment in the King's Tower. His palm was callused, used to gripping a sword.

She shivered as the wind tossed her curls. "It's growing colder," said Ruan. "Perhaps there's a war in the Otherworld, like you said."

Branwen laughed. "You *were* listening."

"*Comnaíde*," Ruan replied in Ivernic. *Always*. He winked.

Switching to her native tongue, Branwen said, "Would you speak to me in my own language?" The request came out more earnest than flirtatious.

He turned the key in the lock. "I will do my best," he said, acceding to her wishes.

"Thank you, Ruan," Branwen told him as she realized just how much she needed to hear it. To do this on her terms. She never felt quite herself when speaking Aquilan.

The wind whistled between them.

"I'll warn you that my rooms aren't the tidiest." Ruan pushed open the door for her. Brushing past him, "I'll consider myself warned," Branwen said.

Ruan hurried to light an oil lamp. "I wasn't expecting company this evening."

"Oh, no?"

"No, Branwen." He lit another lamp. "Not all rumors are true. But some are useful."

The orange glow of the lamplight spread through the room. She glanced around her. The table was piled high with books and maps. Clothes were strewn over a settee and several chairs. The canopy bed in the corner was only half-made.

"You *are* a bit of a slob," Branwen said, smiling. She found it endearing that the dashing, arrogant King's Champion should be messy, too.

"I don't know if I would say *slob*," Ruan countered, a tad defensive, but laughing. "Just . . . untidy."

Branwen closed the door and walked toward the prince. He met her in the middle of the room. The space between them thrummed, like the air before lightning struck.

Ruan ran his tongue along his top lip. "This isn't how I expected my Long Night to end," he told her.

"Long Night is over," Branwen said. "Do you know what today is?"

Shaking his head, Ruan lifted a hand to her cheek. "What day is it?"

"My birthday."

"Why didn't you mention it?"

Her cousin had forgotten, and Tristan had never known. Branwen shrugged. "It didn't seem important," she said.

"How old are you?" Ruan's hand followed her cheekbone. He

skimmed his thumb along her mouth. Branwen made a sound halfway between a moan and a sigh.

"Twenty summers."

His hand continued down the length of her neck. "And am I your present?"

Branwen trapped it against the swell of her breasts and stared Ruan in the eyes. "Only if you want to be," she said.

He snaked his other hand around her waist and pressed her flush against him. "You know I do, Branwen."

She sighed as her body quivered with relief, anticipation.

"Ruan, I made a mistake once," said Branwen. "I didn't have the courage to be honest with someone and it . . . ended badly." Her lips tightened at the memory of giving Keane her ribbon. "I don't want there to be any misunderstandings between us."

"I'm listening, Branwen." And, indeed, his eyes had never shone with so much intensity.

"I'm not in love with you. I don't know if I will ever—if I *can* ever—fall in love again," she told him. "But I desire you. And I want you to take me to your bed as your lover."

Ruan inhaled a long breath through his nostrils, then exhaled heavily. For the length of that breath, Branwen feared she'd been too brazen. Yet she longed to be brazen.

"You fascinate me, Branwen of Iveriu. And I want to be your lover."

His mouth crashed against hers, and Branwen's entire body became a riot. His hands were everywhere, and so were hers. Ruan threaded his fingers through her hair and wrapped his arms around her, towing her nearer. Branwen moaned. She hungered for him to be closer still. Her hands scrabbled over Ruan's tunic, ripping it over his head.

She stroked the firm muscles of his torso, delighting in the sensation, wanting to press her own naked skin against his. She pulled away for a moment to look at him. The flesh of his shoulders was covered with raised pink scars, lines that began around his collarbone and continued down Ruan's back.

She traced one of them with her forefinger. Ruan met Branwen's gaze, and his was unblinking.

"You were whipped," she said. Repeatedly, she didn't need to add. The wounds had healed well, treated properly. Some were at least a decade old.

"My father had exacting standards. I didn't meet them."

"I'm sorry."

"I don't want your pity, Branwen. Especially not in this moment."

She pressed her lips together. Her hand dropped to the laces at the front of her dress. She tugged, and they began to loosen.

"What are you doing?" he said.

Branwen let the front of her dress fall to her waist, her bare flesh on display. In the lamplight, the Shades' bite marks were hearth-red.

"I have scars, too, Ruan."

"Who did this to you?" Rage tipped his question.

"The pirates who attacked our ship from Iveriu."

Ruan cursed extensively in Kernyvak. Cautiously, he touched the wound on Branwen's stomach made by the one-eyed Shade.

"I don't want your pity, either," she said.

He raised his eyes back to hers. "You are nothing but beautiful to me."

All of a sudden, his arm came around Branwen's knees, and he lifted her from the floor and carried her to his bed. Her dress fell away as he began to kiss her scars.

Branwen nibbled her way from Ruan's throat to his belly button, and he laughed. A real snort. "You're ticklish?" she said.

"I am."

"I promise not to tell."

"Thank you for that." Ruan drove his fingers into her curls and pulled Branwen back up for another kiss. He emitted a growl against her mouth. She teased him by catching the skin of his throat between her teeth—gently.

His life pulsed beneath her lips, her kiss. Ruan cupped her breast, and Branwen became aware of her body in a whole new way. His desire made her feel both powerful and vulnerable at once. She gasped.

His hand went still. "Do you want me to stop?" he asked.

"No." Branwen tugged at the waistband of Ruan's breeches. The material was sleek between her fingers. She fumbled with the knots. "*Off*," she told him with a grunt of frustration.

Ruan chuckled. "As my lady commands." He shimmied out of his trousers and rolled onto his side, propping himself on his elbow, and gazed down at her.

Branwen caressed one of his naked thighs; then the other. A tremulous sigh lifted Ruan's rib cage. His eyes drank her in as he traced the curve of her waist. Gooseflesh followed in its wake.

She wanted Ruan to finish what she'd started.

"Yes," she said to the unasked question in his eyes. "*Yes*." She burrowed her fingers through his golden hair, grasping at his scalp, bringing him down on top of her.

Ruan held Branwen's hand as their bodies joined together. The muscles of his back were hard, his scars soft, as she held on to him.

There was pain at first, a burning, and then all of Branwen was on fire. It wasn't the Hand of Bríga—this fire was of their own making.

When Branwen had envisioned her First Night, she had thought she would find peace in the arms of a lover. This was something else. Something deep and wild and true. A part of herself she never knew existed.

She cried out as euphoria surged through her. Branwen kissed Ruan. Hard. His mouth opened to her. His body rocked against hers, shuddering.

Breathless, he laid his head against her breast and kissed the flesh above her heart.

"Are you all right?" Ruan asked between pants.

She nodded, embarrassed. "I didn't know it would be so . . . much."

Ruan kissed Branwen's cheek as he slid off her. Their sweaty bodies glowed in the lamplight. She turned onto her side.

"Thank you for being my first time," she said.

He worried a knuckle against his lower lip. "You're—you were a maiden?" His voice was troubled.

Ruan's eyes, still round with desire, swept the length of Branwen's body. She followed them to the sheets.

No blood.

No. Blood.

A viselike hand tightened around her heart.

Branwen tilted her head, letting her hair cover her face, trying to veil her shock. "You don't believe me?" she seethed at Ruan, still staring at the spotless sheets, because she couldn't believe what she was seeing. Or what she *wasn't* seeing. How could there be no blood? Was there something wrong with her?

"No, Branwen. Of course I believe you." Ruan threaded their fingers together. "It's just—I . . . I assumed from the way you were talking, from the fact that you suggested coming back to my room . . ." He swallowed. "I didn't think it was your first time."

He brought her hands to his lips, kissing her fingertips. "Was it . . ." Ruan trailed off. "What you expected?" She could almost laugh at how bashful he looked.

"I—I didn't know what to expect," Branwen admitted. "But it—it was wonderful." Her voice had gone shy. She pressed one hand to Ruan's cheek. "I'm glad I chose you."

Relief loosened his shoulders. "I'm glad you chose me, too." One corner of his mouth lifted. "I've heard talk." Ruan coughed. "At taverns . . . that not all maidens bleed." He raised his shoulders. "I won't pretend to be an expert, though."

"Won't you?" Branwen said.

Anger sliced through her happiness. Disbelief. Did Seer Casek know that a virgin might not bleed? Had it all been a game? A very, very dangerous game.

When Branwen had started her monthly bleeding, her aunt had explained that she would also bleed when she first lay with a man, and not to be afraid. Why hadn't Queen Eseult warned her that she might not? Branwen gnawed at her lower lip. Most likely because her aunt didn't deem it important—because it shouldn't be.

The Mantle of Maidenhood was never anything but hollow. An empty symbol. All it represented was submission. Nothing more.

Branwen had nearly done something unforgiveable, and it would have been for nothing.

"Branwen?" Ruan said her name gently. "I didn't mean to upset you. Are you having regrets?"

So many. Too many. But not about him. Not about what they'd shared.

"No, no." She flashed a half smile. "And don't worry—it doesn't change what I said before."

"About what?"

"About not being in love. I won't start following you around like the puppy from the village."

Something dimmed in Ruan's eyes. "No, we wouldn't want that."

Branwen nibbled his earlobe to make him laugh, tickled his chest. "I like tickling you—I like the way it makes you smile," she told him.

"You can tickle me anytime you want," Ruan said with deadly earnest.

Branwen snorted, and it became a giggle. She couldn't remember giggling since she was a girl. "I promise not to tell anyone that you can giggle," Ruan said, and tickled Branwen right back, making her giggle again, nearly making her forget everything else.

Having such liberty with somebody else's body was exhilarating. They discovered new parts of each other and talked until Ruan yielded to sleep.

Branwen watched him for a little while, marveling at what they had done, wondering who the boy was beneath Ruan's scars. Then she dressed herself, kissed him, and left him dreaming.

She stumbled down the hill into the gardens and watched dawn light the water.

From behind her came a familiar voice.

"You went through with it."

Tristan came to stand shoulder to shoulder with Branwen. She could smell drink on him. She peered at him sidelong. His eyes were bloodshot.

"I told you that I would."

He jammed his eyes shut. "You kept the peace with your body."

Almost. Wheeling on him, Branwen said, "I gave up my honor for peace because it was the only honorable thing to do."

Believe me. Believe me. Believe me.

But if Branwen had followed the seers' rules, the rules would have broken her—and the peace.

The only way to satisfy the lie of the Mantle of Maidenhood was with another lie.

Tristan fell to his knees before Branwen. "You are the True Queen of Kernyv."

"Get up, Tristan."

Branwen hauled him to his feet. He tripped and clutched at her shoulders. "I don't care that you lay with Marc. I *don't*," he said. "Just tell me if you could ever love me again? The way you did in Iveriu."

The solace she'd found in Ruan's bed was fading, making way for resentment.

"In Iveriu, you told me Marc had no time for family life," she reminded Tristan. "That wasn't true. He's in love with a merchant who spent last winter at Monwiku." It wasn't hard to discern that the Xandru who sent Marc flowers for his garden was also his *karid.*

"I wanted to tell you. So many times, I—"

"You upheld your duty to your king—to your brother, and I don't blame you," Branwen told him. Tristan hung his head at her words. "We were never free to love each other first."

"But there's nothing keeping us apart now, Branwen. You know all of my secrets." A tear slid from the corner of his eye. "You paid for my mistakes tonight, and I will spend every day for the rest of my life earning your forgiveness. And Marc's."

The laments of the sea howled in her ears. Branwen might know all of Tristan's secrets, but he could never know hers. If she told him that she hadn't given her body to Marc, she didn't trust that Tristan might not one day tell Eseult, and Eseult needed to believe Branwen's sacrifice had been real if there was any hope of keeping the lovers apart. Branwen wouldn't risk the peace merely to unburden herself, to save her reputation in Tristan's eyes.

"Do you remember, the night you returned to Iveriu—what you said at the welcome feast?" she asked. Tristan scrubbed a hand over his face. "You said that if keeping me safe meant marrying me to your uncle, you would do it. Even if my presence tormented you every day and you could never show me your heart."

Brow furrowed, "I don't—" Tristan started.

"Tell me that isn't how you feel now." Branwen stepped toward him, very close. "Tell me you're not protecting Eseult by pretending not to love her."

The strain in his jaw, the hesitation in his dark eyes—that was all Branwen needed to see. "You have your answer," she said, and Branwen had hers. "We will never love each other again as we did in Iveriu, Tristan. I am not selfless enough to share you."

"Emer," he rasped.

"Stop, Tristan. *Please*. Emer and Tantris were only ever a dream. And now we're awake."

Branwen left Tristan on his knees and walked to the sea. The chimes in the trees called back to the lonely waves.

PART II

INTO THE WRECK

QUICKENING

A CROWD OF VILLAGERS STREAMED toward the beach to catch a glimpse of the king and queen.

Branwen held herself back. Ruffling Senara's forelock, she tied the palfrey's reins to a wooden post. In the past month, Branwen had traveled across most of the Kernyvak peninsula, accompanying her cousin as King Marc introduced the new True Queen of Kernyv to his people. The welcome tour had been exhausting and she was grateful that the festival they were attending this morning would be the last event.

Inhaling, she wended her way toward the water. The wind carried a hint of spring. At Castle Rigani, they would soon be celebrating Imbolgos, the feast sacred to Goddess Bríga. The Iverni believed it was Bríga's fire that melted the frost, sending winter on its way and quickening the land.

How much had changed since last Imbolgos—before she'd met Tristan, when Keane had asked her to dance.

Up ahead, Tristan stood at a protective distance from the True

Queen. Both he and Branwen had been present for the inspection of the Mantle of Maidenhood. Branwen watched as Seer Casek inspected her blood and declared that the union between King Marc and Eseult had been sanctified.

Branwen had returned the *kordweyd*'s tepid smile with a dark one of her own. Where he saw victory, she saw only his defeat. She had outmaneuvered the seer. She wouldn't underestimate the threat Casek posed, but neither would she play by his rules again.

"You look rather miserable, Healer Branwen."

Branwen jumped. Seer Ogrin chortled at her side. "*Dymatis*," she said. "What are you doing here?"

"I come to the festival every year." His smile was open. "And I brought some friends." He pointed to a thatch of auburn hair in the crowd. Lowenek was walking with one crutch to support her weight, Talorc holding her other hand.

Branwen's lips tilted upward. "She's recovering well."

"She is. Thanks to you, Healer Branwen. We've missed you around the temple."

"I'll come for a visit as soon as I can."

In truth, Branwen would be delighted to escape her duties at the castle and the constant, silent friction between her, Tristan, and Eseult. They had succeeded in their deception but there was no triumph in it.

"I know Ailleann would be glad to see you, too," Seer Ogrin added.

Branwen touched her fingers to Lady Alana's brooch. Earlier, when they'd been riding through the forest, she'd sensed the White Moor in the distance, as if it were calling to her. On Long Night, she had nearly lost control of the Hand of Bríga and what scared Branwen most was how much she'd enjoyed it—the thrill of her rage.

"I wouldn't have thought a Wise Damsel and a seer would be friends," she said, tamping down on the memory of her fire. Too vivid. Too tempting.

Amusement beamed from Ogrin's round face. "Ailleann was my first friend in Kernyv. Many, many seasons ago." He rubbed his head. "When I had more hair."

The seer's robe dragged in the sand as they came to a halt amidst the press of bodies.

At the water's edge, King Marc was stepping into a rickety rowboat.

He had tired eyes. Branwen suspected the fact that Prince Kahedrin had departed Kernyv without a formal farewell wasn't the only thing keeping him awake at night. She suspected Marc's heart ached from the wedding vows he had made and intended to keep.

The chattering of the villagers petered out as they watched Ruan hand King Marc a pair of oars. Sea foam lapped against his boots.

Branwen's cheeks warmed. It was a strange thing to know what a man looked like without his clothes—strange in an exciting way. She hadn't returned to Ruan's bed, but she'd thought about it. More than once. She didn't know what she wanted from the prince. Ruan cracked a grin at Marc, chuckling as he said something Branwen couldn't hear. Warmth spread through her body. She did want *something*.

King Marc surveyed the crowd, then glanced at Eseult who stood closer inland, out of the tide's reach. Tristan positioned himself between his grandmother and the queen; Endelyn and Andred just behind. Against Branwen's advice, the Queen Mother, who grew weaker by the day, had insisted on coming with them.

Ruan passed Marc one half of a pair of antlers and the king raised it above his head. As the crowd cheered, Seer Ogrin explained to

Branwen, "Carnonos is the Lord of Wild Things, and that includes the creatures of the sea. King Marc will honor them with an offering. He will ask the Horned One to bless the sea and keep the fishermen's nets full."

Branwen recoiled. She knew what kind of wild creatures lurked in the sea and they didn't answer to the Horned One. The vision she'd had of the Shades attacking Monwiku was never very far from her consciousness.

She kept her eyes pinned to the king's boat, watching for any sign of dark shapes beneath the waves.

Caught up in her own thoughts, Branwen forgot entirely about Seer Ogrin's presence until he patted her elbow. "Come back to us soon," said the seer, and wandered over to Lowenek and Talorc.

Branwen moved toward Queen Verica, offering an escort back from the beach to the center of the village, which resembled the coastal settlements along the Rock Road. From the corner of her eye, she spotted Andred working up the courage to speak to Lowenek, bringing the girl one of the fish pies that King Marc had gifted his people to mark the festival.

"What's making you smile, Lady Branwen?" the Queen Mother asked. She faltered a step, and Branwen secured her with an arm around her shoulders.

"You see the girl with Andred? She was injured in the mining disaster. Andred's been helping me care for her and the others."

"He is a clever boy, and kind," the queen said. "Nothing like his father."

"He's a diligent apprentice." Branwen pressed her lips together, wondering if Andred carried similar scars to Ruan. "Prince Edern, he . . . I've heard he was a severe man."

"Thank the Horned One he wasn't the firstborn son. Marrying Kensa made Edern nearly as rich as the king." She paused. "But it didn't make him king."

Branwen mulled over the queen's words. "Prince Edern married Countess Kensa for her family mines," she said, pitching her voice low.

"It wasn't for love," Queen Verica said as a cough overwhelmed her. "He didn't know the meaning of the word."

Branwen had never met the man but she couldn't help but be glad he was dead.

At that moment, King Marc strolled toward them with Eseult on his arm. He had told Branwen that he'd wanted a partner, someone to share the burden of ruling. Observing them together now, their postures rigid, they appeared more like acquaintances than husband and wife. Tristan and Ruan remained a few paces behind, giving the royal couple privacy while remaining within striking distance.

The Champions never seemed at ease with each other. How had Ruan given Tristan his scar? Why? And what would Ruan do if he ever learned that Tristan had betrayed his king? Branwen cast her eyes back to her cousin.

Eseult's complexion was wan in the bright midday sun. She'd only picked at her food for the last couple of weeks, Branwen had noticed, but she could detect no sign of serious illness. And while she registered her cousin's unhappiness, she couldn't bring herself to offer any consolation. Revealing Branwen's plan to Tristan was, perhaps, a small betrayal compared to others. Still, it had slammed a door in Branwen's heart.

Marc smiled at his mother in greeting and, more tentatively, at Branwen. "Lady Branwen, are you enjoying the festival?" he said.

"The start of spring is always welcome," Branwen said, somewhat stilted. She'd been in Marc's company nearly every day for the past month, and he'd made many attempts at conversation. Her guilt warred with her desire to accept his friendship. He had given up much for this peace, and Branwen had wronged him. But, she also knew without a doubt that he had orphaned her.

"Yes," Marc agreed. "Monwiku will be in full bloom soon enough."

"Branwen was telling me that some of her patients from the mine are here," Queen Verica said, ever the diplomat. It was a shame she and Branwen's aunt would never meet.

"Oh?" Marc looked to Branwen. "How do they fare?"

"Better. Much better, thank you." He nodded. "Actually, there is a girl. Her parents perished in the disaster," Branwen said to the king. "Seer Ogrin asked if we might be able to find a place for her at the castle. Perhaps she could help in the gardens?"

"Of course," Marc answered without hesitation. He held Branwen's gaze as he said, "It's a hard thing for a child to lose her parents."

"*Mormerkti*," Branwen said quietly. Did he ever wonder whether the woman he'd watched die left behind children of her own?

"Is the girl from Iveriu?" Eseult asked, her attention being drawn back to the conversation from somewhere else.

"No, Lady Queen," Branwen told her.

Her cousin flinched at the reminder of who she was to Branwen now. Branwen needed that distance. Loving her cousin was too painful, a pebble she could never dislodge from her boot.

"And the mines," Eseult said, angling her shoulders at Marc. "Are the working conditions safe?"

"All of the floodgates have been reinforced." Marc turned to meet his wife's eyes. "Mining is never entirely risk-free—but I am satisfied with the precautions that have been taken to avoid another calamity."

Eseult sniffed, not entirely placated. "I see."

"I can summon the engineers to the castle to make a full report to you," the king offered. Tension saturated the small gap between the monarchs.

"No, that won't be necessary," Eseult said. "I have another proposal." Her eyes latched on to something behind Branwen. Branwen turned and saw that Seer Casek and Countess Kensa approached from behind. Regrettably, they had also come for the festivities.

"What is the proposal?" Marc prompted his queen.

She cleared her throat. "During the past month, I have seen much of Kernyv. There are many people—both Iverni and Kernyveu—whose livelihoods prove dangerous. Whether they be miners or fishermen."

"Indeed." Marc kept his eyes steady on Eseult, listening attentively.

At Branwen's side, she also felt the Queen Mother tilt forward to hear what the True Queen would say next.

"I would like to care for my people as we do in Iveriu." Catching Branwen's eye, Eseult said, "I propose the establishment of a royal infirmary."

Branwen's lips parted in surprise.

Casek jerked his shoulders back, as he joined the circle. "But, Lady Queen, the temples already provide adequately for the sick."

"I don't believe they do," the True Queen replied.

He tapped the antler shard rapidly. Countess Kensa displayed no reaction. She watched the king, gaze artful. Was ambition enough to survive marriage to a man like Prince Edern? A cruel husband had been Branwen's greatest fear for her cousin. Brief, unwanted sympathy flared for Ruan's mother.

Marc looked between his wife and the seer. He tugged at the bristles on his chin.

"You have a gracious heart, my queen," he began, choosing his words carefully, like someone trying to avoid woodland snares. "We can certainly dedicate more resources to helping those in need. We could fund an expansion of the clinic at the temple in Marghas."

"There are many people who would find traveling to Marghas difficult, my Lord King," Eseult replied. "And it's far from the mines. It would be better to build an infirmary where it can help those who are most in need."

"And where would you suggest?" Seer Casek spoke too offhandedly to the woman who was his True Queen. King Marc shot him a dark look. "My queen," the *kordweyd* added.

"On the moors, near Seer Ogrin's temple." Eseult looked from Casek to Marc. It was a good suggestion. The True Queen had been shy and withdrawn on her official visits, not seeming to take much interest in her new kingdom. Branwen had underestimated her. Hope swelled that her cousin was starting to embrace her duties.

"Building a new infirmary would be costly," Casek appealed to the king.

"Seer Casek poses a valid concern," Countess Kensa said. "Especially since the nobles will struggle to pay their taxes this year with the new cost of labor." The countess's expression was as sweet as rotting meat.

"A valid concern," said Queen Verica, looking between Kensa and her son. "But not an insurmountable obstacle. I would be happy to donate a portion of my estate to the project."

"Queen Mother," said King Marc. "That is very generous."

"I can't take it with me when the Horned One calls me to be

judged," she said as she held her son's gaze. "The True Queen's project is an excellent idea."

"Thank you, Lady Queen." Eseult shifted her weight, taken aback at the support. "I would like Lady Branwen to oversee the plans."

Eseult's green eyes shone as she turned them on Branwen. "My cousin's birthday has just passed." She had remembered after all. "Lady Branwen always puts the needs of others above her own," she said, a hitch in her voice, and Branwen felt tightness in her chest. "My cousin is an expert healer and would do much good with a clinic of her own. I can think of no better gift for her—or for her patients."

Tears pricked Branwen's eyes. Love and gratitude diluted her anger. Despite everything, Eseult knew her better than anyone. Her cousin discerned the one thing that might bring Branwen joy. Lasting joy. More than a night in a lover's embrace. True fulfillment.

"Thank you," Branwen said to Eseult in Ivernic. Since they were girls, her cousin had apologized best with gifts. The gesture levered open the door in Branwen's heart, just a crack, but enough to let in the sun.

"I couldn't agree more," Queen Verica said, turning a cold stare on Seer Casek. "Lady Branwen is perhaps not aware that Matrona, the mother of Carnonos, was herself a healer. It's why *all* healers are beloved of the Horned One."

Branwen quirked her lips. "I wasn't aware, no."

"Yes, she was. Isn't that right, Seer Casek?" prodded Queen Verica.

"Yes, Queen Mother."

"Queen Eseult," said Queen Verica. "With my donation, I would like to request that Matrona be made the patroness of the new infirmary."

"I—" Eseult started, reluctant, and looked toward Branwen.

"I have no objection to that," Branwen said.

"Do you have any further objections, Seer Casek?" the Queen Mother said. The look in her eye reminded all present that her body might be frail, but she was still a queen. And a formidable one.

"No." A meager sound. Casek speared Branwen with a glance, and she knew this was far from the last of their battles.

"Stargazy pie! Stargazy pie!" Andred broke the fraught moment with a laugh. He hurried to Marc's side and held out a thickly crusted pie. Pilchard heads stuck out through the slats in the pastry, eyes glassy.

Taking a step toward Eseult, Andred said, "We call it Stargazy pie because the fish are gazing up at the stars. See!" He raised the pie up to the queen's nose, and she went completely green.

She lifted a hand over her mouth as if she were about to be ill. Panic lanced Branwen. The queen pushed the pie away with her other hand, and Andred's face fell.

"I'm—I'm sorry, Andred . . . I think—" Eseult's shoulders heaved. She made a gurgling sound and then broke into a sprint.

Branwen immediately followed. The True Queen of Kernyv raced down the beach, only stopping when she reached the water. She clutched at her stomach and then she began to retch.

Branwen pulled Eseult's braid away from her face. She shushed her, rubbing her back. When the queen was done, Branwen wiped a dab of spittle from the corner of her mouth.

"I don't know what happened," Eseult said, cheeks pinking with embarrassment. "The stench was just too much."

"Strange. You've always loved pilchards."

"I know. A lot of things have been making me feel ill lately. I don't know what it could be."

"This isn't the first time?" The queen shook her head. "Are you sure?" Branwen grabbed her elbow.

"Yes, I'm sure!" Her tone grew petulant, and panicked. "Why?"

"Have you had your monthly bleeding?" she asked her cousin in a whisper.

"My monthly—no, no . . ." Eseult's eyes rounded.

"When was the last time?"

"In Iveriu." Three moons ago.

"Eseult! Queen Eseult!" Tristan called out, rushing toward them headlong.

"Oh, Branny," said the True Queen. "I'm not—it was only once. I—I couldn't be . . . Am I?"

Branwen slanted her gaze at the man running through the sand.

"Pregnant," she said.

And the father was Tristan.

Branwen thought she might retch, herself. The wind whipped her face, and she heard the waves laugh.

ONWARD, ARMORICA

BRANWEN CLOSED HER EYES AS Senara carried her through the forest. She trusted her mount to stay on the path more than she trusted herself.

Blood and bone, forged by fire, we beseech you for the truest of desires.

The Queen of Iveriu's truest desire was that Eseult should bear a child that united Iveriu and Kernyv in one bloodline, one legitimate heir to both kingdoms. The birth of an heir would also put Eseult's status as True Queen of Kernyv beyond question.

Branwen shivered as if she had a fever.

The birth of a child who resembled the Queen's Champion rather than the queen's husband would mean war. War within Kernyv, and war between Kernyv and Iveriu. There would be no denying the evidence of their treason.

The second vision she'd had while casting the spell flooded Branwen's mind. She had seen Tristan drifting on the sea—the way she'd found him—and herself being tied to a pyre, set alight. She'd seen the Land wither and die.

"Taking a nap, Lady Branwen?"

Her eyes flipped open at Ruan's teasing voice. He spoke to her in Ivernic whenever it was just the two of them. His blond hair gleamed, messy in the breeze, as he guided his stallion alongside hers.

"It's been a busy few weeks," she said, fiddling with the reins.

"That it has. But things should calm down now." Branwen swallowed at Ruan's words. They were already in the midst of a storm he couldn't see. Involuntarily, her gaze was drawn to Tristan. He rode just behind Eseult and the king. All of the men had believed Branwen when she'd said the queen was suffering from simple indigestion.

Ruan leaned in her direction, halfway out of his saddle. "We'll soon have more free time for other pursuits," he told her.

"What pursuits would those be?" Branwen kept her tone light.

Dropping his voice, he promised, "Highly imaginative ones." The tip of his nose grazed her cheek before he pulled away. Tingles radiated from the spot.

On the wedding night, she'd foolishly hoped that the Mantle of Maidenhood would be the end of her many deceptions. Ruan was the King's Champion. Their loyalties would always be divided. No matter how much her cousin might hurt Branwen, she would never let any harm befall her. Letting Ruan get close to her was a risk Branwen shouldn't take.

"I think I'll have my hands full with the royal infirmary," she said.

"Yes, your cousin has a talent for getting her own way."

"Doesn't a queen always get her way?"

"Perhaps." He laughed. "Mother will be fuming all the way back to Illogan."

Branwen suspected as much. She was glad that Countess Kensa wasn't returning to Monwiku with them. Seer Casek had also, mercifully, departed separately for Marghas. Branwen glanced around the wood. Endelyn accompanied Queen Verica in the carriage trailing at the back of the convoy. Andred rode beside them on his steed, chatting away to Queen Verica. Endelyn ignored her younger brother as usual.

"Andred seems happy," Branwen noted. "I think he plans to teach Lowenek the name of every flower in the castle gardens."

A pensive expression came over Ruan's face. "He does. He likes being your apprentice, and he's never had many friends. My father . . ." He paused, and Branwen sensed protectiveness in him. "Edern didn't like having a cripple for a son, he said." His lips curled at the memory. "Andred was scarcely allowed to leave the villa until Marc appointed him his cupbearer. My father couldn't refuse a king's request."

Ruan glanced at Branwen, gauging her reaction. She was beginning to understand why he kept himself so well guarded with innuendo and cavalier statements.

"King Marc is a kind man," Branwen said.

Holding her gaze, Ruan said, "Does the queen think so, too?"

"Of course. They're getting to know each other—slowly." Branwen shifted her weight so that her shoulder touched his as their horses walked. "You're kind, too, Ruan. Despite your attempts to hide it."

He pulled back, trying to recapture her gaze. Ruan's voice was deep as he began, "Branwen—" Then abruptly, he broke off. He jerked his head forward, following something with his eyes.

"*Rix!*" he shouted.

This time Branwen heard it, too. The sound of an arrow whizzing through the air.

And another.

And another.

King Marc's stallion reared as an iron tip pierced its shoulder. The beast crashed back down to the ground, letting out an agonized cry. Marc rolled deftly from the horse's back before it could crush him.

"Get low," Ruan directed Branwen and galloped straight for his king.

Dread paralyzed her. This was how her parents had died. Ambushed.

Arrows continued to sail through the air, lodging in the trees with a wretched *thunk* sound. A woman's scream cut through her fear.

Eseult. Her cousin. Her *queen*. Branwen's right hand twitched. The urge to protect her cousin was violent, and Branwen's magic was more potent than a sword. But did she dare reveal it? Would the *kordweyd* condemn her powers?

In her moment of hesitation, she saw Tristan pull Eseult from her saddle onto his horse. Another arrow whirred through the air, striking the king's mount again, embedding in its left flank. "Marc!" Tristan yelled as Ruan charged his stallion in between the king's felled horse and the direction from which the arrows seemed to be coming—inland, east from the moors.

Praise the Old Ones, Eseult had been riding on the king's right. Marc shouted back at Tristan in Kernyvak. Even from a distance, Branwen could detect the anguish that contorted Tristan's face.

Marc's voice was furious, and the only word she understood was *Rixina*.

Queen.

Tristan's eyes were locked with his king's. A moment later, grimacing, he gripped Eseult tighter around the waist and kicked his steed into a gallop.

Tristan's first duty was to protect the queen—and that was what King Marc had ordered him to do.

Ruan brandished his sword, shielding the king with his body, as Tristan's horse disappeared between the trees.

The queen's mare whinnied, frightened, and took off after her mistress. Several more arrows pursued it.

Twisting around in her saddle, Branwen dashed a glance at Queen Verica and the others. The Royal Guardsmen driving the carriage had taken defensive positions around the Queen Mother and Endelyn. As had Andred, even though he didn't have a weapon.

No arrows were being launched at the back of the convoy. King Marc was the target.

Instincts taking over, Branwen urged Senara toward the king. Alarm spread across Ruan's face as he realized what she was doing. She kept her body low against her horse's neck.

"Stay back!" Ruan shouted at her. Branwen ignored him.

Another arrow zoomed toward the king. But this one came from the west.

Marc howled as it struck him in the right shoulder. A blossom of blood darkened his tunic. For less than one heartbeat, Branwen saw him as the boy he was—the boy who had ambushed her family in exactly the same way.

Resolve erased resentment. He was Branwen's king now, the Land's Consort. Her magic simmered beneath her skin, almost as if it recognized him.

Marc stumbled, his foot catching on a gnarled tree root, and he fell back against his writhing mount. All of Branwen's senses sharpened. The sounds of the forest grew crisper. The red of the king's blood and the blue of the sky became more vivid.

It was as if she'd once more passed through the Veil. Something dark, something that didn't belong caught her attention. Branwen squinted. A woman's shadow wavering between the trees to the west.

A skeleton dressed in flowing silk.

Chills erupted across Branwen's chest. This was a Death-Teller. The skull opened its mouth and began to sing: a bloodcurdling lament. The shriek stopped her heart.

No! Branwen wouldn't let the Death-Teller take the king. She yanked Senara's reins and steered her mount toward the Otherworld woman. Branwen had no weapon, but she hadn't needed a weapon to defeat the Shades. The Wise Damsel had been right.

Branwen was the weapon. The Hand of Bríga ended the Shades' living-death, and she prayed it could stop a Death-Teller. She would defend King Marc as she would defend the Land.

The Death-Teller floated toward Branwen at breathtaking speed. Branwen didn't let up on her mount's pace. Just as Senara was about to run down the Death-Teller, Branwen was blinded by a starburst of light. The palfrey balked.

"Branwen!" Ruan screamed. She turned her head toward him. He had leapt down from his horse. "Move!" Ruan shouted at her again. Vision still blurred with dark spots, Branwen didn't think she could trust her eyes as the Death-Teller dissolved and took on the form of a man.

"Onward, Armorica!" hollered the man, eyes wild.

Branwen recognized the Armorican motto—they were the only

Armorican words she knew. The man waved a dagger in jagged motions. He was perhaps forty summers, his white skin weather-beaten, dressed in fisherman's clothes.

When the steel caught the sun, it blinded Branwen again. Senara neighed in distress, hooves flying into the air.

The Armorican man dodged the hooves and sprinted toward King Marc. Ruan raised his sword, planting his feet in front of the king. Marc had regained his footing, but he was cradling his shoulder. Branwen jumped down from her horse and ran after the Armorican.

She managed to grasp the tail of his tunic, throwing him off balance just as his dagger clashed against Ruan's sword. He wheeled on Branwen.

The Armorican's expression changed from aggression to fear. She looked down at her hand. A flame danced on her palm. Her heart line had turned black.

He regarded her the same way that the captain of Dhusnos's Shades had during the assault on the *Dragon Rising*. When Branwen had looked at the Armorican, she had seen a Death-Teller.

What did he see when he looked at Branwen?

Thankfully, his body blocked Ruan's view of her flame. The King's Champion wasted no time in using the man's distraction to his advantage. He bashed the Armorican over the head with the flat of his sword.

The man pivoted to defend himself, and Ruan cracked the pommel of his sword against the Armorican's temple. The dagger went limp in his hand and slid to the ground as he keeled over.

Branwen's flame vanished. Ruan took two predatory steps toward the unconscious man. He pressed the tip of his sword to the Armorican's throat.

"Stop!" Branwen barked. She dropped to her knees beside the man. She pressed two fingers below his jaw. "He's still alive."

"Yes, that's what I'm trying to correct." Ruan was breathing hard. "I know you're a healer. But this man doesn't deserve your mercy."

"Mercy?" She looked up at Ruan. "This isn't about mercy. We need him alive so he can be interrogated."

"Branwen speaks wisely," Marc said, hissing against the pain. He pushed himself to standing and walked toward his attacker. Surveying him, he said, "He'll be unconscious for a while. Bind his hands and feet, and we'll take him back to the castle."

Ruan glanced around them. "We don't know how many there are."

"No," the king agreed. "But we need to find out." He and his Champion argued with their eyes. The forest was silent. Whoever the man's accomplice was must have run off when he was captured.

Branwen approached Marc, touching a gentle hand to the elbow of his injured arm. He gritted his teeth. She panned her gaze along the shaft of the arrow; its head was firmly lodged inside the flesh.

"I need to remove the arrowhead. But I'd prefer to do it with all of my surgical instruments."

Marc showed her a half smile. "I think I'd prefer that as well."

Branwen stooped down to pick up the Armorican's dagger. Closing her palm around the handle, she noticed her scar had returned to white. The king looked from the knife to Branwen's face.

"I don't think I'd survive your attack," Marc told her. He wheezed a laugh. The king had no idea that she could have ended his life on his wedding night. How close Branwen came to surrendering to her darkest impulses.

Ruan snorted. "I don't think anyone could, *Rix*."

Branwen huffed a breath. "I need to trim the shaft of the arrow so it doesn't cause more damage on the journey back to Monwiku."

"Of course," said Marc.

"Ruan, your sash." Branwen held out her other hand, and he laughed as he pulled it over his head. "I'm going to need to have more of these made," he remarked.

The king's maimed stallion released another doleful cry, discordant against Ruan's laughter. Tying the sash tightly around Marc's upper arm, Branwen told him, "This should stem the bleeding until we reach the castle."

"*Mormerkti*," he replied.

King Marc turned toward his mount, sadness rinsing his features as his eyes swept over the beast's wounds.

"He's in pain," he said to Ruan. His Champion nodded, expression becoming solemn. He kneeled beside the horse and used his sword to slit its throat.

The immediate quiet made the air heavy. After several moments, Marc put his lips together in a whistle that sounded like a birdcall.

Branwen raised her eyebrows in question. "It's a signal Tristan and I made up as boys," the king explained. "To let each other know that we're safe. The danger's passed."

She lifted the dagger and began sawing through the shaft of the arrow.

ALL THAT WE ARE

THE PALE LAVENDER OF TWILIGHT streamed through the windows of the king's study. Branwen rushed in without knocking, healing kit under her arm.

"*Nosmatis*," she said. The king was seated at the table toward the back of the room. Pain was etched into the line of his jaw.

The return journey to Monwiku had been slowed by the pace of the carriage. Marc had sent Tristan on ahead with the queen, but Branwen insisted the king travel with his mother to avoid jostling the arrow.

"Queen Eseult is resting comfortably?" King Marc said as Branwen neared. His brows were drawn. "I promised her she'd be safe in Kernyv."

At this very moment, the would-be assassin was being transported by Ruan and the other guards to the dungeon.

"She's fine. Unnerved, but fine. Endelyn is with her. And Tristan." In truth, Branwen hadn't had time to look after her cousin. "The queen has an aversion to blood, but she's thinking of you."

One corner of Marc's mouth lifted. Dropping her satchel onto the table beside him, Branwen scanned him with her healer's eye. Luckily there were no outward signs that the arrows had been poisoned.

"Are you feeling hot?" she asked.

"No." He shook his head.

Branwen lifted her hand to check for herself but hesitated before pressing it to his forehead. "May I?"

"Treat me like any other patient."

As her skin made contact with his, Branwen swallowed a lump in her throat. She hadn't been alone with the king since she'd lain beside him in his marriage bed. She feared that she might somehow trigger a memory, that he might suddenly realize it had been her with whom he'd spoken in the dark, but he gave no sign of it.

The king's brow felt a normal temperature. Branwen exhaled. "Infection is the worst complication from an arrow wound," she said.

"I know. I've seen." He didn't need to explain it had been while raiding.

"As have I."

Marc nodded. "Tristan told me you work miracles. I know I'm safe in your hands."

Just how much had Tristan disclosed about how he'd survived the poison-tipped spear? Branwen cast her eyes to the blood-soaked tunic. A short section of the arrow's shaft still protruded from his right shoulder. She removed Ruan's sash and tore at the fabric of the sleeve with her fingers, but the tunic was made from thick wool.

Retrieving a slender blade from her bag, Branwen sliced through the fabric around the wound. The sound of ripping filled the room. She cut the sleeve free and exposed the sea-wolf tattoo on King Marc's forearm.

She couldn't help but purse her lips. Marc noticed. "Wolves of the sea," he said. "I know that's how the Iverni view us. And, it would seem, the Armoricans, too. Is that all that we are?"

Their eyes met. Branwen had posed the same question to herself many, many times.

"I think that depends on you, my Lord King."

His face darkened. She saw grief there. "I got this tattoo when I was Andred's age. Before my first raid." Branwen couldn't breathe as Marc spoke. "Our bards sing of glory in battle. They don't sing of the hollow that grows inside you when you take a life—of how it's never refilled."

The king blanched. "Forgive me, Lady Branwen." His lips quirked. "I didn't mean to—to . . . unburden myself with you. The pain must be addling my mind."

She broke his gaze. "I'm going to feel around the entry point," Branwen told him, focusing on the task before her. The arrow was embedded in the muscle at the top of the shoulder. She needed to determine if the head had pierced the bone.

Marc hissed as Branwen twirled the arrowhead. "Your god has favored you," she announced. "The tip failed to spear the bone. If I enlarge the wound, I should be able to slide it free."

King Marc gave a soft laugh. "I think the Horned One favored me with your presence, my lady. If you hadn't seen the assassin, I might yet be on the forest floor. I don't know how you spotted him."

Branwen inhaled. She didn't understand how she'd seen the assassin, either. Not truly. It was as if the Otherworld had layered itself over this one, like when she was on Whitethorn Mound.

This was different from the fox or the blackbirds she had seen in Iveriu. The Wise Damsel was the only person Branwen knew who might have answers. She'd been avoiding her, but she could stay away no longer.

"I won't soon forget that you put yourself in harm's way for me, Lady Branwen," Marc said, tilting closer. "But, why? I wouldn't blame you if you agreed with the Armoricans."

She met his probing stare. "You're my king. My cousin's husband. I am loyal to you. Iveriu's fate is now tied to yours."

He drew in a heavy breath at her statement. "Yes. We are all of us bound together." Taking Branwen's hand in his, Marc turned it over and nodded his chin at the scar from the wedding ceremony. "You have bled for me, Lady Branwen. Believe me, I would bleed for you."

"I do." The flesh of her palm tingled as she realized she truly did. "I believe you. But I hope it doesn't come to that," Branwen said as she withdrew her hand from his. "I'm going to give you something to dull the pain. It won't be pleasant when I remove the arrowhead. You may feel woozy."

She turned toward the table and began to search her satchel. Marc released another groan.

Her hand closed around a vial of ground *derew* root. Without the other ingredients she'd used to prepare Medhua's tears, the root would solely numb Marc's mind to the pain in his body.

A decanter of Mílesian spirits and several goblets rested on a sideboard. With precise movements, Branwen poured the spirits into a glass and added the *derew* root.

"Here," Branwen said to the king. "Drink." Marc put the goblet to his lips with the same trust as he had on the night of the wedding.

Perhaps it was guilt that led Branwen to confess, "I understand the hollowness."

Marc finished the spirits and set down the goblet. He waited for her to continue.

"I killed a man once. In Iveriu. I was defending myself."

"A Kernyvman?" he asked.

"No."

His posture loosened, either in relief or from the effects of the *derew* root.

"I'm sure it was justified," Marc said. "But I'm sorry you feel the hollowness, too."

"It's a hungry kind of empty," she said.

"It is." The king sighed. "I didn't expect Prince Kahedrin to make good on his threats so soon."

Neither had Branwen.

A knock came at the door. "Enter," said the king. Tristan's face appeared in the entrance. He looked from the protruding arrow to Branwen and walked toward them. "How is he?"

"I'm about to take the arrow out," she replied.

"Can I help?"

"No—yes." Branwen changed her mind when she saw how the king was slumping in his chair. "Lift him onto the table for me."

Coming to stand beside her, Tristan said, "How are *you*?" His dark eyes searched her. She felt them as keenly as if he were touching her.

Many responses ran through Branwen's head. "Uninjured," was all she said.

"In the forest, she was fearless," Marc told him, his words slurring slightly, eyes dilated.

A smile wavered on Tristan's face. "I don't doubt it."

"Help the king up," Branwen said, unsmiling. His smile vanished as well.

Tristan was lifting Marc to his feet when the door banged all the way open and Ruan strode toward them. "The prisoner is secure," he reported.

"*Mormerkti*," said the king. He blinked rapidly.

Ruan skidded to a stop before Marc. "Here, let me—"

"I've got him," Tristan interrupted, rebuffing his cousin, as the king sagged against him.

"He's not your responsibility," snarled Ruan. "Go back to the queen."

"The queen is safe, and Marc is my brother," Tristan told him. "How did you let an assassin get so close to him?"

Ruan shrunk back as if the other man had struck him. Marc looked from Ruan to Branwen. "Red-hot ashes," the king murmured. "It's what you said to me in the garden." His thoughts had started to skip like a stone across a brook. "We still haven't played Little Soldiers."

His gaze slid toward the *fidkwelsa* board in the corner of the room. "I have a feeling you'll beat me."

"For Otherworld's sake," Branwen exclaimed at the two Champions. "*Both* of you, lift the king onto the table!"

Bristling, Ruan knelt down and grabbed King Marc's feet. "Be careful," Branwen warned. She moved her satchel to the sideboard together with the candelabra that had already been lit for the coming evening.

With extreme caution, Tristan and Ruan set their king on the long wooden table.

"Hold him down," she ordered them.

"I won't move," Marc tried to protest, the words growing more sluggish. Tristan looked to Branwen; she shook her head.

"What did you give him?" Ruan asked.

"Something for the pain," Branwen said, flustered.

"Branwen is very skilled at potions," Tristan told him.

"I know how skilled the lady is."

Tristan looked between Branwen and Ruan, brow creasing.

"Do it now," Branwen ordered the Champions in a furious whisper. Tristan pinned one of Marc's arms to the table, and Ruan pinned the other. Branwen picked up the same slender blade and held it to the candle's flame. She grimaced as heat traveled down to the handle.

She pressed the tip of the blade to Marc's shoulder, just above the entry point, and made an incision the length of a knuckle. Then she repeated the procedure beneath it.

Fresh blood began to stream from the wound. Marc grunted and Branwen dashed a glance at his face. His eyes were closed, his breathing deep. She'd given him a very liberal dose of *derew* root. The knife made a clattering sound as she laid it on the sideboard.

Tristan and Ruan watched her avidly. The love that both men had for their king was fierce. Ruan tensed as Branwen wrapped her hand around the shaft of the arrow.

Gently, she levered it back and forth, trying to pry the arrowhead loose.

The king was lucky to have received only one arrow wound. Most well-trained archers could shoot more than ten in a matter of minutes.

With the same gliding motion as she would pull a needle through a piece of embroidery, she dislodged the arrowhead.

She stared at the blood-covered steel. Such a small thing—the size of her pinkie finger—and it had the power to destroy three kingdoms.

"You did it," Tristan said, exhaling with relief. Ruan met her eyes and his shone with gratitude.

"I still need to stitch up the wound." Branwen dropped the

arrowhead on the sideboard and plucked a salve that prevented infection from her satchel. She rubbed it into the wound, Marc's blood covering her fingers. The scent of the salve was fresh.

Branwen poured some of the Mílesian spirits over her hands. Ruan gave a small laugh. "I believe that vintage was a gift from the King of Míl himself," he said.

She shrugged. "Tristan, your sash," she said.

Tristan removed it immediately. As the Queen's Champion, his sash was embroidered with the standards of both Iveriu and Kernyv. Branwen used it to dry her hands. Smearing the lion and the sea-wolf with the king's blood.

"I will need clean bandages when I'm done stitching up the wound," Branwen said, avoiding Tristan's eyes, and rummaged in her satchel for a needle and thread. "Can you find something in the castle laundry?"

His boots clicked on the stone, and she only turned back to her patient when she heard the door close.

The king groaned as Branwen began to sew his flesh together with the same love-knots she had used on Tristan. Sweat beaded on her top lip as she worked. Her own shoulders and neck began to ache from the meticulous work. Finally, she tied off the last knot. She rolled her shoulders as she inspected her web of stitches.

"Marc's going to be all right," Ruan asked in a quiet voice.

"The herbs I gave him for the pain will likely make him sleep through the night," Branwen told him. "It will be safe to move him to his bed once I've bandaged the shoulder."

Ruan nodded. "Thank you, Branwen." The look on his face was one of misery. "I'll treble the guard outside the king's chamber. Andred, too, I suspect, will insist on standing watch. The scamp's furious with me for ordering him to stay with the Queen Mother. I didn't want him getting in your way."

"Andred is very capable."

Ruan's expression grew even grimmer. "Then I'm sorry I kept him from helping." He ran a hand through his now-matted locks. "I'm failing everyone today."

"You didn't fail anyone, Ruan. The king is still alive."

"Tristan was right. The assassin never should have got so close."

Branwen put down the needle. She placed a hand on his elbow. "Tristan was wrong. He did his duty and you did yours."

"I should have taken Kahedrin's threats more seriously."

"We can't be certain it was him."

"Of course it's him. Who else could it be? The assassin proclaimed it himself."

"But doesn't that strike you as strange? Why send an assassin to murder a foreign king and let his people know whom they should invade? It doesn't make sense."

"I know you liked Kahedrin, Branwen. But Marc's death only serves Armorica."

Branwen flattened her lips. Could it be that Ruan was unaware of the threats from within Kernyv that King Marc had spoken about on the wedding night?

"We'll find out when he's regained consciousness, I suppose," she said.

Ruan's face softened somewhat. "Branwen, about before, with Tristan. I'm sorry. I would never do anything to compromise your honor."

She stepped toward him. "Do you think I've compromised my honor, Ruan? By making you my lover?"

Ruan pushed one of Branwen's loose curls behind her ear. "Today you fought an assassin with your bare hands. You saved my king." He stroked the edge of her ear with his thumb. "I'm in awe of your honor."

He tilted forward until Branwen felt his breath on her face. She wanted nothing more than to lean into him.

"I won't use what we have as a weapon against Tristan. It's beneath me."

"Thank you."

The door creaked open. Branwen and Ruan split apart as Tristan returned. Cheeks burning, she blew out a large breath. Branwen bandaged King Marc's shoulder while he slept, and then the two Champions carried him to his bedchamber.

She would have preferred to stay with the king, but she retreated toward the Queen's Tower. Branwen and her cousin had many things to discuss, and she had no inkling where to start.

She would rather face another Death-Teller.

THE WORLD YOU THOUGHT YOU LIVED IN

ARTHEK BARKED FROM QUEEN ESEULT'S lap as Branwen pushed open the door to the royal apartment. Her cousin sat at the window, expression weary, picking at a plate of cured meats. For a moment, Eseult resembled her mother completely.

Quieting the puppy with a kiss atop his wrinkled head, Eseult said, "How's the king?"

"Sleeping. I removed the arrow. He'll recover," Branwen replied, and her cousin nodded, face brightening a smidge. She crossed toward the queen, stretching her shoulders. "He was more concerned for your safety," she said.

Eseult stroked Arthek between his ears, her chest deflating further. "He's been very attentive. Considerate."

"He has. You should visit him in the morning. I think—I think he would make a steadfast friend."

"I will. I was worried, but I knew you'd heal him." The queen lifted her eyes to her cousin as Branwen took the seat opposite hers. "In the forest, I was so scared for you, Branny. I told Tristan to go back for you but he . . . wouldn't."

The flame of a beeswax candle flickered on the windowsill. Outside, night had stolen over the sea. "Tristan was following the king's orders," Branwen said.

"But he's the Queen's Champion and I wanted him to save you."

"Tristan will always choose the queen first." Branwen swallowed. "He must. It's his duty to his kingdom."

"*You* matter more to me than any kingdom," said her cousin.

"But I shouldn't."

"Not you without me," Eseult said stubbornly. With a sigh, Branwen answered, "Not me without you."

Her cousin coiled a flaxen strand around her finger. "Are you— are you pleased about the infirmary?" She gave Branwen a small, hopeful smile, with a hint of mischief. It reminded her of the times her cousin would fill Master Bécc's inkwells with honey.

"I am. We'll create a bit of Iveriu in Kernyv."

Eseult nodded in satisfaction. Taking a breath, Branwen steeled herself and said, "We need to talk about what happened at the festival."

The queen cast her eyes downward. "There's blood on your sleeve. Would you like me to have a bath drawn?"

"Perhaps later."

"You must be hungry." She pushed the plate of untouched food across the table toward Branwen. "I don't have much of an appetite."

"Eseult." Branwen glanced around them. "Where's Endelyn?"

"I sent her away. I wanted to be alone." The queen gripped the strand of hair tighter. "But I don't think I could be pregnant, Branny," she said in a whisper. "It's probably just indigestion, like you told the king." Her cousin gathered Arthek closer to her breast, clutching the puppy as if it could protect her from the truth.

Leaning across the table, Branwen said, "Men have very little understanding of women's bodies." Although she wondered whether Queen Verica or Countess Kensa might suspect the cause of Eseult's nausea.

In a cajoling tone, she asked, "Do you remember precisely when you had your last bleeding?"

"I—I think it was the week of the Farewell Feast."

"King Marc hasn't shared your bed since the wedding." It was more of a statement than a question, but Branwen had to be certain. She hadn't seen the king visit the Queen's Tower at all.

"No." Eseult pressed her lips together. "He said—he said he would wait to be invited. The king is kind to me, Branny. But I don't love him." She scratched Arthek between his ears. "I wish I could."

The hungry emptiness Branwen had spoken of with Marc expanded inside her. If there had been no Loving Cup, might Eseult have learned to appreciate Marc for his own qualities?

"You have time to get to know him," Branwen said, but observing her cousin, she noticed her cheeks were a little fuller than normal. They had arrived in Kernyv slightly less than three moons ago. In a few weeks, the queen's condition would become apparent to the untrained eye.

She dragged her chair closer to the queen's. "Essy," she began. Since the wedding night, Branwen had used her cousin's title as a weapon, but she couldn't do that anymore. If not for the Loving Cup, Essy wouldn't be facing impossible choices. Guilt threatened to devour Branwen like a wolf.

"Essy," she repeated. She traced the symbol for hazel on her cousin's hand. "I can fix this," Branwen told her. "No one ever need know you were pregnant."

The queen's lips trembled.

"There are herbs that will bring on your bleeding," she explained. "They'll make you ill for a few days, but it will pass."

Eseult lurched back in her chair. Arthek leapt from her lap in protest, letting out a small whimper.

"Branny, no. I can't." She dropped a hand to her belly. "This is Tristan's child."

Branwen dug her fingernails into her palms as surprise turned to terror. She had assumed the queen would be relieved. "I know, Essy. But he's not your husband," she said. How could her cousin not see the danger they were both in?

The danger Branwen had put them in.

"I'll stay by your side the whole time," she promised Eseult. "Don't be scared."

The queen squeezed her eyes shut for a moment. She traced her belly in concentric circles.

"What Tristan and I shared, it was joyful. More joy than I thought I'd ever know."

Branwen allowed herself a few steadying breaths. "If you give birth to Tristan's child, you will both be executed as traitors," she said. "The child will likely be put to death. Kernyv will be plunged into civil war and Iveriu along with it. I don't want to lose you—*please*."

"This isn't fair," Eseult rasped, tears springing to her eyes. "Every choice has been taken away from me."

Her words enlarged the hollow inside Branwen, a void in which lay only darkness. Fate had taken away her cousin's choices, but so had Branwen.

"I'm sorry. I know it's not fair. But, Essy, do you even want to be a mother?" she said softly. She reached for her hand again. "You've always hated the idea."

"I don't know. I didn't before," Eseult admitted. "I didn't want my sole value to be producing heirs." She pulled at the fabric over her stomach. "But now . . . this is different. Being with Tristan, it wasn't because I was useful. It wasn't because of politics. And he—he would be a loving father."

In the back of her mind, Branwen heard a low keening. Having a family of her own had never been a goal; she had always thought her place would be by her cousin's side when she became queen. Perhaps it had been fear, too, of orphaning someone else. Tristan had been the first man to make her reconsider.

"One day, Tristan will get the chance," Branwen said. "But he can't know you're pregnant. Not ever." Her voice grew harder with each word. "Tristan would die to protect you. There would be no stopping him from lying to King Marc about what happened between you— from saying he forced himself on you. Marc would have no choice but to put him to death."

Eseult moaned and rested her head against Branwen's shoulder. "You're right," she whispered. "He would. We can't tell him."

Branwen edged closer. She stroked her cousin's back as she wept.

"Oh, Branny. I don't want this to be true. I've tried so hard to pretend that Tristan is nothing but my bodyguard. I just . . . carrying his child, it doesn't *feel* wrong."

"In another world, it wouldn't be, perhaps," Branwen said, tongue growing thick. "But you are who you are, and he is who he is. Your love was never meant to be."

Eseult pulled back. "I don't know if I can believe that."

Desperation burned through Branwen's guilt. "Essy, I know this is a hard thing. We've both done hard things for peace."

Her thoughts spiraled. It couldn't all have been for nothing. If the True Queen gave birth to a child born too early to be King Marc's, who looked like the king's nephew, both Tristan and Essy would be sentenced to death. No matter the hurt they had caused each other, Branwen didn't want to live in a world without her cousin.

Eseult tugged at her scalp. "Why is everything always taken away from me?"

"I'm still here."

Tears dripping down her cheeks, she nodded. "I—I need time. Time to think." She swiped at them. "Maybe you're mistaken, Branny. Maybe my bleeding will come naturally."

"Maybe," Branwen allowed. She watched the conflicting emotions on her cousin's face: both hope and fear that she wasn't carrying Tristan's child.

"I'll prepare Ériu's Comfort for you, Essy, and then you *will* have a choice." She cupped her cousin's cheek. "You won't have to do it alone. I'll be here, whatever you decide." Branwen knew what she would choose, what the safest choice was, but it was not her body. If Eseult chose not to take the herbs, Branwen would find a way to protect her—and Iveriu—somehow.

Eseult nodded again. She glanced toward the darkened sea outside.

"I think I need to sleep."

There was a chill to her cousin's words. A lifetime had taught Branwen that further talking would do no good tonight.

"Rest well," Branwen said, and kissed Essy's brow.

The last thing Branwen could do was sleep. She exited the Queen's

Tower in a rush and nearly lost her footing on the last stone step. She caught herself before flying into Tristan's arms.

"Lady Branwen?"

"The queen is fine. I'm going to check on the king."

Tristan's shoulders immediately relaxed. "Thank you for what you did today." He dared a step closer and lowered his voice. "Did you have to use your magic on Marc?"

Branwen wet her lips, eyes falling to the Hand of Bríga. "No," she said. "The wound didn't require it."

"You would have, though, to save him."

Tristan's gaze fixed onto a few snowy strands amidst the raven-black that Branwen had tucked behind her ears. It didn't matter how often she plucked them. Since the Shades' attack, the hairs always grew back white.

"Yes, I would have. I've come to agree with you, Prince Tristan," Branwen told him. "King Marc is a good ruler. A fair one. I wouldn't let him die."

"I always told you how alike you and Marc were," Tristan said, almost smiling, but not happily.

"You did." Inhaling, she said, "I'm—I'm glad you weren't hurt," and stepped past him.

"Wait." Tristan touched a tentative hand to her elbow, then dropped it. "*Bran*—Lady Branwen, I've accepted that you can't forgive me. You will never look at me the same way and I will learn to live with that."

Branwen bit her lip. She had also caused him great harm—and she was keeping yet another secret from him this very instant.

Tristan straightened his spine. "All I hope is that we might become allies once again." She recognized the determination in his stance, in the set of his jaw.

"Allies are hard to come by," she said.

"Especially at court."

He held her with his eyes. Branwen darted a glance up the stairwell, toward where Endelyn dwelled. She tugged at Tristan's tunic, pulling him through the archway into the courtyard.

"Ruan thinks the assassin was sent by Prince Kahedrin," Branwen told him in a whisper.

"You don't?" he said, confused. "He declared he was doing it for Armorica. Everyone heard him."

"I'm aware. But when I spoke with Kahedrin at the wedding, he seemed like a man who wanted to stop his people from being attacked. Not someone who would provoke an all-out war by assassinating Kernyv's king."

"There's been tension with Armorica for some time." Tristan ran a hand through his curls; Branwen used to love that gesture.

"I know. Still, not all of the barons are happy about the alliance with Iveriu. There are, perhaps, others who could benefit from a Kernyv in chaos."

"The person who has the most to gain by King Marc's death is the queen—followed by me," Tristan told her.

"What do you mean?"

He lowered his voice further. "Eseult is the True Queen now. She would remain sovereign in the event of Marc's death. And, after Eseult, I am the next-in-line since they don't yet have a child. Not that the nobles would let me take the throne without a fight," Tristan said in a rush. "House Dynyon resents that their lands in Liones were given to my mother, and Baron Gwyk dislikes anyone not of *pure* Kernyvak blood." His lip curled.

Branwen pressed a hand to her heart. If anyone ever discovered

Tristan and Eseult had conceived a child together . . . it was more disastrous than she had even imagined.

"Why can't the king control the pirates?" Branwen asked.

"My grandfather used to fund them in exchange for a percentage of the . . . spoils." He swallowed. "It allowed him a degree of control. Marc refused to continue staking their raids. Now he only controls the Royal Fleet."

By trying to do the right thing, King Marc may have brought his kingdom to the verge of war.

"There's something amiss here, Tristan. I don't know what it is." Branwen let herself meet his eyes. "Ruan's guilt is clouding his judgment. If you're sincere about us being allies, you will counsel the king caution. I don't want Iveriu swept up in another war."

"I *am* sincere, Branwen," he said, switching into Ivernic for the first time in weeks. "I don't want war for either of our kingdoms. I—*we* have already done so much for peace."

She could see how heavily Tristan's betrayal of Marc weighed on him, left dark smudges beneath his eyes. The betrayals clawed at Branwen, too, as if there were a beast beneath her skin. Scratching, always scratching, clamoring to get out.

"We have. We're so close. Let's try being allies," Branwen replied in Ivernic. The corners of her mouth flickered. "Thank you, Tristan. I'll go see to the king's bandages."

"Branwen—" he said, and she stopped mid-step. "I see how Ruan looks at you. You may not think I'm in a position to judge, but I don't want to see you get hurt."

"Like you hurt me?"

"Yes." It was guttural. "Like I hurt you."

"You once said I deserved some happiness of my own." Branwen canted her head. A gust of wind teased her loosened plaits. "You don't get to tell me where to find it."

"I'm not. That's not—"

"Ruan told me he gave you that scar." She skimmed it with her forefinger. "What did you do to warrant it?"

"I'd rather not say."

"*Nosmatis*, Prince Tristan."

✟ ✟ ✟

Eight guards were posted outside the king's bedchamber. It would require a small army to breach. Inside, Branwen found Andred and Ruan. King Marc's chest was rising and falling at a steady pace. The king's canopy bed was very similar to the queen's, but the rest of the furnishings were sparse. As if he'd only just moved in.

"I've checked the bandage," Andred informed her. "No pus. Just blood."

Branwen gave her apprentice a tired smile. "Well done." She swayed slightly on her feet. Ruan's brow crinkled. He rounded the bed and stood next to her.

Ruan stroked Branwen's upper arm. "You look weary."

"I'm flattered."

He grinned. "Andred, I'm going to take Lady Branwen to find some refreshment."

"I'll be here if the king needs anything," the boy said earnestly. Ruan ushered Branwen past the guards to find refreshment—in his chambers on the ground floor of the tower.

"I thought you had retired to the Queen's Tower for the evening," he said as he filled two goblets with wine.

"I was restless," Branwen said. The settee in the center of the room was large enough for two. Branwen flung a spare tunic that was draped across it onto the floor and sank against its maroon velvet cushions.

"That tunic was clean, Lady Branwen," Ruan said with faux-admonishment. He handed her a silver goblet.

"Was it?" She accepted the goblet and took a sip, trying not to sneeze. She'd almost become accustomed to the spice the Kernyveu put in their wine. Almost.

Ruan shrugged. "Maybe not." He laughed and drank from his own goblet, ensconcing himself beside her. They drank in silence for a minute or two. Then, gently, he traced the slope of Branwen's cheek. "What's making you restless?"

"Besides the obvious?"

"Besides the obvious." Ruan fixed his eyes on hers. Tonight, in the light of the oil lamps, they were a less brilliant topaz. More mellow, like thick honey.

"In Iveriu," Branwen began, "Eseult and I lived in the same tower. But I had my own rooms. When that wasn't far enough, I had a favorite cave." She took a sip of wine, putting the man she'd shared it with far from her mind.

"Ah. I see." Ruan pressed the goblet to his lips. "Growing up, when I was restless, I would escape to the mines. The land around Villa Illogan is depleted now. As a boy, I preferred the fields to being cooped up indoors."

"Is that how you learned Ivernic? From the miners?"

"Mostly." He nodded. "Branwen, whenever you need a place to escape—feel free to come here."

Not knowing what to reply, Branwen kissed Ruan, feather-light, on the lips. He kissed her back fiercely. She became liquid fire.

Ruan's goblet clinked as he set it on the stone floor; then he plucked Branwen's from her hand as well. Ravenous fingertips caressed the outline of her torso. She released a soft moan before rapping at the door startled her.

"What is it?" Ruan yelled. A male voice replied in Kernyvak.

Branwen looked up in alarm. "It's all right," Ruan assured her. "Nothing to do with the king. Just something I need to deal with." He kissed her again, nipping her lower lip. "Stay—will you stay? I'll be right back."

She shouldn't. She really shouldn't. But Branwen was too worn out to go anywhere else. "I'll stay," she said.

He smiled at her like he did the first time she called him just Ruan. He dashed another kiss on her forehead and leapt to his feet. When he was gone, Branwen's eyelids fluttered and before she knew it she was asleep.

Sometime later, she became aware of a warm embrace, of strong arms lifting her and laying her atop a bed. "Good morning," Branwen said dreamily.

Ruan laughed. "Not quite morning yet."

"Oh, good," she said.

He laughed again and stroked her brow. "You can keep sleeping."

Ruan pulled his tunic over his head and threw it on the floor. Unable to stop herself, Branwen reached out and brushed the back of her hand against the finely packed muscles of his abdomen. He let out a groan.

"Did that hurt?" she said, perplexed.

"Only in a good way." He lay down on the bed, turning onto his side to face her. "I think we could both do with some sleep." Ruan gave her a wicked grin. "I want you to experience me at my best."

"I thought you told me you were never a disappointment."

Ruan stroked her cheek, sobering. "You're the first woman I'm afraid I might disappoint." He held her gaze, and she felt a pinch in her chest.

"I asked Tristan why you gave him his scar," she said. "He wouldn't tell me."

"Branwen," he said, inhaling her name. "I'll tell you—if you'll tell me what's between you and Tristan. From the moment you stepped off the ship, I've known there was something."

Her thoughts whirred. So many lies, too many. So many shades of truth that Branwen had become color-blind. "There might have been something between us, under different circumstances," she told Ruan. "Now, we're allies. We serve the same queen."

"Allies," Ruan said. "Nothing more?"

Branwen rolled onto her back and stared up at the canopy. It was a green so dark it was nearly black.

"Sometimes you wake up and the world you thought you lived in is gone."

Ruan twirled one of her curls around his pinkie, considering her words. Branwen snuggled into the crook of his arm and traced her finger around his belly button.

"Tristan caught my father beating me," he said. Immediately, she darted her eyes to his. "I was twelve. Tristan about eight. He threatened to tell."

"Tell who?"

"I don't know." A regretful laugh. "I just knew it would be worse for me if he did. And I was twelve—I thought I was a man, that I should be able to take it."

"Did your mother know?" Branwen said, gentle.

His eyes grew unfocused. "There was nothing she could do. I'd rather he hit me." Branwen kissed his shoulder. Ruan inhaled. "I found Tristan, and I punched him, threatening him with worse if he told. He fell and cut his face on a flagstone."

Ruan twirled and untwirled Branwen's curl. She let the silence surround them.

"I became my father in that moment," he said. Gazing down at her, he said, "I swore to myself that I never would again. And I haven't. I *won't*."

She propped herself up on her elbow. "I know you won't. I don't see that rage in you." Branwen had seen it in Keane, even before he had turned it against her.

"When the Armorican attacked Marc, all I felt was rage," Ruan said quietly.

She stroked the line of soft, pink scar tissue that traveled across his collarbone.

"You are not your father, Ruan."

He wrapped his hand around her neck and pulled her into a kiss that was deep, yet gentle as the spring rains that brought the buds to life.

His breath on her lips, Branwen said, "Why do you and Tristan still dislike each other? That was years ago."

"I was . . . vicious to him for a long while after that. I was scared he might change his mind and tell. I feared what he thought of me and my father. I felt ashamed every time I saw the scar, saw what I was capable of." Ruan sighed. "And I was jealous. Queen Verica has always adored him, as did King Merchion. I was closer in age to Marc, but Tristan is his brother. His best friend. I'm not proud of my behavior."

"You must have been hurt when he chose Tristan as King's Champion."

He gave her a chagrined smile. "Furious. I thought I deserved it. But I failed him today so perhaps he was right to appoint Tristan."

"We all underestimated the threat, Ruan. If you failed the king, then so did I. And I failed my queen, too."

"You fought like a Champion, Branwen. And you didn't even have a weapon," he said. Her heart panged. Could she ever reveal her magic to Ruan? She feared what his mother or Seer Casek would do with the knowledge.

"Although I might wish you weren't so brave," Ruan added, kissing her ear. "Most Champions don't die gray-haired in their sleep."

"But then I wouldn't fascinate you."

"You do more than fascinate me." He drew Branwen back against his chest. "I've never told anyone any of this." Shaking his head, Ruan said, "You must be a healer, because I feel better when I'm with you."

"I feel better when I'm with you, too."

The shadows from the lamplight flickered as the oil ran out.

Branwen was lulled to sleep by the thump of Ruan's heart.

WAYS OF SEEING

THE STREAM GURGLED BENEATH A TINKLING OF BELLS.
Branwen had sensed the dawn and left Ruan sleeping. She
had been selfish to seek out his company last night. She knew it—
she knew it, and yet she could only half regret it.

She had just lifted her hand to knock when the door to the Wise
Damsel's cottage flew open.

"*Enigena*," said Ailleann, expression severe. Cloudy sunlight accen-
tuated the wrinkles around her eyes.

"Greetings," Branwen said. "Seer Ogrin said you were asking
after me."

"A couple of moons ago."

The Wise Damsel turned on her heel and retreated inside the
cottage.

She left the door open.

Branwen hesitated on the threshold a few moments. She had come
here seeking answers, but this woman was not her aunt. She had not

raised her. She wouldn't coax or flatter her. Branwen touched her mother's brooch and stepped inside.

Ailleann was feeding some twigs to the hearth. The kindling crackled.

"Something happened yesterday," Branwen started. "Something I don't understand."

The Wise Damsel raised her eyes from the fire and peered at her sidelong.

"I saw a Death-Teller." The Wise Damsel betrayed no reaction at her revelation. "I was traveling with the king and queen," she continued. "We came under attack in the Morrois Forest. Everything sharpened around me. I saw the skeletal face of a Death-Teller, but it turned out to be a man. An assassin." The words rushed out of her.

"Have you seen things like this before?" Ailleann asked.

"Since I was a girl, I've had dreams. And, in Iveriu—there was a fox. It told me to save the man who was poisoned." Branwen coughed. "Afterward, I caught glimpses. Echoes of the Otherworld, I think. But nothing so distinct. It felt as if I were both in this world and seeing the Otherworld around me. How is that possible?"

The Wise Damsel fed another twig to the fire. "The goddess you call Bríga, she has three faces."

"Yes." Branwen nodded. "The Fire of the Hearth, the Fire of Inspiration, and the Fire of the Forge."

"Your Goddess Bríga speaks to poets," Ailleann said. "She transports them temporarily to the Otherworld where they can see truths, connections, that are invisible in this world. This is what mortals call inspiration." Tristan's music had always transported Branwen outside herself, somewhere the seas were an infinite blue.

"You are Otherworld-touched, *enigena*, and your power of sight is growing. Despite your neglect. You see the fissures between the worlds now."

Branwen strummed her finger along the ridges of the wood, feeling scolded. "I've been practicing with the flame," she said. "Controlling it."

"Good." The Wise Damsel glided across the room toward her.

"I think my magic has been flaring when it senses danger," she confessed. "Could that be?"

"The in-between is a place of rebirth—but first there must be death. Destruction comes before creation. Your power is both. You sensed death approaching," replied the other woman. "And it senses you."

Branwen wished she could say the Wise Damsel was wrong.

"Does that mean the Iverni are right about the gods?" she asked.

Ailleann laughed. "Why would you say that?"

"Because I saw the Death-Teller, and she looked the way she's described in our legends. She was terrible," Branwen said, meeting the Wise Damsel's stare. "And her song. It made my bones want to crumble."

"We see as we believe. You saw the death you expect."

Branwen curled her fingers, catching her fingernails in the grain. "But what am I supposed to *do* with this Otherworld sight? If I use all of my magic, you warned that I'll burn myself out." A splinter lodged itself beneath a nail. "How do I know *when* to use it?" Frustration transformed her questions into accusations.

"What do the Old Ones *want* from me?" Branwen yelled. Instantly, she slapped a hand over her mouth.

The Wise Damsel stared at her a long moment. Then she threw back her head and laughed. Bellowed. Her crimson hair swung about her waist.

"I'm—I'm sorry. Forgive my impertinence, Wise Damsel."

"We're not at court now. Magic requires honesty above all—honesty with yourself." Her gaze bored into Branwen. "What is it that *you* want?"

"My aunt said I was gifted the Hand of Bríga to protect the Land. I just want the Old Ones to tell me how." How could she protect Eseult from herself? How could she protect Tristan from the treason she had caused?

"Your aunt is the Queen of Iveriu, is she not?"

"Yes," Branwen replied, confused as to the question.

"Your aunt has chosen to use her gifts to support her kingdom, as well she might. But your magic is *yours*, Branwen. You must choose what you want to do with it—you cannot live somebody else's life. Seeking permission, approval from the Old Ones for your choices will not free you from their consequences," she said, drawing in a long breath.

"You must be prepared to live with them, *enigena*. The Old Ones cannot do that for you. They have given you the tools, but we all build the houses we live in."

Branwen glanced around the cottage. She knew the Wise Damsel was not referring to this collection of red snakestones. The other woman pointed at a bucket next to the door. "Fetch that for me," she said. "I collected water from the stream this morning."

Cheeks still aflame, Branwen followed her orders.

"You came here today because you're scared," Ailleann said from behind her. "You had no control over your power in the forest because your heart is still divided."

I know that, Branwen nearly shot back. She carried the pail over to the table, arms straining at the weight.

"With practice, you can choose when to let the Otherworld in, and when to keep it at bay," said the Wise Damsel. She set a shallow bowl on the table and nodded at Branwen to fill it. The surface of the water was still, orange light from the hearth gleaming atop it.

"Water is neither air nor earth, but something in-between. It acts as a conduit, a focus for your Otherworld sight."

Returning to her seat, Branwen leaned over the bowl but only saw her own reflection, hazy and darkened.

"I see only myself," Branwen said.

"That's a start." The Wise Damsel leaned across the bowl and tapped Branwen's chest. "The truth is here. The sight comes from your heart, not your eyes. When you're honest with yourself about what you want, your magic will obey."

But Branwen wanted things that couldn't be. As much as she denied it, she wanted to be Emer again. Emer loved innocently, her conviction absolute. Sometimes Branwen wanted it so much she would be willing to tether her soul to Dhusnos for the chance to reclaim who she once was.

The Wise Damsel stared at Branwen. "What is the question most pressing on your mind?"

So many crowded inside her that she could scarcely choose. Had Prince Kahedrin truly sent the assassin? How long could she continue to hide what was between the True Queen and her Champion? Threats loomed on all sides.

"I want to defend the Land. The people I love," Branwen told Ailleann. "That *is* my choice, not my aunt's. I want to know the greatest threat to peace. I want to fight."

"Very well, *enigena*. Seek guidance in the water."

Branwen gazed down at the shallow bowl. There was a temporary calm in the darkness. She heard the stream and the crackling fire, as if nothing else existed.

Her breathing grew deeper. The stillness, the glow of the water enveloped her. She was both gazing into the bowl and not. The interior of the cottage fell away.

Waves roared in her ears.

Branwen stood on the bow of a ship. Overhead, a *kretarv* circled. There were men surrounding her, heavily armed, but they didn't notice her. Almost as if she were a Death-Teller.

In the distance, Branwen spied another vessel. Its sail gleamed white against the horizon. A sea-wolf danced in the wind. The ship must belong to Kernyv.

She glanced back at the sail billowing from her own ship: black. Fear hammered her. Branwen was aboard a war ship. One with no allegiance. *Pirates.*

The *kretarv* cawed. Squinting, she recognized a familiar coastline, the silhouette perched atop the cliffs. Castle Rigani.

War was closing in on her home, the seas rough. The ship lurched violently, sending Branwen to her knees.

Who was attacking them? Who was threatening Iveriu?

Tell me!

Her gaze dropped to her hands as Branwen began pushing herself to her feet. She froze. Her hands were red; blood leaked from them, staining the deck of the ship.

A sob racked her body before it became a desperate laugh. Branwen had never needed to look further than herself. Hot tears sluiced down her cheeks.

Branwen was the greatest threat to the peace.

She pounded the deck of the ship with her bloody hands. The vision dispersed as the bowl of water jumped, and Branwen's fists banged against the table.

Her tears rippled in the water.

It took Branwen a few moments before she risked meeting the Wise Damsel's gaze.

"Did you get the answer you wanted?" the older woman asked.

Branwen got the answer she needed. The one she should have already known. She dabbed angrily at her damp cheeks and rose from her seat.

"I must return to the castle," she said. But she didn't want to. Branwen wanted to run, she wanted to run until she turned to fire, then smoke. She wanted to run far away, too far to hurt those she loved any further.

"*Enigena*." The Wise Damsel stood to meet her. "What you see in the in-between is meant to guide you. But it is mutable. Water is not stone."

Branwen shuddered another breath. Her worst fear had been confirmed. Why had she ever doubted it?

The Loving Cup had set them all on the course for war.

"Darkness is coming," Branwen said. "I don't know that I can fight it."

"Darkness comes every evening, and it leaves every morning." The Wise Damsel lifted a shoulder, unperturbed.

"What if I'm the darkness?"

"You must choose to be the light."

✦ ✦ ✦

Branwen exited the stable feeling both heavy and empty. She raised her hand against the strong midday sun. Wild, blond hair shone against the shadows of the doorway.

"Ruan?" she said, panic prickling her skin.

"I was about to saddle my horse and come find you," he said. Worry roughened his tone. "The guards at the gate told me you departed at dawn, seeking a medicine for the king. Where did you go?"

Branwen fidgeted with the strap of her leather satchel. That had indeed been the excuse she'd given the guards, which they'd accepted easily.

"I didn't realize I need your permission to leave the castle," she replied, her tone like vinegar. She wasn't ready to discuss her visit to the Wise Damsel, or her magic, with Ruan just yet.

Ruan scowled, rubbing his lower lip. "Branwen, we were attacked yesterday. You should have woken me. I would have escorted you wherever you needed to go." He lifted a hand tenderly to her cheek, and Branwen's pique was mitigated by his concern. She rested her hand on his, lowered it from her cheek and threaded their fingers together.

"You smile in your sleep, you know," she told him.

"Probably because of who was sleeping beside me." He squeezed Branwen's hand with another smile. Then, growing serious, he said, "I need your help. The prisoner won't wake up."

"Is he breathing?" Ruan nodded. Branwen straightened her shoulders. "Take me to him," she said. The Armorican needed to live so they could get the truth from him.

She dropped Ruan's hand and matched his fleet strides toward the guardsmen's barracks, which were located halfway up the hill, the dungeon beneath it.

The eyes of the soldiers were alert, their swords ready. They murmured tense greetings.

Branwen followed Ruan down a serpentine staircase lit by a solitary torch. The dungeon had been dug out of the earth and the stone was slippery with moisture from the humid climate.

When they reached the bottom, it remained eerily quiet. The murk was interrupted by oil lamps at intervals along the walls. There were three cells on either side of a corridor, but only one of them was occupied.

"We aren't used to prisoners at Monwiku," Ruan said under his breath. A guard stood outside the cell containing the Armorican, glaring at the man who had attacked his king. The Royal Guardsman looked to be around Branwen's age, with light brown skin and closely cropped hair.

He bowed. "*Penaxta.*" Ruan replied in Kernyvak, and the guard opened the cell, his twisted lips betraying his unease.

Ruan entered first, hand poised on the pommel of his sword. The prisoner was lying in a heap on the floor, which was covered with a smattering of hay. The cell was compact, and Ruan had to step back to let Branwen pass. She crouched beside the prisoner and tugged at his shoulder to examine him.

Blood leaked from his nose and one eye was swollen shut. The other was framed in black and blue.

"I don't remember him having these injuries," Branwen said, keeping her voice neutral. She felt the Kernyvak guardsman's gaze on her, uneasy, perhaps because she was speaking Ivernic with Ruan.

"He woke last night," Ruan told her. "The guards tried talking to him."

Branwen swallowed. When she'd stopped Ruan from finishing off the Armorican in the wood, she'd known the Royal Guard wouldn't interrogate him by asking politely.

Ruan squatted beside her. "Can you bring him around? The King's Council is meeting tomorrow. We need to know who his accomplices are and where they're hiding."

"I'll do my best." Branwen lifted one of the prisoner's eyelids. The pupil was enormous. "There's too much pressure in his skull," she said. "One more punch and he won't be able to tell you anything. No more beatings."

"He fought back," Ruan said, strained. Branwen glanced at him sideways and the conflict in his eyes was plain as day. "But the guards were following my orders. I won't fail Marc again."

Under his breath, he told her, "I'm not a brute, Branwen."

The pain beneath his words drilled into her. Branwen had killed Keane when he threatened Eseult. Yesterday, she had nearly killed the man at her feet to protect her king. And she had watched both her uncles behead Kernyvak prisoners of war. These were the stakes of their world. She was no better or worse than Ruan.

Branwen touched his elbow. "I know you're not, Ruan. Just give me some space to work."

"The Armorican's still dangerous."

"Not at the moment." She and Ruan stared at each other. With a grunt, he rose to standing. "You should return to the king," she said. "I'll come to his chambers as soon as I'm done here."

"As you wish. Tutir will stand guard."

"I can't work with him hovering. Ask him to wait upstairs." She removed her cloak.

Ruan ground his teeth. "At least keep this." He withdrew a small knife from his boot. Its handle was emblazoned with a golden lion.

Reading Branwen's reaction, Ruan said, "It's not what you think. I didn't get it raiding. The blade was a gift."

She eyed him, innate suspicion flaring. Then she nodded. She didn't see why he would lie. "Thank you," Branwen said as she accepted the knife. She also had a far deadlier weapon in her right hand than the blade.

Ruan exited the cell. "Be safe," he said.

Water dripped from the walls, collecting in a pool beside the Armorican's head. She set to the work of reviving the prisoner, rubbing some of Andred's garlic paste into his visible cuts and abrasions.

The water fell in a steady rhythm.

Branwen pressed an ear to the prisoner's chest. There was no indication of fluid in his lungs. Was this man simply a cutthroat for hire as Ruan believed? He didn't seem terribly skilled. His attack had been frenzied, not dispassionate or professional. Surely the King of Armorica would employ a better assassin?

Drip. Drip.

Her eyes were attracted to the small puddle. She exhaled a long breath. Before Branwen had made a conscious decision, her gaze lingered on the grimy water, her vision growing blurry.

The prisoner was on his feet again, running toward a beach. A beach where a ship with black sails had landed. The tide frothed pink and red, bodies strewn haphazardly across the sand.

The man staggered among the corpses, searching. Branwen felt the thrashing of his heart in her own chest.

He stopped before a girl of seven or eight. Ringlets graced her sunburned forehead. She looked as if she were sleeping.

Blood wept from her middle, soaking her tunic. The girl would never wake up.

A cry of despair rent Branwen's lips. Feet pounded on the stairs, breaking her trance.

"My lady?" It was Tutir. His sword was drawn.

The prisoner groaned.

"F—fine," Branwen said, embarrassed. "I'm fine," she repeated in Aquilan, but her shoulders heaved. Tutir sheathed his sword.

With some difficulty, she pushed to her feet. Dizziness permeated her senses. She was both seasick and voraciously hungry. She swayed as she gathered Ruan's knife and her jars of salves into her satchel.

Branwen gripped the bars of the cell. "When the prisoner wakes, give him water," she instructed Tutir. "If he doesn't vomit, start him on gruel."

He nodded, but she sensed his suspicion. She hoped he wouldn't report her outburst to Ruan.

"*Mormerkti*," she said.

"*Dymatis*," the guard replied. Branwen felt his quizzical gaze on her back until she was out of sight.

✛ ✛ ✛

Afternoon had faded to evening when King Marc awoke, ate a small supper, and returned to slumbering. Only then did Branwen allow herself to return to the Queen's Tower for a much-needed bath. Eseult helped wash Branwen's hair but she refused to broach the subject of her pregnancy, and Branwen was too tired to push. Despite the utter exhaustion brought on by the Otherworld visions, however, she couldn't find any rest in the small room that adjoined her cousin's.

The face of the dead Armorican girl flickered behind Branwen's eyes. She had no reason to doubt what she'd been shown. The assassin had motive for wanting revenge on Kernyv. The question was whether he'd been sent by either Prince Kahedrin or his father. Was he working alone or at the behest of his king?

The scene of carnage had been like so many others that had played out on Ivernic shores, like the Skeleton Beach massacre Keane survived as a boy but from which he'd never recovered.

Finally, the moon high and her hair still damp, Branwen threw on her cloak and hurried across the inner bailey. She bid *Nosmatis* to the guardsmen posted at the entrance to the King's Tower.

She didn't head for the stairs. Quietly, not wanting to disturb him, she opened the door to Ruan's chambers.

He bolted upright in his bed, illuminated by a single shaft of candlelight. It winked off the sword in his hand. "Branwen?"

"I'm here to escape."

Ruan lowered his sword and spread his arms. "Your escape is here."

ALLIES

DAWN CAME TOO SOON.

A few hours later, the King's Council had been assembled. Marc asked Branwen to join them as she changed his bandages. Following him down the corridor toward his study, she could already hear arguing from behind the door.

"I suppose I can't keep the council waiting forever." He sighed.

"Well, you're the king," said Branwen. "I think you can."

Marc let out a laugh, then winced from the movement of his shoulders. He'd declined to wear a sling.

"Would you escort me?" Branwen asked, touching his elbow.

His lips quirked in understanding. "Forgive my manners, Lady Branwen." She accepted the king's left arm, leaning in close so that she could take some of his weight as they entered the study.

The loudest of the voices—belonging to Baron Dynyon—ceased mid-sentence when he spotted King Marc. He smoothed the ends of his fiery mustache. The other half of the heated exchange appeared to be the elderly head of House Julyan. His liver-spotted hand was wrapped tightly around his cane.

Everyone sitting rose immediately to their feet and began to approach the oblong table upon which Branwen had operated on the king. Seer Casek had been interrupted mid-discussion with the younger Baron Chyanhal, seated on opposite sides of the *fidkwelsa* board in the far corner.

Countess Kensa gave Branwen a look as cold as moonlight when she saw her on the king's arm. She stood beside Baron Dynyon, with the inordinately tall Baron Gwyk completing their group. His glass eye reflected a shaft of sunlight.

"My king," said Baron Dynyon as he bowed. "*Kernyv bosta vyken!*"

"*Kernyv bosta vyken,*" King Marc affirmed. He relinquished Branwen's arm.

The other councillors lifted their goblets and toasted to Kernyv forever. The last Kernyvak king to die in battle had been before the Aquilan retreat from Albion. Despite the fact that Marc had narrowly escaped death, the barons believed in the permanence of their kingdom.

"Apparently the debate has begun without me," said the king.

"Not at all," Baron Julyan said. His wizened eyebrows drew together.

Noticing King Marc was without a goblet of his own, Andred hurried toward his older brother who had the decanter of Mílesian spirits in hand. Ruan leaned against the sideboard, refilling his glass generously, as well as that of Baron Kerdu.

Ruan had a robust tolerance for drink, but Branwen suspected he was maintaining his well-cultivated image among the nobility as a cad. His eyes trailed to hers languorously, and an unwelcome heat rose in her cheeks.

"Please, everyone, take your seats," King Marc said, part request, part command.

Tristan escorted his grandmother to a chair at the far end of the table, closest to the windows. Marc walked toward the Queen Mother and the True Queen, as the council members complied. Eseult caught Branwen's eye and beckoned her.

"You look well, my son," said Queen Verica.

Eseult gave her husband a shy smile. "You do," she agreed. "Very well."

Marc returned the smile. "Thank you for visiting me yesterday," he told her, somewhat reticent. "I'll try not to fall asleep next time. I promise it wasn't the quality of the conversation." He offered a self-deprecating laugh.

"Oh, I don't mind. I might be quite dull only no one dared tell me because I was a princess."

"I very much doubt that's possible." They shared another smile that soon became awkward. "Here," Marc said, pulling out the chair at the head of the table. "I am filled with gratitude that you are attending your first council meeting as my wife and my True Queen."

Eseult's creamy complexion grew rosy. "*Mormerkti*, my Lord King."

"*Sekrev*." He kissed Eseult's hand as she lowered herself into the chair.

Branwen's stomach revolted as she observed them and watched Tristan observing them. Another night of escape in Ruan's bed was not enough to make her forget all of the suffering she had caused.

As if summoned by her thoughts, the prince appeared at her side, proffering her a silver goblet. "My younger brother seems to have forgotten you," Ruan said, nodding at Andred who was handing the king spiced wine. "Is he still your favorite?"

Ruan's eyes danced. Branwen pried the goblet from his fingers, letting a scratch on the back of his hand be sufficient answer. He licked his lips.

"Let's turn to the matter at hand," the king said to his councillors as he wandered back to the other end of the table. Ruan followed.

Seer Casek had seated himself in the chair directly to the king's left; Ruan flanked his right. As at other formal occasions, the barons from Houses Julyan, Kerdu, and Chyanhal also filled out the right side of the table, while Countess Kensa, Baron Gwyk and Baron Dynyon rounded out the left. Tristan pulled out a chair between Baron Julyan and his grandmother. The divisions among the nobles couldn't be starker.

Andred had wisely made himself scarce, decamping to the corner of the room.

Standing behind the chair at the head of the table, Marc said, "Baron Dynyon, please, let us begin with your concerns."

"But, my Lord King, we have a guest," Countess Kensa interrupted. She dazzled Branwen with a poisonous smile. "Lady Branwen is not a member of the council and there is no chair for her."

"I invited her," King Marc said. His words were steel. "She is welcome."

The head of House Chyanhal rose. His chair creaked. "Please, Lady Branwen, take my seat. I'm glad to stretch my legs after a day of hard riding." He pulled the chair out farther.

"*Mormerkti*, Baron Chyanhal."

Countess Kensa's lips twisted as if she'd tasted something sour but raised no further objections as Branwen took the baron's seat, next to Ruan. King Marc showed Baron Chyanhal a reserved smile of thanks. Ruan allowed his knee to rest against Branwen's beneath the table, a sign of support.

"Now that that's settled," said the king, "Baron Dynyon?"

The baron touched two fingers to his crimson mustache. "Sire, I had suggested to the esteemed head of House Julyan that the Royal Fleet set sail for the south coast," he replied. "Once our ships have amassed at Illogan, they can cross the Southern Channel from the headland with ease. The fleet can reach the Armorican capital of Karaez before the end of next week. With favorable winds."

Branwen went rigid in her seat, pressing her spine against the leather back.

"And I suggested to Baron Dynyon," said Baron Julyan, white eyebrows lifted, "that he was being hasty."

"Hasty? The Armoricans tried to kill our king!" Baron Dynyon shot back.

Seated on Branwen's right was Baron Kerdu, who said, "We have long had a friendly relationship with Armorica." He rested his elbows on the table and leaned forward, the cream of his tunic contrasting against the brown of his skin.

"Prince Kahedrin didn't behave like a friend when he attended the royal wedding," Ruan said, looking from Baron Kerdu to King Marc.

The king was quiet a moment, calculating. "Prince Kahedrin expressed his . . . frustration with ongoing raids on Armorica's northern coast," King Marc said finally, countenance neutral.

Ruan twisted in his seat to meet Marc's eye. "He *threatened* you."

"I was also present for the conversation, Prince Ruan," Branwen reminded him. "He appealed to Kernyv to put a leash on the pirates." Ruan turned in Branwen's direction, stunned, hurt. She broke his gaze.

Countess Kensa scoffed. "Nobody puts a leash on the pirates." To King Marc, she said, "The Seal of Alliance with Iveriu precludes subjects of the crown from buying goods or prisoners taken from our True Queen's homeland." She darted a sideways glance at Eseult. "But the pirates can't be prevented from finding other sources of . . . revenue."

From where he stood behind Branwen, Baron Chyanhal stroked his angular cheekbones and said, "Armorica is an important trading partner. They rely upon our white lead."

"No, they don't," the countess told him. "Which you would know if House Chyanhal had any mines." The younger baron bristled. "White lead is flowing into Armorica from the kingdom of Míl."

Her expression was bloodless. Baron Gwyk nodded in agreement. Beneath the table, Branwen bunched the skirts on her thighs. Countess Kensa appeared utterly unconcerned with the Armoricans being terrorized, only with her business interests. Had she always been so callous, or had it been years of marriage to a heartless man?

Baron Julyan coughed. "House Julyan has mines. I am aware of the competition from Mílesian lead. However, I do not believe that King Faramon would sanction an assassination attempt on our king solely because Armorica is no longer dependent on our minerals."

Branwen panned her eyes around the table, trying to read the expressions of the other councillors. Baron Dynyon fiddled with the end of his mustache, shaking his head. Baron Gwyk's lips were also pursed.

She locked her gaze on Tristan. His dark eyes showed his worry. If there were anyone she would trust with her vision, it would still be Tristan. But what she'd seen was inconclusive at best.

"I agree with Baron Julyan," Tristan said, looking down the table at King Marc. "Before we consider launching an assault on the Armorican capital, we should send an ambassador to King Faramon." He briefly glanced back at Branwen before returning his gaze to Marc. "I would be happy to lead a diplomatic mission."

Queen Eseult inhaled sharply, and Branwen sensed her dismay. Her cousin dropped a hand to her belly.

"Why should we send an ambassador when they sent an assassin?" Baron Dynyon exclaimed. He pounded a fist on the table.

"Because war is not something to be courted," Branwen said, her own vehemence surprising even herself. Beneath her skin, she felt her magic stir.

"Who are you to speak about what Kernyv should or shouldn't do?" Baron Gwyk reprimanded, fixing her with his one good eye.

"Kernyv and Iveriu are united now," Branwen told him. "If Kernyv becomes Armorica's enemy, so will Iveriu. Prince Kahedrin made that clear."

"*See*," said Ruan, agitation mounting. "Kahedrin made very free with his threats."

"Beneath his threats was desperation," she said. "*I* have felt that desperation." Branwen shifted in her seat, beseeching Marc directly. "My kingdom has known nothing but war my entire life. It's enough."

King Marc lifted his right hand to his beard out of habit and winced. He lowered it slowly to his lap.

"What does my True Queen say?" he asked. All eyes snapped to Eseult.

She looked to Branwen. Branwen lifted her brow, uncertain what the True Queen would say. "I believe, my king," her cousin began. She visibly swallowed. "I believe that I came to Kernyv for peace."

The queen pressed on her abdomen, drawing in a breath. "We should find a way to keep the peace with Armorica."

Her green eyes were moist. Had the danger of her situation finally impressed itself upon her cousin?

"You speak wisely, my queen," King Marc said.

Queen Verica leaned forward. "King Faramon has always been a reasonable ruler. I support my grandson's proposal. Send an envoy."

"And would you be willing to give them Prince Tristan as a royal hostage if they aren't interested in diplomacy?" Countess Kensa asked, voice needle-thin and piercing. She knew that the Queen Mother's love for her grandson was one of her few vulnerabilities.

"I have taken greater risks on the battlefield," Tristan countered.

"Responding to an assassination attempt with diplomacy is a mistake," Baron Dynyon said, a low hum threading through his words. "It tells the other kingdoms we're weak."

"I have to agree, my king," Ruan said. "Prince Kahedrin was often in the company of King Cunacus at the wedding, and Ordowik has always been a difficult neighbor."

"Seer Casek," King Marc said, pointing his gaze at the *kordweyd*. "What is the opinion of the temple?"

The seer took a long, dramatic breath. "The Horned One teaches us mercy, but he died to protect his father, and all of the Kernyveu would die to protect you, my king. The opinion of the temple is that a threat against a king who has accepted the truth of the Horned One cannot go unanswered."

Light winked off the precious stones that encased the antler shard around his neck.

"But what if the assassin wasn't sent by the King of Armorica?"

Branwen said hotly. "Should innocent people be slaughtered because of the actions of one man?"

Seer Casek opened his mouth to reply when King Marc held up his hand.

All fell silent.

"Let us ask him," said the king. "Ruan, fetch the prisoner."

The King's Champion leapt to his feet and exited the study without glancing at Branwen. This would undoubtedly be the first of many disagreements between them. She sent a silent prayer to the Old Ones that the Armorican was awake.

Countess Kensa raised her goblet to her lips and took a long sip.

"I presume the plans for the royal infirmary will be put on hold, given the circumstances." She did nothing to hide her gloating.

"On the contrary, Countess." King Marc looked down the length of the table to his wife. "The True Queen's project is even more paramount if we are soon to have war wounded to care for. We will not change our course in the face of danger."

He stared around the table at each of his councillors. "*That* would be weakness."

Every now and then, Branwen saw the menace in King Marc—the fortitude—that had allowed him to survive his raids, much as he regretted them.

The barons drank in silence. The waiting became almost unbearable.

Sooner than Branwen expected, Ruan burst back into the king's study.

Alone.

"He's dead," he said. "The prisoner is dead."

THE TOUCH OF DHUSNOS

RUAN'S CHEST CONTINUED TO HEAVE. He must have sprinted up the hill from the dungeon. Branwen glanced at the other members of the King's Council: Their expressions ranged from shocked to furious.

"How?" King Marc asked Ruan, careful to betray no emotion.

The room was still enough to hear nothing but the surf.

Ruan looked from the king to Branwen. She clasped her hands together, worrying one thumb over the other. The prisoner should have recovered. Unless, of course, the guards had tried interrogating him again.

"I'm no expert, *Ríx*, but . . . it looks like poison," Ruan told Marc, eyes still on Branwen.

At the far end of the table, Eseult gasped. The shock and indignation on the faces of those assembled became tainted with fear.

Was there another assassin within the castle walls?

King Marc pushed to standing. Branwen noticed his knuckles tighten against any pain he might feel.

"Take me to the body." The conciliatory, diplomatic king was gone. "Lady Branwen," he said, and the tension in his voice wound around her heart. "You're a master of the healing arts. I'd like your opinion."

"Of course, my Lord King."

Seer Casek rose to his feet. "Allow me to lend my expertise as well, sire."

"As you wish," Marc replied, curt. The *kordweyd* worked his jaw. Surveying the barons and the rest of his council, the king said, "Thank you all for coming. Return to your homes. I will advise you of my decision in due course."

"But, my Lord Ki—" Baron Dynyon began to protest before seeing the fierceness in Marc's gaze and shutting his mouth.

To Tristan, the king said, "Please escort the Queen Mother and Queen Eseult to their rooms," and then pivoted toward the door.

Branwen hurried to King Marc's side and quietly offered him her arm for support. Ruan and Casek followed closely behind. As she and the king began descending the stairs, the din of arguing voices once more filled the air.

The king said nothing as they walked down the path to the barracks at a brisk clip. No one else dared to speak, either. Marc was ready for a fight, Branwen could feel it. She'd seen the battle-lust in men's eyes before. But there would be no fight at the dungeon. Only a dead man.

The guards at the entrance to the barracks straightened as their king approached, Tutir among them. He kept his eyes on the ground. He had failed in his duty to keep the prisoner alive to face the King's Council.

Marc barked at the Royal Guardsmen in Kernyvak. Ruan stepped forward to his side, pointing at Tutir and another, older guard who was blond and had a scar bisecting his left cheek. Branwen couldn't catch everything that was being said, but she inferred that they had been the two guards on duty when the prisoner was found dead.

Ruan spoke to them in a lethally soft tone. Then, switching to Aquilan, he said to Branwen, "Please come this way, my lady. *Rix*," and she followed him once more down the murky stairwell to the dungeon. King Marc and Seer Casek filed behind them.

At the bottom, Branwen spied the cell door flung open and the Armorican flat on his back, arms and legs sprawled on the floor like a serpent-star. As they neared the cell, Ruan stepped aside to let Branwen enter. The king and the seer also remained on the other side of the bars.

Branwen knelt beside the dead assassin. Even in the dim light, the bloody froth on his blue lips confirmed what Ruan suspected.

She looked up to meet King Marc's avid eyes. "The prisoner appears to have drowned in his own blood."

The king swept his gaze over the dead man's swollen eye and broken nose.

"Could he have succumbed to his injuries?"

Shaking her head, she said, "When I treated him, I believed he would recover."

Branwen lowered her face to the Armorican's and took a deep breath. The scent of something astringent clung to him.

Seer Casek took a step closer, peering at the prisoner's lips. "I concur with Lady Branwen. Poison seems the most likely cause of death."

Branwen's mouth parted at the shock of the *kordweyd* agreeing with her.

Ruan clenched his fists. King Marc drew in a long breath. "Who was last alone with him?"

"I was," said Branwen, the air trapped in her chest.

"No. Tutir fed him this morning," Ruan told the king. "He was alive." His eyes met Branwen's, and she saw sympathy, ferocity.

"What did he eat and drink?" Marc asked his Champion.

"Lady Branwen left instructions to start him on water when he was conscious, then gruel." Ruan looked between Branwen and his king. "Tutir informed me this morning that the prisoner was hungry. I ordered gruel to be sent from the kitchens." Each word grew heavier; she could taste his guilt.

"There must be someone loyal to Armorica within the castle," said Seer Casek, tone grave. "Someone afraid the assassin would reveal their plans."

Unconsciously, King Marc touched the elbow of his injured arm.

"Ruan," he said. "I want you to begin questioning the kitchen servants—but be discreet. I don't want word to spread. And I don't want panic."

"Yes, *Rix*."

"Ask Tristan to help conduct the interviews," the king instructed. Ruan gritted his teeth, but Branwen thought she was the only one to notice. "And make preparations for the body to be removed from the island and interred."

"The *kordweyd* in Marghas can arrange the burial," Seer Casek offered.

"Thank you," Marc said.

"King Marc," Branwen began, hesitant. "In Armorica, they burn their dead. There is an Old One that the Armoricans call Ankou. They believe that burning the body makes it easier for her to collect the soul."

Ankou, Branwen knew, was like a Death-Teller but more powerful—almost a goddess.

Seer Casek scoffed. "We're in Kernyv, Lady Branwen."

The king stroked his beard once. "True, Seer Casek. But if I die abroad, I would want my body treated according to my beliefs." He met the *kordweyd*'s stare.

"I'll see that the body is burned," said Casek.

The Armorican's eyes were still open. Had he seen a Death-Teller approach him? Had he seen the death he expected? Gently, Branwen closed the man's eyes.

"I can clean the body," she said to the king. The Armoricans, like the Iverni and the Kernyveu, washed their dead.

Marc nodded in approval. "Seer Casek, thank you for your assistance," he said, and it was a dismissal.

"The temple is always at your service," said the *kordweyd*.

"Ruan, ask the guards to bring water and fresh linen to Lady Branwen on your way out," Marc said. Another dismissal. Seer Casek headed up the spiral staircase first. Ruan hesitated a moment, hurt welling in his eyes, and then left.

Branwen's heartbeat accelerated once more, wondering why the king had stayed behind.

When the other two men had disappeared from view, King Marc leaned against the open door of the cell. He groaned.

"Can I give you something for the pain?" Branwen asked.

"No, thank you." Marc slid his gaze back to the prisoner's face. "Is it possible to determine the precise kind of poison that was used?" he said.

"I—I suppose that it is, but I'm afraid that I'm not well versed in poisons," Branwen said, apologetic. Perhaps she would need to make a study of them. "I can tell you that the prisoner's blood has a bitter scent, which isn't natural."

She slowly lifted the dead man's arm from the floor and let it drop again.

"And the touch of Dhusnos is not yet upon him. His limbs move easily." Meeting Marc's eyes, Branwen said, "The Armorican has only been dead a couple hours at most."

"If I can't even control what happens within the walls of my own castle, how can I control an entire kingdom?"

Branwen remained quiet. She rubbed her scarred palm. She understood why the king didn't want anyone to know that the prisoner had died without his command. King Marc was reliant on his councillors holding their tongues, and Branwen thought that highly unlikely.

She raised herself from the floor and walked toward him.

"My king, may I speak to you as a . . . friend?" she said. At the beginning of last spring, the suggestion that Branwen might one day consider the King of Kernyv a friend would have seemed impossible.

"You saved my life, Lady Branwen. You may speak to me however you wish."

"Then, as a friend, I would counsel you caution. Someone didn't want the assassin to be able to speak to you. But whether it was an agent of the Armorican crown—or someone else—we don't yet know. I—" Branwen swallowed. "I hope you might still consider Tristan's suggestion of a diplomatic envoy."

"The line between caution and weakness is a difficult one to tread," Marc said.

"Yes."

"Like in *fidkwelsa*," he said, and Branwen showed him a small smile.

"I won't be forced to move before I'm ready, Lady Branwen. And I'm not without my own agents abroad."

"Of course."

"But, thank you. I am glad to count you among my friends." Marc sounded sincere and relieved. "I will help you clean the body."

"You will?"

"This man was my enemy, he wished me harm, but I will honor him in death. I did not honor my enemies as I should have in the past."

Branwen envisaged the younger Marc leaving her mother where she lay dying, but she no longer felt rage. Only sadness. Sadness for her parents, for herself—but also for the man in front of her.

"*Mormerkti*," she told him. "Friend."

JUST ONCE

WIND HOWLED OVER THE MOORS.

"Here," said King Marc from astride his new mount, easing the reins back one-handed. His wounded arm rested in the sling that Branwen had convinced him to wear while riding.

"Right here."

The sun broke through the clouds, casting a cold light on the Stone of Waiting.

Marc glanced at his queen, who rode beside him, and then at Branwen, who was just behind. He had surprised the cousins that morning by announcing that he'd selected the location where the royal infirmary should be built, and that he'd like to show it to them.

Ruan had spent the last week interviewing castle servants trying to find another assassin to no avail. Too many people had had access to the prisoner's food and water: Everyone and no one was a suspect. It was a relief to leave the castle, if only for a bit.

Sensing that his king had stopped, Ruan raised a hand, signaling the other guards to follow suit. The King's Champion rode at the front of ten Royal Guardsmen who formed a defensive ring around the king and queen, as well as Branwen and Andred. Tristan rode at the rear of the party. Both Champions scoured the surrounding area for any sign of danger.

King Marc gestured at the flat landscape. Spiky yellow gorse lent the moors a bleak but bright beauty.

"Eseult," he said, not sounding entirely comfortable addressing his wife without her title. "I believe this spot would be the ideal location for your infirmary. It lies equidistant from the mines and the sea, easily accessible to both." Beneath his cape, the king pulled at the fabric of the sling. "And the Stone of Waiting is a landmark that can be seen from leagues away."

Sunlight sparkled on the dark green longstone like ice.

"Would this—do you find it suitable?" King Marc asked his queen. She bowed her lips into an uncertain smile, looking back at Branwen.

"What do you think, Branny?" she said. Eseult wanted her gift to please her, Branwen knew, but she was growing exasperated with the queen. Her cousin had returned to a state of denial about her pregnancy. Branwen tried introducing the subject of perhaps hiding the baby, giving it to someone trustworthy, but Eseult refused to entertain the discussion.

The king turned toward Branwen as well, gaze expectant.

"I think this an excellent location," she said, finally, a strain in her voice, as she glanced from Eseult to Marc.

"Me too," Andred piped up from beside Branwen.

"Well, that's the important thing, scamp," Ruan ribbed his brother, joining the conversation. He grinned at Andred. His eyes met Branwen's and the grin faded.

Ruan had been unusually aloof, his comportment around Branwen diffident, since their disagreement at the council meeting. He hadn't desired her company, so she hadn't requested his, either.

Branwen returned her attention to the king. "We're not far from Seer Ogrin's temple," she said. "Perhaps he can also tend to patients here?"

"My thoughts exactly," said the king. To Eseult, Marc said, "We will build a new, stronger Kernyv—together. Our enemies will not derail our plans."

The muscles tightened in Ruan's neck as he agreed, "Of course not, *Ríx*."

King Marc reached into his saddlebag, emitting a groan, and retrieved a silver flask. Andred immediately sidled his pony next to him. "Has the water been tasted?" he said, eyeing the flask.

Branwen glimpsed Marc's hesitation in the tightening of lips. Appointing a new cupbearer would be a grave insult to both Andred and House Whel, but the danger in the position now seemed imminent, and the king's reluctance to put his young cousin in harm's way was evident to all.

"*Ríx*," said Andred with a seriousness that belied his fourteen years. "I might not be able to serve Kernyv on the battlefield, but there are other ways to fight." The boy thrust out his hand. "I swore to protect my king like any other member of the Royal Guard."

King Marc took a breath. "Indeed you did." He let Andred take the flask from his grasp. Everyone watched as the boy put its lip to his mouth, and swallowed.

Unconsciously, the king cradled the elbow of his injured arm. Branwen stole a sideways glace at Ruan: His expression was a mixture of pride and fear.

At last, Andred nodded. "With Lugmarch's blessing," he said, and returned the flask to Marc. The king expelled a relieved breath.

Taking a drink, he said, "We'll break ground before summer," and dropped the flask back into the saddlebag.

Tristan walked his stallion closer to the king, coming to a halt beside Andred's pony, as the rest of the guardsmen fanned out farther.

"Grandmother will be glad to hear it," he said. "She was sorry she couldn't join us today." Tristan cast a quick glance at Branwen, eyes troubled. Endelyn had surprised her by volunteering to remain with the old queen at the castle.

Everything Ruan had told Branwen about his father inspired sympathy in her for Endelyn, and the princess's affection for Queen Verica appeared genuine, yet the disdain with which she treated Branwen was hard to overlook.

"The Queen Mother has always loved the moors," Marc said. He fidgeted with the reins in his good hand. He, too, worried for his mother. Her black cough was growing worse and Branwen doubted she would live to see the foundation stone of the infirmary laid.

"Since we're not so very far from Seer Ogrin's temple," Andred began, the pitch of his voice growing higher, "perhaps we could pass by?"

Ruan shook his head. "We need to return before high tide."

"Lowenek will be joining us at the castle soon enough," Branwen told Andred. She patted his elbow, amused at his blush.

"I wasn't . . . ," the boy began to protest.

His older brother threw his head back in a laugh. "Oh, I see. Andred's in love!"

"I'm not!"

"Well," said King Marc. "We are at the Stone of Waiting." His expression broke into one of his rare full-faced smiles.

"I'm not," Andred repeated, muttering mostly to himself.

Eseult wrinkled her nose. "What does the Stone of Waiting have to do with love?"

A chill wind billowed Branwen's cloak.

Marc coughed. "The Kernyveu believe that if you come here on a full moon, you'll see the face of your true love."

Eseult's gaze swept from Tristan to Branwen. "Oh," she said. Branwen heard all of her own sadness in her cousin's voice.

King Marc's shoulder blades drew together, and he shifted in his saddle.

"Lady Branwen has no interest in true love," Ruan pronounced.

"She doesn't?" Tristan said.

"That's what she told me, cousin."

Eyes still locked with Ruan's, Branwen felt Tristan's gaze on her cheek; she couldn't meet it. Pressure expanded inside her chest. She flicked a glance at Eseult, instead, and then at the king.

"I've never cared for ballads," Branwen told Marc. "But duty is a true form of love, and I believe in that."

"As do I, Lady Branwen," the king said.

Eseult's mount stomped her hoof. "Lí Ban agrees," said the queen with a soft laugh, turning the horse to face Branwen. "My cousin is the most loyal woman I know."

Love bled through her words, and the frustration that had been simmering inside Branwen all week transformed into guilt. "Also serious," Eseult added. "*Too* serious. Even when we were girls."

"That I believe," said Ruan. Branwen made a small, annoyed noise. She wouldn't apologize for counseling diplomacy.

Eseult glanced between Branwen and Ruan. "Except when Branny has too much elderberry wine," she told the prince, while baiting her cousin with a wink.

"Is that so?" Ruan gave Branwen a long look. King Marc laughed. Tristan remained silent.

Cracking a mischievous smile, the queen said, "Come on, Branny, I'll race you. Like we used to."

"I'm not sure that's a wise—"

"See? Too serious." Eseult surveyed the faces of the men. "I bet none of you can catch us!" The queen gave her horse a swift kick and bolted across the moor. Panic instantly widened Tristan's eyes.

"It's me she wants," Branwen said to him. She slapped her own mount's rump and Senara broke into a gallop.

The moors whizzed by as Branwen kept her eyes trained on Eseult's blond plaits. She heard the rumble of hooves, like the gathering of thunder, as the rest of the royal guards began to follow in pursuit. Branwen spoke words of encouragement to Senara and the mare rewarded her with a gait that matched the wind.

In their many childhood races, Eseult had never realized that Branwen had always let her win.

Shock parted the queen's lips when Branwen came along beside her.

"Slow down! It's not safe to run off!" she admonished her cousin.

"You run away all the time!" Eseult hollered back, voice frayed by the wind. "Why shouldn't I!"

"You know why!"

"Admit it, Branny!" her cousin said, words punctuated by hoofbeats. "You like this! You wanted to flee as much as me!"

Branwen couldn't deny it. She had been desperate to escape the shadow of the Stone of Waiting. Escape from the expectations of Tristan, Ruan, and the king.

"But I'm not the queen!" Branwen shouted.

Her cousin kicked Lí Ban faster. "I wish you were! Then I could be free!"

"Stop, Essy!"

"No! I feel like I'm flying!" Her laughter held a trace of desperation. The memory of her cousin jumping from the waterfall as a little girl instantly resurfaced.

The True Queen zoomed ahead, straight for the forest. Branwen released a sigh and leaned her chest against Senara's neck, digging her heels in farther.

At the forest's edge, she gained ground on the queen's palfrey. Senara neighed in complaint at the dirt being kicked in her face. Branwen's breaths came in pants, nervous energy flooding her. Nervous, but also resolute. Magic bubbled in her veins.

Just once, Branwen didn't want to let her cousin get her way. She didn't want to let her win.

Her mount shared her sentiments. Senara nipped at Lí Ban's hindquarters as she overtook the mare.

"Looks like I'm flying, too!" Branwen taunted Eseult, passing her by. The queen grunted in frustration, puckering her lips.

Branwen let out a shout and pressed onward. The hoofbeats of the queen's mount pounded in her ears, getting closer, ever closer.

Senara galloped into a copse, and sunlight momentarily eclipsed Branwen's vision. The palfrey neighed. Branwen pulled back on the reins just before she would have forced her mount into a boulder that reached the horse's chest.

The True Queen continued to pursue Branwen from behind. "Essy, watch out!" she called, motioning at the boulder.

Her cousin laughed. "You might be scared, but I'm not!" Eseult charged Lí Ban straight for the boulder, and Branwen saw her cousin's posture prepare to jump.

The front legs of the horse sailed over the craggy rock. Just as Branwen's shoulders began to sag in relief, one of Lí Ban's back legs caught on the top of the boulder. The palfrey recovered her stride.

Her rider did not.

Eseult screamed as she toppled to the forest floor. Branwen leapt from Senara's back. "Essy!" Branwen shrieked, rushing toward her. Her cousin had stopped screaming.

All of the rage, all of the pain, every grievance Branwen had been harboring against her younger cousin—it all melted like snow in the sun.

Twigs snapped as Branwen dropped to her knees beside Eseult.

"Oh, Essy." The queen had fallen sideways. She lay in a crumpled heap. "Essy, Essy, Essy," she repeated like a prayer.

Branwen rolled the queen onto her back, lowering her face to her cousin's. *Thank you, Bríga.* Eseult was still breathing. Branwen poked the queen's thigh, and her foot twitched involuntarily. *Praise Ériu.* She would walk again.

"Eseult!"

A man's voice sheared the forest, so agonized it was nearly bestial.

Branwen glanced up. Tristan drove his stallion straight for them— for his queen. For the woman he didn't want to love, and the woman he had loved first. King Marc and Ruan were less than a horse length behind the Queen's Champion.

Tristan's mount hadn't fully halted when he jumped down beside them.

"Branwen," he said. Her name was a question, and it was full of terror.

"She's alive."

Tristan stroked the line of Eseult's cheek; blood leaked from a few shallow cuts on her forehead. There was no mistaking the tenderness with which he touched the queen, the affection—like a lover would.

A shadow fell over them. Ruan. He watched as Tristan caressed the queen.

"What happened?" the King's Champion demanded.

"Essy tried to jump her horse over that boulder," Branwen replied between uneven breaths. She directed a glare at Tristan. Recovering himself, he removed his hand.

Ruan glanced at the enormous rock. "She's unconscious," Branwen said. "But nothing seems broken."

"By the Horned One's mercy," Marc said, still atop his horse. He cut the air with two fingers. All of the color had drained from his face. "Ruan, help me down." His shoulder prevented him from dismounting on his own.

The Royal Guardsmen surrounded their king and queen as Ruan helped Marc from the stallion, one-armed. He approached his wife, anguish knitting his brow.

"Forgive me, brother," Tristan said to Marc. His voice was hoarse.

"It's my fault," said Branwen. "I should have let her win." Tears leaked from her eyes. "Why didn't I let her win?" she whispered. Before she could wipe them away, Tristan had lifted his hand to her cheek.

"It's not your fault, Branwen," he said, and Ruan grunted faintly as he watched them.

Marc dropped a hand on Tristan's shoulder. "It's no one's fault. Just an accident." He squatted next to Branwen. "What does the queen need?"

"Rest."

"I'll carry her on my horse," Tristan said.

"*Mormerkti*, Tristan. I would, but—" Marc pulled at his sling, exhaling in irritation.

"Of course."

Ruan looked from his king to Tristan. "I'll help," he said. "Saddle yourself and I'll lift the queen up to you."

Tristan jammed his lips together, grieved, then nodded. He rose to his feet.

Branwen kissed Essy between the eyes and retreated, allowing Ruan to gather the queen into his arms. Marc pushed himself to standing and offered Branwen a hand, which she accepted.

"Branwen," said Ruan with the icy calm of true fear. Her jaw dropped as she lifted her eyes. One of Ruan's arms supported the queen's shoulders, the other her upper thighs.

Beneath the queen's traveling cloak, the back of her gown was stained with blood.

Tristan pivoted at Ruan's tone and let out a shout, instinctively reaching for his sword. "What did you do?" he screamed at his cousin, brandishing his weapon.

Ruan's mouth fell open at the accusation. Tristan had never shown such rage.

Marc looked from Tristan to Eseult to Branwen. Her own knees went weak.

"I'm sorry, *Rix*. I'm—" She paused, trying not to lose her composure completely. Branwen had been right about the pregnancy. She wished she wasn't—so very much.

"My Lord King," Branwen started again, inhaling through her nose. "It appears Queen Eseult is miscarrying."

Tristan audibly swallowed. "She's pregnant?"

"She was."

His gaze remained fixed on Branwen, and for the first time, he looked at her with true suspicion.

"Will she live?" King Marc said in a hush, eyes running up and down the length of Eseult's inert form.

Branwen willed away her own fears. She couldn't let them control her. Not when her cousin needed her. "Miscarriages are common," she told Marc, taking his hand and squeezing it as if he were any other worried husband, as if the bleeding woman was not the sister of her heart.

"But we must make haste for the castle. When she wakes, there will be pain."

Marc shouted at the guards in Kernyvak. Tristan jumped onto his mount, and Ruan lifted the queen into his waiting arms.

There would be blood and there would be pain, and Branwen would stay by Eseult's side, clinging to her like a vine.

MATRONA

WATCHING TRISTAN CARRY ESEULT UP the stairwell of the Queen's Tower, unconscious and bleeding, Branwen's guilt consumed her like shadow-stung flesh does the healthy tissue that surrounds it.

Many boots tromped on the stone steps behind Branwen. Endelyn popped her head out from the door to her chamber on the second floor landing. Alarm rippled across her face when she saw the blood trickling from the True Queen's skirts.

Arthek barked, his nails scrabbling against Tristan's ankles as he flung open the door to Eseult's suite. He hastened toward the canopy bed and lowered his queen onto the coverlet with great care.

Branwen was immediately at his side, watching as her cousin's eyelids fluttered. Eseult made a soft moaning sound as her eyes opened on Tristan. Disoriented, she lifted a hand to his face. "Tristan," she said. "You're here."

The longing in her voice cleaved Branwen in two.

"I'm here," he replied.

Branwen stood next to Tristan, but he was all her cousin could see. And beside Branwen, Ruan and King Marc had stopped in their tracks. In her peripheral vision, she saw Ruan curling and uncurling his hands. A breath caught in her throat.

"Where am I?" Eseult asked her Champion.

"We're at the castle. You fell from your horse."

Voice tight with fear, she said, "Branny?"

She stepped closer. "I'm here, too." Eseult let her hand float from Tristan's face down to the quilt, reaching for Branwen.

Eseult gripped the quilt beneath her fingers and cried out, writhing as a fresh bout of pain overtook her. "Branny," she said, her name almost a gasp. "What's happening?"

Arthek whined at his mistress's suffering. Branwen pushed Tristan to the side and took her cousin's hand. "Get the dog out of here," she told him roughly.

"No," said Eseult. "Don't go, Tristan. Not again."

Branwen gave Tristan a stern look. Eseult was too delirious to censor her feelings. As her Champion, he needed to protect the queen from all threats—including herself. Tristan met Branwen's gaze, his eyes tormented. With tremendous effort, he nodded woodenly.

"I won't go far," he promised his queen. Eseult clutched at her stomach with one hand, moaning, and dug the brittle fingernails of the other into Branwen's palm, gripping her tight.

Arthek barked again as Tristan scooped the puppy into his arms, heading for the door. Branwen lowered herself beside Eseult on the bed, feeling her brow with her free hand. It was clammy. "Branny—it *hurts*," the queen mewled.

"I know, Essy."

King Marc took one step closer to the bed. "It's worse than on the ship," Eseult said to Branwen, scarcely aware of her husband's presence.

"It will pass."

Eseult shook her head back and forth on the pillow, her pallor a terrifying white. "I feel like I'm dying."

Marc muttered something in Kernyvak under his breath. Branwen could only make out the word *Matrona*.

"You're not dying, Essy," Branwen said, voice firm. "I won't allow it. Not you without me."

"I know you won't." Then Eseult's eyes trailed down the length of her body for the first time.

As her gaze fixed on the blood between her legs, the True Queen let out a heartrending sob.

"Please," King Marc said into Branwen's ear. "What can we do for her?"

"What about the tea she takes for her nerves?" Andred asked.

Immediately, he covered his mouth with his hand. His cheeks went pink at having betrayed her confidence.

"It's not strong enough," Branwen replied tersely. Pointing toward the door that led to her small room, she said, "In my healing kit, find a glass vial. It contains a crushed root. Purplish-brown. Bring it to me."

Andred moved toward the door. "I'll help," Endelyn told her brother. He snapped, "I don't need your help," as she followed at his heels.

Returning her attention to Marc, Branwen explained, "It's the same pain reliever I gave you before I removed the arrow."

He nodded. Eseult wailed again. "What can *I* do?" the king asked Branwen.

Branwen gestured to the other side of the bed. "You can comfort her," she said. Marc immediately complied. He lowered himself on the other side of his wife and gently took her hand.

Branwen felt a hand press against the small of her own back. She whipped her eyes up. It was Ruan. A wounded look crossed his face at her reaction. He removed his hand, and she missed the reassurance of his touch.

The door clicked as Tristan reentered the queen's bedchamber.

"Arthek's locked in my room," he announced. He walked a straight line toward Branwen and Eseult, his brow creased with worry. Ruan retreated toward the window.

Endelyn hurried toward Branwen, holding out the vial of *derew* root. Andred was a half a pace behind his sister. "Andred," Branwen said. "Just a pinch will be enough. Dissolve it in water."

His sister scowled as he pried the vial from her grasp. Endelyn accompanied him to the sideboard where a decanter of water rested beside two bronze goblets.

"Branny," Eseult said in a whisper. Branwen leaned in closer to her cousin. "Branny, was it . . . is the baby—" She broke off when she saw the expression on Branwen's face, and she clenched her eyes shut.

Andred approached Branwen, holding out the goblet. *Mormerkti,* she mouthed.

"Essy," she said in a coaxing tone. "I need you to drink this. It will ease the pain."

Her cousin didn't reply, but she allowed Branwen to cup a hand behind her head and set the goblet to her lips. She drank eagerly.

Stroking Eseult's forehead, Branwen said to the room, "The queen needs to sleep." Ruan looked to Marc, who nodded at his Champion.

"I'll be just outside the door," Tristan said. As he moved to leave,

Eseult said, "I love you," although her eyes were closed. Tristan's posture went rigid.

"I love you, too, Essy," Branwen replied, and Tristan kept walking. She prayed it was enough to cover the moment.

Ruan exited next, followed by Andred and Endelyn. It only took a few minutes for the *derew* root to send the queen into a deep slumber.

Branwen continued holding Essy's hand, as did the king. They both listened to the hum of her breathing.

Branwen's mind kept spinning like a potter's wheel, replaying the same memory. She had been nine or ten years old, and she'd just begun helping her aunt in the infirmary at Castle Rigani. One of her first tasks as an apprentice was to restock the jars of herbs and bottles of tonics. Dubthach often harassed Branwen and pulled on her plaits while she worked because he didn't dare take revenge on the princess for her many practical jokes.

On a particularly hot summer's afternoon, Dubthach snatched at Branwen's braid, throwing her off balance as she stepped onto a footstool with a bottle of disinfectant in hand. The thick glass hit the stone floor, and Dubthach vanished down the corridor. At first, it didn't appear to be damaged, so Branwen put it back on the shelf. Only later, when the fresh scent of juniper that filled the room was potent enough to make her eyes water, did Branwen realize there was a crack in the glass.

She should have reported the damage to her aunt. She should have—but she didn't. She was afraid that the queen would determine Branwen was too young or clumsy to be her apprentice.

Later that evening, the Queen of Iveriu came to the garden beneath the south tower where Branwen and Essy were playing.

"The infirmary smells like winter," said her aunt. "Would you know anything about that, Branny? Did you spill the juniper tonic?"

Branwen had stared at the grass between her toes, shamefaced. Before she could muster a reply, Essy told her mother, "I did it. Dubthach and I were playing leapfrog."

The queen had frowned, giving her head a little shake of exasperation.

"How many times have I told you not to play in the infirmary, Essy?"

"I'm sorry. I won't do it again." Her cousin's tone had been contrite, and yet she couldn't refrain from a grin.

"See that you don't," the Queen of Iveriu had scolded her. "And Branny, next time, tell me. I can't fix what I don't know is broken."

After her aunt was gone, Branwen had asked Essy, "Why did you lie for me?"

She'd simply shrugged. "I don't mind when Mother scolds me. But I know you do." Then her cousin had kissed Branwen on the cheek, yanked her plait, and chased her once more around the hazel tree.

As her cousin moaned in her sleep, Branwen could only see the girl who had lied for her, who had taken her scolding. She would do anything to suffer in Essy's place now.

King Marc raised his wife's hand to his mouth and kissed it. *Menantus.* He murmured a word in Kernyvak that Branwen had learned was both an apology and the name of a particularly rapid brook that never froze, not even at Long Night.

Becoming aware of Branwen's gaze, Marc said, "I don't like feeling helpless."

A season ago, she never would have believed the King of Kernyv could ever feel powerless. "Neither do I," she said.

"You always know what to do, Lady Branwen."

"Would that it were true." Her heart twinged. "I'm sorry for—your loss," she said. "But there is nothing to prevent you from having another heir."

Marc gave one sad laugh. "Heirs have a cost," he said. "Men die in battle and the bards praise their bravery. I was with my sister just after she gave birth." He dragged down a breath. "Gwynedd was dying, and she knew it. She put Tristan in my arms and told me that he was mine to protect."

The king's eyes had grown wet with tears. "I was only seven, but I gave her my word. Gwynedd was braver in that moment than I have ever been."

His admission affected Branwen deeply, and she understood yet another reason why he wasn't pressuring her cousin to visit his bed.

"Eseult will recover," she told him. "You will share more than this loss."

Under any other circumstances, Branwen would have welcomed the chance to love Essy's child, a niece or nephew she would never know. But she had loved her cousin first, and she would never trade her cousin's life for that of another. Eseult would survive this loss, and then she would be safe. Tristan would be safe.

"*Mormerktí*, Lady Branwen," said the king. "Like Tristan, your cousin is also mine to protect. I would rather die than let harm come to her. And yet, I find myself a man without weapons."

"You called on Matrona earlier," Branwen said. She reached across the bed and touched his elbow. "I don't know your gods, but I believe you're a man worth helping."

"Will you call on yours as well?" Marc asked. She held his gaze, then nodded.

Branwen and the king watched the True Queen sleep as day faded to night, the room filled with silent prayers.

LIKE A DRAGON

THE HOUR HAD GROWN LATE when King Marc insisted that Branwen take a break from her ministrations of the queen. Fastening her cloak around her shoulders, she'd only taken a few steps down the corridor when the sob she'd been suppressing racked her body. *Essy.* Her cousin had been dealt yet another heart wound today. It was too late for Branwen to apologize for the pain she'd caused her with the Loving Cup—it was too late to explain.

She gripped the wall and broke a nail against the stone.

"Branwen." Her eyes were lured toward Tristan's voice. His stance was battle-ready, and he didn't move to soothe her.

"Tristan." She breathed in his name. "The queen is sleeping. Nothing has changed." Branwen blotted her tears with her sleeve.

He prowled toward her in the same manner he had his competitors at the Champions Tournament, with a lethal kind of grace. The hazel flecks of his eyes glittered with a hardness that Branwen had never seen in them.

"Did you know?" he said. She didn't reply. Tristan only stopped coming closer when they were standing toe-to-toe.

"Did you know the queen was pregnant?" he challenged her again.

Branwen's torrent of emotions coalesced into anger: familiar, powerful.

"Yes," she told him.

Tristan emitted a *tsk*ing sound. "Of course you did. You hoard secrets like a dragon."

"I'm not the only one." She stared at him hard.

"I'm the Queen's Champion, Branwen. Protecting her is my duty. I deserved to know."

"The truth wasn't mine to share. Like you, I serve the queen first."

"Maybe," he growled. "Or maybe you just don't let yourself trust anyone. Maybe you *like* not trusting anyone!"

The words were a blow. Raising her voice, Branwen said, "We were trying to protect *you!*"

"Protect *me?*" Tristan said, incredulous. "Why would you need—" He clamped his lips tight. Fear brightened his eyes. Tilting his face down to Branwen's, close enough to kiss, he started, "Was it—"

Branwen pressed a finger to his lips, silencing him. "Yes," she said.

She watched as several emotions passed over Tristan's face. Nearly six weeks had elapsed since Long Night. He must have assumed that Marc and Eseult had shared a bed. Tristan took a step backward, pressing a fist to his chest as understanding settled in his heart. Then he swung it sideways, pummeling the wall.

"*I* did this to her. She's suffered so much because of me." He pounded the wall again. "One night of madness. She must hate me."

"She doesn't. Essy doesn't hate you at all. It would be better if she did," Branwen whispered, and the words burned her throat. "She thinks what you shared . . . she doesn't regret it."

Tristan scrubbed a hand over his face; the knuckles were raw.

"Then why didn't she tell me?" His voice cracked. "She must have been so scared. I should have—I don't know, I should have done something."

"She was, and she was afraid you might do something rash."

He glanced at Branwen pointedly. "*You* were afraid," he said. "You must have had a plan. You always do."

"We were *both* afraid, Tristan." Branwen had had no plan. If Essy had insisted on keeping the baby, she would have helped her. Her mind had already been scrambling for a way to smuggle the infant out of the birthing room, convince King Marc the child had died, but any solutions were far from guaranteed.

"Neither of us wants to see you dead," Branwen said, the last syllable wobbling. "The peace destroyed." She balled her own hands into fists. "Tell me we were wrong."

Tristan slammed his right hand against the wall hard enough to break it. Blood smeared the wall.

"*Stop it!*" she barked, grabbing his wrist. "You can't defend the queen if you can't wield a sword, and I only have so much magic!"

His expression grew desolate. His shoulders quaked.

"Your goddess never should have chosen me, Branwen. You should have let me die on that raft."

She and Tristan had done so much damage to each other, but here he was, standing in front of her and ripping himself apart. She had stolen his honor, her hands would forever be marked; she had stolen it and she couldn't give it back.

All at once, Branwen threw her arms around him, holding Tristan up, holding Tristan tight, as the air rushed out of him. He gripped her back, fingernails curling into the fabric of her cloak. He clung to her, heartache seeping between them.

Their love had never been uncomplicated, and it was no longer innocent, but Branwen stayed exactly where she was. Torchlight flickered through her tears.

"For months, I've wanted nothing but to regain my honor. To make things right with you, with the queen, with Marc. To prove that I'm more than one betrayal," Tristan rasped. "Seeing Eseult in so much pain—I know I'm not."

His body shuddered against Branwen's. "You *are*, Tristan. You can be." Branwen wanted the same thing, hoped it was also true for herself.

"How can you say that? You risked your life for me. You gave me your *magic*. And look what I've done." His fingers dug into her back.

I did that. It was me. She held him closer, needing his support as much as he needed hers.

"I know it was a mistake," Tristan said. "The worst thing I could have done. And yet, I feel this brutal sadness. Loss for something I . . . never had, that I couldn't want, shouldn't want. Isn't that strange?" An ache welled inside Branwen at his words that pervaded her bones, every part of her.

"I don't think it's so strange," she said, voice scratchy. "Loss is still loss."

Tristan pressed his cheek to hers, and it was damp. She squeezed him tighter.

"I imagined *our* children, Branwen. The day Marc's men came looking for me, as they rowed me back to the ship, I thought of the family we might have had." He trailed a finger down her forearm. "A girl with freckles and as stubborn as her mother."

She released her hold on him.

"I never intended to hurt you," he continued. "I didn't think it was possible to care so deeply for two people at the same time."

"I can't hear this from you, Tristan. Not now. Not ever." *It's too hard.*

"Branwen, we'll see each other every day for the rest of our lives. You said we could be allies. How do I make peace between us?"

It was a spear to the gut. Branwen had been waiting, expecting, *wanting* the Old Ones to punish her, but she was already living her punishment.

"*Tell me,*" he repeated.

"I don't know how to make peace between us, Tristan. I don't know how to find it for myself!"

Branwen pushed past him and dashed down the stairwell of the Queen's Tower, taking the steps two at a time.

She found herself in the terraced gardens as fresh tears marred her vision, and she buried her face in the delicate blooms of childhood's end, which were beginning to wilt. The smoky aroma clung to her tongue.

Her ears pricked at the clack of boots on stone. A lifetime of anticipating raiders had Branwen's hand reaching for the knife that Ruan had given her. Without thinking, she retrieved it from her boot and turned to greet the intruder.

Ruan looked from Branwen to the blade. Lantern light glistened on the golden lion of its handle.

"You're crying," he said, brow furrowed.

"And you're following me."

"I saw you run out of the Queen's Tower like you were being

chased, and I was concerned," Ruan told her. "Do you want me to leave?"

Branwen stared at him. With a shaky breath, she shook her head. She didn't want to be alone right now. Ruan dared a step closer.

"Is there anything I can do—for you?" he said. "I know how much your cousin means to you. How worried you must be."

"No, but *mormerkti*, Ruan."

He took another step, stopping when there was only the knife's blade between them.

"Would you mind putting that away?" he said.

"Do I make you nervous?"

"All the time." Ruan's laugh was tired. "Although it makes me glad you're carrying it. I thought you might have tossed my present into the sea."

"Why would you think that?" Branwen slid her thumb along the grooves of the lion's head.

"You've barely said a word to me since the council meeting."

Tucking the knife back into her boot, she corrected him. "No, *you've* barely said a word to me." She raised herself back to standing, and Ruan was standing very close indeed.

"So, you haven't been avoiding me?" he said, rubbing his thumb against his lip. "Because we disagreed about Prince Kahedrin?"

"Yes, I disagreed with you—I still do. But, no. It's not personal. It's politics."

"I'd say you were a born politician, Branwen. My mother dislikes you because you remind her too much of herself."

"I'm nothing like Countess Kensa."

With an arched eyebrow, Ruan said, "You both fight for what you want."

Her shoulders sagged, conceding the point. Ruan tucked a loose curl behind Branwen's ear. In a gravelly voice, he said, "You're my first lover, Branwen. I don't know how to do this. I've never not been able to walk away before."

"Do you want to walk away?"

"Part of me wants to run." But Ruan twirled her curl around his finger, tugging Branwen nearer.

"Lovers can fight, Ruan. I think we'll probably disagree about a great number of things."

"And that doesn't scare you?" Laughing, he answered his own question. "Of course, it doesn't. Nothing scares you."

"Many things scare me."

Ruan twisted his lips, dubious. "Fights in my household didn't end well," he told Branwen, and he was no longer laughing.

"It doesn't have to be that way."

"When I heard the screams in the forest today, my first thought wasn't for King Marc. It was for you." Ruan swallowed. "That should more than scare me."

"Does it?" Branwen asked, voice quieter than the night.

He lowered his lips to hers. His kiss was soft but firm, demanding. She savored his desire. Pulling back, he said, "I'd like to ask King Marc's permission to court you, Lady Branwen of Castle Bodwa. Formally."

A cord pulled taut inside of Branwen at the thought. "You have my permission, Ruan," she said. "You don't need the king's."

"I could write to King Óengus, if you prefer?"

"I hardly think your mother would approve," Branwen deflected. It wasn't Tristan that made her hesitate, and it wasn't Ruan, either. Not exactly.

"Oh, she isn't your biggest supporter, but she's had her eyes on the lands that Tristan gifted you in Liones for years."

Branwen snapped her head back. "And would you also like my lands, Prince Ruan?"

"If I wanted to court a woman for her lands, I might start with one of Queen Verica's many princess nieces in Meonwara," he replied crisply.

Nodding in apology, Branwen pressed her right palm flat against Ruan's heart. In Iveriu, Tristan had said that she was skilled at finding reasons for them not to be together. Perhaps it was more that she didn't want to be ruled by the laws of men, especially men like Seer Casek, any more than she already was.

"I would like what we have to be just for us, Ruan. No talk of titles or lands," Branwen said. "I don't want to be gossiped about at court. I want something that's just mine."

Ruan's face took on a look of wonder. "And you want that something to be me?" Branwen gave another nod. "I understand the feeling," he said.

With a smile, Branwen slid her hand behind his neck and brought the prince's mouth to hers, parting his lips with her tongue. Ruan wrapped his arm around her waist and held her fast. When he'd kissed Branwen breathless, she laid her head on his chest.

The surf broke against the sandbar that lay to the west of Monwiku.

Ruan caressed Branwen's spine in long, whisper-soft strokes. "I should get back to the queen," she said.

"Stay a minute longer. I'm sure Tristan is at your cousin's side. He also seems very . . . devoted."

Branwen craned her neck to meet Ruan's eyes. "He's her Champion. He's as afraid as you were when King Marc was attacked."

"Of course," came Ruan's reply, but it lacked conviction.

"If you question my cousin's honor, then you question mine."

"I—" He paused; wet his lips.

"Perhaps your jealousy of Tristan is making you see things that aren't there."

Branwen stepped out of his embrace and Ruan clutched at her hand, tugging her back. "I've always wondered why a lion was the symbol of Iveriu when there are no lions on your island," he said. "Now I see I was wrong. You're a lioness, to be sure."

He cracked a half smile. "I like that you're honest with me, Branwen. Maybe I am still jealous." Ruan pulled her closer. "Truce?" he said.

Overhead, the lanterns squeaked in the breeze. Tristan thought her a dragon; Ruan thought her a lion. Perhaps Branwen's heart was a hybrid beast.

A truce might be the only peace she would ever know.

She let another kiss be her answer.

ÉRIU'S COMFORT

IN HER DREAMS, THERE WAS music. An ancient lullaby. Branwen stood at the foot of Whitethorn Mound. The full moon shone off the crescent-shaped blade in her hand.

She raised the moon-catcher in supplication to the Old Ones, begging them for something, but she couldn't remember what. All she felt was yearning, yearning that was strangling her from the inside like a honeysuckle vine.

Branwen sliced her palm with the blade her aunt had gifted her. She offered her blood to Bríga. She offered her blood to Ériu.

How much more did she need to bleed?

Her eyes dropped to the whitethorn blossoms that had fallen at her feet. A trickle of night. Beads of blood glistening like jealous stars leaked onto the petals.

Gasping for air, Branwen raised her gaze back to her palm.

Wildness stirred in her heart as she watched the river of her own black blood gush forth, flow ever more freely.

It scorched the blossoms until there was nothing left.

✠ ✠ ✠

She woke in her own bed, drenched with sweat, panting. The Otherworld melody echoed in Branwen's ears. The longing held in each note clung to her skin.

Stumbling to her feet, thirsty beyond measure, she followed the music. Was she still in the dream? She mopped her damp brow with the sleeve of her nightdress and pushed open the door into the queen's adjoining chamber.

Her eyes caught on silver strings and nimble fingers.

"Tristan?" she said.

The music stopped. Branwen dabbed at the perspiration on the bridge of her nose. Scanning the room, she half expected it to fade away and to find herself back on Whitethorn Mound. She hadn't had a dream so lucid since arriving in Kernyv. Perhaps it was more than a dream. Sleep was a place of in-between, too.

"*Dymatis*," Tristan replied as Branwen stretched her arms above her head with a groan. Tristan was perched on a stool at the bedside of the True Queen, cradling the golden body of the *krotto* between his arms. Endelyn listened to his song from the armchair by the window. She wrinkled her nose at Branwen's disheveled state.

"What time is it?" Branwen said, finger-combing her knotted curls and avoiding Endelyn's stare. The sun was high. "You should have woken me."

Eseult shook her head. "You've been working too hard, like always," she said from where she lay, tucked snugly beneath the coverlet. Her lips formed a quarter smile, but there was a leaden quality to her cousin's voice that dragged on Branwen's spirit as well.

Several days had passed since the queen's accident. There was no physical reason why she couldn't leave her bed. Eseult reached a hand toward Branwen. How Branwen wished she possessed a salve or tonic that would relieve the weight pressing on her cousin's chest. The Loving Cup had caused nothing but pain and Branwen hated herself more with each passing hour.

"I hope the music didn't wake you," said the queen. Branwen drew closer and gave Eseult's hand a squeeze. "No," she assured her.

"I'm glad. Tristan is going to teach me to play the *krotto.*"

Branwen and Tristan traded a glance. His demeanor had also been subdued since the accident. She wanted to be his friend, support him in this, but her own regrets overwhelmed her.

Tristan's hold tightened on the harp. "With your permission," he said, and Branwen's gaze slid back to her right hand, intertwined with the queen's, relieved there was no black blood streaming onto the coverlet.

She couldn't shake the floating feeling, the sensation that she wasn't entirely present in this world.

"You don't mind me using Lady Alana's *krotto*, do you, Branny?" asked her cousin.

It hurt Branwen to see them together, sharing songs as she and Tristan once had, but she was grateful for anything that lifted her cousin's spirits.

"No, no." She squeezed her hand again. Branwen had found refuge in Ruan, and she couldn't deny Tristan or Eseult a respite from their grief.

Forcing a smile, she said, "I think my mother would have liked for you to play it, Essy. You always loved to hear her sing."

"I think I remember." The queen fingered a limp strand of hair.

Branwen thought her cousin must have been too young to carry the memories, but Branwen remembered Essy sitting on her lap beside the hearth, Lady Alana's melodic voice washing over them, only days before she died.

Eseult patted the quilt next to her. "Join us."

Branwen hesitated. She wanted nothing more than to mend her cousin's spirit after this loss, she did. Still, sitting here between Tristan and Eseult, sharing in their heartbreak, in their music, was more than she could bear.

"Let me dress myself first," she said. Releasing Eseult's hand, Branwen caught another strain of the Otherworld melody, even though Tristan's fingers were still.

"What were you playing—just now?" she asked him. "I—I recognized it, but I can't place it. Can you play it again?"

As his hands began to glide over the strings, Tristan said, "I don't think you could have heard the song before, Lady Branwen." His fingers moved deftly, plucking chords that brimmed with remorse. "It's a ballad I'm composing. I haven't finished yet."

"Does it have a title?"

"'The Dreaming Sea,'" he told her, holding her gaze, and continued to strum the *krotto*. Branwen's stomach somersaulted; then she startled as the door to the queen's chamber flew open.

"I didn't realize the duties of the Queen's Champion included serenades, cousin," said Ruan, shoulders thrown back, as he sauntered into the room. His eyes circled its occupants. "And you have not one, but three ladies hanging on your every word."

Branwen studied Ruan's profile. Something was very wrong.

Tristan's fingers tensed on the strings. "Why have you barged into the True Queen's chambers, cousin? She needs peace and quiet to heal."

"I have been sent by the king to summon Lady Branwen for questioning."

Ruan turned toward Branwen, making eye contact for the first time. His eyes were as shuttered as the day they'd met at the Port of Marghas.

Questioning? Branwen's pulse skittered, and her magic thrummed.

Tristan set the harp on the floor and leapt to his feet. "What does King Marc need to question Lady Branwen about?" he demanded, taking the words out of her mouth.

"Concerns have been raised regarding the lady's care for her patients," Ruan informed Tristan. His words were clipped, officious. Branwen felt as if she'd been punched.

"Do *you* have concerns, Prince Ruan?" she asked. *How dare he?* Branwen had let herself cry in front of him, let herself be vulnerable.

Ruan swallowed. "The queen never should have been allowed to go riding while she was with child," Endelyn sniped, as her brother remained silent. Tristan pivoted to face the Kernyvak princess, his nostrils flaring, and she sunk back in her chair, a flush crawling up her neck.

Branwen continued to stare at her lover as if her gaze were as lethal as her magic.

"My cousin is a healer, Prince Ruan," said Eseult, straightening against her cushions. "She would never harm anyone. The king's concerns are misplaced."

The queen's defense made Branwen's heart twinge. With everything that had passed between them, her cousin still trusted Branwen without question. They had both done things that couldn't be undone, but spring was the season of renewal. Perhaps they could start again.

"Lady Queen, I am the King's Champion and I follow his orders." To Branwen, Ruan said, "Please, come with us." His voice quavered ever so slightly, and she looked over his shoulder to see that he was accompanied by two other members of the Royal Guard.

Branwen pressed her palms together, trying to quell her magic. It wanted to fight.

"Would you allow me to change into more suitable attire, Prince Ruan?" she said as calmly as she could manage.

He gave her a long, unreadable look, then nodded.

"Thank you," Branwen told Ruan in Ivernic, and he ground his teeth together.

She refused to hurry. She walked into her room and shut the door. Heart pounding in her ears, Branwen changed into a dress made from wool the color of ripe elderberries.

The practice sword Uncle Morholt had given her peeked out from beneath her cot. It should have been burned along with all of his other possessions when he was denounced as a traitor. Branwen couldn't say why she'd kept it and brought it across the sea. Perhaps because her uncle had been willing to die for what he believed was the right fight, and she would do the same.

Wavering between fury and panic, Branwen plaited her tangled black locks into a single braid that swung against her back. The dream must have been a warning. Tingles spread from her right palm up her arm and across her chest, until it became a numbness, her limbs nearly weightless.

A rapping came at the door. "Ready?" Ruan asked as she opened it. Taking a shallow breath, Branwen nodded. His expression softened a fraction.

"Just answer the king's questions," he said in a whisper.

"Gladly. I have nothing to hide, my prince." Branwen brushed past him with some force as she reentered the queen's bedchamber.

Eseult was on her feet. "Branny, you don't need to do this." She took her hand and sketched their private symbol, urgently, nicking Branwen's skin. "I am the True Queen of Kernyv and I say it isn't necessary." The pitch of her voice was sharp like a badly tuned instrument.

Branwen cupped her cousin's cheek. "It's all right, Essy." She gave the queen a meaningful look. "You have nothing to fear."

"I will accompany you, Lady Branwen," said Tristan. He secured his sword at his waist. Glancing at Endelyn, he barked, "Stay with the queen until I return."

The floating, disoriented feeling returned as Branwen accepted Tristan's arm. Ruan and the Royal Guardsmen escorted them from the Queen's Tower.

Tristan leaned in close as they crossed the inner bailey and whispered in her ear.

"I'm right by your side, Branwen."

✛ ✛ ✛

Countess Kensa glanced at Branwen haughtily as she entered the king's study. Involuntarily, Branwen squeezed Tristan's arm. The countess was seated between Seer Casek and Queen Verica at the table in the center of the room. Andred sat on the other side of the Queen Mother. The look on his face was crestfallen.

King Marc pushed to his feet at the head of the table. "*Dymatis*, Lady Branwen," he said, his countenance devoid of emotion. "Thank you for coming." He nodded at Ruan, who stepped from Branwen's path and came to stand beside his king.

"I am always at your disposal, *Rix*," she said. Releasing Tristan's arm, she curtsied. "I am confused as to why I required an escort."

Marc pulled at the fabric of his sling. He wore the sling as little as possible. Countess Kensa's arrival at Monwiku must have caught the king unawares.

Ruan dismissed the other guards.

"I, too, would like to know the reason for Lady Branwen's escort," said Queen Verica. She coughed into a silk handkerchief, a guttural noise. She should be in bed.

"Countess Kensa," began the king. "It is your right as a member of the King's Council to request an audience with Lady Branwen." He stroked his beard. "Ask her your questions."

Branwen looked between Ruan and his mother. Countess Kensa sat forward in her chair, almost preening. She withdrew something from her lap and held it up for all to see.

Pinched between her thumb and forefinger was a dried leaf, similar in shape to a fern but dark red rather than green.

"Do you know what this is?" the countess asked Branwen.

"It's a leaf from a plant we call Ériu's Comfort in Iveriu. I don't know your name for it in Kernyv."

"False Heart," Andred supplied, barely a whisper.

"As a healer, you must know the uses of the plant," said the countess, as if Branwen were a mouse caught in a trap.

"I do."

Agitated footsteps were heard from the hallway. Branwen and

Tristan twisted toward the door as Queen Eseult burst into the study, Endelyn at her heels.

Eseult's blond hair was unbraided, whirling around her and gleaming in the sunlight like liquid gold. Her teeth were bared, expression ferocious. She stormed toward her husband.

"I demand to know why you sent your Champion—" Eseult sneered at Ruan. "To arrest my cousin!" She gestured at King Marc with a closed fist.

The king took half a step backward. "Lady Branwen isn't under arrest. According to Kernyvak law, the King's Council has the right to summon any subject for questioning."

"Even when that subject is in the service of the True Queen?" Eseult glanced at Branwen, her cousin's jaw set with the same determination she'd seen many times throughout their lives. Branwen wasn't the only lioness that had crossed the waves from Iveriu.

Directing another glower at her husband, the queen said, "How dare you question Branwen without me! Without telling me what she's being accused of!" Her voice bounced off the high ceiling. "Branwen is my family and you will not take her away from me!"

King Marc shifted uneasily, bewildered at Eseult's vehemence. He had never seen her lose her temper before.

"I'm sorry, my queen. I thought you were too weak to leave your bed." Regret stained his features. A muscle flickered in his jaw. "I didn't want to overtax you."

"I'm feeling much better," Eseult said, livid.

"I can see that, and I'm greatly relieved." Marc extended a hand toward her, and she avoided his touch.

"By the Horned One's mercy," Seer Casek interjected, cutting the air with two fingers.

Eseult glared at the *kordweyd*. "It has nothing to do with the Horned One. I owe my recovery to Branwen." She aimed her gaze once more at her husband. Pointing at the sling, she said, "As do you, my Lord King."

"Indeed," Queen Verica said, eyeing her son with consternation.

"Do you know what this is, Lady Queen?" Countess Kensa asked. She held up the red leaf.

"No," Eseult said tartly, and rested her hands on her hips.

"Ah." The countess arched an eyebrow in the exact same way that her eldest son often did. "Andred informed me that when brewed as a tea, it brings on a woman's bleeding." Looking from Eseult to King Marc, she said, "It makes a woman miscarry."

Eseult swept a panicked glance between Branwen and Tristan.

Branwen's legs trembled from the effort of forcing herself not to react.

"Endelyn found the False Heart in Lady Branwen's healing kit," Countess Kensa announced, brandishing the leaf at the king.

"I—" Branwen started, but Tristan spoke over her.

"I'm afraid I don't follow your logic, Countess," Tristan told her. But Branwen did. If the nobles believed that the queen had purposefully miscarried Kernyv's heir, she didn't know what would happen. Branwen's mind filled with the vision of Eseult walking toward a pyre.

To Endelyn, Tristan demanded, "Why were you rifling through Lady Branwen's things?"

The princess cringed, her ears turning scarlet. "Lady Branwen asked me to fetch something for the True Queen's pain. I noticed this in her box of herbs."

"She asked *me*," said Andred, and his sister's eyes became slits.

Queen Verica peered at Countess Kensa sideways and said, "I have to agree with my grandson. What is your question for Lady Branwen?"

Appealing once more to King Marc, the countess said, "My Lord King, it is my understanding that Lady Branwen is in the habit of preparing a tea to steady the True Queen's nerves. Just before the wedding, she asked Andred for directions to the White Moor because she was missing an ingredient."

Eseult's shoulders hitched as she drew in a breath. She slid another glance at Branwen; Branwen shook her head, almost imperceptibly.

"There is nothing wrong with a calming tea," said the king.

"No, but it would be easy enough for Lady Branwen to brew a tea from False Heart instead."

Branwen's jaw dropped, and rage erupted in her breast. She pressed her right hand to her stomach, curling her fingers, digging into the wool of her dress. Countess Kensa wasn't bold enough to accuse the True Queen outright, but she clearly wanted to sow discord between the king and the Iverwomen.

"The queen fell from her horse!" Tristan exclaimed. He looked from the king to Ruan. "You were there, cousin. As were you, *Ríx*."

"I was," said Ruan.

"Agreed," King Marc said. "Countess, I cannot see any reason why Lady Branwen would poison the queen. What do you believe her motive to be?"

Branwen looked toward her cousin, but her cousin refused to meet her gaze. Eseult's complexion was pallid. Her bottom lip quivered. The queen shifted her weight, unsteady, and Branwen felt unsteady, too. The world tilted around her.

Eseult knew of a reason why Branwen might want her to miscarry.

Did she—*could* she believe Branwen would poison her? Dark laughter rolled through the back of her mind. She was drowning in it. Lost, buffeted.

She scarcely heard Countess Kensa charge, "Armorica would like to see Kernyv without an heir, and Lady Branwen appears to be in league with Prince Kahedrin."

"In league with Prince Kahedrin?" Tristan gave a shocked laugh. "Marc, you can't seriously be entertaining these accusations. Lady Branwen is no spy. She is loyal to her cousin above all."

"To Iveriu," Eseult said under her breath. "She is always loyal to Iveriu."

The vine from Branwen's dream strangled her anew, strangled her where she stood only nobody else could see. Branwen longed to embrace her cousin, shake her cousin, make her see the truth.

She couldn't stand for Essy to doubt her motives for even a single heartbeat.

King Marc crossed his arms. "Do you have any proof upon which you're basing your charges, Countess?"

"Seer Casek," she prompted.

"Sire," the *kordweyd* began. "Too much False Heart could cause the internal bleeding that killed the Armorican prisoner."

"You're accusing her of murder, too?" Tristan cried, fingering the pommel of his sword.

The king swung his gaze from the seer to Branwen. "My lady, can you explain why you have the False Heart in your possession?" He asked the question carefully, without menace.

Branwen interlocked her hands behind her back, resisting the urge to strike someone. She was guilty of many betrayals, but not of those which she was being accused.

"Yes, my Lord King. False Heart, as you call it, when taken in small doses, is used to treat many female ailments."

"Such as?" Seer Casek said.

"It prevents pregnancy," Andred told the seer, then blushed as he glanced at Branwen. "That's what I've read." He lowered his eyes toward the table.

"Yes. Andred is correct," Branwen said. "It does." At her side, Tristan stiffened, and his stare grazed her cheek. She flicked a glance at him, at his dark eyes bright with guilt, and then looked directly at the King's Champion.

"The False Heart belongs to me, and me alone."

Ruan's jaw went slack. His shoulders slouched forward.

"Why would you have need of such a plant?" said Seer Casek, contempt tipping his words.

"I think you have questioned the lady's honor quite enough," Tristan roared. He knew full well why Branwen might have needed it on Long Night.

Eseult remained quiet. She pulled a blond strand from the crown of her head and watched it fall to her feet.

"I don't mind answering," Branwen told him. "Seer Casek, I suppose that the drawback to all of the *kordweyd* being men is that you do not possess the knowledge which is passed down between gifted women." It took all of her strength to maintain her composure as she spoke.

"In addition to preventing pregnancy, False Heart can also ease the cramps that come with a woman's monthly bleeding. This is why we call it Ériu's Comfort."

"I prefer that name," Queen Verica said, her voice croaky as she coughed, cheeks sunken. "Your knowledge will be invaluable at the royal infirmary, Lady Branwen."

King Marc inhaled through his mouth and everyone went quiet.

"Lady Branwen's answer has satisfied me," he said. "Her use of the plant is her choice and that is her right."

"*Mormerkti*, my Lord King." Branwen bowed her head. Humiliation rippled beneath her skin, and she would not soon forget who had been responsible for it.

"But, sire, it still leaves the question of who murdered the Armorican," Countess Kensa protested. "Is it not true that Lady Branwen tended the assassin alone? And that a disturbance was heard by a guard?"

Kensa looked directly at her son, and Ruan nodded. So Tutir had reported Branwen's outburst, after all. Why hadn't Ruan mentioned it to her?

"Lady Branwen had ample opportunity to administer a lethal dose of False Heart. And she demanded that the body be burned—to disguise her crime, perhaps."

"The prisoner was still alive after Lady Branwen's visit," Ruan said to his mother, voice growing steely. He caught Branwen's eye. Seething, she dropped her gaze. His defense was too little, too late.

"Depending on the dose, however, it might have been a few hours before it took effect," Seer Casek said, addressing King Marc.

"Lady Branwen was attending the king before the council meeting," Andred said. "With me." He darted a look of apology at Branwen.

"But we don't know where she was before that," said Countess Kensa. "Endelyn says she wasn't present in the Queen's Tower that morning. She could have slipped into the castle kitchens."

"You have a tremendous imagination, Countess Kensa," Tristan scoffed. "I'd almost think you were a bard."

Endelyn stepped out from behind Queen Eseult. "My Lord King,

Lady Branwen wasn't present in the queen's chamber when I arrived to wake her." She looked at Eseult. "Was she, Lady Queen?"

Eseult lifted her head in a jerky motion. Her eyes were dull. Pitching her gaze between Endelyn and Branwen, she started, "I don't—"

Ruan interrupted the True Queen. "I know where Lady Branwen was that morning, *Rix*. She was with me." He took a step toward Branwen, his hands hanging at his sides, palms up as if in supplication. "Lady Branwen was with me until she arrived at your chamber to tend your wounds."

"From the moment she woke?" asked his mother.

"Yes." It was a hard syllable.

Tristan's head swung in Branwen's direction, as did Endelyn's. Apparently the Kernyvak princess wasn't as diligent a spy as she thought she was. Branwen's fingernails cut half-moons into her palms to keep from exploding. So much for having a lover—having anything—that was hers and hers alone. She could almost hear her magic crackle in the air as she leveled Ruan with a glare that made him gulp.

"I've heard enough," King Marc declared. "My apologies, Lady Branwen. Countess Kensa, you are ignorant of a most important fact."

"Which is?"

"When we were ambushed in the forest, it was Lady Branwen who stopped Ruan from finishing off the Armorican so that we could question him. She had nothing to fear from letting him speak to the King's Council. She did not want him dead."

"But—"

The king's eyes were a tempest. "The next time you bring slanderous allegations against a trusted member of this court, Countess, you had better have substantial proof. Not wild speculation."

Utter shock blanketed the countess's face. Branwen had never heard King Marc castigate anyone so thoroughly, and it would appear neither had the countess.

"Lady Branwen is sister to my wife, which makes her sister to me. And she saved my life. She protected me without a weapon, with no thought for herself," he said gruffly. "If we turn on each other, we won't need the Armoricans to destroy us, Countess Kensa."

"I only sought to protect you," the countess said, somewhat obsequiously. "You are my nephew, after all."

"Of course," he said. Surveying the room, the king added, "While you're all assembled, won't you join me in congratulating Lady Branwen on her new appointment?"

"Appointment?" asked Seer Casek.

To Branwen, King Marc said, "I am appointing you as the official Royal Healer. If you'll accept?"

"It would be my honor." Branwen's shoulders shuddered. Of her many crimes, Countess Kensa's charges were not among them. If King Marc had believed Branwen—and Iveriu—to be complicit in his assassination attempt, the Otherworld only knew what revenge Kernyv would take on her beloved homeland.

Relief made her light-headed. Branwen lifted her eyes to the True Queen with a timid smile.

The queen didn't smile back.

Nothing but Sand

KING MARC DISMISSED EVERYONE SAVE his queen. His brow had been deeply creased as Branwen took Queen Verica's arm to escort her back to her suite. Her cousin still wouldn't meet Branwen's gaze as she exited. Each nerve was a needle beneath her skin.

The Queen Mother acquiesced immediately to Branwen's suggestion that she take to her bed, which emphasized how frail the proud woman had become.

She returned slowly to the Queen's Tower, the air temperate as it teased the wisps at Branwen's hairline. The Festival of Belotnia was still more than two moons away, but, perhaps, summer came earlier to Kernyv than it did to Iveriu.

Tristan leaned against the archway that led up to the True Queen's chamber. His sword rested against his hip.

"How is my grandmother?" he asked, tension in his voice. The truth of the old woman's weakening state was hard to conceal. Still,

Branwen had given Queen Verica her word not to make her illness common knowledge.

"She's having a nap until dinnertime."

Tristan pressed his lips together at her reply. The wind blew between them. From the gardens, the chimes rang out.

"Thank you," Branwen said to Tristan in her native tongue. His eyes lit with surprise. "Thank you for defending me."

"Branwen." He took a step closer. "I owe you my life many times over. I will always defend you." He paused, composing his next words. "Please trust in that if you can trust me in nothing else."

A lump welled in Branwen's throat. "I release you from your obligation."

"I don't want to be released."

"Then consider us even."

Tristan gave his head one shake. Branwen didn't know how to respond but before the silence stretched on too long, Tristan's shoulder blades drew together. His gaze focused on something behind her.

"Ruan." His cousin's name became an accusation.

"I would like to speak with Lady Branwen," Ruan said. Tristan returned his gaze to her and she clutched her skirts, keeping her back to Ruan.

What did Tristan make of the revelation that Branwen had spent the night with his cousin?

After a beat, Tristan said, "I doubt the lady has anything to say to you."

"The lady can speak for herself," Ruan retorted.

"Yes. She can." Branwen pivoted toward the Kernyvak prince. His complexion was ashen. "What do you want to say to me, Ruan?"

"Alone," he said, glaring at Tristan. He flicked his lips with his tongue. To Branwen, he implored, "*Please*," in Ivernic.

The unbidden memory—the sensation—of his hands, his kisses moving over her body, and the way he smiled at Branwen when she wore nothing but her scars sparked in her mind. But he'd done nothing to prevent such outrageous claims from being brought against her.

"*Please*," he repeated.

"I'll give you a moment, and no more," Branwen relented. Better to rip the bandage from a wound than to let it fester.

Tristan drummed his fingers on the flat of his sword. "I'll see if the True Queen needs anything."

"Like a serenade?" said Ruan. Tristan grimaced as he headed into the stairwell. With his cousin's footsteps receding, Ruan reached for Branwen. She dodged his hand.

"This is your moment," she said. "Don't waste it."

"I was only doing my duty, Branwen," he said. "I must do as the king commands."

"And your mother—do you also do as she commands?"

A breath hissed through Ruan's teeth. "She arrived at the castle this morning. I had no idea as to the source of her intelligence."

"Your sister, apparently."

"Endelyn is . . . don't blame her. She thought she was doing the right thing by reporting to our mother." Branwen crossed her arms, and Ruan blew out another frustrated breath. "My sister and my mother—it's complicated."

"From where I stand, it's very uncomplicated. Your entire family would like to see me branded a traitor to the throne."

"No, Branwen. *No*." Ruan extended his hand toward her once

more, then stopped himself. "Andred is devastated. He idolizes you. He's afraid you hate him."

"I could never hate Andred," she said. He was the lone member of House Whel whom she bore no malice. Doubtless the boy had told Countess Kensa the uses of False Heart in an attempt to be helpful. He possessed a genuine passion for herbs and healing, and he craved the approval of both his mother and older sister.

"Why did you cry out when you were in the cell?" Ruan asked. "Did the prisoner hurt you?" Concern infused his question.

"No. I pricked myself with your knife," she lied. "You could have asked me sooner." She was glad that she hadn't disclosed her vision to anyone at the castle.

Ruan's shoulders rolled forward. "I'm sorry, Branwen. Do you hate me?"

"If you think me capable of murdering the Armorican prisoner—a defenseless man, that I could poison my own cousin, then *you* should hate *me*, Prince Ruan!"

"I never believed you did anything of the kind. I feel the opposite of hate for you, Branwen."

The admission filled the air between them.

"And now everyone in Kernyv knows I shared your bed!" Branwen said, voice rising as her indignation mounted. "Congratulations. Your mother and the other nobles will enjoy gossiping about how you made a conquest of the Ivernic lady's maid."

"That isn't what I wanted. My only thought was to give you an alibi," he said. "But, why not let me court you openly? It would silence any wagging tongues."

"I've told you I have no interest in marriage. Certainly not to a man who would accuse me of treason!"

"Branwen, I felt sick. I felt sick when the king sent me to fetch you. If anyone has made a conquest, it's you who has made one of me." Ruan waved a pleading hand. "But Marc is my king—I have to investigate any and all threats to his crown."

"I understand."

"You do?"

"Yes." She held his gaze. "I let you know me more than any other man in this world, and I understand now that it was a mistake." Branwen had known before the wedding night that making the King's Champion her lover was a dangerous, foolhardy thing to do—and yet she'd done it, heedless.

She took a step under the archway and Ruan hooked her elbow.

"You said lovers could fight."

"We are no longer lovers." Branwen jerked her arm from his grasp and retreated into the darkness of the stairwell.

✦ ✦ ✦

Eseult sat alone in an armchair, framed by shafts of streaming light. Her shoulders were hunched; her eyes red and raw.

"Did something happen with the king?" Branwen asked as she closed the door behind her. Arthek yelped and raced across the room, nails clacking, and pressed his nose against Branwen's ankles like he was digging for something in her skirts.

Eseult absently stroked her belly. She gazed out the window toward the sea.

"Ériu's Comfort," she said. "Did my mother give it to you?"

Branwen pinched her lips together at the question. "Some time ago."

"She never gave it to me."

"I used to suffer with my monthly bleeding. You know I did."

Eseult nodded in a vague way. "Mother wants me to bear an heir for Kernyv and Iveriu. It's all she's ever wanted." Her laugh was brittle. "Little does she know I nearly fulfilled her wish."

"I'm sorry, Essy. So sorry. I would carry this loss for you if I could."

"Are you?" The True Queen seared her with a look. "Are you truly sorry? This is what you wanted."

Branwen took several quick steps toward her cousin. Arthek thought she was giving chase and he followed, yipping excitedly.

"You can't believe I wanted you to fall from your horse. I tried to warn you, Essy. But you wanted to win—like you always do."

"You've won this time, Branny." Eseult pushed to her feet. "You're the most gifted healer in generations, that's what my mother always said. And yet you couldn't stop me from losing the pregnancy? Maybe you just didn't *want* to?"

Branwen's jaw dropped. "There was no way to prevent nature from taking its course."

Wasn't there? A voice at the back of her mind taunted. Could the Hand of Bríga have saved Essy's pregnancy? It hadn't occurred to Branwen to use it.

"How do I know you *didn't* drug me like you did the king on our wedding night?" Eseult charged, and Branwen balked.

"Are you forgetting *why* I drugged your husband?" She thrust out a hand. "*Why* I needed Ériu's Comfort?"

"I haven't forgotten. But you didn't do it for me." She sucked her lips together, expression forlorn. "You did it for Iveriu. And it seems you've found other uses for the protection, too—with the King's Champion."

Branwen closed the Hand of Bríga in a fist. Her cousin had always known the deepest and most effective ways to cut her.

"I won't apologize for trying to protect our people—and that includes you, Essy," she said raggedly. "I won't apologize for not wanting to see you executed!"

"Was it me you didn't want to see executed, or was it Tristan? You lied to me about your love for him in Iveriu. Maybe you poisoned me to save him!"

"Essy, how can you say that? I tried to talk to you about ways to keep the baby—you wouldn't listen!"

"You wanted to give it away! You wouldn't let me keep it!"

"Of course not! There was no other way!" Branwen shouted. "The chances of getting caught were still enormous—but I would have done it! I would have done it for you!"

"I guess we'll never know." Tears collected on the True Queen's lashes. "Ever since we were girls, I loved you more than my kingdom, Branny. I used to think you loved me more, too."

I did. The words were stuck on the tip of Branwen's tongue. She had conjured the Loving Cup because she'd loved Essy more than the Land. And look what her love had done—look what she had done to her cousin, to the king, to the man who had wanted her to be his bride.

"When we boarded the *Dragon Rising*," the True Queen said, "you promised me it would be us against the world. I believed you."

"Essy, please. I would never hurt you."

Her tears began to fall. "The trouble is, I don't know if I believe you. I don't know what I believe. I'm not who I was. And neither are you."

Branwen's magic flared. Something deep inside her cracked.

"What are you saying?" she rasped.

"Since you've been appointed the Royal Healer, I have asked King Marc to find you accommodation in keeping with your new position,"

Eseult told her. "A room in the West Tower beneath Queen Verica's apartment is being prepared for you as we speak."

"Essy—"

"I am the True Queen of Kernyv, and this is my decision. You told me that I needed to learn to stand alone, Branny." She gave her a fierce look. "I'll have your things sent to your new chambers directly. You may go."

Branwen stood motionless. "Go," the queen commanded.

She had no choice but to obey.

She rushed out of the tower faster than even Senara could have carried her and raced into the gardens, nearly colliding with a birdbath made from granite. Her knuckles scraped against the stone.

Cursing, Branwen plunged her hands into the water to soothe the sting.

She watched the ripples as they began to still. The surface of the water reflected a much younger Branwen.

She recognized the scene: Her forehead scrunched as she built a many-tiered sandcastle for her parents. It was the day they died.

A high-pitched giggle trilled across the beach. Essy catapulted toward the castle that Branwen had spent hours building. Long-forgotten anger flooded her.

She knew what came next.

Only it didn't. This time, when her cousin launched herself at Branwen, just at the moment they tumbled together on top of the castle, Essy disintegrated in her arms.

The castle remained standing and Branwen was left hugging nothing but sand.

Icy sweat beaded on Branwen's top lip. She removed her hands from the water, leaving a swirl of blood behind.

FALSE FLAG

A WEEK HAD PASSED SINCE the True Queen of Kernyv had exiled Branwen from her apartment. They hadn't spoken since. The queen informed King Marc that she was feeling too tired to leave her chambers and Branwen didn't contradict her. Only the sound of Lady Alana's *krotto* signaled that her cousin was safe and well.

Branwen paused in the middle of the courtyard and let the music settle over her as it drifted down from the Queen's Tower. The wistful melody raised the tiny hairs on her arms.

The morning after Branwen's banishment, Talorc had escorted Lowenek to Monwiku. She was gratified to see that the girl no longer required a crutch to support her weight. Branwen asked King Marc's permission to have Lowenek attend the Queen Mother and, absently, he'd agreed. His countenance had grown more reticent, brooding.

Late at night, Branwen often spied him from her window pacing the garden. She couldn't sleep, either. Regret kept her awake, disbelief that her cousin could believe she would ever intentionally harm her.

Branwen had always been the one to soothe Eseult's pain. She didn't know how to do anything else, even when it hurt her. Branwen's longing for her cousin's company was just the near side of rage.

Queen Verica had sent Lowenek to summon Branwen to her chambers, but she remained rooted to the spot, letting the melancholy chords of Tristan's song wash over her for a few moments longer.

Somehow Branwen had made new friends in Kernyv and, for the first time in her life, she had an official status and occupation that had nothing to do with being Eseult's cousin. She should take some satisfaction in that, and yet, her heart was a blue sky with a black hole where the sun should be.

"He's not half-bad. My cousin."

Branwen's eyes flipped open on Ruan. "You make it a habit of startling me."

"You don't startle easily."

"I still have your knife."

He gave her a long look, but his expression was guarded. "Good," he said. Ruan hadn't engaged Branwen in more than pleasantries for the past week. She suspected he was the kind of man who only apologized once.

Ruan thrust his chin at the True Queen's bedchamber window. "Tristan and Eseult make beautiful music together," he said.

"Is that what Endelyn tells you?" Branwen replied.

"No." Ruan caught her eye with a crafty grin. "On the contrary, she says the True Queen is a rather terrible harpist."

"She's just learning," she said. Defending her cousin was the habit of a lifetime.

"And Tristan is a most attentive teacher. She'll soon be a master musician."

King Marc was too focused on Armorica to notice how many harp lessons Tristan was giving his queen. The King's Champion was not.

"*Dymatis*, Prince Ruan," Branwen told him, and resumed walking toward the West Tower, leaving him behind. Her palms grew sweaty as her magic tingled in her veins, fiery and cold. Grief was a wounded animal, and Branwen tried to keep her own caged. She feared the queen would let hers run free.

The West Tower's layout was identical to the others. The room that Branwen had been given beneath Queen Verica's suite was the same as Endelyn occupied in the Queen's Tower. The king had been using the space to store his excess maps and manuscripts.

Branwen suspected that Eseult hadn't offered the room to her before because she wanted to keep her cousin close. And now, she didn't.

Lowenek opened the door to Queen Verica's chamber the moment Branwen knocked. From farther back in the room, the Queen Mother said something to the girl in rapid Kernyvak. Lowenek smiled sweetly at Branwen and left.

"I told her to help Andred with his flowering box experiments. We need a moment in private," Queen Verica explained. "It's nice to see the children working together."

Branwen thought Andred would protest at being called a child, but her lips curved as she closed the door behind her. She surveyed her patient with a critical eye.

The Queen Mother was formally dressed in a gown of burgundy damask and her silvery hair had been intricately plaited. She was seated at the small table near the hearth, dice resting in front of her. She hadn't left her bed for days.

Queen Verica touched her crown of plaits and smiled knowingly at Branwen's scrutiny. "Lowenek has agile fingers. She'd make a skilled surgeon," she said. "I wanted to look my best." A cough racked the Queen Mother's diminished frame and she raised a glass of Mílesian spirits to her lips.

Beckoning with her other hand, she told Branwen, "Come, sit with me."

Branwen pulled out the finely whittled chair opposite the old queen. Rain started to fall as Queen Verica picked up the dice and tossed them. *Plink, plink.*

Both dice landed on the Aquilan numeral for one: the worst possible pair.

"A gambler must always know when to walk away," said the Queen Mother. "The time has come for me to do just that."

She drained the remainder of the spirits.

"I wanted to hold on through the wedding, and I did. I've been greedy with time. As you grow older, Lady Branwen, you'll find it's the one thing you can never get enough of," Queen Verica told her. "I wanted more time with Tristan, with my son. I wanted to help my daughter-in-law navigate the Kernyvak court."

She sighed. "And you, Lady Branwen. I wish I could stay to see all that you'll accomplish." The Queen Mother circled her wrists. "But it's not to be."

Meeting Branwen's gaze, she continued, "I am heartened that you accepted the position of Royal Healer. You will be much needed, I fear, in the coming months."

Branwen dropped her eyes to the Queen Mother's now empty glass.

"How much time do you have left?" she asked.

"An hour. Maybe two. The *kordweyd* in Liones prepared an elixir for when my body could take no more." She smiled. "I feel better than I have for seasons."

"I'm glad." Branwen laid her hand atop the old woman's.

"I apprised King Marc of my illness after the wedding. Thank you for keeping my confidence," she said. "Lest Countess Kensa should accuse you of poisoning me, I have also told him of the elixir—and my decision."

She nodded. "*Mormerkti.*"

"The countess serves only herself. She must see you as an obstacle to something she wants, Lady Branwen."

"I don't know what that could be."

"Unfortunately, neither do I." The Queen Mother toyed with the dice. "I retreated to Castle Wragh after my husband Merchion's death. I didn't want to undermine Marc's authority as a new king. A young king. Now I regret leaving court. But it's too late, and regrets will do me no good."

Queen Verica shifted in her seat. "I have left instructions with Marc that the income from my dower lands in Meonwara should be used to fund the royal infirmary. In perpetuity. This will not please Seer Casek." Her smile broadened. "But I would not have Matrona forgotten in Kernyv," she said.

"Like your Goddess Ériu, Matrona brings comfort to women. I want there to be a place where female healers can share their knowledge. It will be a legacy worth leaving my people."

Branwen was overcome at her words. "Thank you for your generosity, Queen Mother. For your faith in me." She swallowed. "And in the True Queen."

Queen Verica nodded, smile wavering, while her gray eyes remained acute.

"When I was a girl," she began, "I summered at an old Aquilan villa on the coast of Meonwara. There was rock jutting up from the sea, just beneath the cliffs that sailors call the Two Sisters."

She coughed thickly. "Many ships are wrecked upon it." She raised a silk handkerchief from her lap. "The locals say that one sister fell from the cliff top and that the other jumped after her because she couldn't live without her."

Branwen chewed her lip. "Don't take it too much to heart if Queen Eseult needs time to herself in the next weeks," the Queen Mother told her. "I lost several pregnancies between Gwynedd and Marc. There is always a period of mourning for what might have been. She will come back to you when she's ready."

Branwen broke Queen Verica's gaze, shame flooding through her. All she could do was nod.

"May I ask you another favor, Lady Branwen?"

"Of course."

"You have saved the lives of both my son and my grandson. Watch over them for me. The king will need all the allies he can get. And Tristan—he cares for you deeply. I had expected another betrothal by now."

"I—" Branwen started, but there was too much she would never be able to explain. "I will do my best," she promised the Queen Mother.

The old queen glanced at the darkening sky. "Time is running short. Will you find Tristan and Marc, and send them to me?"

Branwen stood at her request. "I'm also leaving you my dice," said Queen Verica. Hazy light shone on the alabaster. "Even if you prefer Little Soldiers, I think you're more of a gambler than either my son or my grandson."

They shared a final smile.

The rain cooled the hot tears on Branwen's face as she crossed the courtyard and entered the King's Tower.

She heard voices coming from inside the king's study as she climbed the stairs. She knocked on the door, which was already ajar.

King Marc whipped around at the sound. His face was whiter than the crest of a wave.

Encircling him, wearing equally bleak expressions were Tristan, Ruan, and a man that Branwen had never seen before. The stranger had a lithe build, his skin golden-brown. His long, dark hair was pulled back with a leather string at the nape of his neck.

He gave Branwen a look that was neither friendly nor unfriendly, then glanced back at Marc.

"What is it?" she asked. Bile surged up her throat. "What's happened?"

Tristan stepped forward. "Crown Prince Havelin is dead. Kahedrin is the new heir to the Armorican throne."

Her lips parted, but she couldn't even gasp. "An assassin?"

"Pirates."

"Pirates flying the flag of Kernyv," Marc spat. He curled the hand of his uninjured arm into a tight first.

"But, why—why would they do that?"

It was the stranger who answered. "To start a war, my lady. To start a war."

DEATH IN THE NIGHT

WIND LASHED THE CLIFF TOP as Queen Verica was laid to rest.

Branwen had washed her body tenderly, with reverence. In the short time they'd known each other, the older woman had grown dear to her. As she'd prepared the queen for her burial, Branwen's thoughts had lingered on her own mother, wondering how her aunt had felt as she'd cleaned her sister's body.

To mask the stench of death, Branwen had rubbed rose oil into the creases of the Queen Mother's skin. The body was then transported to the castle cellars, which were cool enough to slow decay, while messengers were sent to Meonwara and throughout Kernyv with news of Queen Verica's death. King Marc sat vigil beside his mother's body every night, and met with his councillors during the day.

For ten days and nights, fear had coiled around Monwiku Castle like a serpent.

Two of Queen Verica's nieces and one nephew from Meonwara

had finally arrived at the castle yesterday. Branwen recognized the sandy-haired man, roughly the same age as Marc, from the Champions Tournament.

This afternoon, the sky was a lonely pewter-blue as Branwen watched Tristan, Ruan, Andred, and the king raise the Queen Mother's litter aloft and carry it into the burial mound. King Marc winced as his shoulder ailed him, but he would not be dissuaded from this final act of love for his mother.

Countess Kensa, Endelyn, and the True Queen followed the body inside. Only members of the Kernyvak royal family were permitted entry to the sacred site.

Branwen remained on the cliff top with the other mourners. Wild daisies were opening at her feet. Representatives from all of the Kernyvak noble Houses, as well as the prince and princesses from Meonwara waited in silence.

The burial mound was ancient. It rose imperiously above the headland, resembling a small hill. Thousands of black and white stones decorated the circumference of the mound. The pattern mesmerized the eye.

During the procession from the castle, Andred had whispered to Branwen that no one knew who had constructed the resting place of the kings and queens of Kernyv. Lugmarch himself, perhaps. Or giants. One day, Eseult would be laid to rest among these ancient monarchs.

Branwen fidgeted a piece of white quartz between her fingers. The edges were uneven. Andred had pressed the pebble into Branwen's hand, explaining that mourners in Kernyv offer a white stone to the deceased with the wish of peace in the afterlife.

The custom was much older than the belief in the Horned One. The *kordweyd* disapproved, but they did nothing to halt the practice.

Branwen slid her gaze over the faces of the crowd to Seer Casek. He, too, held a piece of quartz in his hand.

Queen Verica had been resourceful and strong. The court at Monwiku would be more dangerous for Branwen—and the True Queen—without the support of the king's mother. The late queen had told Branwen to give Eseult time to heal, but with each passing day, she feared her cousin would never return to her.

An unnatural quiet wove itself around the funeral guests. Not only the nobility, but commoners, too, had come to pay their respects. Lowenek stood with the other castle servants, together with Talorc and Seer Ogrin.

Talorc had stayed on at the temple to look after the pigs, which was less grueling work than returning to the mines. Lowenek held his hand and Talorc ruffled her hair, gazing down at her with grandfatherly affection. Both of them had lost their families in the mining disaster, but at least they had found a new one in each other.

Branwen doubted Talorc, or the other freed Ivernic prisoners, could feel much grief at Queen Verica's death. If she had opposed King Merchion's raids on Iveriu, she hadn't put an end to them. But she'd raised a son who had. Branwen lamented that she would never get to know all of the Queen Mother's complexities and contradictions.

Waves battered the rocks below. Armorican ships might soon be crossing the Southern Channel toward Kernyv—and Iveriu. More prisoners of war might soon be taken from both kingdoms. Branwen had thought she was fighting the right fight, made both sacrifices and mistakes, and yet everything was on the verge of coming undone.

She clutched the white quartz so tightly with the Hand of Bríga that she hissed. A watchful pair of eyes landed on her.

They belonged to the man who had brought news of Crown Prince Havelin's death. His face was a bland kind of handsome: inviting, but not too memorable. Before he'd been introduced to her by name, Branwen had realized that this man must be King Marc's agent abroad. And then she learned his name: Xandru.

Xandru was no simple merchant. The king's former lover was a spy.

Branwen darted him a quick smile as she loosened her grip on the stone. He returned it. Since his arrival at Monwiku, she and Xandru had been observing each other with cordial smiles the way one surveys a battlefield.

What did it mean that King Marc had recalled his *karíd* to his court? The only person she could ask was Tristan, but he had been avoiding her since the night Queen Verica died.

A seagull circled overhead. The gull's cry was wretched, at odds with the somber quiet of the mourners.

King Marc was the first to reemerge from the burial mound. His face was blank. He coughed into his hand. Raising his voice against the wind, he spoke first in Kernyvak, and then in Aquilan.

"Thank you for joining me to honor my mother, Queen Verica of Meonwara and Kernyv. Please offer her your wishes. Kernyv forever."

Murmurs of *Kernyv bosta vyken* were carried out to sea. Peasant and royalty alike approached the tomb with white pebbles extended on open palms like pearls in oysters.

Xandru walked straight for the king and flanked his left side. Ruan had stationed himself at Marc's right. Both men scoured the crowd for possible assassins. No one knew how the Armoricans would avenge the death of their crown prince.

Branwen still doubted that the first assassin had been sent by

Kahedrin; she no longer had any reason to doubt that the next one might be.

The True Queen stood just behind her husband in the shadowed mouth of the burial mound. Endelyn held her cousin's arm, and Branwen clenched her jaw against the bite of jealousy. She hoped Eseult didn't make the mistake of believing the Kernyvak princess was anything more than her mother's informant. Whether her cousin believed her or not, however, Branwen would continue to protect her.

She made her way through the crowd to the edge of the hill. Up close, Branwen saw that the black and white stones covering the tomb were each perfectly round in shape, symmetrical in size. She crouched down and laid her quartz pebble at the foot of the mound.

May you find Matrona beyond the Veil, Queen Verica. May she comfort you.

Branwen released a sigh. "*Damawinn* was fond of you," Tristan said, squatting beside her. He placed his own stone on the mound.

"I was fond of her."

He peered at Branwen sidelong, anguish burning in his eyes. "You could have warned me. She raised me. She was as much my mother as she was Marc's."

"Tristan, I'm sorry. She wanted to keep her illness secret, and that was her decision to make. A healer has a duty to her patients."

"I know. *Damawinn* asked me not to be angry with you. But I am." His voice was hoarse. "I *am*."

Branwen recoiled. Tristan leaned into her. "You knew she was sick at the wedding." He lowered his voice further. "When you threw the secret I kept for Marc back at me. *You knew.* You could have let me have more than a rushed goodbye." The accusation was raw.

"You never put anything before your own honor, Branwen. I used to love that about you. I—" Tristan broke off, shaking his head. "You were right," he said. "You never loved me first. You never *wanted* to."

Regret splintered Branwen's heart. "I'm sorry for everything you're going through." She placed a hand on Tristan's shoulder. "What can I do to make it better?"

He gave a ragged laugh. "You mean the great healer doesn't know?" Tristan had never spoken to Branwen with spite before.

"No," she whispered.

"Neither do I."

Tristan pushed to his feet abruptly, and just walked away.

Branwen stared at the black and white stones until the pattern lost all meaning. She breathed in and out. She had lost Tristan and Eseult all over again.

As she collected herself, she glimpsed a tall woman with dark red and silver hair farther down the cliff top, away from the crowd. Branwen hadn't expected the Wise Damsel to attend the funeral.

She straightened up and began weaving through the mourners. The other inhabitants of Monwiku Castle started to mount their horses. The carriage that had transported Queen Verica's body was decorated with bowers of white clover. It would return to the castle empty.

The Wise Damsel stood beside bushes of prickly yellow gorse, which trimmed the cliff top for leagues in both directions.

"Greetings, Ailleann."

"Greetings, *enigena*."

Branwen's chest pinched at being called daughter today of all days. Glancing back at the burial mound, she said, "What are you doing here?"

The Wise Damsel opened her hand. A smooth, clear piece of sea glass glimmered in the gray light.

"I'm here to offer my wishes. Queen Verica came to Kernyv when she was barely out of girlhood. She became a steadfast queen."

Queen Verica was at least ten summers older than Ailleann, and yet the Wise Damsel was speaking as if she remembered the Queen Mother as a girl.

Holding up the sea glass, Ailleann said, "There was a time when the people of this land believed that the stars were gods. They saw death in the night, and in the earth where they buried their dead. They covered the graves of their loved ones with white stones because they resembled the stars."

Her shoulders lifted as she inhaled. "The ancient Kernyveu hoped that the god-stars would care for their friends and lovers in the long night of death. So strong was their belief that white on black became the symbol of their kingdom."

Branwen liked the idea of the old queen slumbering among the stars.

Just then, a high-pitched whinny attracted Branwen's attention. It was Lí Ban. Eseult kicked her palfrey into a canter as she departed.

Turning toward the Wise Damsel, "There's someone who needs me," Branwen confessed. "Someone I've caused a great deal of pain. I don't know how to help her—I would do anything to take it away."

"Not physical pain."

"No. I broke her heart."

"You broke your own."

"Yes," Branwen said, more a gasp than a word. "We were two halves of the same whole. I shattered them both." *Not you without me, not me without you.* She would do anything to renew that vow.

"Time is the only salve for wounds such as these, *enigena.*"

"I don't *have* time." Branwen held out her scarred palm. War

353

was on their doorstep; she heard Tristan's ballad of the Dreaming Sea every night. "My magic senses danger, Ailleann. The darkness is growing closer."

The other woman didn't respond to the frustration in her tone.

"Have you seen another Death-Teller, as you call them?" she asked.

"No, but I saw something else." The vision of Essy disintegrating in Branwen's embrace tortured her. "I need to take away her pain—her loss," Branwen rasped. The cousin she loved was disappearing before her eyes, becoming someone else. Someone cold, hard. Worse than a stranger.

"I must fix my mistake before it's too late."

"Branwen of Iveriu, you have worked this kind of magic before." Ailleann pierced her with a stare. "You know the risks. If you want to make the heart forget the source of its pain, you must be prepared to sacrifice something else in exchange."

Branwen brushed her fingers over her mother's brooch. "What kind of sacrifice?"

"A memory. A binding one. You will not know which until it's gone. Or you may never know. But it will be a memory stitched into the fabric of your very self." The Wise Damsel closed her hand around the sea glass.

"I would not make such a trade," she said.

The True Queen's palfrey followed a bend in the coastal path and slipped from view. Could there be a higher price than what Tristan and Eseult had already paid?

"But if I did—if I did want to make such a trade," Branwen said, "how would I do it?"

"Whatever you're trying to erase, you must burn its most potent symbol." Raising the sea glass to the sky, Ailleann said, "Who's to say the ancients weren't correct? The stars may yet be gods. Or Old Ones. Burn the cause of the pain where you can see nothing but stars. Stars and love. Feed its ashes to the broken heart to erase the pain of memory."

Branwen had hoped the effects of the Loving Cup would wane, or that the lovers could fight it, but it had only brought them misery. Perhaps magic was the only way to fight magic.

"Thank you," said Branwen.

"I don't believe in trying to stop another Wise Damsel from the path that she is determined to follow. But first ask yourself if there is a better path, *enigena*. Before you go too far."

"Lady Branwen?"

Branwen spun toward the sound of Andred's voice. He waved at her, holding Senara's reins. The boy had a puzzled expression on his face.

"Coming!" she called. When she turned back to the Wise Damsel, she was gone.

Branwen stood alone among the gorse.

A THOUSAND SEAS

KERNYVAK FEASTS FOR THE DEAD were held at night. While the other noble funeral guests were being served refreshments in the Great Hall, King Marc had assembled his council to make an important announcement.

Ruan glanced at Branwen as she entered with his younger brother. He wore a suit of black velvet; his white sash now made Branwen think of a falling star.

The barons also wore suits of black while Seer Casek had donned his habitual dark robes. Countess Kensa had accented her black gown with a sea-wolf brooch made from diamonds. Queen Eseult had pearls threaded through her plaits. Endelyn must have arranged them. Branwen missed the feel of her cousin's tresses sliding through her fingers, the way she hummed ballads as Branwen worked.

As the members of the King's Council took their seats around the table, she also felt the absence of the Queen Mother profoundly. Tristan took his grandmother's place beside the True Queen at the opposite end of the table from the king. He motioned for Andred to sit between him and Baron Julyan. The elderly baron must not have expected to outlive Queen Verica.

Branwen remained on her feet, as did two newcomers: Morgawr and Xandru. She hadn't noticed the captain at the cliff top.

"I won't keep you too long from sharing in the feast to celebrate my mother's life," King Marc began, grim-faced. "She always preferred feasts of the dead because she said at least the dead are quiet dinner companions." He attempted a meager smile and there was muffled laughter. That of Baron Dynyon and Baron Gwyk seemed particularly disingenuous.

"There have been many losses at this court," King Marc continued, and his eyes found the True Queen. "I am not eager for there to be more. After careful deliberation, I have come to a decision about the Armorican threat. Captain Morgawr, Captain Xandru."

He waved a hand toward the men who stood at attention behind him, inviting them to approach.

Morgawr met Branwen's stare and tipped his head, his jaw taut. He was dressed in his Royal Fleet uniform, a white clover pinned to his collar.

"Tomorrow morning, Captain Morgawr will lead a convoy of ships around the tip of Liones," King Marc disclosed. "Word has already been sent overland to Captain Bryok at Illogan to expect reinforcements. Together, they will fan out along our southern coast in a defensive net."

"We will not be breached, *Rix*," said Captain Morgawr.

Marc nodded. "The shallow waters that surround Monwiku will protect us, but Countess Kensa, Baron Gwyk, Baron Dynyon: Your territories are the most in danger from an attack by sea. When you return to your homes tomorrow, you should start fortifying your beaches."

Baron Gwyk turned his good eye on the king. "Will the crown be providing funds for these new battlements? The cost of labor has increased and our revenue from trade has decreased in recent months, my king."

"Now is hardly the time to haggle over your taxes," Tristan said, nostrils flaring.

"I agree," said Baron Chyanhal. While he was slim, his shoulders were broad, and when he threw them back his normal reserve vanished.

"Which is easy for you to say, seeing as your lands lie here on the north coast," countered Baron Dynyon.

Tristan leaned forward suddenly. "We are on the brink of war, and we have just laid my grandmother to rest. Can you not think of your kingdom rather than your coffers for one solitary day?" His outburst stunned the barons into silence.

Countess Kensa shifted in her seat. "Prince Tristan is right," she said. "We should have better fortified ourselves long before now. We've been complacent, Baron Dynyon." The baron looked at her askance. As did Branwen. Although, for once, she agreed with the countess.

To King Marc, Countess Kensa said, "House Whel will do its part to defend our lands."

"Thank you, Countess."

"*Rix*," Tristan said, capturing his uncle's gaze. "Grant me leave to return to Castle Wragh. Liones is also vulnerable to attack from across the Southern Channel."

"No." It was the True Queen who spoke. She shot Tristan an anxious glance, twiddling one of the pearls in her plaits.

Meeting the queen's gaze, he said, "I should be there to defend it with my people."

"No." She gripped the sleeve of his tunic. "You're my Champion. I need you here." The quiet desperation in Eseult's voice clawed at Branwen.

Branwen tilted her gaze at Ruan, whose face had become an enormous scowl. Could King Marc see what his Champion did? She rubbed her right hand several times against her skirt.

"As you wish," King Marc told his wife.

"Tristan, we will send reinforcements to Castle Wragh," he added.

With a quick, pained look at Eseult, Tristan said, "But, *Rix*, the people of Liones are mine to protect."

"Surely your obligation to Liones is not more important than your duty to the True Queen of Kernyv, Prince Tristan?" said Countess Kensa.

The other barons watched for Tristan's reaction. If he didn't yield to Marc in this, he would be declaring the needs of Liones greater than those of Kernyv. By making Tristan heir to Liones, Queen Verica and King Merchion had brought the permanent specter of civil war to their kingdom. Tristan would always be a threat to the crown.

"Of course, *Rix*." Tristan swallowed hard. "My place is here, with you and the True Queen." He swung his gaze to Eseult, who relaxed into her seat. She folded her hand around a pearl that she'd yanked from her braid.

Countess Kensa was unable to suppress a smirk. Ruan's expression didn't change.

As King Marc looked over his shoulder at Xandru, the corners of his mouth creased. With concern, Branwen thought.

"Captain Xandru Manduca has volunteered to sail for Karaez. As many of you know, the Manduca family in the Melita Isles has been trading with Armorica for generations. The captain is also a distant cousin to the Armorican queen."

Marc shifted his gaze to the left-hand side of the table and spoke directly to Seer Casek, Countess Kensa, Baron Gwyk, and Baron Dynyon. "Captain Xandru will be our ambassador to King Faramon and Queen Yedra."

There were a few startled grunts among the nobles at King Marc's pronouncement. Tristan's face registered no such surprise.

The king swallowed, unable to keep the apprehension from his eyes. "Captain Xandru is a neutral party in this. He assures me that King Faramon and Queen Yedra will grant him an audience to explain that the attack that killed Havelin was not sanctioned by the Kernyvak crown."

Baron Kerdu cleared his throat and said, "Sire, might it not be a mistake to admit that we no longer have control of our own waters? That the pirates fear no repercussions from us?"

Baron Dynyon leaned back in his chair, folding his arms and nodding in agreement.

"There *will* be repercussions." King Marc's tone was flinty. "But first, I will make one last attempt at diplomacy with Armorica." Returning his gaze to Xandru, he said, "All of Kernyv owes you a great debt, Captain."

Tristan shifted in his seat. Did he regret not being sent as envoy? Given the death of Crown Prince Havelin, it would be distinctly unwise to send a prince of Kernyv.

"No doubt the captain is being paid handsomely for his trouble," said Baron Gwyk. "The Manduca family isn't known for its charity."

King Marc's eyes flashed. Xandru took a step forward. "My dear

Baron Gwyk," he said. "It is not in the interest of my family that war make the Southern Channel too dangerous for our merchant ships to traverse."

Branwen suspected Xandru's motives for aiding the King of Kernyv were not purely financial. She grabbed Tristan's gaze, but he immediately looked away.

"My services in this instance are therefore free of charge," Xandru continued. "But not without reward." He gave the one-eyed baron a winning smile, and the baron clamped his mouth shut.

The king bit down on a smile of his own. Frowning again, he said, "Thank you all for coming. Let us go and toast to the Queen Mother."

"*Rix*," Branwen interjected. He lifted his brow. "My Lord King, what of Iveriu?" she said, and the True Queen gave her a barbed look.

"A fast messenger ship has been sent to warn King Óengus, Lady Branwen," King Marc replied. "I pray that no harm will come to your island."

"*Mormerkti*," she said.

The rest of the night passed in a somber haze. After the feast of the dead had been consumed, the funeral guests were invited to the gardens for the final rite: a toast to the stars. If the stars were gods, it made sense to appease them with drink, Branwen supposed. The moon had risen during the meal, and the air was chilly. Branwen had dashed back to the West Tower to grab her cloak.

Fastening it about her shoulders, she ducked into the Great Hall to fill a goblet with spiced wine. The hall was empty, the oil in the Aquilan lamps burning low, emitting a warm light on the snakestone. She stole a small sip of wine from the gods.

Carrying her drink toward the darkened entryway, she heard the hushed murmur of voices. It was King Marc with Xandru.

"I hate to leave you, with everything—" Marc was saying. Branwen froze a few paces away. They didn't see her.

"I always hate to leave you," Xandru told the king.

"And I hate putting you in danger. I won't be able to sleep while you're in Armorica."

"When do you ever?" He gave a soft laugh.

"Xan." The name was a tease, a sigh. Branwen had never heard King Marc sound so unguarded. Not like a king at all.

Xandru lifted a hand and stroked the line of King Marc's jaw. "I'd cross a thousand seas for you, Marc." Tenderness glowed on his face. The king shuddered a breath.

Branwen's grip tightened on the goblet. This moment wasn't hers to see. She retreated a step.

"I wish I could go with you," Marc said.

"You know you can't. Besides, Queen Yedra has Manduca blood, and we'd rather turn a profit than cut off heads."

The king sighed. "At least promise me you won't take any undue risks."

"Define *undue*." Xandru toyed with Marc's earlobe. "You always cut yourself in the same place," he said. "I can't die because you need me to shave you." Another soft, flirtatious laugh.

Branwen took one more quiet step backward, trying to escape without notice.

"You can't die because Kernyv is falling apart with you gone, Xan. And me, I'm—" Marc wrapped his hand behind Xandru's neck and pulled him close. The motion was violent, jagged. Desire gripped the king's face.

"*Karid*," he said huskily against the other man's lips.

The heel of Branwen's boot caught on the hem of her dress. Before she could balance herself, the goblet was flying from her grasp. It clattered against the stone as she fell on her bottom with a yelp.

Xandru's head snapped up. He raced toward her, dagger halfway out of the sheath at his hip. "Lady Branwen?"

His hand remained on the hilt of the weapon. His jaw was tensed as he glanced sidelong at King Marc. It was a question. Branwen's heart thundered.

She looked at Xandru and saw herself the night Keane had threatened to expose Eseult's affair with Diarmuid. Marc was Xandru's absolute, the way Eseult was hers. He would eliminate any threat to the king and his rule, and he wouldn't be overly plagued with qualms about it.

"Let me help you up," King Marc said, offering Branwen a hand. She accepted; his palm was clammy.

"*Mormerktí*," she said.

Xandru looked between Branwen and Marc. With some reluctance, he dropped his hand from the blade. "My apologies, my lady. We're all on edge at the moment."

"Forgiven, Captain."

"Would you mind giving me a moment alone with Lady Branwen?" Marc said.

Xandru straightened his shoulders. "Take all the time you need. The crew of the *Mawort* awaits. We sail at first light, and I should be returning to port."

Mawort was what the Aquilans called their god of war, and it seemed an ill omen to Branwen.

"Yes, of course," said Marc. He touched the spot where he'd nicked himself shaving. "Safe travels, Captain Xandru."

"And to you, King Marc."

363

Xandru pressed two fingers to his lips, and then his heart. Perhaps it was a customary salutation on the southern continent. Branwen suspected it held a private meaning between the two men.

The captain departed as silently as a shadow. Branwen could practically feel the air around Marc growing solid as he watched the other man leave.

Scrubbing a hand over his face, the king said, "Let me get you another drink." He walked over to one of the long feasting tables, not looking at Branwen, and began checking for an unused goblet among those left behind.

She followed him, unsure what else to do. Metal made a muted *thunk* sound on the wood as he turned over each cup.

"Lady Branwen," said the king. "I don't know what you saw—"

"I didn't—"

He pivoted to face her. "You must think me a terrible husband. You must . . . I don't know what you must—"

"I don't," Branwen interrupted him. "I don't think you're a terrible husband."

Marc winced as if she'd said the opposite. "On the wedding night, I promised you I'd cherish your cousin. I am committed to our marriage. To peace." He turned over another goblet. "Xandru and I meant a great deal to each other. Once. I hope you can understand. What you saw—it doesn't change the vows I made."

He flexed his hand around the rim of a goblet.

"If I could beg you a favor, Lady Branwen. Please, let me be the one to explain to Eseult what you witnessed. This should come from me."

Panic streaked through Branwen. After everything that had happened, she had no idea how her cousin might react. "I saw nothing that requires an explanation, my king. Two old friends parting—nothing more."

"I don't understand." King Marc squinted at her.

"You buried your mother today." Branwen worried a loose thread on the hem of her cloak. "I remember when I buried mine. We do—we seek comfort from those who love us."

For her, it had been Essy. Always Essy. She had caused her oldest love the deepest pain. "I—" She stopped and started again. "Every truth has its season, I think. My cousin is still grieving her own loss. I don't think it's the right time for a discussion of your past."

The king held her gaze. "Xandru understood my choice. Why I have to put peace above all else. He was with me on my first raid."

Branwen stood immobile. "I don't know how to reach Eseult," King Marc continued. "Maybe I haven't tried hard enough. I, too, feel the loss." He swallowed. "I will find a way." Determination glinted in his eyes. "The queen is fond of the harp. Maybe Tristan can teach me, too."

Branwen's mouth grew dry as she said, "That's a nice idea."

"Thank you for your understanding, Lady—may I call you Branwen?"

"Of course, *Ríx*."

"I see you as family now, Branwen. Won't you call me Marc?"

Tears pricked her eyes. She was deceiving him in so many ways, but still, "I'd like that," she told him, because it was the truth.

His answering smile was sad, but real. "I'm afraid your cloak is stained," he said. Marc dabbed at it with the sleeve of his own tunic, right next to her brooch.

Cocking his head, he stepped back a pace. He pulled the sleeve tight over his hand. "Branwen," he said. "This brooch you always wear . . . is it a common style in Iveriu?"

Their eyes met. "No. It's the emblem of Castle Bodwa. It belonged to my mother." Her lips trembled. "She was wearing it when she died."

"When she was killed by raiders?"

Branwen nodded, and Marc paled. "I've seen you wearing it for months," he said. "It was somehow familiar. I dismissed the thought, but the truth has been tugging at the back of my mind." The king searched her face and cursed.

"You look just like her."

"Who?"

"Your mother." Marc covered his face with his hands. "I have wronged you, Branwen. It's my fault. Your parents are dead because of me."

The admission struck Branwen like a firebolt. She already knew, of course. Yet hearing him say it aloud made it more real. As if she were seeing the *kretarv*'s vision for the first time.

"What happened?" she whispered. Branwen needed to know if Dhusnos had shown her the full truth.

"I didn't want to hurt your mother. I was letting her go. But she didn't believe me. Why would she?" He shook his head. "Your mother killed herself rather than risk being taken by raiders."

Marc rubbed his eyes. "By the Horned One, I see her now in you. She was fearless in the face of death—like when you charged the assassin."

Daring to look up at her, he said, "Branwen, I knew shame in the moment of your mother's death that I will never stop feeling. And I decided to bring peace when I became king. I will never stop making amends. Xandru knows this. I want you to know it, too."

Branwen blinked at her own tears, which now flowed freely. "I do know, Marc. I grew up hating the raiders who killed my parents." She touched his shoulder. "That hate is in the past."

"I have hated *myself* every day since it happened, I swear to you. It will be fourteen years soon."

"Yes." A breath rushed from Branwen that he also remembered the day her parents died. "Fourteen years is long enough for hate. I forgive you."

She wished with her whole heart that she could ask Marc for his forgiveness, too: for the Loving Cup—for everything.

Marc wrapped his arms around Branwen. "Thank you." He breathed deeply. "Thank you, sister. Iveriu won't know any further death because of me."

"I believe you, brother." This was no longer the boy who ran away from a suffering woman; he was a man who stayed so that his people would not suffer, who took their suffering onto himself.

Drawing back from his embrace, Branwen held out her hand.

"Let's toast the stars."

THE TRUE HEIR

BRANWEN HELD ON TO HER cloak, hugging herself close in the cold moonlight.

The castle gardens teemed with opening buds and mourners raising a glass to the departed queen. Marc was set upon by courtiers offering condolences the moment they entered the gardens, and Branwen excused herself.

She roamed among the spear-leafed trees alone. The Queen Mother had asked her to watch over Tristan and he was obviously in tremendous pain. After what he'd said to Branwen at the burial, she didn't know if he'd accept her sympathy. All the same, she wandered the gardens until her eyes caught on the bright white of his sash.

He, too, walked alone. She followed him as he descended the stone steps to a lower terrace. He looked to either side of him. Deserted. Dragging in another breath, he kept going down to the level of the gardens that met the sea. A secluded part.

Branwen was about to call out to Tristan when she saw that he was no longer alone.

Queen Eseult stepped out from the shadows.

Terror tore through Branwen. From the terrace above, she followed them as Eseult took Tristan's hand in hers and led him to a bench enclosed by rose bushes.

Fewer lanterns swung from the trees on the lower levels of the gardens. Branwen concealed herself between the spindly tree trunks, clinging to one at the edge of the terrace.

Tristan slumped onto a bench beside Eseult, weariness rolling off him. Eseult began to rub his arm. Neither of them suspected Branwen's presence.

They spoke quietly, but not as quietly as they should have given the unnervingly still night. Even the lapping tide showed its respect for the dead.

"I found your message," Tristan said. "We shouldn't be meeting like this."

Eseult swept a hand along the line of his jaw. "I didn't want you to be alone tonight."

"The castle is full of people."

"It's not the same."

"No." He sighed. "Thank you."

"You've been the only one to support me in my grief, Tristan. The only one who understands what I—what *we*—lost," Eseult said, tender and defiant. "I want to be here for you. I know how close you were with Queen Verica." Her cousin had always had a talent for loving people, and her love was difficult to resist.

Regret spread through Branwen as she watched them together.

Marc had sought Xandru in his hour of need, and Tristan had sought out Eseult. She didn't want to begrudge Tristan his solace, yet fear held Branwen tight—fear and resentment at her own losses. A bone-deep remorse that she was no longer his sanctuary.

"Thank you," Tristan repeated. Grazing his cheek with the back of her hand, Eseult told him, "You were lucky to have her in your life as long as you did. Not everyone feels the same way about the woman who raised them."

Branwen's guts twisted. Queen Verica had known she needed to raise a king in Marc, but Tristan was her joy. The Queen of Iveriu had also tried to mold her daughter into a queen. Maybe intimacy always fell victim to duty.

Tristan leaned back to meet his queen's gaze. "Eseult," he said. "I should go to Liones."

"I need you here."

"Monwiku is secure."

"No, I need *you*. I have no one else." Eseult framed his face with her other hand. "Don't abandon me, too."

Branwen gripped the tree, its bark splitting her nails. She knew what it was to be needed by her cousin—the temptation of that need. She had done terrible things because of it. Branwen had never left the queen, even when she had devastated her, but her love was never enough.

"If I'm to be trapped here," Eseult said, leaning in closer to Tristan, "let us be trapped together."

"I will always serve you," he told her.

"I don't want you to serve me. *Kiss me*, Tristan," Eseult whispered. "Touch me like you did on the ship. Just once. I miss you every day I'm with you."

She traced Tristan's full lips with her finger. "There must be more to life than *this*—this grief. When I look at you, I see the life I want—just out of reach."

Something savage tangled itself around Branwen's guilt. She had once gazed upon Tristan and glimpsed the future she'd wanted, too. But she hadn't loved him best. She had loved the Land. Perhaps Branwen's kind of love had never been what Tristan wanted.

"Let me comfort you," said the True Queen.

As Tristan's resistance flagged, his fingers weaving through Eseult's plaits, bringing his lips down to hers, Branwen heard footsteps. They were coming from behind her.

She reeled around and saw Ruan on the stairs, staggering down to her level of the garden. In a few moments, he would be able to see Tristan and Eseult for himself. He would witness their treason with his own eyes and there would be nothing Branwen could do to explain it away.

The wind chimes sparkled in the branches above her. She did the only thing she could think of to prevent disaster. Jumping as high as she could, Branwen slapped the metal chimes with all her strength. The shafts of white lead clanged together, rang out like discordant laments. The lovers broke apart.

Tristan and Eseult both swiveled toward the sound and spied Branwen between the trees. By the starlight, Branwen saw Tristan's eyes grow wide.

"There you are, Lady Branwen," Ruan said as he approached. He slurred. "Avoiding me as usual." He took a sip from his goblet. Tonight his inebriation didn't seem feigned.

"I wasn't thinking of you at all," Branwen countered. She walked out from the trees, willing her racing heart to slow.

"And yet I can't stop thinking of you."

"You're drunk."

"Perhaps." Ruan glanced at his goblet. With a shrug, he finished the remainder. "Now? Yes."

New footsteps distracted him. Tristan escorted Eseult up the stairs, posture rigid. Correct. As a Champion should escort his queen.

"*Nosmatis*, cousin," he said to Ruan in his most formal tone. "Lady Branwen."

"*Nosmatis*, Prince Tristan," Branwen replied, acerbic, precise. "Queen Eseult."

Tristan should know better. They both should know better. She could barely look at them.

"The queen was feeling unwell," Tristan explained as Eseult showed Ruan an embarrassed smile. "I've had too much wine," she said.

"Haven't we all?" Ruan's reply was light, but Branwen heard the danger in its undercurrent.

"Indeed, cousin," Tristan said, eyeing Ruan's goblet. "I'll escort the queen back to her chamber."

"Lady Queen," said Branwen. "Would you like some willowbark tea?" How many times had Branwen given her cousin the remedy when she'd pilfered too much of Treva's elderberry wine?

"No. Thank you," Eseult answered, voice tight. "*Nosmatis*, Lady Branwen."

Tristan and Eseult continued up the stairs. Ruan followed them with his eyes until they vanished from view. He shifted his jaw side to side.

"I wonder why Endelyn isn't with them?" he mused.

"Doubtless she's not far."

Ruan twirled his empty goblet by its stem. "Doubtless. My sister keeps hoping Tristan will look at her the way she looks at him." He paused. "But my cousin prefers Ivernic ladies—and I can't blame him."

"Stop making threats against my queen," Branwen told him.

"When will you see that I'm not making threats? I'm trying to *help* you."

"Help me? By accusing me of treason?"

Ruan threw the goblet to the ground and muttered something under his breath in Kernyvak. "I'm trying to warn you, Branwen. If Xandru's mission to Armorica fails, we'll be at war. Marc will insist on fighting beside his men because that's who he is. And if he dies, whomever the True Queen marries will become the next King of Kernyv."

Branwen exclaimed, "You think Tristan wants Marc dead so he can be king?"

"People are scared. Armorica has a fleet to match our own."

"Now you know how Iveriu has felt all of these years!" she said.

"*Yes*. Yes, we do. The Armoricans are bearing down on us and we have an Ivernic queen on the throne. A queen who—by her own admission—feels like a hostage in our land. And we have a dead assassin in our dungeon."

"Are you accusing the *True Queen* of plotting to kill the king now?" Branwen's fear came out as laughter.

Ruan covered her mouth with his hand. "No. *Shh.*" He removed his hand as outrage lit her eyes. "Shh. I'm only telling you how it looks when the queen spends more time in the company of her Champion than her husband."

Branwen's heart rate accelerated once more. "And what do you expect me to do about your suspicions?" she demanded.

"*Branwen.*" When Ruan said her name, it was despondent. "This is coming out all wrong. I don't want this court to tear you apart. I want to *protect* you."

"I don't need your protection."

Tristan and Eseult were trapped together, and it was Branwen's doing. Hostages to their desire. Only she could release them from it.

If she dared.

Branwen knocked into Ruan's shoulder and, as she barged past, he whispered, "Wait," in Ivernic. Her shoulder remained pressed to his. "Wait, Branwen," Ruan said again. His breath was hot against her cheek. The scent was spicy like the wine.

Ruan dared to run his hand over her plaits and then took a step back, looking her in the eye. "I know you think I betrayed you," he said. "The only way I see to regain your trust is to give you the power to ruin me."

"Ruan. You don't have to." Branwen had been betraying him since the day they met.

"No, I want to tell you." He cast his eyes toward the sky. "Maybe it's the wine. Maybe it's the stars. The last funeral I attended was my father's," he said.

"I'm sorry."

"I'm not."

On impulse, Branwen took his hand. She understood why he'd feel that way, and why he'd wanted to get drunk tonight.

Ruan blew out a long breath. She waited for him to speak when he was ready.

"After King Merchion died and Marc became king, my father—Edern—grew ever more volatile. I was too old, too strong for him to bully."

He intertwined his fingers with Branwen's, and his tension bled into her.

"One night at dinner, he hit Endelyn." Ruan paused. "You never met Prince Edern. He wasn't fair-haired."

Her stomach dropped. "What are you saying?"

"I'm saying that Andred is his only true son." Ruan rubbed his thumb along hers. "Endelyn and I—we're the children of an Ivernic prisoner. A miner. Edern didn't discover the affair until I was seven or eight." He began speaking more rapidly. "My father—my real father—died badly. That's when my whippings began."

"Oh, Ruan." Sympathy streamed through every part of her.

"The night he hit Endelyn, my mother finally hit him back. Edern was no longer in his prime, but he punched her so hard in return that she lost a tooth."

Ruan squeezed Branwen's hand. "I saw my mother and my sister bloody, and I—I lost control." Staring into the dark, into the past, he continued, "I hit Prince Edern, and I couldn't stop hitting him. He was strong enough to hit women, but he was no match for me."

Branwen swallowed. "You did what you had to do."

"My mother cleaned up the blood. Hard to imagine Countess Kensa scrubbing a floor, isn't it?" His laugh was a little desperate. "My mother wasn't always as she is now. Edern made her life—difficult. I think she truly loved my real father."

"Your father taught you Ivernic," Branwen said.

Ruan nodded. "Endelyn was too young to learn much before he died. She doesn't remember him."

"What was his name?"

"Conchobar. The knife I gave you—it was his."

Branwen's heart panged. The gift had been far more significant than she'd realized.

"You should have it back," she said.

"You're the only person I would want to have it, Branwen. Whether you ever let me court you or not."

She compressed her lips, lost in a bevy of emotions.

"I confessed my crime to Marc," he said. "My mother was furious. Terrified. Marc forgave me. I owe him my life, and I would die to protect him. He's the kindest ruler Kernyv is ever likely to know."

Ruan brushed Branwen's lower lip with his knuckle.

"Marc knows I killed my father. He doesn't know Edern *wasn't* my father. Neither does Andred. No one knows I'm a bastard except for my mother and my sister—and now you."

Branwen placed her hand flat against Ruan's chest. He had given her a weapon that could destroy his entire family. His legacy. Everything.

"I understand your love for the king, Ruan," she said as she fiddled with the sash that denoted his Champion's status. "And what binds you to your mother and Endelyn." Branwen paused. "I was hurt by what happened. And angry. But I understand better now."

She looked up to meet his gaze. "We all act rashly to protect the people we love. I won't betray you with what you've shared."

"My entire life is a lie, Branwen. I'm not Prince Ruan. I'm just Ruan: bastard son of an Ivernic prisoner."

So many things about him made more sense now. Starting with why he saved the Iverman at the mining disaster.

"I've always liked Ruan better than the prince," Branwen told him.

His hand slipped around her waist, splaying against her back.

Heat spread through her. "I've had enough of the stars," he said. "Shall we go to bed?"

Branwen looked him up and down. Part of her wanted to go with Ruan. Very much. But he was drunk and vulnerable, and she wondered if he'd regret his confession in the morning.

"Not tonight," she said. "I'm not saying never. Just not tonight." Raising herself onto the balls of her feet, she kissed Ruan gently on the mouth.

"I'll wait," he said against hers.

Branwen kissed him again. "*Nosmatis*, Ruan." Reluctantly, she extricated herself from his warm embrace.

There was someone else who couldn't wait.

A BETTER PATH

R UAN WASN'T THE ONLY MOURNER who had toasted the stars too much. There would be many sore heads at Monwiku Castle in the morning.

Branwen strode toward the Queen's Tower. The moon was already beginning its descent. Torchlight illuminated three figures beneath the entryway.

Tristan leaned against one side of the arch beside two other members of the Royal Guard.

"*Nosmatis*," Branwen said, looking first at the other guardsmen, then settling her gaze on the Queen's Champion.

"*Nosmatis*, Lady Branwen."

Their eyes locked and she saw every smile, every kiss, every tear that had led them to this place. From the misery etched on his brow, Tristan did, too.

"King Marc ordered extra security for the True Queen while we have so many guests at the castle," he said.

"Prudent." Also fortunate for Tristan that she couldn't speak her mind in front of the other soldiers.

"I need to see my cousin," she told him.

"She's—she's most likely asleep."

"I very much doubt it, and I've brought her a remedy for too much drink. To prevent a headache."

Tristan inhaled shortly. "Of course, my lady."

Tiny red crescents marked Branwen's palms by the time she reached the third landing.

Branwen didn't bother knocking. Arthek barked as she entered the queen's bedchamber. Eseult was pacing by candlelight. Her blond hair was loose about her shoulders, one strand taut around her forefinger.

"What are you doing here?" demanded her cousin. "Have you brought the King's Champion with you?"

When Eseult was in the wrong, her instinct was to attack. Branwen welcomed it. She slammed the door behind her. Arthek barked again.

"What you did was absurdly stupid!" she yelled at Eseult.

"I didn't ask your opinion. And I don't need your permission, Lady Branwen."

Branwen closed the distance between them. "Are you trying to get caught? Do you *want* to be accused of treason?"

"You're the one who wants me caught!" the queen volleyed back. "You brought Ruan to spy on us!"

"I *saved* you!" The Hand of Bríga awakened, stirred to life with Branwen's escalating pulse. "All I ever do is save you!"

"No one asked you to! Why were you even there? Were you *following* me?"

"I was looking for Tristan—to console him!" Branwen shouted.

"He has me."

"But he *can't*, Essy. You're married to his uncle. His king!"

"I'm sorry it hurts you to see us together." Eseult's voice gentled. She exhaled. "Really I am. But whatever you and he shared in Iveriu— it's finished."

"Yes, it is," Branwen agreed. "But that doesn't change the vows you made. Or the promise you made to me when I went to your husband's First Night bed." She thrust out a hand. "You promised never to look at Tristan as more than your husband's nephew."

"I tried. I *tried*, Branny. But then, the baby . . . it brought us closer again."

"You didn't try hard enough. Do you remember when you said a man would never come between us?" Branwen said. "Why can't you choose *me*, Essy? You said you loved me more than any kingdom, but you've never loved me more than yourself."

"And you have always loved your kingdom more than me. For what?" Eseult drew in a ragged breath. "War is still coming. It doesn't matter what I do, it doesn't matter what you do. I married a man I don't love. I can't be with the man I do love. Tell me what it's all for, Branny!"

"For peace! For your people!" Branwen pleaded. "If we go to war with Armorica, we'll need the True Queen more than ever."

"I would trade my royal blood for sovereignty over my own life in a heartbeat."

The truth filled the space between them. Branwen wished it was within her power to grant. But it wasn't.

"The Old Ones saw fit to make you sovereign over two kingdoms, Eseult. They chose you for a reason."

"No, Branwen. It wasn't the Old Ones who made me a True Queen. It was my mother," Eseult said, a quiet howl. "My mother who didn't think it necessary to warn me what I would be facing in Kernyv."

Branwen pressed her palms together. "She didn't warn me, either."

"Yet you're still loyal to her—and her schemes. Why? *Why*, Branny?"

"Because she's my queen. She's the Land. As are you," she replied automatically. But, in the most private part of her heart, Branwen had started questioning her aunt's decisions. She and the Queen of Iveriu shared the blame for the Loving Cup. It was their magic, not the Old Ones, that had tried to steer fate.

"I never would have done that to my child," Eseult said. She dropped a hand to her belly and pain washed over her face. "I would have loved my child more than all the gods."

Branwen's chest rose and fell, her cousin's unbearable sorrow tempering her rage.

"I know you would have, Essy. Please, for your own sake, let Tristan go to Liones. Release your hold on him. Before you both get yourselves killed."

"Is that a *threat*?"

"No, it's a fact. I'm trying to protect you," Branwen said, exasperation growing. "And if you burn, Iveriu burns with you. What will it take to make you understand?"

"I'll tell you what I understand." Her voice turned to ice. "I understand what it is to have no power, to have your choices taken away. My entire life, I felt like I was running toward a precipice. One day I would be pushed off that cliff and into a marriage with a man I didn't know, a lifetime full of obligation I didn't want."

"Essy—"

The True Queen silenced her with a look. "I hated my future, and I turned that hate inward. I hurt myself because I hated how pathetic I was." She touched her fingers to the scars Branwen knew lay beneath her plaits.

"Now I see that was wrong. When I felt a new life growing inside of me, a future that could be filled with love, it changed things. It changed *me*," Eseult said. "Why should I hate myself? Shouldn't I hate the world that hurts me? I don't deserve to hurt. From now on, I will put my hate in the right place, and I will attack those who hurt me—who try to take away what I love."

Branwen stood stock-still. "Does that include me, Lady Queen?"

"If you try to take what's mine. Don't forget I could have you executed for my miscarriage at any moment, Lady Branwen."

Branwen took another step toward her cousin. When her face was less than a handsbreadth away, she said, "As long as *you* don't forget that I have the power to destroy you, Lady Queen. I know all of your secrets."

"And I know yours."

"Tristan wouldn't love you if he knew you as I do."

Smack. Eseult's open palm connected with Branwen's jaw before she could even flinch.

Arthek barked, pawing at his mistress's skirts.

Without another word, Branwen turned away from her cousin, rubbing her cheek, and walked out the door.

Tristan's eyebrows lifted at the fury on Branwen's face. Emerging from the stairwell, she said, "Prince Tristan, do you have my mother's harp?"

"It's in my chamber."

"I need it back." She massaged her aching jaw.

"Now?"

"Right now."

✠ ✠ ✠

Tutir was one of the guards stationed at the gate of the first perimeter wall.

He passed a quick glance over Branwen as she swept past him on her mount. If he thought it strange that Branwen had a harp strapped to her back, he gave no indication.

The Wise Damsel had asked Branwen to consider whether there was a better path.

There wasn't.

The spell needed to be performed where she could see nothing but stars and love. Branwen knew of one place that fit that description.

As her mount galloped across the causeway, her mind traveled back to the first night that she'd hidden Tristan in her cave. Raiders had been spotted along the coast. Raiders who had not been authorized by King Marc. Branwen now knew that Queen Verica had sent raiders to retrieve her grandson from Iveriu, but she certainly hadn't sent the pirates who'd attacked his ship in the first place.

The King of Kernyv had been losing his grip on power for far longer than anyone in Iveriu had realized.

Branwen reached the Stone of Waiting under a pale moon. The orb dangled so low over the moors that she could reach out and wrest it from the sky.

Since her arrival at Monwiku, she'd been fighting her magic. In these hours between night and day, Branwen would give herself over to its power.

Only magic could undo the pain the Loving Cup had caused. The illusion of love that courted destruction.

Tristan and Eseult were trapped in an illusion of truth. Despair was transforming her cousin into someone she never would have become. Not without Branwen's magic. If Branwen lost part of herself in its unbinding, so be it. It would be no more than she'd already lost.

Although she barely drank any wine this evening, time moved dreamily around her. She dismounted her palfrey in the shadow of the crooked stone, black rather than green in the pre-dawn. From her saddlebag, Branwen retrieved a glass jar.

Last summer, if Branwen had waited long enough at this stone, she would have expected to see Tristan's face.

She walked farther across the moor before she sank to her knees. Slinging the harp around from her back to her front, she pulled the leather strap over her head. Lady Alana had often carried the harp in this way when they went on seaside picnics with her father. Lord Caedmon claimed it was her mother's singing voice that had first enchanted him.

When Branwen's aunt had gifted the *krotto* to Tristan, she'd believed they would be wed in Kernyv. Before Tristan and Eseult had imbibed the Loving Cup, Eseult's heart had softened toward the Kernyvman when he'd serenaded her aboard the *Dragon Rising* and called her a hero.

Their love had begun with music. With this harp. It had to be destroyed.

Branwen would save her cousin one last time. She would save the kingdom.

Only the *krotto*'s ashes might undo the terrible wrong she had done to Tristan and Eseult—and to Marc. She caressed the curve of its gold-painted frame. She plucked the silver strings. They reverberated across the empty moor.

As the last note faded, Branwen heard the sound of her own abandonment. Of that cavern inside herself that had been emptied on the day her parents died, refilled by the love of her cousin, and emptied again.

A gasping, hungry sob racked her body. Branwen forced it down.

She raised the Hand of Bríga. She summoned her spark.

Blue flame flickered against a melancholy horizon.

Branwen wrapped her right hand around the neck of the *krotto* the way her mother had instructed her when she was still too small to manage the harp's weight. She had sat on her mother's lap because she'd wanted to learn. She gripped it tight.

Crackling filled her ears. Fire ignited silver and gold. Releasing the burning frame, Branwen sat back on her knees. A vision appeared in the flames.

The Belotnia Festival of her twelfth year. She had just begun her monthly bleeding. Queen Eseult had explained that Branwen was on the cusp of womanhood. The prospect was both frightening and intriguing. For the first time, she was invited to attend the Festival of Lovers.

Essy wasn't included because she was still a child. Her cousin begged Branwen not to leave her alone that night. Despite her curiosity about what the festival might entail, Branwen had capitulated.

When the bonfires could be spotted in the distance from the princess's bedchamber window, Essy stuck her tongue out at them. She grabbed Branwen's hand and dragged her down to the garden beneath the south tower.

"Let's dance!" Essy had said. She and Branwen twirled until they were dizzy. Falling down between the roots of the hazel tree, they erupted into fits of giggles.

"Aren't you glad you stayed behind at the castle with me?" her cousin had said, and Branwen knew the only acceptable answer was, "Yes."

With a stolen kitchen knife, they carved their names into the tree.

"We don't need lovers, Branny. We have each other. I'll always love you best."

"Me too."

The burning harp hissed. The vision danced in the flames, enveloped her, the past and present merging.

As young Branwen lay beneath the hazel tree, a spark jumped from her hand to the roots. Fiery red streaked up the gnarled bark to the honeysuckle vines that clung to the trunk. Essy shrieked as the names they'd carved were eaten by flame.

Yellow petals swirled in the air, singed, and landed on Branwen's tongue.

It tasted sweet.

DON'T SPEAK

SENARA NUDGED HER AWAKE.

Branwen's back was stiff from sleeping on the ground. Sitting up, she felt the joints of her neck crack. She wiped the slumber from her eyes.

The sun was drifting westward across the moors. She must have slept the day away. Still groggy, her gaze fell on the grass beside her. White strands of hair wavered atop a pile of ash.

Her mother's harp was gone.

Urgency swept through her. Branwen removed the glass jar from her skirt pocket and scooped up a handful of ash. She stoppered it with a cork.

Her mind strained to recall what the Old Ones had shown her as she worked the spell. Like the night in Kerwindos's Cauldron, Branwen could only clutch at fragments.

A honeysuckle vine burned in her mind. Why would the Old Ones show her that plant?

Tucking the glass jar firmly into the recess of her pocket, Branwen pushed to standing. She would mix the ash into spiced wine, serve it to Tristan and Eseult, and the anguish of the Loving Cup would be erased.

Patting Senara's shoulder, Branwen thanked her for staying, and lifted herself into the saddle. She didn't want to wait another moment. She gripped the reins and her mount galloped toward the forest.

Most of the funeral guests would have started their return journeys this morning and afternoon. With any luck, amidst the hustle and bustle of departures, Branwen's absence from the castle wouldn't have been noted too widely.

As she and Senara followed the coastal path into the Morrois Forest, Branwen spied several ships in the far distance, specks against the sea. Did any of them belong to either Morgawr or Xandru? She prayed to the Old Ones for their safekeeping.

Branwen tapped the pocket of her skirt, feeling for the jar.

Twilight began to shower the forest floor in amethyst light. An hour passed as Senara cantered through the wood, eager to return to her stall. From the branches above, the birds trilled their evening songs. Up ahead, her gaze landed on something bright white, out of place in the darkening forest. The sash of a Royal Guardsman. Branwen felt the downy hairs of her neck prickle.

Drawing closer, she recognized Tutir. He had stopped his stallion in the middle of the bridle path, blocking her route. She pulled back on Senara's reins.

"Halt, Lady Branwen," he called out, his Aquilan unpracticed.

"Has something happened?" Branwen asked him. Panic gripped her mind, showing her many potential scenarios where either the king or queen lay dying.

"I'm on an errand for the True Queen. I need you to dismount."

"What errand?"

"Please dismount, my lady."

A lament more spine-tingling than any call of the sea overwhelmed Branwen's senses. It became a scream. The scream of the lost.

From the corner of her eye, she glimpsed a skeletal face. Branwen lurched backward in the saddle, splaying her body along Senara's back, just missing an arrow that whizzed through the air and lodged in the nearest tree.

Tutir swore. He hadn't heard the Death-Teller's warning. Senara reared her front legs, and Branwen's feet slipped from the stirrups. She slid sideways, tumbling to the forest floor.

As she fell, she watched in horror as the glass jar dropped from within her skirts.

It smashed against a rock. The shards were beautiful, blue glass twinkling amidst the ashes.

"No!" she screamed. It was too late. A breeze rolling off the Dreaming Sea scattered the glass and ashes through the Morrois Forest.

No, no, no . . .

Tutir approached Branwen with steady steps. "I'm sorry, my lady. You've betrayed the True Queen of Kernyv."

She scrabbled backward on the ground. Twigs and rocks scratched her palms. The guardsman kept coming. Panic tangled her thoughts.

The knife, said an insistent voice. The knife Ruan had given her was still concealed in Branwen's boot.

She reached for the blade just as Tutir dove on top of her. *No.* Branwen had sent the Shades running back to the Sea of the Dead. She would survive this. She swiped the dagger at Tutir's torso. The guardsman groaned as the blade made contact, but the cut was shallow. Too shallow. And Tutir was strong.

He grabbed Branwen's right wrist and slammed it against the ground with ferocious strength. And again.

"Stop!" Branwen yelled. "There's been some mistake! I haven't betrayed the queen!"

"I'm sorry. I have my orders." The knife slipped uselessly from Branwen's grip. Tutir grabbed it and hurled it into the forest.

Approaching at a diagonal, she saw another guardsman. The blond one with a scar on his left cheek. She remembered him, although she didn't know his name. He'd also been on duty when the Armorican assassin was discovered poisoned.

"Please!" Branwen said, looking between Tutir and the man with the scar. "Take me back to the castle! Let me answer to the king!"

Tutir glanced at the other man. He shook his head.

"Be still," Tutir told her. "I'll make it quick, my lady. You won't feel any pain."

The guardsman thought the knife had been her only weapon. She laughed. Her knife would have been a mercy.

Branwen pressed the Hand of Bríga to his chest. Tutir stared at her, confused.

Please, Bríga, hear my call! Help me!

Before the guardsman could take another breath, he ignited. He seized the way Keane had in the stairwell at Castle Rigani.

Senara released a hysterical whinny at the sight of the burning man. The horse bolted into the wood, away from her mistress.

Branwen pushed Tutir off her and leapt to her feet. He continued to smolder. His flesh melted from his bones. Branwen's rage was a beautiful, powerful thing.

Blood drained from the other guardsman's cheeks; then he ran.

Branwen pursued him, fueled by need—a dark need. A consuming need. A need that was sweeter than any wine. She was drunk on it.

The scarred guardsman tripped on loose rocks and fell to the ground. "Please, no," he said. "What *are* you?"

Branwen shrugged. "I don't know. But you should be afraid." She lowered herself beside him. "Who sent you after me?"

"We received a message from the True Queen. That's all I know. It had her seal. Please, show me mercy."

She considered. "Would you have shown me mercy?"

Branwen read the answer in his eyes. She pressed her hand to his heart.

He began to shake. She raised herself to standing and walked away from the guardsman.

Branwen let him burn. His screams filled the wood.

And then there was silence.

✢ ✢ ✢

Night fell over the castle as Branwen made her way back on foot.

Her cloak was stained with smoke and ash, with dirt from the forest floor. Wild curls tangled in the breeze, escaping her lopsided plaits. Her feet ached.

The tide had started to rise again when she reached the causeway. Water lapped at her boots as she followed the elevated stone path. Moonlight brightened the slippery stones.

Her cousin had sent men to murder her.

Branwen knew too much, and she had lost her trust.

She kept repeating the truth in her mind, turning it over, kneading it like dough, trying to give it a form that made sense. Branwen had doomed Eseult, and Eseult wanted to kill her for it—even if she didn't know the full truth.

How could Branwen not have seen what her cousin was capable of? Was it all the fault of the Loving Cup?

Her mother's harp was gone. The True Queen's assassins had thrown any chance of healing Eseult's heart to the winds.

Branwen reached the gate at the bottom of the island. Did the other guardsmen wonder where Tutir had disappeared to? Or the scarred man whose name she didn't know?

When the bodies were found, they would be unrecognizable.

Branwen had tried so many times to save her cousin.

She no longer knew why. She reached out for a reason and found nothing: a night without stars. What had driven Branwen to risk so much for a woman who would see her dead?

"Lady Branwen," said a tall guard with brown skin. Some weeks ago, she'd sutured a laceration the man had sustained during single combat practice.

"*Nosmatis*," Branwen replied, leery. Which other Royal Guardsmen might be in the queen's employ?

The man gave her a rapid scan. "Are you hurt?"

"I was thrown from my horse." She flicked up the corners of her mouth in a tight smile. "Nothing serious. Just a few bruises."

"Glad to hear it." He opened the gate. "*Nosmatis*, my lady."

Relief flitting through her, Branwen thanked him and picked up her pace as she climbed the hill. What might the True Queen have told King Marc? Would he have sanctioned her unceremonious execution in the woods? Branwen found that hard to believe.

Several times on her walk back to the castle, she'd considered running away, abandoning Iveriu to whatever fate the True Queen was weaving for it. Why not let her cousin think Branwen had passed into the Otherworld? Escape to a distant land?

But she couldn't. Branwen had made vows, too. She touched her mother's brooch on her cloak. Her last vestige of Lady Alana. The right fight had become clearer to Branwen than the crystal waters of the River Bóand.

Something between excitement and terror swirled inside her. She caressed the inside of her hand.

It wasn't solely the promises she'd made that propelled Branwen toward the Queen's Tower—into a potential nest of enemies.

No, she wanted to see the look on her cousin's face when she realized Branwen was still alive. Dhusnos had tried to kill Branwen. What made her cousin think she would succeed where the Dark One had failed?

There were no guards at the entrance when Branwen reached the tower. Perhaps with the funeral guests departed, King Marc thought the threat to his queen diminished.

He had no way of knowing Branwen was the greatest threat to the True Queen's safety this evening.

She proceeded purposefully to the third floor. Its corridor was also empty. No sign of the Queen's Champion.

A low, dark laugh rumbled at the back of Branwen's throat as she pushed open the door to the queen's suite. Her gaze fixed on the intertwined form of Tristan and Eseult.

They stood in the center of the bedchamber, the Champion embracing his queen, brushing a tear from her cheek with his thumb.

"I wish I were surprised," Branwen remarked.

"Branwen." Eseult made her name a gasp.

Tristan instantly dropped his hand, breaking the embrace, and moved back from Eseult. Turning toward Branwen, he took a step in her direction, hands up.

"This isn't what it looks like," he said. "I'm saying goodbye. I'm leaving for Liones tomorrow."

Ignoring him, Branwen walked toward her cousin. "Didn't expect to see me again, did you, Lady Queen?"

Eseult's brow creased. "I don't know what you mean."

Surveying Branwen's disheveled state, Tristan asked, "What happened? Where have you been?"

"Where have I been?" Branwen repeated. "Where *have* I been? Trying to cover up for my queen yet again. For my selfish, spiteful queen!"

"Branwen, I'm sorry for what you saw last night. It was a grave mistake." Tristan captured her gaze. "It won't happen again."

"This woman you think you love." Branwen slashed a hand through the air at Eseult. "She just tried to have me killed."

Shock blanketed his face. "No!" Eseult protested. "No, Branny. How could you think that?"

"Last night you threatened to have me executed for your miscarriage. And this afternoon, I was attacked in the forest by two Royal Guardsmen—on your orders!"

"Eseult?" Tristan whispered.

"*What?* Oh, Branny!" She reached a hand to Branwen's elbow, and Branwen jerked away. "You can't believe I would try to have you killed! I was furious last night. You threatened me, too. But I would never—*could* never do that!"

"Lady Queen, I don't believe you."

Eseult's lips quivered. She took Branwen's hand in hers and began tracing a symbol with her finger. Branwen didn't know what it was.

"What are you doing?" she demanded.

Eseult traced the pattern with more force. Her touch stirred something within Branwen, some kind of echo—but the meaning slipped like sand between her fingers.

"Not you without me," said her cousin. "Not me without you." Branwen could only stare at her blankly. "We promised that to each other," Eseult insisted. "No matter what, I wouldn't hurt you, Branny."

Branwen shook her off. "I don't know what you're talking about, Lady Queen. I've never made such a promise to you. The oaths I've sworn have been to the Land."

Her cousin made a low, wretched sound. She stepped back a pace. Tears began rolling down her cheeks. "Don't be cruel, Branny. Since the day we carved our names into that tree, it's been you and me. Don't pretend you don't know what I'm talking about!"

"What tree?" Branwen was genuinely mystified. "I don't know anything about a tree! But I do know that your assassins failed." The True Queen hiccuped a sob.

Looking from her cousin to Tristan, Branwen said, "Did you know? Did you pick the guardsmen yourself?"

"Of course not!" he roared. "I'll kill whoever attacked you!"

Branwen held up the Hand of Bríga. Exhilaration soared through her.

"No need," she told him.

Eseult let out another gasp. "Branny? Branny, you're on fire!" she exclaimed.

"Yes," Branwen said. "The Old Ones gave me this power to protect Iveriu."

The queen's eyes were as big as moons. "How long have you known you had magic?"

"Since I saved Tristan at the Champions Tournament."

"When you were in the fever," said Eseult. "I thought you were in the Otherworld because you were close to death. But it wasn't that. You—" Her cousin looked from the flame in Branwen's hand to Tristan. The tendons protruded from his neck, but his expression remained stoic.

"You knew?" rasped the queen. Tristan gave a swift nod.

"I killed Keane because he found the letter you wrote to Diarmuid," Branwen told Eseult. "He threatened to announce your treason to your father—and to Tristan." She swung her gaze from her cousin to the man she had once loved.

"You think you're the first man my cousin wanted to betray her kingdom for?" Branwen laughed. "No, she pinned her heart on that crown-chasing northern lord long before she met you, Tristan. She wanted to elope with Diarmuid on the night of the Farewell Feast."

Eseult pulled at her hair. "You read the letter?"

Branwen's flame grew brighter. "Keane found it and threatened to ruin you. I made him a Shade."

Tristan cursed and ran a hand through his curls. "You never told me," he said to Branwen, disbelief shearing the edges of his words.

"I told you Keane threatened the peace. I spared you the details because I wanted to protect my cousin. I traded my heart to protect hers—and look how I've been repaid!"

"Traded your heart?" said Tristan.

"The wedding toast you two drank on the ship." Branwen swept her gaze back to her cousin. "It wasn't one of Treva's spirits." Something akin to a smile played on her lips, an unhinged smile at the absurdity of what had happened—at the tragedy.

"Remember how you asked me to make a love potion for you and Diarmuid?" she said.

Eseult brought a hand to her mouth. "*No.*"

"Yes." Branwen curled her fingers, extinguishing the flame. "I begged Queen Eseult to help me. I didn't want you to live your life without love, Essy. I wanted you to be happy. More than I wanted anything for myself. Only now, I can't remember why."

The revelation was cruel, and part of her—a growing part—reveled in that cruelty.

Eseult fell to her knees. "No. Please, *no.*" She began to bawl in earnest. Arthek scurried to her side, whimpering.

Tristan squared his shoulders, staring at Branwen. "You never trusted me," he said. "If you had only told me of your plans, I—"

"You would have what, Tristan? Let me work magic on your king?"

"We'll never know. No wonder I could never reach you, Branwen— you built a wall of lies between us." Tristan looked at Eseult, waving a hand. "*You* did this to her. You did this to *me!*"

Tristan hammered a fist against his heart. "For so many months, I've hated myself. I've asked myself how I could betray you. Betray Marc. But you *knew*, Branwen. You knew how it was possible and you still let me believe it was my fault. You let me think I was a man without honor!"

"It was the only way to preserve the peace."

Tristan made a face like he was going to spit. "You are not the woman I thought you were. Your heart isn't noble. You kept telling me you weren't Emer. I didn't believe you." He sneered. "Now I do."

"*This* woman has brought peace," Branwen retorted. "She's killed for it. She would die for it."

His lips twisted further. "We're not friends or lovers or allies. We're not even enemies, Branwen. We're *nothing.*"

Tristan's words struck her like daggers, and Branwen threw hers right back at him.

"I've tried to protect you, Tristan. Both of you. I gave my body, my heart—all of me." Branwen whirled on her cousin. "My allegiance is to the Land. Not to you. Come after me again, Lady Queen, and I *will* end you."

Tristan's hand moved to his sword. "And you," Branwen told him, spearing him with a look over her shoulder. "Peace above all."

The right fight was for Iveriu. For far too long, she had confused her cousin with the Land. No more.

"I can't look at you," Tristan said to Branwen. Glancing at Eseult, he added, "Either of you."

He fled from the queen's chambers.

Branwen continued to glare at her cousin, who was dry heaving on the floor. "I didn't send those men after you, Branny. I *didn't*. I swear!" the True Queen managed between shudders. "Why didn't you tell me about the love potion?"

"Because I wanted you to believe your love for King Marc was real." Branwen scoffed, mostly at herself. "You've always wanted to be loved for yourself, Essy. You threw yourself at feckless Diarmuid because of it. At Lord Conla before him. But you never were. All these months, you thought Tristan loved you—but that wasn't real, either. It was only a spell."

A sob rent Eseult's entire being. "But why didn't you tell me what I feel for Tristan wasn't—*isn't* . . ."

"Would you have believed me?"

"I—" Realization settled in her cousin's green gaze. "You didn't trust me. You've *never* trusted me."

"You were never worthy of my trust." Branwen dipped into a curtsy. "*Nosmatis*, Lady Queen. Sleep well."

She swept out of the queen's chambers as her cousin began a

fresh round of weeping. As she exited the tower, a familiar profile approached her.

Lantern light beamed on Ruan's hair. "I didn't see you at dinner." His eyes searched Branwen's face. "You're crying. Again." He nodded across the inner bailey. "I saw Tristan running from the tower a minute ago. He always makes you cry."

She wiped the tears from her cheeks.

Ruan's gaze panned across Branwen's cloak, her sullied dress. His eyes landed on her right wrist, which Tutir had bashed against the ground. It was starting to swell.

"Did something happen?" he asked, anger in the question. Branwen could guess where his thoughts would lead him.

"I went for a ride and fell from Senara," she said. "It's nothing."

Ruan lifted her injured wrist gingerly to his lips. "Whatever it is, you can tell me, Branwen," he said. But she couldn't.

The True Queen had tried to have Branwen killed, and yet the Land needed her cousin to remain on the throne of Kernyv.

Perhaps there was no way to serve your kingdom without betraying someone who trusted you. Perhaps that was the real Truth of the Ruler.

Branwen stroked her bruised hand across Ruan's chest, then slid it around his neck. "Don't speak," she said. "I don't want to speak." She kissed him hard, biting his lower lip.

"Don't speak," she repeated.

She took his hand and led Ruan to her room. Branwen needed to laugh, and she needed to scream. She didn't need to speak.

NO EXIT

THE STARS HAD FANGS. BRANWEN dove into the blackened waters to escape them. The songs of the drowned bubbled along her skin.

Her arms pulled her through the depths, her legs kicked with ease. The waters welcomed her, beckoned her. Farther, deeper, plunging toward the bottom.

She couldn't breathe. She didn't need to breathe. There was a secret on the sea floor, just out of reach—a prize she wanted.

Branwen glanced upward, something pulling at her mind, a cord she needed to cut.

Fire danced upon the waves. On the surface lay a ring of fire and devouring stars.

She dove faster into the dark.

✦ ✦ ✦

A man's scream startled Branwen awake. Ruan bolted up in the bed next to her. The candle on the bedside table was guttering. The flickering flame was enough to reveal the fear on Ruan's face. Each of his muscles tensed.

The man shouted again in Kernyvak. It was coming from the courtyard below.

"Attack," Ruan said. "The castle is under attack." He stroked the curve of Branwen's cheek, a frantic gesture. Leaping out of bed, he searched the floor for his breeches.

"Stay here," he told her. "I need to find the king." He cursed as he pulled on his trousers, tying the strings of the waistband.

Branwen threw the quilt aside. "I'm coming with you." The stone was cool beneath the soles of her feet as she sprang to the floor.

"No, Branwen. We don't know what we're up against."

Ruan had no idea how dangerous Branwen could be—the damage she could do to whoever was attacking them. "I've faced pirates before," she reminded him. "And assassins. I'm a healer. The guards might need me. Or the king."

Tristan would get the queen to safety; King Marc would fight. Branwen rummaged on the floor for the gown she'd hastily tossed aside a few hours earlier, and slipped it over her head. There was no time to bother with breast bindings or her undershift.

"Help me with the laces," Branwen said to Ruan.

"You do like giving me orders." His hand hesitated against her spine; his touch on her naked skin sent tingles rushing from the spot, memories.

"Please," she said.

With a harsh exhale, Ruan threaded the laces of Branwen's dress and tied it closed. Swiftly, he reclaimed his tunic, then his boots.

Heart thumping, magic thrumming, Branwen pulled on her own boots. Danger was nearby, and her magic wanted to meet it. Anticipation invigorated her.

"Take the knife with you," Ruan said. Cautiously, he opened the door. He peered into the hallway, then nodded back at Branwen.

"I—I'm not sure where exactly it is," she replied. *Liar.* His father's dagger was somewhere in the Morrois Forest. "I'm sorry."

Ruan grunted. "We'll find it later." He unsheathed his sword. "Stick close to me." He took Branwen's hand and pushed her behind him, shielding her with his body.

The din of fighting men grew louder as they hurried along the corridor, and down the two flights of stairs toward the inner bailey. Wind agitated the torches; shadows wavered across the courtyard. Ruan and Branwen sprinted together for the King's Tower.

Running up the stairwell, they nearly careened into King Marc on the first landing. He brandished a sword, as did Andred, at his side. The boy's jaw was set, determined.

Branwen's mind returned to Cadan. Not again. She couldn't watch another boy die in battle.

"*Rix*," Ruan said, terse. "Are you hurt?"

Marc gripped his sword, thumb tapping its crossguard. "I'm fine."

Ruan nodded, glancing at Andred. "I'm fine, too," his brother assured him. "Have you seen Endelyn?"

"No, scamp. I'm sure she's safe in the Queen's Tower."

"Lowenek?"

Ruan glanced at Branwen. "She'll be safe in the servants' quarters," Branwen told Andred, hoping it was true.

"The castle is surrounded," King Marc informed his Champion.

"How?" Branwen asked. The king shifted his gaze from Ruan to her. He showed no judgment at finding them together in the middle of the night.

"Dinghies. Fishing boats. Clever. Brazen," Marc said. "The waters around Monwiku are too shallow for long-distance ships." He shook his head. "I thought we were safe from siege."

Andred stepped forward. "They're landing in the gardens. I saw the men from my window."

"Who is it?" Branwen asked, dreading the answer. "Pirates?" Her voice trembled with hope.

"They're flying Armorican colors," Marc said. He pressed his lips together. "Xandru is too late."

Ruan swore. "How did our fleet miss them?" Frustration and guilt knitted his brow.

"Nobody was looking for dinghies. *Brazen*," Marc repeated, something close to respect tinting the word. "One storm and they would have been sunk. And nobody expected an attack on our northern coast."

"Can we get a message to Captain Morgawr? Signal his convoy to return?" Branwen asked.

"Not in time," said the king. "We're alone in this." To Ruan he said, "How many guardsmen reported for duty at last watch?"

"Three companies. Although two men failed to return to the barracks."

"Which two?" Marc gritted his teeth.

Branwen tasted acid at the back of her throat. "Tutir and Bledros," Ruan replied. Bledros must have been the man with the scar. "I'll find out where they are, *Rix*."

"Three companies. Sixty men," Marc said. "Not enough to defend the circumference of the island. Not nearly enough." He tapped his thumb against his sword's crossguard more rapidly. Looking at his Champion, he said, "Ruan, I need you to secure the True Queen."

"Tristan is more than capable of protecting her," Ruan countered. For once, he didn't sound jealous. His cousin's talent with a sword could not be denied, and he was relying on it.

"I promised Eseult she'd be safe in Kernyv. Tristan is just one man," Marc said. He took a heavy breath. "If I should fall, she must live. An empty throne would spell disaster for the kingdom."

"But, Marc—"

"That's an order. Defend the True Queen with your life. Keep her alive at all costs."

Ruan nodded. Branwen could see how much it pained him, but he deferred to his king.

Marc returned his attention to Branwen. "Go with Ruan," he said. "He'll keep you safe, too."

She swallowed. If Marc should die, Branwen doubted whether Eseult could hold on to her crown. Civil war in Kernyv would mean more chaos for Iveriu.

Her right palm throbbed. Branwen was her mother's daughter and she would do anything to ensure King Marc survived the night.

"I'm the Royal Healer, and I will be needed," Branwen said. "I'm coming with you, *Rix*."

"So am I," Andred chimed in.

"No." Ruan's reply was unyielding.

"I can fight. You taught me," protested his brother.

"You've never been in a real fight, scamp. *No*."

"We're outnumbered." Andred raised his sword. "The castle needs every man." He shot a pleading look at King Marc.

"Andred, go with Ruan. Help him keep the queen safe. And your sister."

His chest deflated as he obeyed. "Yes, *Ríx*."

"We go now," said the king, and the four of them raced down the stairwell of the King's Tower. When they reached the bottom, before Ruan darted out from beneath the archway, he seized Branwen's hand. "You're too brave," he said.

He kissed her fiercely. The kiss of a man afraid it was his last.

King Marc cut the air with two fingers as his Champion loped across the courtyard. Andred followed his brother.

The clash of steel carried on the breeze. "You *are* too brave," Marc told Branwen. "But, thank you."

He lifted his sword, grimacing slightly. His ligaments were not yet fully healed from where he'd been shot. "Pray to your gods," he said, and dashed toward the gardens.

Branwen followed the king through the shadowy passage between the towers.

The flower bushes were ablaze. Flaming arrows were being fired from the water into the spear-leafed trees. Fighting men bellowed, lunged at one another with hacking blows.

Fire and sea and fighting men. Branwen could never escape her childhood nightmares. The Kernyvak guardsmen were attempting to prevent the Armoricans from reaching the upper levels of the garden. If the invaders reached the top terrace, there would be nothing to prevent them from overrunning the castle.

From one of the towers above, Branwen saw the Royal Guard return fire against the dinghies. There were at least thirty small ships. Several of the square sails burned against the moonlit sky.

King Marc stormed down the steps to the second terrace. The

smoke that wafted over Branwen as she followed was both floral and acrid. Marc's dream of making something grow was being turned to ash.

She had seen this attack coming. The night King Marc announced that her cousin would become the True Queen, Branwen had seen this moment.

Why had the Old Ones warned her if there was no way to prevent it from coming to pass? Why give Branwen foreknowledge if it did nothing but torment her?

She skirted around the legs of a dead man who had fallen face-first into a rosebush. He wore the yellow tunic of Armorica. At least he couldn't feel the thorns.

Branwen seized the sword that lay on the steps beside him. A *kladiwos*. The Iverni and the Armoricans shared many things, including their weaponry. The sword was long and thin, and rested heavily in Branwen's injured hand. The skin of her wrist had purpled while she was sleeping.

A slender figure caught her eye. It streaked toward the king on the second terrace. Another Armorican. In the smoke and starlight, Branwen couldn't make out the man's features. He moved with grace, almost like an acrobat.

"*Rix!*" Branwen screamed. Marc rounded on the graceful Armorican. He waited several long heartbeats, then elbowed the attacker in the face. Branwen heard the *crunch* of a broken nose. The Armorican crashed to his knees, dead or unconscious.

Marc continued his progress down the steps, racing toward the thick of the fight. Branwen's momentary relief was erased by the sight of yet more attackers landing on the lowest part of the garden. Why had the Kernyveu never thought to build a wall?

If they lived through the night, many walls would be built all across the kingdom.

"Lady Branwen!" shouted a familiar voice. She had just reached the first of the garden terraces. Branwen turned on her heel toward the voice.

Prince Kahedrin. Any remaining hope that this raid hadn't been sanctioned by the Armorican crown was shredded. Sweat darkened Kahedrin's red hair.

"I have no desire to hurt you, my lady. Throw down your weapon!"

Branwen gripped the *kladiwos* more firmly. "I can't do that, Prince Kahedrin. You're attacking my castle."

"You've chosen the wrong side in this war," said the prince advancing toward her. She held her ground. If the sword was Branwen's only weapon, she would lose this fight.

But it wasn't. "This is a mistake!" she told Kahedrin.

"Kernyv made the mistake in murdering my brother!"

"The king didn't send the pirates," Branwen shouted back at him. The screams of other men blurred her words. "King Marc didn't kill your brother!"

Prince Kahedrin—the new Crown Prince of Armorica—gave a jagged shake of the head, holding up his sword. "The time for diplomacy is done, Lady Branwen."

"Yes, it is, Prince Kahedrin," said King Marc from over Branwen's shoulder. "I told you that sailing your fleet into Kernyvak waters would be seen as an act of war."

Marc pushed Branwen forcefully out of the way. He brought his sword down hard against Kahedrin's *kladiwos*.

The Armorican prince bent his knees and used all of his strength to throw off Marc's blade.

This was Final Combat with no rules. Prince Kahedrin was first in line to his father's throne. He would either kill or be killed. Branwen didn't see how King Faramon could ever make peace with Kernyv if he lost both his sons.

Branwen tasted blood as she bit the inside of her cheek. She stood, rapt, watching.

Prince Kahedrin slashed at Marc's ankles. The king jumped, tucking his knees into his chest. Branwen had seen Tristan use the same maneuver at the Champions Tournament. Of course they must have trained together.

Marc counterattacked. Kahedrin barely dodged the sweep of his sword, leaping sideways. The king grunted. Marc and Kahedrin were evenly matched.

The crown prince forced Marc to retreat a few paces, backing him up against one of the narrow tree trunks. He took a swipe, grazing Marc's thigh. The king cried out.

He let Kahedrin move in a little closer before bringing his own sword up at an angle; Marc bashed the crown prince on the temple with its hilt. Blood welled from the wound.

"Branwen!" Marc hollered. "Behind you!"

She twirled on the spot. An enormous Armorican with dark hair lunged at Branwen. He snarled something she didn't understand. She swung her sword at him sloppily; she'd never trained with more than the practice sword her uncle Morholt had gifted her.

The Armorican wielded a double-headed ax. The same kind that Keane had favored. Branwen's attacker scythed his weapon downward against the length of her *kladiwos*. The sword fell from her grasp, and he laughed.

Branwen was about to retaliate with the only weapon she had left at her disposal when a flaming arrow pierced the Armorican's neck. Blood spurted from his throat like a fountain. The ax fell onto the garden path as the man tipped backward, dropping over the edge of the terrace, and landed like a boulder on the flower beds below.

Darting her gaze from the slain Armorican to the king, Branwen saw that Marc had also lost his weapon. He was on his knees. Kahedrin loomed over him.

One solitary blow, and everything Branwen had sacrificed would be for naught.

Gentle people didn't survive in this world. Branwen was no longer gentle but she still wanted to make a better world for those who were.

A feral cry tore from her lips. She grabbed the double-headed ax with both hands. Battle lust gave her the strength to heft it.

King Faramon might never forgive Kernyv the loss of his sons, but Kernyv couldn't survive the loss of its king.

Branwen took two long strides and brought the blade down against Kahedrin's spine. It landed with a horrible cracking sound. The blade embedded deeply.

Dark, wet blood soaked the yellow of Kahedrin's tunic as if Branwen had spilled an inkwell.

He crashed to his knees in front of Marc. Branwen hoisted the blade from his back, panting. The squelching noise set her teeth on edge.

"*Kahedrin!*" A woman's scream sliced the air. Branwen looked to the terrace above but she only saw the slim man whose nose Marc had broken. Even from a distance, Branwen felt the hate in the other man's gaze, blood smeared against golden-brown skin, features indistinct in the shadows. Then he ran toward the castle.

Branwen released the ax. Kahedrin began to flop forward and

Marc caught him. Branwen had broken his back. Marc laid the Crown Prince of Armorica on his lap, and Kahedrin bared his teeth at him. Blood stained the gleaming white.

"I see Ankou," he said.

"We'll burn your body," Marc told the prince. "We'll honor you."

He gurgled a laugh. "Now...you'll deal...Alba." Marc and Branwen exchanged a confused look.

Kahedrin drew his last breath. Branwen hoped he would be greeted by the face of his goddess.

Marc's shoulders curled forward. "*Mormerkti*, Branwen. Sister." Panning his gaze across the death-filled gardens, he said, "Someone orchestrated the attack on Armorica so that they would be forced to seek revenge. It seems I'm not the King of Kernyv, after all."

He gave a bitter laugh. "It will be an honor to die fighting by your side."

"No," Branwen growled at him. "I'm not ready to let you die."

Marc's smile was sad. "I never thought I'd live to know such forgiveness. We've been outsmarted, Branwen. And we're about to be overrun. Not even my mother would stake a wager with these odds."

The king was right. The castle was almost lost. Except...except that in her vision, Branwen had seen the Shades streaming through Monwiku.

Could she...*dare* she...Branwen looked down at the Hand of Bríga: From the same source came creation and destruction. The Queen Mother always gambled with loaded dice.

Branwen's healing powers couldn't save the people she loved. Not this time. The Land couldn't save them.

She pitched her eyes toward the pitiless depths that surrounded the island, that carried enemy ships to their shores. Slowly, Branwen looked back at the king.

Steeling herself, she called forth her flame.

Marc sucked in a breath. "The Old Ones sent me to Kernyv to protect the Land, and her chosen Champion," Branwen told the king. "*You.*"

She skimmed her burning palm over the blade of the ax. Blood trickled down her wrist.

"Just stay alive," she said.

Branwen leapt to her feet and sprinted through the battlefield toward the sea.

BECOME THE DARK

BRANWEN'S PATH THROUGH THE CARNAGE was unimpeded. Almost as if she'd become invisible. Except to the Death-Tellers. She saw them prowling the gardens, and they saw her. Branwen couldn't hear their cries because they weren't for her. Not tonight.

She passed the bench where she had spied Tristan and Eseult embracing. She hoped they were safe, she did, but Branwen couldn't think about them. Or Ruan. Or Andred and Lowenek. If this gambit failed, they would all be dead or hostages in a few hours.

When Branwen was marked with the Hand of Bríga, the Queen of Iveriu had told her that sometimes a leader's path ran with blood.

She reached the water's edge. In her dream, before she was woken by the guard sounding the alarm, Branwen had dove straight into the night-shaded waters, eager. They had welcomed her.

There was no time to hesitate. She extended the Hand of Bríga, let her blood flow toward the sea.

Her teeth chattered as the words she'd spoken on Whitethorn Mound spilled from her lips once more.

"This is my body! This is my love!" Branwen's eyes fixed on the choppy waters. "I give it to the Sea of the Dead. I offer you everything I am!"

She inhaled a long breath, arced her arms above her head, and plunged into the depths.

The coming spring had not yet brought any warmth to the sea surrounding Monwiku. It wouldn't be long before Branwen's body grew too numb to move. But she had already offered herself to the dead.

She allowed herself one backward glance at the surface.

Only fire. The stars were hiding.

Branwen let herself sink. She had put her trust in the Old Ones on Whitethorn Mound. Now, if not her trust, she put her belief that the Dark One had been watching her, listening, to the test.

Blinding white flashes illuminated the waves. Thunder shook the darkness. Nobody knew where the Veil between this world and the Otherworld lay in the sea, but Branwen's senses prickled in the same way as when she neared the White Moor.

A whirlpool opened like a crater in the sea, enveloping her. Branwen's warm blood streamed more quickly. On Whitethorn Mound, the Old Ones had sent a whirlwind for her offering. The swirling water was even more voracious as it embraced her, consumed her. She was losing too much blood.

Lightning streaked through the waves as Branwen saw the silhouette of a skull emerge from the vortex. A skull with black voids for eyes.

This was the true face of Dhusnos. The face she had seen as she languished with the destiny snake's venom in her veins. He was the starless tide.

The water quivered with laughter around Branwen, needled her frozen limbs.

Branwen of Iveriu, said the Dark One. His voice resounded in her ears as if she were at the bottom of a well. *At last. The Land has asked too much. You've come to join my House.*

No. Water streamed up her nose, burning.

No? Dhusnos laughed. *You hear my call. When you stop lying to yourself, it's my voice you hear.* The water-skull surged closer. *Your heart has darkened. The ties that bound you are gone—you severed them. If not to join me, then why?*

Branwen clamped her mouth shut. *I'm here to ask for your help.*

The carrier of the Hand of Bríga asks for my help. You are a curious child.

Thunder rumbled as another bolt of lightning turned the black waters blinding.

My people are dying.

Your enemies.

They're my people now, Branwen countered. She could have sworn she felt water-skull's breath on her face, as if it were an excited, rabid beast.

You want me to save your people because the Land cannot help them, Dhusnos surmised. *She is too weak.*

Yes.

I want something, too, Branwen of Iveriu.

She squirmed as seaweed wrapped around her ankles, itchy tentacles.

You will make me a Shade. To replace the one you destroyed, the god said. *Keane, you called him. His rage was beautiful. Like yours.*

Branwen thrashed as she saw Shades gathering at the edges of the whirlpool.

You will kill of your own volition. Not in self-defense, not in the defense of another—but because you want to, Branwen of Iveriu. Goddess Ériu also deals death. She condemned me to be what I am. We are not so different. That is my price.

Branwen pictured Marc, Ruan, and all of the other friends she'd made at the castle. Tristan. Even Eseult. They would perish if she didn't agree.

It was no deal at all, but Branwen told Dhusnos, *I accept.*

I will give you until next Samonios to offer me my Shade. If you do not procure the soul by the new year, I will take the soul of one you love.

Before Branwen could protest at the Dark One's added condition, she was being spit out of the Sea of the Dead.

She flew into the air, then smacked against the surface of the Dreaming Sea. It sounded like the crack of a whip. Branwen ached all over; her skin smarted.

Fires glowed from the gardens of Monwiku. At this distance, it was beautiful. She struggled to take in air, spitting out seawater.

Exhausted, she floated atop the waves.

Larger ships suddenly appeared behind the dinghies belonging to the Armoricans. Their sails winked in and out of view. Dark exhilaration coursed through Branwen.

These ships belonged to the Shades. They cast their monstrous grappling hooks onto the fleet of dinghies. The smaller boats didn't stand a chance against them.

Some capsized immediately. Terrified shouts rose up from the ones that were boarded.

Branwen no longer felt the cold. She felt hotter than the fires of Belotnia. She fought the rough waves, each stroke onerous, as she made her way back to shore.

Overhead, an entire flock of *kretarvs* circled Monwiku Castle, gliding together like a giant wing. Screams flew out of the mouths of the Armorican fighters as the *kretarvs* dove toward them, talons ready, beaks open.

Their caws made Branwen's flesh crawl. She knew that each victim would be lured, enthralled by the *kretarv* using the voice of a loved one. Right before the vile bird moved in for the kill.

Waves buffeting her, Branwen clutched at the rocks surrounding the base of Monwiku island. Her nails broke and bled. Chest heaving, she pulled herself up.

Another ragged breath. She scrambled to standing and raced back into the garden.

Shades charged past her. Branwen had almost forgotten how hideous they were. Half-men, half-*kretarv*, their bare chests were covered with tiny, insatiable beaks. The souls claimed by Dhusnos left a trail of blood and seawater.

They cried out to be fed.

The Shades stalked the castle gardens, appearing and disappearing at will, more liquid than solid. Branwen watched as the Armorican raiders grew slack in Shades' lethal embraces, their life forces being drained to sustain the afterlife of Dhusnos's crews.

The men drowned where they stood, withered.

Branwen's vision had come true. Shades were using Monwiku Castle as a hunting ground. Only *she* had been the one to invite them in.

She had asked the Sea of the Dead to obliterate her enemies, and the Dark One had answered her call.

Destruction was the only thing that could save the kingdom. And she couldn't regret what she'd done.

Not if King Marc survived. Not if the True Queen survived.

Her right palm tingled. Branwen lifted it to eye level. The scar had become a shimmering black. She called forth her flame.

It was the color of a moonless night.

Darkness spread from the scar through her veins, like a vine wrapping around her arm. The Wise Damsel had told Branwen magic required honesty, and Branwen wanted this.

She wanted to watch her enemies burn. She hadn't felt this alive for months.

A man in a yellow tunic barreled toward her, holding his sword aloft.

She ran to meet him, black flames climbing from her right hand. His mouth fell agape. He looked at her in the same way the Armorican assassin had. In the same way the scarred Royal Guardsman had.

Branwen was the face of his death.

The Armorican hacked the air between them with his sword, and she felt no fear. From behind, a Shade grabbed the man, clutching him with his black-feathered arm.

The creature bayed through its ulcerous gums. It pressed the beak in the center of its left palm to the Armorican's heart. He began to waste, dessicate before Branwen's eyes.

The Shade nodded at Branwen. It was protecting her.

She left the Armorican in the arms of the man-beast and went in search of her king.

From farther out at sea, a great wave headed straight for Monwiku. The wall of water hit what was left of the Armorican fleet. It burst apart, blood and water, like watching a mountain disintegrate. The wave left nothing in its wake.

Dawn glimmered through its mist, black fading to grayish-purple.

Branwen spotted Marc on the terrace above and hastened toward him. An Armorican lunged at her. She flung her right arm at his chest. Black flame made his entire body spasm. Branwen left him where he fell and kept running.

Marc rattled his sword at a *kretarv* feasting on the eyes of a dead man who wore a yellow tunic. He regarded Branwen warily as she approached.

The Shades were beginning to retreat. Their hideous forms winked in and out of Branwen's vision as they returned to their ships.

The Armoricans were defeated.

Decimated.

With a final, bloodcurdling shriek, the flock of *kretarvs* took to the sky, flew out to sea, back to their master. King Marc's gaze trailed after them.

"*Rix*," said Branwen, rasping.

"You . . . Morgawr told me about the Sea of the Dead. About the monsters that attacked the *Dragon Rising*. I didn't . . ." Marc looked from the bodies that littered his garden, watering the earth with their blood, to Branwen.

"Sister," he said. "Are you all right?"

Branwen didn't know the answer to that question.

"My offering was accepted," she told him.

The king's garden smoldered. "Whatever you did . . . I'm grateful." But he looked haunted.

"Please—please don't tell the *kordweyd*," Branwen said. "Don't tell . . . anyone."

"You have my word. You saved the castle." Marc took her right hand in his. She tensed. The black flame had evaporated, but the king watched as the vine-like strands of power receded from Branwen's veins to the center of her palm. The scar had blackened, almost like a tattoo, and it had changed shape.

Peering closely, she recognized the symbol: a letter from the Ivernic language of trees, and fresh horror flooded her. Each letter had two meanings. The first was innocent enough: a fern—a flowerless plant. The second, deeper meaning was the truth.

Slayer. Killer.

"Is there anything I can do for you?" King Marc asked Branwen who failed to contain her shivering. She shook her head.

"You stayed alive," she said. The king answered with a troubled smile, nodding.

"*Rix!*" Marc and Branwen glanced above them. It was Ruan. "*Rix!*"

He was alive. A breath rushed out of her. *Thank the Old Ones.* But it wasn't the Old Ones who had saved her lover. It wasn't the Old Ones who had saved Monwiku.

The King's Champion sped toward them. There was blood on his cheek.

Revulsion contorted Ruan's face as his gaze circled the garden and settled on the dead. On the misshapen, unnatural corpses.

When he reached Branwen, he rubbed her arms. "Thank the Horned One you're alive." He crushed her into an embrace and she didn't correct him. Ruan kissed her cheek, her temple, between Branwen's eyes.

Turning to his king, all relief fled the Champion's face.

"The queen?" Marc asked. "Is she secure?"

Ruan swallowed. "She's missing."

"Missing?" Marc's eyes bulged.

"Andred and I found Endelyn, but not the queen. I told Andred to stay with his sister while I searched the castle. I've looked everywhere."

"And Tristan?" Marc asked.

"Also . . . missing." Ruan's jaw shifted. He seemed nervous. Angry, and nervous. "I couldn't find him, either, but . . ."

"But what?" King Marc demanded. He pulled at his beard.

"I saw no sign of a struggle in the queen's chamber. Or in Tristan's."

"Of course there was a struggle!" Marc shouted.

"Did you check between the walls?" Branwen asked. Ruan nodded. "Maybe—maybe Tristan got her somewhere safe," she suggested to the king, then to his Champion.

Ruan met her gaze. "Maybe."

"If Eseult's been kidnapped, the Armoricans won't get far without their boats," Marc told Ruan. "Gather any able-bodied men and find her!"

"Of course, *Ríx*."

Branwen heard the Dark One's laugh. It was her own. Hysterical. Furious.

Honest. *Slayer.*

She sank to her knees. "We'll find your cousin," Marc promised, dropping a hand on Branwen's shoulder. "I swear, we'll find Eseult— even if I have to go to Armorica myself to get her back."

Branwen buried her face in her hands. In her heart, her midnight-colored heart, she knew that the True Queen hadn't been kidnapped. She peered up at Ruan.

He knew it, too.

Tristan and Eseult were gone.

They were gone, and Branwen was left among the ruins of their love. She'd saved the castle, but lost the peace.

The new day glittered like a vicious smile on the sea.

Odai eti ama. There were no more songs in Branwen's heart.

ACKNOWLEDGMENTS

It's hard to believe that the second part of Branwen's story has already come to a close. Thank you so much to all of the readers who have championed *Sweet Black Waves* this year—it means the world to me. Thank you for the messages and tweets and bookstagrams.

I am incredibly lucky to have worked on this installment with my editor, Nicole Otto, who understood the journey that Branwen needed to take and helped me get it just right. My agent, Sara Crowe, is a Wise Damsel who gives incredibly wise counsel, and I don't know where I'd be without her.

I will always be grateful to Rhoda Belleza for giving me a home at Imprint, and to Erin Stein for supporting the series so fully. A huge thank-you to Brittany Pearlman, Jo Kirby, and Katie Halata for everything you do to put my books into the hands of readers. Ellen Duda has created another amazing cover that captures the heart and soul of *Wild Savage Stars*. Thank you to Linda Minton for your close reading and helpful comments.

A shout-out to Liane Worthington, Crystal Patriarche, and Courtney Floegel at BookSparks for your tireless efforts to introduce Branwen to the world—as well as the sage advice. Over here in London, I am deeply grateful to Laura Dodd, Stevie Finegan, and Jamie-Lee Nardone for your support (and wine!), and the entire Super Relaxed Fantasy Club crew.

Wild Savage Stars is a deeply personal book for me and deals with several difficult issues. From the bottom of my heart, I want to thank my early readers for providing important and necessary feedback. Thank you to Kelly deVos, Somaiya Daud, Lucy Hounsom, Rebecca Barrow, Christopher Keelty, Carlie Sorosiak, Amanda Hall, Sara Polsky, and Georgina Cullman. As ever, thank you to Dr. Geraldine Parsons for your help with the Old Irish linguistics.

Nothing prepares you for your debut year and I wouldn't have gotten through it without the Class of 2K18 or my fabulous girlfriends: Deborah McCandless, Kitty Harvey, Ame Igharo, Brooke Edwards-Plant, Andrea Ledoux-Richards, Annie Stone. ¡Mil gracias a todas #LasMusas! Being part of the wonderful KidLit community, I've met so many extraordinary writers who I'm also fortunate to consider friends: Kamilla Benko, Ali Standish, Karen M. McManus, Alice Broadway, Heidi Heilig, Kaitlyn Sage Patterson, Dhonielle Clayton, CB Lee, Katie Locke, Sarah Ahiers, Vic James, Elizabeth Lim, Natalie C. Parker, Zoraida Córdova, Sara Holland, April G. Tucholke, Melissa Albert, Sangu Mandanna, Stacey Lee, Lexa Hillyer, Kayla Whaley, Megan Bannen, Lydia Kang, Rachel Lynn Solomon, Elsie Chapman, Elly Blake, Marieke Nijkamp, Julia Ember, Rebecca Schaeffer, Laura Lam, Beth Revis, Amie Kaufman. If you're still reading, run don't walk to buy all of their books!

Last but not least, to my husband, Jack: *Not you without me, not me without you*—not even primordial magic can break our vow.

GLOSSARY

A NOTE ON LANGUAGES AND NAMES

The languages used in the Sweet Black Waves Trilogy are based, fairly loosely, on ancient and medieval languages. As I have adapted the Tristan legends for my retelling, Ireland has become Iveriu, Cornwall has become Kernyv, and the Roman Empire has become the Aquilan Empire. I have taken liberties with history and linguistic accuracy while trying to postulate how the political realities of my world might influence the development of its languages.

Today, nearly half the world's population speaks what are known as Indo-European languages. This group includes English, most of the European languages, but also Sanskrit and Persian. One branch is the Celtic languages, which are now spoken primarily in northwestern Europe: Ireland, Cornwall, Scotland, Wales, Brittany, and the Isle of Man (as well as small diaspora communities), but during the first millennium BCE these languages were spoken as far afield as the Iberian Peninsula, the Black Sea, and Asia Minor. The Celtic languages are further divided into two groups: the Goidelic (Irish, Manx, and Scottish Gaelic) and the Brittonic (Cornish, Welsh, and Breton).

Since the nineteenth century, scholars have been working to recreate the Proto-Indo-European language—the hypothesized common ancestor to all Indo-European languages. Celtic linguists have also made significant headway in the reconstruction of Proto-Celtic, the language from which all Celtic languages derive.

Therefore, my fabricated Ivernic language is based on Old Irish and Proto-Celtic, whereas my Kernyvak language is based on Proto-Celtic and the Brittonic languages. For the Aquilan language words I have looked to Proto-Italic—the forbearer of Latin—for inspiration. Given that the Aquilan Empire occupied the island of Albion for hundreds of years before Branwen's story begins, I have also allowed for there to be some linguistic influence of the Aquilan language on Kernyvak. Since the Aquilan Empire never invaded Iveriu, their languages would have remained quite separate. Although, of course, Branwen and the rest of the Ivernic nobility speak Aquilan as a second language.

In creating the place-names for Branwen's world, I have tried to incorporate relevant aspects of the Celtic tradition. For example, rīganī is the reconstructed Proto-Celtic word for "queen," and since the Land is a female goddess in Iveriu, it made sense for me to name the seat of power Castle Rigani. Likewise, bodwā is the Proto-Celtic word for "fight," which is fitting as the name of Branwen's family castle given that their motto is *The Right Fight.*

The ancient language of trees that Branwen calls the first Ivernic writing is a reference to the Irish Ogham alphabet. It was devised between the first and fourth centuries CE to transfer the Irish language to written form and is possibly based on the Latin alphabet. Ogham is found in approximately four hundred surviving stone inscriptions and is read from the bottom up. In addition to representing a sound, the letters of the Ogham alphabet have the names of trees and shrubs. The Ogham letter coll translates as "hazel" and represents the /k/ sound as in *kitten.* The Ogham letter *uíllenn* translates as "honeysuckle" and represents the /ll/ sound as in *shell*. Hence, when Branwen and Essy trace their private symbol, they are only writing two letters rather than a whole word.

The legend of Tristan and Isolt has been retold so many times in so many languages that simply choosing which form of the character names to use also poses somewhat of a challenge. Two possible origins for Tristan's name include Drustanus, son of Cunomorus, who is mentioned on a sixth-century stone inscription found in Cornwall, or a man named Drust, son of King Talorc of the Picts, who ruled in late eighth-century Scotland.

In the early Welsh versions of the legend, Drust becomes Tristan or Drystan. Tristan was the name propagated by the French poets, who employed its similar sound to the French word *tristesse* ("sadness") for dramatic effect. Another consistent feature of the legends is Tristan's disguising his identity by calling himself Tantris—an anagram of his name—and I therefore decided to do the same.

While the name Isolt is probably the most easily recognized, it is in fact derived from the Welsh name Essyllt. The French poets translated her name as Yso(lt) or Yseu(l)t(e). I have therefore synthesized the two for my Eseult.

In the Continental versions of the story, Isolt's lady's maid is usually called Brangien or Brangain. However, this is a borrowing from the Old Welsh name Branwen (br.n "raven" + (g)wen "fair"). This choice was also inspired by another Branwen from the Middle Welsh *Mabinogion*, the earliest prose stories in British literature. The Second Branch of the Mabinogi is called *Branwen uerch Lyr* ("Branwen, daughter of Llŷr"), the meaning of the patronym *ap Llŷr* being "Son of the Sea," and the connection that the Branwen of The Sweet Black Waves Trilogy feels for the sea was inspired by this forerunner.

The Branwen of the Mabinogion is a member of a Welsh royal family who is given in marriage to the King of Ireland to prevent a war after one of her brothers has offended him. When Branwen arrives at the Irish court, the vassals of the King of Ireland turn him against his new queen and she is forced to submit to many humiliations. Her brothers then declare war on Ireland, and Branwen is the cause of the war her marriage was meant to prevent.

Several prominent Celtic scholars have made the case that the Welsh Branwen can trace her roots to Irish Sovereignty Goddesses or that both the Welsh and Irish material derive from the same, earlier source. Particular evidence of this is that Branwen's dowry to the King of Ireland included the Cauldron of Regeneration, which could bring slain men back to life, and which served as the inspiration for Kerwindos's Cauldron in my own work.

While there is no evidence of a direct connection between the Branwen of the Mabinogion and the Branwen of the Tristan legends, I find the possibility tantalizing, and so I have merged the two into my Branwen as a forceful female protagonist with magical abilities and a strong connection to the Land.

IVERNIC FESTIVALS

Imbolgos—Spring Festival of the Goddess Bríga
Belotnia—the Festival of Lovers
Laelugus—the Festival of Peace
Samonios—New Year Festival

IVERNIC LANGUAGE VOCABULARY

derew—a pain-relieving herb
comnaide—always

enigena—daughter

fidkwelsa—a strategy board game

Iverman/Ivermen—a person or persons from Iveriu

Iverni—the people of Iveriu

Ivernic—something of or relating to Iveriu

keylos—a traditional Ivernic musical band

kladiwos—an Ivernic type of sword

kridyom—heart-companion

krotto—an Ivernic type of harp

lesana—ring-forts belonging to the Old Ones

ráithana—hills belonging to the Old Ones

silomleie—an Ivernic type of cudgel made from blackthorn wood

skeakh—a whitethorn bush or tree

KERNYVAK FESTIVALS

Long Night—the shortest day of the year

Hunt of the Rixula—takes place the day before Long Night

Blessing of the Sea—a festival to mark the beginning of spring

KERNYVAK LANGUAGE VOCABULARY

damawinn—grandmother

dagos—better/good

dolos—pain

dymatis—"hello"/"good day"

karid—beloved

Kernyv bosta vyken—"Kernyv forever"

Kernyvak—something of or relating to Kernyv

Kernyvman/Kernyvmen—a person or persons from Kernyv

Kernyveu—the people of Kernyv

kordweyd—a seer of the Cult of the Horned One

kretarv—carnivorous seabird

menantus—an apology/a deep brook

mormerkti—"thank you"

nosmatis—"good evening"

penaxta—prince

sekrev—"you're welcome"

rix—king

rixina—queen

rixula—"little queen"/a red-breasted bird

AQUILAN LANGUAGE VOCABULARY

ama—"I love"

amar—love

amare—bitter

de—of

eti—and

est—"is"

fálkr—a broad, curved sword

la—the

misrokord—a thin dagger; literally means "mercy"

odai—"I hate"

SOURCES, LITERARY TRANSMISSION, AND WORLD-BUILDING

The legend of Tristan and Isolt is one of the best-known myths in Western culture, and arguably the most popular throughout the Middle Ages. The star-crossed lovers have become synonymous with passion and romance itself.

When I first decided to write Branwen's story, I put on my scholarly hat and reacquainted myself with the most influential versions of the Tristan tales, then followed their motifs and principle episodes backward in time before arranging them into a frame, a loom onto which Branwen's story could come to life. Despite the numerous retellings of Tristan and Isolt throughout the medieval period, the structure remains remarkably consistent.

The names of the main characters can be traced to post-Roman Britain (sixth or seventh century CE). There was no real Tristan or King Arthur, but there are tantalizing stone inscriptions in the British Isles that suggest local folk heroes whose names became attached to a much older body of tales, some mythological in genesis. And while there is evidence that some motifs may have been borrowed from Hellenic, Persian, or Arabic sources, the vast majority are Celtic. Rather than viewing these Celtic stories as direct sources for the Tristan and Isolt narratives, however, most scholars agree the medieval Irish and Welsh material should be viewed as analogues that presumably stem from the same, now lost, pan-Celtic source.

These oral tales were probably preserved by the druids, and our earliest surviving versions were written down by Christian clerics in Ireland between the seventh and ninth centuries, and in twelfth-century Wales. Because Ireland was never conquered by the Roman Empire, it didn't experience the same "Dark Age" as elsewhere in Europe. Women in early medieval Ireland also had many more rights and protections under the law, enshrined in *Caín Adomnáin* (Law of Adomán), *ca.* 679-704 CE, than their Continental counterparts— which is echoed in the strong female protagonists of its literature.

There are three Old Irish tale-types that feed into the Tristan legend: 1. *aitheda* (or, elopement tales), in which a young woman runs away from her older husband with a younger man; 2. *tochmarca* (or, courtship tales), in which a woman takes an active part in negotiating a relationship with a man of her choosing that results in marriage; and 3. *immrama* (or, voyage tales), in which the hero takes a sea voyage to the Otherworld.

The Old Irish tales that share the most in common with Tristan and Isolt's doomed affair are *Tochmarc Emire* ("The Wooing of Emer"), a tenth-century *aithed;* and *Tóraigheacht Dhiarmada agus Ghráinne* ("The Pursuit of Diarmuid and Gráinne"), an *aithed* whose earliest text dates to the Early Modern Irish period but whose plot and characters can be traced to the tenth century. In these stories, the female characters wield tremendous power and are closer to their mythological roots as goddesses. Other tales that are reminiscent of Branwen's complicated relationship with Isolt include the ninth- or tenth-century *Tochmarc Becfhola* ("The Wooing of Becfhola") and the twelfth-century *Fingal Rónain* ("Rónán's act of kinslaying").

When the Romans withdrew from Britain in the fifth century, many residents from the south of the island immigrated to northern

France. For the next five centuries, trade and communication was maintained between Cornwall, Wales, and Brittany. The Bretons spoke a language similar to Welsh and Cornish, which facilitated the sharing of the Arthurian legends, to which they added their own folktales. By the twelfth century, the professional Breton *conteurs* (storytellers) had become the most popular court entertainers in Europe, and it was these wandering minstrels who brought the Tristan legends to the royal French and Anglo-Norman courts—including that of Henry II of England and Eleanor of Aquitaine, famed for her patronage of the troubadours in the south of France.

The Breton songs of Tristan's exploits were soon recorded as verse romances by the Anglo-Norman poets Béroul, Thomas d'Angleterre, and Marie de France (notably, the only woman), as well as the German Eilhart von Oberge. Béroul's and Eilhart's retellings belong to what is often called the *version commune* (primitive version), meaning they are closer to their folkloric heritage. Thomas's Tristan forms part of the *version courtoise* (courtly version), which is influenced by the courtly love ideal.

The twelfth century is often credited with the birth of romance, and Tristan is at least partially responsible. Which is not to say that people didn't fall in love before then, of course (!), but rather that for the first time, the sexual love between a man and a woman, usually forbidden, became a central concern of literature. The first consumers of this new genre in which a knight pledges fealty to a distant, unobtainable (often married) lady were royal and aristocratic women and, like romance readers today, their appetite was voracious. While the audience was female, the poets and authors were male, often clerics in the service of noblewomen. The poetry produced at the behest of female aristocratic patrons might therefore be considered the first fan fiction.

However, while the courtly lady may have appeared to have the power over her besotted knight, in reality noblewomen were rapidly losing property and inheritance rights as the aristocracy became a closed class ruled by strict patrilinear descent. Legends like that of Tristan and Isolt provided a means of escape for noblewomen who were undoubtedly in less than physically and emotionally satisfying marriages of their own, while also reinforcing women's increasingly objectified status. The portrayal of women in the Tristan legends therefore exemplifies the conflict between the forceful protagonists of its Celtic origins and the new idealized but dehumanized courtly lady.

It is this conflict that particularly interests me as a storyteller and which I explore through my own female characters. Because the legend as I have inherited it is a mix of concerns from different historical epochs, I decided to set my retelling in a more fantastical context that allowed me to pick and choose the aspects of the tradition that best suited Branwen's story. In this way, I also followed in the footsteps of the medieval authors who, while they might make references to real places or kings, weren't particularly concerned with accuracy. The stories they produced weren't so much historical fiction as we think of it today but more akin to fantasy.

During the nineteenth century, the German composer Richard Wagner drew on his countryman Gottfried von Strassburg's celebrated thirteenth-century verse romance of Tristan as inspiration for his now ubiquitous opera. Gottfried had, in turn, used the Anglo-Norman version of Thomas d'Angleterre as his source material, demonstrating the unending cycle of inspiration and adaption. The Tristan legends started as distinct traditions that were grafted onto the Arthurian corpus (possibly in Wales, possibly on the Continent) and became forever intertwined with the thirteenth-century prose romances.

Concurrently with Gottfried, there was a complete Old Norse adaption by Brother Róbert, a Norwegian cleric, and the Tristan legends gained popularity not only throughout Scandinavia but on the Iberian Peninsula and in Italy. There were also early Czech and Belarusian versions, and it was later translated into Polish and Russian. Dante also references the ill-fated lovers in his fourteenth-century *Inferno*, and Sir Thomas Malory devoted an entire book to Tristan in his fifteenth-century *Le Morte d'Arthur*, one of the most famous works in the English language.

The popularity of Tristan and Isolt fell off abruptly during the Renaissance but was revived by the Romantic poets of the late eighteenth and early nineteenth centuries, who sought an antidote to the changes enacted by the Industrial Revolution—although they viewed their medieval past through very rose-tinted glasses. Nevertheless, the preoccupation with Tristan and Isolt, as well as their supporting characters, has persisted for more than a millennium and it would be surprising if it did not persist for another.